MW00810314

Hold Up The Sky

Susan Palardy Egan

This story is a work of fiction. Names, characters, and events are either products of the author's imagination or used in a fictitious manner. Any resemblance to actual persons, living or dead, is coincidental.

E. LAWRENCE PRESS

Copyright © 2018 Author Name

Library of Congress Control Number: 2018909831

All rights reserved.

ISBN: 10 17326747-0-1
ISBN-13: 9781-732674707

DEDICATION

Beth's story is dedicated to my parents Edna and Fred for a childhood filled with love. Their particular personalities and their particular love story have provided me with too many interesting, poignant and happy memories to recount.

CONTENTS

ACKNOWLEDGMENTS

My heartfelt thanks— TO ALL

…to my faithful reader friends Anne, Sharon, and Sheryl for spending many hours of your personal time reading my story carefully, chapter by chapter. For months, you generously met with me as a group to go over Beth's story as it unfolded. You created a safe space for me to hear solid, constructive feedback.

…to Nancy, for your enthusiastic faith in me that I could pull this off and for your willingness to dive back into this crazy time period with me whenever I needed. You encouraged me to go forward, trusting myself always.

…to Patti for your ongoing and loving interest in Beth's story and your gobbling up every chunk of chapters I sent you with the message to "send more, please!"

…to Jennifer and Ben for giving me loving and constructive feedback when I worried over including troublesome events, and for acting as a sounding board for me when I got lost in MSWord's functioning, and when I *literally lost* sections of my MS that I hadn't properly saved.

…to Jennifer and Ben, as well as to Sharyn, for your invaluable help in reading my ending sections and helping me to keep my focus on Beth's journey and her ties to Jack. You expressed your confidence in my ability to finish Beth's story when my own was waning.

…to Sydney. While in a challenging and sad space yourself, you gobbled up Beth's story even as I worried out loud to you that reading it might add to your woes.

…to Maggie, because you wanted to read Beth's story and accepted my answer, gently asking when you *might be old enough to read it*! (God bless you, honey. You definitely are now!)

…to my entire family for being supportive, even when you might have wondered if I would ever really finish telling my story.

…to Deb, for texting, talking on the phone and meeting at Coffee Bean to allow me to access your encyclopedic knowledge of music—songs and lyrics, as well as applicable anecdotes. You got what I was trying to do.

…to Robin, for being that friend who finds time to help with the mundane work of downloading and uploading and all in between and for coffee meetings to deal with fonts and style and just holding my hand through the process.

…Of course, to my life-long sweetheart and partner in all things, Richard, for being the king of champions where Beth's story is concerned. You helped me to remember details and you reminisced with me through your own memories. Even when the events were hard, you listened and responded thoughtfully.

…Lastly, to my editor, Suse. You have given me your straightforward comments and suggestions while unreservedly cheering me on. You made this endeavor possible. I have embraced your edits and appreciated your carefully pointed questions. And I have loved your witty emails. Thank you, my dear friend. It's been a wild ride.

PROLOGUE

August, 1965

Softly, I will leave you
Softly, long before you miss me
Long before your arms can beg me stay
For one more hour or one more day....

~Georgio Calabrese and Tony De Vita

Anna's first sensation was blessed relief as she felt herself ascending airily. But then, abruptly, came an awareness of her physical self, crumpled on the seat of the car. No marks clearly indicated violence, yet she–her body–lay lifeless. She knew what this meant, but, at this moment, she felt no regret. Instinctively, she embraced this release of the life that had meant disappointment, yearning, and constraints.

Then, a new recognition took hold. There, on the seat next to her old physical self, groaned her darling daughter, her special one who never stopped needing her, who had always provided her life with purpose. It had always been Margaret, beside her in her dreary chores for a large, unappreciative family; Margaret beside her, listening patiently, mimicking her as she made her way in her narrow society of church, family; Margaret, always depending on Anna to champion her through the directionless days.

With these thoughts, her new freedom felt a heavy tug. How could she leave her beloved girl? Now, she allowed the scene's vivid horror to come to life. There lay her own inert body, with Margaret to her right, and, to her left, in the driver's seat, her husband, Jack, covered with blood and clearly fighting to hold on to the life she had so serenely let go. In the back seat sat another precious charge, Laurie, mutely staring as she was helped out of the car by a dark-haired boy. As he guided Laurie out of the car and onto a narrow stretch of ground, he spoke softly to this frightened one of her heart.

"Laurie, are you okay? Come on with me," he crooned as he gently helped her into his waiting arms. Once she was safely seated on the grass, the boy moved quickly back to speak to Margaret and Jack. He got close to Jack, whose face seemed crammed in the steering wheel and spoke firmly, "Mr. Lawrence, can you hear me? I'm going to get everyone out of here. Someone stopped up the road. I think help's coming. I'm not sure I should move you just yet. Hang in there. Okay?" Jack's only response was an unintelligible groan. The boy turned his attention to Anna's lifeless body and whispered, "Mrs. Lawrence? Can you hear me, Mrs. Lawrence?" He grasped her condition quickly, and turned his attention to the others in the car, who, when questioned, murmured in response.

Anna was momentarily perplexed. Who was this boy? How did he know her name? Why was he here? Finally, she pulled back a little, taking everything in. Even though she was removed from the scene, she didn't feel separated from it. Focusing once again on her own still body, Anna knew instinctively that soon she would free herself from this scene forever. She summoned up the woman she had been: devoted mother to her five children and any other stray children who came her way, and compassionate caregiver who had clucked with concern while listening to sad stories of others' hardships. Ever the quiet introvert, she had instinctively suppressed her emotional responses to her family's frequent insensitivity, their easy ways of expecting her to be all things at all times, and their subtle criticisms of her when she was not. Intuitively, she now realized that no, she was wrong: they loved her, needed her; they would feel the loss of their lifeline.

Now, she dispassionately inspected what she would never miss: the imperfect body that revealed the rigors of 55 years: breasts heavy, sagging over a bloated belly, a torso that had once been slim, beautiful; thin legs with varicose veins that mapped the years of carrying babies too heavy for her tiny frame and toting endless loads of laundry that had to be hung on the clothesline to dry then taken down to be folded or ironed…just so much to be ironed. She was surprised to note that the face, though lined, was still pretty. Streaks of gray ran through the dark hair that framed her no longer heart-shaped face, but she could see the soft, smooth texture and sweet quality of her features. Oh, it was all so dear after all!

Anna took another look at her husband of 25 years: there lay a hopeful man who resisted freedom from pain, instead clinging tenaciously to the thread that bound him to the earth, to the others, to her, although she sensed he was already aware that she had gone. Oh, come with me, Jackie. Why not come with me?

A new impulse came unbidden: the desire to provide comfort before she melted away, one last act of love for those here as well as her other children, who blithely lived without a thought as to the agony to come.

Love for the daughter on a high school outing they'd been driving to visit; love for the sons at home, expecting the family back intact in two days even as they enjoyed some quiet time. Time for her, Anna knew, was no longer a concern. But as she pondered the time to come for her family, she remembered her own endless grief at the wasting away of her mother and father, in spite of her best attempts to care for them. How long ago that had seemed! And then, after leaving that behind to find a life out west, the persistent pang for her handsome, sensitive, brother Daniel who had cheered her with funny, thoughtful letters brimming with his plans to move to California. How could death rob her again? And so suddenly? The same black illness that took her parents had felled him as well. She remembered how, in her devastation, she had considered entering a convent.

Her older siblings, except Daniel, were married, but she had seen no prospects. Still young and pretty—although at 27, she hadn't thought so—she had seen no hope for a life with a family of her own. It was Daniel who had urged her to visit their cousin in California, get some sun, defer a permanent decision. Here, she had met Jack, who seemed to instantly adore her, called her his little doll. For the first time, the dream of a future had awakened within her. Still, she'd been torn by the thought of being across the country from Daniel, who'd done his best to replace their parents and give her a "cheerleader" for once in her life.

After the flurry of her romance with Jack and their hastily arranged wedding and honeymoon, and after they had settled into their apartment life, loneliness for her Midwestern ties had begun to gnaw at Anna. One baby arrived, and then another, filling her with exquisite joy, but always, it seemed, the ache had persisted. Then, happily, Daniel had announced his decision to move west, a suggestion by his doctor because of Daniel's frail constitution and their parents' medical history. All too soon, the telegram had come, telling her it was not to be. Daniel had taken ill and died a month before his planned relocation to California. Though she had a young, thriving family, this loss had magnified the others. It had seemed to Anna, from her current vantage point, to have set the tone for too much of her life.

Oh, now that she could see it objectively, she knew she had decided well when she said yes to Jack. He certainly had never quite gotten over the thrill of finding and winning her over, and he'd let her know that. He'd wanted to do more than provide for Anna; he was determined to make her know her petite prettiness, to coax her dark, shining eyes into a smile just for him. He was her Jackie, and he'd wanted to hold her endlessly, at least in the early years. Yes, he'd wanted to sing to her and with her, to boast about her beauty and cooking, basking in one and sharing in the other. Jack had been more than a good decision. Only now could she see what she'd withheld from him: her open and freely-given love, for while she had keenly felt it, she could not overcome her familiar inhibitions to allow the delight she felt to flow and, at the very least, reflect his passion. In fairness, each early loss had been another hammer blow and, for a time, after Daniel died, Anna had given up trying. But Jack, ever the optimist, never gave up on her. When the war came, taking him away for those painful years, she had yearned for him, writing to him every day, determined to keep him alive through her words, her prayers, her love. Miraculously, Jack had returned to her, gratefully embracing the family they'd created. In the years after, he'd rarely let Anna into any dark moments of that experience, instead sharing comic antics of him and his war buddies.

Anna's mind wandered to Jack's business after the war, after Bethie's birth. So very consuming, the business had demanded as much from her as from Jack because of the financial burden it had placed on their family and because of the time spent nurturing it instead of their growing children. The boys had needed their father's manly attention, guiding and supporting their own burgeoning maleness, the girls had needed their daddy's playful personality doting on them, petting them in that charming way that he had. They'd all desperately needed the family fabric to be strong, to stretch and give, but without tearing. For some reason, Anna now recognized that their fabric had been too delicate. Where the family unit had needed silk, she and Jack had produced tulle. Why was that? Surely, they'd loved their children fiercely…but had they truly known or understood them?

James, their oldest, had been only three when Jack shipped off to the Philippines; Anna had called him her "little man" during those lonely years. Already six when his father returned, Jimmy had watched cautiously as Jack dove into the role he had been dreaming of for the previous three years. That's how Jack had done everything: eagerly, boisterously, just so full of life. And when he'd come home from the war, saturated in violence and testosterone, he'd somehow seemed the invader—to her and to Jimmy as well. Maybe the son had resisted what seemed so unfamiliar, certainly very different from the slow moving, deliberate, and soft-spoken single parent she'd been while Jack was away.

And Margaret? No child had ever been loved as passionately or worried about as fretfully as Margaret had been by Anna. When Jack had written home requesting reports on his baby daughter, all Anna could write in return were beautiful descriptions of their "exceptional" little one. Now, Anna wondered whether that had been fair to Jack, who had ascribed different special attributes to his little girl. She knew he had bragged about the child to his buddies. Although Margaret's beauty, with her soft, curly hair and ruby red lips, was beyond question, her inability to walk for so long, or talk until she had labored through years of speech therapy had betrayed the truth of her condition. Yes, it had been stubborn–even mean–to deny Jack the truth in her letters to him. Still, she and Jimmy had looked out for Margaret, and the three of them had gotten by just fine.

Then baby Frankie, the son she and Jack had dubbed the "furlough baby" had arrived, all blond and handsome, cooing and giggling from the start. What had happened along the way to sour him? At three, he had accepted his daddy's presence with glee, quickly becoming the proverbial apple of Jack's eye, ready to be tossed in the air or tickled at any moment, eager for any scrap of Jack's attention. Now, almost a man, his frequent drinking bouts, his sudden sullenness, and his angry opposition to Jack had caused her many sleepless nights.

And then, she considered their other two daughters, Beth, and Laurie.

Laurie, the baby of her heart, was unexpected, born when Anna was 45, going through "the change" and supposedly unable to get pregnant. Laurie had given Anna a last chance at motherhood and youth at a time when she had begun to feel unneeded. But need her Laurie did. Sickly as a baby, shy and awkward as a little girl, Laurie was the polar opposite of her older sister Beth, the child who had dared to climb trees with her brothers and who'd begged them to teach her poker and football so she could play with them and the neighbor boys. Where, at eight and nine, Beth had been all pep and exploration, Laurie, at three and four, had clung to Mommy.

As Beth had grown, so had her horizons. In her teenaged years, she'd wandered farther and farther from the nest on a regular basis. This trip to the Indian reservation symbolized Beth's outlook perfectly, whereas, Anna mused, Laurie's interests couldn't be further from such excitement. Bethie, though, her "little sunshine" for five years before Laurie arrived, Anna's dreams had once rested on Bethie, the daughter who could have it all. Bethie didn't know how her mother marveled at her and rooted for her. She couldn't have known, by virtue of the simple fact that Anna had shone her light on Beth most often when the girl was quiet. How she had loved to hold Beth's feet in her hands as Beth lay on the couch watching TV. Anna would stroke and massage and warm those feet, finally at rest while Beth relaxed into her gentle therapy. And how she had loved washing Beth's little girl hair and rinsing it with vinegar until it squeaked and Beth squealed.

Beth was supposed to grow up to be Anna's confidante. They were going to do the things Anna hadn't gotten to do with her mother. They would be girls together, shopping, talking, laughing. Anna would protect Beth and cuddle her and kiss away her troubles. She would guide her little wild colt, the one, she had once told Beth, who was on an invisible tether that Anna released or reined in, as Beth needed. For a time, this explanation had satisfied Beth; Mommy knew all, Mommy's word was gold.

Too soon, however, Jack's storytelling and singing and laughter had stolen Beth's heart. With Jack, her blue eyes had sparkled with the promise of adventure and discovery—Jack's territory. In her last few adolescent years, as Beth pulled away from her mother, seeming to resist Anna's pleas for consideration, Anna had seen Beth as more Jack's than hers. That pettiness meant nothing now. This daughter, product of both parents, was now eagerly budding into a young woman. Perhaps Beth was not what anyone had expected, but Anna knew she and Jack had both given her qualities that would serve her in her coming hours of need. Beth's strength lay in her resilience, her compassion. She would be tested, but Anna vowed that, somehow, she would be there to help Beth.

But what about Laurie? Laurie, it had turned out, was more Anna's soul mate than Beth ever could have been. Laurie needed her in a special way, not the essential, life-draining way that Margaret did, and not like Beth. No. Quiet Laurie deliberated and brooded the way Anna had, and she enjoyed Anna's attention and presence in her life. She looked up to her mother as someone who knew the answers to life's mysteries. Unlike Beth, Laurie had mostly shied away from Jack's exhausting attention.

Though she now reflected on the unfairness of it, Anna could see she had enlisted Laurie to observe Beth's adolescent acts of rebellion with dismay and disapproval. Her thought had been to protect Laurie from following Beth down a path fraught with danger; but, in reality, she had clung to Laurie's childish trust in her. As Beth moved further from Anna, Anna clung more tightly to Laurie. It was all needlessly complicated. Losing her mother, Anna realized, would impact Laurie severely. Still, this spring and summer, Beth had taken an interest in Laurie. Was it a passing interest in the same way Beth revived and then lost interest in their cat—or Margaret? Anna hoped that Beth would find it in her to nourish Laurie with whatever strength she could marshal. Laurie would need Beth.

The time had passed when Anna could influence the outcome of this drama. Anna felt herself floating away from this scene and these ones whose needs had once consumed her, providing her life with meaning. Now, a mystery was about to unfold for Anna. It called softly to her, compelling her to go. A quiet eagerness began to blossom within her, and a desire to move on.

□

PART 1

1 THE END OF THE WORLD

Why does my heart go on beating
Why do these eyes of mine cry
Don't they know it's the end of the world
It ended when you said goodbye...

~Arthur Kent and Sylvia Dee

August 7, 1965
Journal entry

I can't begin to describe how I feel right now. It seems like a hundred years have passed since this morning when I went shopping with Margie. We were walking out of the store and she said to me, "It's so nice to have a cute, young teenager shopping with me. For a change, the bagboy's helping me with the groceries." At least, this is what I think she said. (Was it really only a few hours ago?) She was leading the bag-boy and nudging her four kids along in front of us toward her car. I know I giggled, but I was embarrassed and probably blushed when she said this.

Margie is just so nice to me, even though she must see how crazy I get at the demands of her kids, kids I'm supposed to be helping her with on this trip. It just seems that one of them is always whining or crying or needing their nose wiped. Now I can't believe how stupid and trivial that attitude was—how immature of me to look at them that way. They're just little kids. I mean, the oldest is only six! Seems really silly and ridiculous now.

Anyhow, what did I think? This is the way I got to come on this trip, agreeing to help Margie and Bill with their kids while the adults built the

Indians' bell-tower. Margie and Bill worked on the reservation last summer, too, but they said it was just too hard to get anything done with the kids needing their attention. I can see why. So, for the trip this summer, they told Father Rex they would pay part of the expenses of a teenaged girl if she would help with the kids. That worked out for me since Mom and Dad said "While a school trip to work on an Indian reservation sounds good, we can't afford it." (Was it fifty dollars—I don't remember—to cover my part of the expenses?) I figured I've done my share of babysitting, and besides, the big job for us girls is supposed to be engaging the Indian kids with games and such. Why couldn't I play with the Niemayer kids as well as the Indian kids? So far, except for the time Margie reminded me that I needed to keep a better eye on her kids, it's been mostly fun. Or it WAS fun.

So here we are today—Margie, me and her kids—grocery shopping on a Saturday afternoon, something I've grown up helping Mom do on any day of the week. Anyway, after the big excursion—that's what it felt like—we get back to the school where we're bunking and eating. I look for Mom and Dad's car, their big, white Mercury or "boat" as Frankie and I like to call it. No sign of it. I remember Mom telling me on the phone that they'd be here by lunchtime. Margie's car clock said 1:30.

Mom and Dad, or, really, Mom, is always late though, so I wasn't that worried. I grab a bag of groceries in one arm and the baby in the other and make my way down the side steps of the school to the cafeteria, chattering away to the baby, something silly like "Polly, Polly, where's your dolly?" Oh, God, I can't even believe it now! Anyway, I keep expecting to see one of my friends—who also volunteered—pop out of somewhere, the idea being I'll scream or jump; the boys, at least, are always goofing around like that. I'll be walking along with one or two of the little kids when we all jump at a sudden "Boo!" as one of the boys leaps out in front of us, following the boo with a sinister, crazy laugh. Or one of them might saunter by with "What's cookin', good lookin'? or "What's free, Bethie Bee?" It always makes the little ones squeal, and usually me, too.

But no, I get to the bottom step and halfway through the doorway, and immediately I sense a heavy silence in the air. I can't really describe it except to say it feels very freaky. I guess it's what people mean when they say they had a sense of foreboding. Then, I spot Terry and John going out the other doorway leading to the classrooms. So I yell, "Hi, you guys!" but they just wave and keep going. It was very weird!

Pretty soon, I'm in the kitchen, and I see Father Rex and Deacon Jim sitting at the long picnic-style table, hands folded, looking very seriously at me. My stomach churns and my heart pounds. I put the baby and the bag down and stand there, looking at them. I guess someone, maybe Margie, grabbed the baby and went back upstairs with him. I don't really know.

"Beth, sit down, please," says Father Rex as he pats the bench next to him. My heart beats so hard, I swear it hurts. I just kind of collapse by him, knowing this is going to be bad. And, Oh, God, it's the unimaginable—my worst-ever fear.

"There's been an accident," he sort of whispers, "involving your folks." I just stare at him. "Your mom, dad, sisters, Mary Ann and Robert."

"Robert?" I gasp. It makes no sense. I couldn't for the life of me figure out why Robert, who I'd only been talking to again for a few weeks, would be with my family and good friend in the car driving to Bakersfield. We were hardly even getting along when I left. In fact, the way he had left it between us, was "Let's call a truce and see what happens when you get back from the reservation."

"Yes," Father Rex says back. "He's okay, but your dad's hurt pretty badly and in the local hospital. One of your sisters has been taken to a hospital in another town, a bigger one, for surgery, but they think she's going to be okay. One of your friends is hurt, but not critically."

"They think? Which sister? What about my mom?" I swear I hear words streaming out of my mouth, but I'm not really talking; I'm not thinking or grasping any of this, that is, until his mouth quietly forms the next words.

"Laurie's okay, but Margaret was in the front seat, and her injuries required more sophisticated equipment. That's why she's at a bigger hospital. But Beth, I'm sorry to say…your mom didn't make it." Immediately, I cover my ears. No. No way. I can't have just heard that. I feel myself falling, losing air, seeing black, being engulfed by it. Then someone catches me, cradles me in his arms. Father Rex. Now, my belly aches. I try to get up, to run somewhere, my guts hurt. Mom gone? No, God. No! "Didn't make it," he had said. Why? How can this be?

"What do you mean? Where is she? I want to see her. Oh, God! Please…I need to see them, please!" Father Rex understands.

"Of course. We'll take you there right now."

He helps me up and takes my hand, leading me back up the steps to his car. The sun blasts us with its light and heat. I feel nothing. Things around me seem washed in muted, blurry shades of color. I move numbly to the car. Deacon Jim gets in next to me and puts his arm around me. This seems weird. He's young, just a few years older than me, and he's preparing to be a priest. I really know, though, that he just wants to comfort me. Oh, my God. No one says anything. I guess I hold my stomach. I don't want to throw up. I just want to get there, now!

When we get to the hospital, I walk in a daze, with Deacon Jim holding one hand and Father Rex holding the other. One of them talks to some hospital staff person, and a doctor stops us for a few seconds and talks to us. Then we go to the room where Dad is, all bloody and bandaged, with his eyes closed. All of a sudden, I don't think I can move. I'm light-headed again. I stop at the door. Is he asleep? Alive? I guess he hears me come in because he opens his eyes, licks his lips and calls me, in a thick voice I can barely hear, "Bethie—oh, Bethie." I don't cry, I can't. I haven't been very close to Dad for a long time. It's very strange, but I know he and I bonded in a huge way at that moment. He wants to know about Mom.

"Where'd they take your mother? Is she okay?" I remember now that, before I walked into that room, the doctor who stopped us in the hall had warned me that he would ask about her. Dad's wounds are "critical," he'd said, and I shouldn't tell him about Mom. But, at that moment, I ask myself how I'm supposed to lie to my dad about my mom? "She's gone," they had told me. Where? Gone where? That's what I wanted to know, what I wanted to shout at them.

"Yeah, I guess so," I try to lie to Dad, but no real words of reassurance come out of my mouth. Then he becomes my father again, and he bails me out, "She's okay. I know she is." I don't correct him. I see that his eyes are closed again, and I walk out. Then Deacon Jim and Father Rex, who must have been hovering outside the door, lead me to see Laurie. So unreal. There she sits on a hospital bed, not crying, just staring into space.

"Laurie, hi. How are you?" I ask nervously as I try to hug her, something I never do. She tells me she has a broken toe, and we kind of giggle.

"How's Margaret?" she wants to know.

"They told me she's at a bigger hospital. She's hurt pretty bad, but she'll be okay," I say. "How about Robert? And Mary Ann?"

"I don't know; I haven't seen them." Truth is, I've forgotten all about them. So now I say, "I think I'll go check. I'll come back and tell you. Okay?"

"Sure." And she looks off into space again. She doesn't mention Mom or Dad. So, so weird is all I can say about this encounter with my little sister. I walk outside the room and see Robert talking to Father Rex. He smiles at me and says something like, "There you are. Are you okay?" I have no idea what I say, but I do ask about Mary Ann. He says she's in with a doctor; her shoulder was hurt in the crash. After a while, a few hours maybe—I honestly don't really know what I've been doing all this time—I see Aunt Maudie and Uncle Ralph coming toward me. They look worried, but they're not crying. They just tell me they want me to go with them to their motel room to rest. I don't argue. I'm sure I acted like a zombie. I still feel like that, too. I say goodbye to Father Rex and Robert. Father tells me he'll see me when I come back.

When we get to the motel, I see Mary Ann's dad checking in at the front desk. Aunt Maudie wants Uncle Ralph to go get me something to eat, but I tell her I don't think I can eat anything. While Uncle Ralph goes to the vending machine to get me a coke, she takes me to the room. I try to lie down on one of the beds, but I can't stay still. Pretty soon, Uncle Ralph comes in with the soda and a candy bar, and right behind him is Robert. He says Mary Ann's parents brought him over. Uncle Ralph motions for Aunt Maudie to go with him out of the room.

Robert and I kinda stare at each other and sit down on the bed, and I guess he grabbed my hand because I remember that we were holding hands. It was all so bizarre! I ask him why he came with my parents, and he says something about wanting to surprise me. We both kinda laugh at that. I think I say something crazy like thanks for coming. So stupid but so what?! After a while, I tell him I have to get back to the hospital. I tell him I just can't stand it here. There's no way I can "rest." I stand up and hold my stomach, trying not to cry, not to puke. He says, "Don't worry. I'll tell your aunt and uncle you need to be where the others are. I'll go with you. It's going to be okay," and he gives me an awkward hug.

When we get to the hospital, I see Father Rex, but Aunt Maudie gets to him first, and she and Uncle Ralph take him aside and the three talk quietly. Finally, they come over to Robert and me. Father takes my hand and, ever so gently, suggests that someone needs to call Jimmy and Frank. He asks me if I want him to do it, and I say no. Somehow, I know this is my job, my family.

"But what will I tell them?"

"About your family, your parents, your mom. Are you sure you don't want me to do it for you? I will," he says. "Or your aunt or uncle can call." And they nod in agreement, just looking at me. I don't know why, but I just know right then that I'm the one to do this. But how? I hardly ever even talk to Jimmy. We don't really have anything in common. And Frankie, Frankie…how can I tell him that Mom is gone? How is he going to take it? My big brother with the golden hair and the beautiful smile. I wished I was with him right then. How can I explain what happened? I wasn't there. I don't know. It makes no sense to me, no matter how hard I try. Right then, I just want to bash my brains in. I still do. I guess I gulped and shook my head.

"No, I'll do it."

Father must have walked me to an empty office where a hospital person got me an outside line. I remember I dialed the number and waited for what seemed like a long time. It was excruciating. Excruciating. That's the word for it. After a few long rings, Frankie answered.

"Frankie, it's me, Beth." I said.

"Hey, Beth. How's it going with the Indians? What kind of Indians are they anyhow? Do they speak English? What kind of clothes do they wear?" God, he can ask such crazy questions!

"I don't know. It's going okay. Fine, I guess. Frankie, something really bad has happened."

"What? Why do you sound so funny? Did Mom and Dad get there

okay?"

"No. They got in a terrible car accident. Dad's hurt really bad. And Margaret, too. Laurie's okay, just a broken toe, but..." How do I say this? My heart is going to burst, it's pounding so hard, like it is now just thinking about it. "Mom didn't make it," I manage to say hoarsely. He must have dropped the phone and run into where Jimmy was because then Jimmy's on the phone and, kind of out of breath, says, "Beth, what's wrong? What happened?" I get through the explanation again, somehow, using the same words about Mom. "Mom didn't make it." Then I add, "She's gone." Silence, utter silence. I add "I love you!"

How or why I say this I don't know. It must have been God talking, because I never say anything close to this to anybody in my family except Mom. Mom. I can hear Jimmy crying and saying "No" over and over; then he says he loves me too and drops the phone. I can still hear him crying. I don't know. Maybe he's hysterical or maybe that's me. I don't know. After a few seconds, I hang up.

Now what do I do? I'm sitting here in this office, watching the hands of the clock. It's seven o'clock. I guess my brothers were eating dinner or at least thinking about it, or maybe watching a ball game on TV, eating a burger from Foster Freeze. Just having a casual Saturday night with the family out of the house for a change. But now...I know this is the worst day of my life, and theirs, too. And I don't know if I can...or how I will...what? Go on? What else do I do?

I'm just wondering...where is she? I don't mean her body. Although I wonder about that too, but I can't really think about that right now. I mean her, my mom, my MOTHER, my only one. Mom, who holds me and rocks me and loves me even when I argue with her, the one who forgives me when I'm mean and sarcastic, the one who makes me cinnamon toast and sits with me at the kitchen table and waits up for me at night and ALWAYS, ALWAYS kisses me goodnight. The one who bustles around the house and does our laundry and soothes my hurt feelings and listens even when I don't know what to say, who loves God and has always made church seem so nice and cozy warm. What can they mean when they say SHE'S GONE?

She CANNOT be gone. If she's gone, that means I will never see her again! I will NEVER see her again! THAT CANNOT BE! I'm not grown up yet. I'm still such a kid. Graduating from high school was exciting at the time, but now, I'm going to start college. I don't know how that's going to be. How am I supposed to do that without her here to talk to when I need to talk, not to just anyone, but to my MOM? I miss her so much already. I want her to walk through the door and tell me it's a huge mistake, that she's here. Ssshhh, it's ok, my honey, my baby. That's what I really am, a big baby, even though they're all treating me like I'm so mature and grown up.

They saw me as a kid this morning; now, I'm grown up? No way! It's just insane.

Aunt Maudie and Uncle Ralph, Father Rex and Deacon Jim—they're all being so nice to me, but they look at me funny, like they're waiting for me to talk, to do something. What?? I have no clue. And Aunt Maudie letting me sit in a motel room with Robert, BY OURSELVES? Me, a good Catholic girl, sitting alone with a boy in a motel room—that's unbelievable. Of course, all we did was hold hands and stare at each other and then the floor. What was there to say?? I want HER. That's ALL I want. I can barely breathe. I don't see how I can go on. I don't think I can do it without you, Mom. I don't see how I can...God, where are you?

2 HOLD THE SKY UP A LITTLE LONGER

Help me if you can, I'm feeling down
And I do appreciate you being 'round
Help me get my feet back on the ground
Won't you please, please help me?

~John Lennon and Paul McCartney

August 9, 1965
Evening

Dressed in shorts and a loose-fitting t-shirt, Laurie lay on the couch in front of the TV, petting her cat. She was only half-heartedly watching the show that was on; most of her attention was consumed by the oppressive August heat and what she could do that might provide some relief. Usually, the onset of evening brought a respite, perhaps even a breeze, but not tonight. It was too hot to move, and anyway, there wasn't anything she wanted to do.

As she scratched behind her cat's ears, she felt—as well as heard—his kitty engine start up and grow stronger, louder. Simultaneously, he stretched his neck as if he could somehow push his way further into the satisfying massage Laurie was providing. Meanwhile, her inner voice began to match his as she softly hummed a tune that only she and Murphy could hear.

The cat lay on her chest, and she had no plans to let him escape. His contentment and her attention to it kept them bonded for now, a bond she sorely needed. In their own little world, this was all that mattered: the two of them, here, right now.

No need to be concerned about anything else—just them and the heat that prevented her mind from wandering to anywhere dangerous. No. Laurie and her black, silky Murphy—they were a pair, a team. Aware that the spell that held her could be broken at any time, she quieted her breathing as she continued to sing softly, keeping her focus on this moment.

"What are you watching, Laurie?" And there it was, the pin popping the bubble; the finger-snap interrupting the trance. Beth plopped down in the big easy chair opposite the couch. "Is this 'The Dating Game'?" No response. "No, I can see it isn't. What are you doing? It doesn't look like you're watching this." Still no response.

"You and Kitty look comfortable, but you couldn't really be comfortable. It's a million degrees today. I thought it was hot on the reservation. Actually, it was hotter than this, but it didn't seem that much worse. I mean, on the reservation, we expected it to be hot. Father Rex even made us take salt tablets every day. They said there in the desert it was a dry heat, ya know, so if we were in the shade, we weren't supposed to feel it as much. I don't know. I'm not sure I really noticed a difference. Ya know what I mean?"

With still no reaction from the stoic Laurie, Beth queried her softly, "You okay? I mean, is there anything I can do?"

"I'm okay. And I'm not really watching the TV, so you can change the channel if you want. I'm just petting Murphy. And yeah, I can't believe it's so hot." Laurie spat out the words in a kind of torrent.

"Okay, okay. I don't really care about the TV. It just seems like something to do. It's so quiet around here."

"Yeah, I know."

"It's so weird, though, isn't it? I mean, when is our house so quiet?"

Now Laurie cringed. She needed Beth to let her be. Small talk, okay. But she desperately wanted to stay away from any topic remotely associated with the events of the last few days.

As it was, their aunt would be back soon, and the reality of their situation would be tantamount to the sky actually falling in or the ceiling suddenly giving way. Soon, she sensed, her world would be strewn with boulders and cement chunks and ash and soot.

It had already begun; voices, eerily familiar but not, had filled most of the rooms of her house with strange and frightening tones—tones way out of the ordinary for this house. Fortunately, she'd found little hiding places where she wouldn't come face to face with them.

Now, with their dad still in the hospital, Aunt Maudie had said she wanted to stay with them for a while…if that was okay. They had agreed. In actuality, Laurie hadn't weighed in. As the youngest in the family, she didn't really have a vote. According to the decision-makers, she, in particular, needed looking after.

She heard that statement and had no comment because she didn't know what "looking after" involved. She knew "they" worried that she wasn't talking much.

What could she say? She couldn't articulate the emotions that rocked her to her core and took her words away. With her aunt coming to stay, she knew—she really knew—she would never be able to go back to the ways things were; she would be stuck in the present. Laurie needed to postpone this inevitability for as long as possible.

But the rest of them, at least her sister Beth and her brother Jimmy, had already accepted what was. She could see that by the way they talked and acted. She supposed her brother Frankie had, too. She didn't know about Margaret, who, like her father, was still in the hospital.

Her situation was dithery, not rational at all.

At twelve, Laurie still lived in a small world: mother as center, the rest of the family—siblings and father—moving around this center, followed by concentric outer circles of best friend, neighborhood/church friends, teachers and so on. Not much had disturbed her thus-far serene life. Laurie had had no inclination to dig into her psyche to discover uncomfortable or troubling feelings.

For sure, when her body began to mature at the young age of 10, she'd been unhappy. Her awkward and uncomfortable new reality had prompted her to go to her mother for explanations, but, for the first time in her memory, her mother had come up short.

Instead of answers, Laurie had found evasion; instead of reassurance, she'd found disappointment. Anna had seemed just as unhappy as Laurie at the early development, plunging Laurie into confusion and tears. Finally, Beth had intervened—much to Anna's chagrin—but eventually, Anna had rallied, calming Laurie and restoring her secure world.

Anna hadn't wanted to see her little girl grow up so soon. That was all. There, there, she'd said in comforting tones, embracing her daughter, and, after that, except for the physical changes that she'd hidden as best she could, nothing else in Laurie's life had disturbed her dramatically. She'd felt a little more grown up, but mostly, she was the same girl she'd always been, and so her life had resumed.

Beth tried again. "What do you think about Aunt Maudie being here for a while?"

"I don't know. It's okay, I guess."

"Yeah, I don't know, either. She's been so nice. I think she just wants to make sure we're all okay. She's a little worried about you." Beth looked hard at Laurie.

"Hmm." Laurie kept her head down, still scratching the cat.

"Well, I told her I would check on you. Things are hard, Laurie, but…"

When her voice broke, Beth got up. No longer looking at her sister, Beth finished her sentence to the room. "We'll get by somehow."

As Beth walked out, Laurie looked after her, curiously, and sighed with relief. Then she began scratching the cat again and continued her wordless song.

3 BURN, BABY

How many roads must a man walk down
Before you call him a man?
Yes, and how many seas must a white dove sail
Before she sleeps in the sand?
The answer my friend is blowing in the wind
The answer is blowing in the wind

~Bob Dylan

It was ten o'clock on a sultry summer night, and a corner of the world was disintegrating. Siren wails punctured the stale air as Beth and Robert sat on her front porch, staring numbly at the smoke and light in the not-too-distant sky. Just then, Aunt Maudie came to the screen door; her voice trembled with fear as she warned "You two better come inside. I don't think it's safe out on that porch, tonight. It's on the news that snipers from Watts are driving around neighborhoods shooting people."

"What do you mean, Aunt Maudie? Why? What's going on?"

"I just heard that people trying to cool off outside are getting shot!" Beth was just about to make a move to obey when Jimmy's voice chimed in from inside. Beth listened, surprised at both Jimmy's tone and what he said to their aunt.

"Maudie, I don't think tragedy's going to strike this family twice in one week. Anyway, so far, those reports are just rumors. And I don't think anyone's talking about our neighborhood. We're pretty far away from the action." Then Jimmy came to the door. "You're okay where you are, Beth."

"Well, I'm turning off the porch light anyway. We can't be too careful," Aunt Maudie said, not one for easy concessions.

"Jimmy, what's going on? There's so much smoke and light in the sky. It looks like an inferno. And ugh! It smells like rotten eggs, really rotten eggs!"

Jimmy came out onto the porch and sat down in one of the green Adirondack chairs.

"Okay, this is what I heard on the news just now. An Afro-American kid got pulled over for drunk driving by a white cop—he was with his brother—and when the cop handcuffed him and started to put him in the cop car, the kid's mom came running up, yelling at the cop, punching him and pulling on his shirt. The newsman said she tore the shirt to bits. Who knows if that's true? Maybe the brother got involved, I don't know, but more police arrived on the scene and arrested the mother and both brothers. It's been so hot that there were lots of people milling around on the streets, and this arrest attracted a crowd of onlookers. Some of them started throwing rocks and bottles after the police car. It looks like more police cars showed up, trying to get control. Now, a rubber factory's burning, and those streets are in chaos. The newsmen are using the words 'possible riot.'"

Beth thought of all the times her brothers would jump in the car at the sound of a nearby siren. Why did some people just have to know what's going on if there's any excitement brewing?

"That's awful. But I still don't get it. I mean, if the kid was drunk and driving, I guess he would get arrested, wouldn't he? I don't see why the mom would start hitting the cop. And besides that, how did it all end up in a riot? Was everyone crazy or something?" Beth looked at Robert, who shook his head.

"It doesn't look like it's just about a drunk-driving arrest, Beth. Some of the people on the street are being interviewed. They're saying people who live in the Watts area, you know, across the railroad tracks, are fed up. They're crammed into a tiny area. A lot of them don't have jobs, and they think the white cops are out to get them.."

"Do you think that's true, Jimmy? do *you* think the white cops have it in for them? I mean, we talked about stuff like this, ya know, in religion class last year, but do you think that the people have a reason to start a riot? I mean, isn't that just going to make their lives worse? It seems crazy."

"Well, I don't know if I'd go so far to say they should all riot. But I would say things aren't always so clear. Sometimes, it depends on your vantage point. If I'd been stopped for suspected drunk driving, I'm not sure I would have been arrested. And if Mom had come yelling at the cop for doing it—and we both know she would never have done that—still, I don't think the cop would have started whaling on me with his nightstick and then arresting every member of our family who happened to be there. So look at the whole picture, Beth. It's hotter than blazes, people without jobs are really unhappy. They're outside, just trying to cool off. They see a commotion and go to check it out. Something that seems really wrong to them is happening, and some of them snap. The sad thing is that those flames and that smell are mostly their own businesses burning, one of them a tire factory that employed a few hundred people. They're also turning cars over and torching them. I just saw on the news that some of the firemen who went to put out the flames got beat up. And the people aren't letting ambulances into the area. It's really bad."

"Joe's dad has a butcher shop in Watts. I wonder if his store's going to get burned up. And if it doesn't, will it be safe for him to go to work? I hope Joe wasn't helping out tonight. Geez, just think if that happened to Dad's store." All three sat there silent, until Robert finally said he better get going, that his parents were probably worried.

A little later, Beth lay in her bed, windows wide open, the putrid smells and screaming sirens invading her room. Nothing made sense. A little over a week before, she had been on an adventure, on a real Indian reservation, playing with and getting to know Indian kids. Away from home, feeling grown up, with a group of teens from her high school and adults from Father Rex's parish, not one of them a family member—she felt something new: life could be delightfully interesting. She saw herself on the verge of experiences that could be hers if she opened herself up to them. Then, three days ago, lightening had struck, shattering the adventure into pieces. Now, she sensed she was witness to someone else's tragedy, very likely the beginning of broken dreams for many girls just like her.

Growing up in middle class Compton, California, Beth had walked or ridden her bike wherever her inclination or a friend's invitation led her—always, of course, with her mother's approval. She couldn't remember many places that were off limits on her girlhood sojourns. On the outskirts of the places her mother had approved lay Wilson Park, located two long blocks from her elementary school, and where the upper grades—fifth through eighth—had the privilege of spending their lunch hours. Beth remembered the excitement of leaving behind the sterile and unforgiving blacktop of St Mary's school grounds for the wide open green of the park where the nuns allowed the children thirty minutes for lunch and thirty minutes organized play time.

For the girls, this meant organized softball, handball and kickball, but usually they found a few minutes to laze about in supposed freedom, laughing and playing on the swings, merry-go-round or rusty teeter-totters. But the park had earned its share of unsavory gossip. Anna had heard that some shady characters had approached a child or two until a nun called the kids away; worse, Anna feared the disquieting whispers about what had happened under a tree or in the bushes to stray girls.

Ever vigilant, Beth's mother had issued strict warnings about walking in twos and never using the bathroom at the park. And never was Beth to venture beyond the railroad tracks that, two blocks over, ran parallel to the west side of the park. This directive had piqued Beth's interest. Somewhere "over there" Anna had explained, stood housing developments for really poor people where some bad things happened. Beth was not to walk or ride her bike on the "wrong side of the tracks." When she thought about it, though...the public library, where many people—including her father—routinely visited, was in that general area. And it hadn't seemed much different from her own neighborhood, except for the industrial feel of the place. Her father certainly had never hurried or looked over his shoulder there, and, in fact, would usually pause at the bottom of the library steps to have Beth jump into his arms.

Sometime during high school, Beth heard that one of the priests at school was arranging for kids to volunteer in Watts, where many children were in need of homework help. Out of curiosity, Beth found her way to the priest's office—it turned out to be Father Rex—and signed up. After tutoring for a few months, Father suggested the volunteers organize a Christmas surprise for the children. The tutors had put big boxes in the classrooms and made announcements during homeroom period. By Christmas break, the boxes were full of canned and boxed food and toys. Father had appealed to local businesses for donations of turkeys and hams. One day after school, he and the volunteers had taken the baskets of food and brightly wrapped toys to the Watts community center. Father Rex took care of the distribution. After the winter break, drill team and a new boyfriend took up her time and interest, and that was that for Beth and Watts until now.

Why? she now asked herself. Why did she give it up so easily, with no thought for the children who might have relied on her? At first, it had been uncomfortable; they were all a little shy. But after the first few awkward times of sitting down with little boys and girls whose noses were runny and whose clothes didn't look all that clean or warm, she started bringing Kleenex and asking them to run and get their sweaters before they got started. Father Rex always brought snacks, which Beth passed out first, and, before long, she would be listening to their labored reading, checking their addition and subtraction, and laughing at cute things they said.

Two children in particular, third-grader Tasha, and her younger brother Devon, had touched her with their affection and diligence. Both of them greeted her with smiles when she knocked on their apartment door, running to get their schoolwork, which they carried in worn binders. They would take turns reading, and tried to help each other if one struggled with unfamiliar words. And the number of words that were not part of their vocabulary stunned Beth. Then they tackled math, and, again, Beth could see clearly that they were behind in the simplest tasks. Still, they worked hard, sure that they were doing well, excited to show off for their tutor.

Other than feeling sad at their lack of space for running around or riding bikes—and the kids she saw mostly had at least a rusty semblance of a bike—she enjoyed her limited experience. After Christmas break, though, her focus turned back to herself.

Now, she thought about the dirty streets with broken down cars and blocks of apartment buildings and to the sweet, eager children who touched her for a moment. Who was helping Tasha and Devon now? Was she that shallow, that self-centered? Her family—at least her mother and brother Jimmy—had suggested more than once that her narrow focus on popularity and boys let other people down, mostly herself. She had to admit that Watts seemed another world from the one she inhabited in her clean and tidy little neighborhood where a group of kids always seemed to be outside playing on the grass in the sunshine, and adults waved to each other, often stopping to share the day's news.

But what was in store for Watts, Beth wondered. How long would it be in turmoil? How long would she lie on her bed listening to sirens and smelling burning tires and businesses? Should she be worried about snipers? What would Mom say about the mess unfolding? Would she be worried for our family? Concerned and sad for the mess unfolding on the other side of town? Before she knew it, she could see her mother at the front door, talking to Beth and Robert instead of Aunt Maudie, clucking her concern, for them, yet simultaneously conveying so much more. Furiously shaking off the image, gulping back the tears and sorrow fighting to spill out of her body. Beth fought for control, fought to force the feelings down, down to her leaden stomach. In rebellion, she sat up, looked around her room and focused on her yearbook and her life a few months before. Suddenly, Father Wade, one of her favorite teachers, came to mind and she cautiously settled back. She wondered what he was doing right now. She knew he'd be riled up, maybe even involved somehow, trying to help or at least talking passionately about the causes of the current furor.

No question about it, her senior religion teacher had challenged Beth and her classmates to "wake up," get their minds off gossip and look around at their world. He had engaged them in discussions about civil rights, asking them "What would you do if someone said you couldn't sit at a particular table because of your color? Would you fight for your equality?' She had nodded her head eagerly in agreement, having no idea what that meant or how she would accomplish it. She had only begun to imagine a life beyond her house, her block, her city. The university where she was to begin classes in a few weeks, only a half hour's drive on the freeway, had seemed immense when she'd toured the campus last spring. But since one brother had graduated from there and one was close to graduation, Beth figured she would find her place and enjoy it. When she made her college plans, she thought she had plenty of time to learn about the big, bad world. Jimmy urged her to take a political science course, read the newspaper, watch the news. She thought she would do all that; just give her a chance.

Chance, however, had something else in store for her. Instead of liberating challenges propelling her forward, tonight Beth felt a 20-pound boulder settling on her chest. How will I ever manage this new world?

She looked at Margaret's bed, occupied tonight by a sleeping Laurie. How bad off must Margaret be—she had to be taken to a hospital bigger than the one Dad's in? Seeing Jack covered in bandages, his arms connected to machines, Beth had shuddered to look at him. Aunt Maudie said his condition was listed as "critical." What did that mean? She hadn't wanted to ask. It was all Beth could do to say a hurried goodbye before coming home with her family, such as it was. But, again she wondered: If her dad's condition is really bad, but he could still be at Porterville hospital, what must Margaret's condition be? When she asked about Margaret, Aunt Maudie said her condition was "grave." At that, she just let the subject drop.

Or did I let Margaret drop? If her condition is "grave," then why aren't we going to her? What's really wrong with her? Is she going to die, too? Would that be better for her without Mom? How can I even think that? Who am I, dammit? I love my sister, don't I? Oh God, what's happened to her. Is she conscious? If she is, how frightened she must be, in pain with no one familiar talking to her and soothing her. How lonely! I had everyone around me.

And suddenly, in Beth's mind's eye, there they all were, circling her pathetic girl self: Father Rex, Deacon Jim, Aunt Maudie and Uncle Ralph—and Robert, of course.

With this image, the heavy feeling increased as confusion crowded into her thoughts, swirling in her brain.

None of this is fair. If Mom hadn't felt I needed checking on, they wouldn't have come. But I had to be such a difficult teenager! Why? My mother's the sweetest, gentlest person I know. She never deserved my snotty comments, my immature…my stupid, STUPID, behavior, NEVER. She always worried about me. If I had been a better daughter, maybe she wouldn't have thought she needed to check on me, to make sure I was all right. No trip, no accident. And I wasn't even all that nice when she called the night before they came. Rather shame on me!"

She shifted in her bed, kicking her feet in anger and throwing off the light sheet that covered her. She didn't think she would ever sleep, yet her body felt heavy, as if she were lapsing into a stupor of lifelessness. She couldn't remember when she had eaten anything, but the mere thought of food shot an arrow of nausea through her. What if she could rewind the past few days, be back in the little school in Porterville? She pictured the other kids, her friends, joking around, trying to get comfortable in their sleeping bags on the hard classroom floors in the stifling desert heat of August. What she wouldn't give to be back there, laughing and complaining right along with them.

Just then, Laurie moved, a murmur escaping her lips. Now acutely aware of this strange sister-child who slept a few feet away in Margaret's bed, she thought of Laurie's little bed in her parents' room. Since Beth could remember, Laurie had occupied a bed in a corner of the big "master" bedroom. She had never questioned this arrangement. In fact, she remembered Laurie starting out there as a baby in a crib, then graduating to a junior-sized bed as a toddler. Somewhere along the line, her parents must have acknowledged that Laurie was growing up--thus, the twin bed.

To Beth, however, Laurie had just been the little, whiny child who always shadowed their mother, seeming like another appendage, along with Margaret. Beth didn't think there was ever a time when she'd done that, except when she'd been forced to help with chores.

She had always loved to be out and about in the neighborhood, looking for excitement or palling around with school friends, though she remembered, as a little girl, loving to sit at the table, having "coffee" (lots of milk and sugar with a touch of coffee) while Anna had told her stories of her young womanhood. But this had been pre-Laurie time. Was it ever a little weird for Laurie, Beth wondered, to sleep practically side by side with their parents?

Suddenly self-conscious, Beth realized that the images coming to mind now embarrassed her, and she went back to her thoughts about the "master" room itself, distinguished from the other two bedrooms by its having two closets.

Her mother's closet was Beth's favorite place in the house. For one thing, Anna kept a box of dress up clothes there. So often, when Beth and a friend wanted to re-invent themselves, they would dig through the box for something that suited their imaginings.

But more importantly, Anna's closet held garments that, over the years, had carried rich meaning for Beth: the everyday housedresses in which Anna hung clothes on the clothesline or swept the floor and did other chores; the black velvet tops with taffeta skirts decorated with tiny sparkling rhinestones that transformed Anna from an ordinary mother into an enchanting sophisticate for special evenings at church; high heels, ranging from black patent leather decorated with grosgrain bows to her very favorites in the collection: the shoes her mother called her "glass slippers"—pumps with clear plastic heels and enclosures for the toes.

How many times did I parade around in those Cinderella shoes, looking at my reflection in the full-length mirror as I struck various poses? And the scent of Mom's fur coat! If she was away at a meeting or running her endless errands, if I missed her or needed grounding and comfort for any reason, I only had to bury my head in that coat to feel safety and comfort.

Beth had never told anyone about this, although she felt sure her mother knew about her daughter's fascination with her closet.

As Beth's mind wandered through this room from the sleeping sister to their mother's closet next door and its belongings, she lingered for a while, deciding that the next day she would go once more to the room and the closet where she could find the comfort of her mother once again.

4 TAKE THE (TINY LITTLE) RING

Miss Lonely Hearts, dear Miss Lonely Hearts
I'm writing this letter to you,
'Cause you're so wise, So please advise
This sad little girl what to

~Aaron Schroede and Wally Gold

August 1965
4 days after the accident

Dear "Abby" if you're out there,

Mom calls me "Dear Abby"; she says I'm always on the phone giving advice to my friends. Well, I need my own "Abby" right now because I need to understand what just happened to me. I don't know who to turn to. The horrible fact is that there really isn't anyone, not one single person. Dad is still in the hospital, even if I could bring myself to talk to him. Laurie is not talking to anybody, period! And forget about Jimmy. He's here, but I've never talked to him about anything like this—wait! That's so crazy! When have I ever experienced anything remotely like this? Frankie's not here. Where is he anyway? He came up with Jimmy to the hospital. I saw him there. But then we came home and he didn't. Did someone say he stayed with Uncle Ralph at the college? Why would he do that? I called Allie, but she's not home. And Robert wouldn't understand. I don't know how I can even talk about this. How can I say it out loud? So, "Abby," you're it. I'm "not talking" to you tonight about the most unbelievable thing I can imagine happening to me.

It's been four days since "The Accident." It's the middle of August, and hot and muggy and miserable in Compton, California. Aunt Maudie is staying with us because of the awful, horrible car crash that took Mom away forever and VERY seriously injured Dad and poor Margaret. Unfair! Horrible in every way! And they were coming to Bakersfield to visit me—yep, me—because I was at an Indian reservation working with kids from my school for a few weeks with Father Rex. Shouldn't that count as a good thing? I guess not, because now Mom is gone! That's it! I'll never see her again. I still can't comprehend what this means. I mean, WHERE IS SHE?!

Aunt Maudie told me that once the funeral is over, the phone calls and visits from family and friends will stop, and I will really get what has happened. First of all, I know she's just trying to prepare me, but WHY does she have to say that? What more is there to get?

Maybe she thinks I don't know my life's been destroyed. What I do know now, for sure, is that when Robert—who was in The Accident—leaves, I start to feel pretty panicky. When he isn't around, I call Allie.

Allie is, without a doubt, my go-to friend right now. And I call nonstop! She just drops what she's doing and rushes over here if she can. Of course—what else is new? These days, I can't even say how much I depend on her. I've also been writing poetry and prayers. I love God so much, and I need Him. Is He there? I'm sorry; I really am, but I have to ask. I feel like I'm going crazy, and everything feels topsy-turvy. I have to stay busy. I can't stand to be alone or quiet. I hate it when I have to go to bed at night for that very reason: it is JUST TOO QUIET! Now, with this latest development, I'm even more at a loss.

A couple of hours ago, after dinner (What a joke! I can NOT eat anything!), Aunt Maudie signals for me to come out on the front porch with her. Our house is pretty small, especially for our family of seven, although now MOM IS GONE, and Margaret and Dad are still in the hospital—or I should say HOSPITALS—and Frankie is…I don't know where, so that leaves three (plus Aunt Maudie). If Dad had been home, and things were NORMAL, he would've been parked in the red reading chair in the living room, and Aunt Maudie and I would never have made it out the front door without his knowing. Of course, if he had been here, he would have been involved, but he would have made everyone get out of the living room so that he and Aunt Maudie could talk to me. We would NOT have gone out on the porch for privacy.

Aunt Maudie is his sister, and she is quite bossy and sergeant like, but I think she's being kinda careful with all of us right now. The thing is, what usually seems funny to me is that Dad actually was a sergeant in the Army in WWII. Anyway, they often butt heads. I'm pretty intimidated by both of them and usually have a hard time having a private conversation with either one. Definitely, it would still have been a strange scene if Dad had been here. But also much better, I'm sure. I could really use my dad right now because, after all, he is still my dad.

Anyway, having Aunt Maudie take me out on the porch felt very weird.

But there it is. That's what happened. We go outside and stand there. It's a big, red porch with two chairs, but we don't sit down. Aunt Maudie, looms over me and looks straight down into my face. Then she says something like, "Now, Beth, I think you should have something very special of your mom's since you're the oldest girl, besides Margaret. Your mom is going to be buried with her wedding ring on, but I think—and your dad agrees—that it doesn't do anyone any good to bury her with both rings. We think you should have her engagement ring, and we believe that's what your mom would want. It would be nice if you decide to use it someday." (I guess, since Margaret's "special," Aunt Maudie was implying that she's never going to need this ring.)

Like I said, I don't really remember her exact words. I remember asking—or at least wondering—if this was really okay with Dad. He and my mom were very close as far as I was concerned, talking over everything. Recently, they had been talking about celebrating their 25th wedding anniversary next month and all. Oh, God! How sad! Why wouldn't he just want to keep my mom's ring or let it stay on her finger? It was hers! I wish he could explain this to me. I love my Aunt Maudie; she's always been a big part of our lives—our only aunt, as far as I know, and our grandparents are all dead. But she's so different from sweet, gentle Mom. Aunt Maudie's bossiness did bug the heck out of Mom sometimes, though she would never come out and say that, but I could tell.

So, anyway, now I'm all confused. She hands me the ring, which is so tiny, silver, with a little diamond in the middle of it. I had never seen it off my mom's hand until that moment, and it doesn't seem right that it's not there now, no matter where she is. I just wish Dad had been the one to ask me if I want it. I might have said no, but Aunt Maudie is so...Aunt Maudie. I went to the mortuary with her and my brother Jimmy to pick out the casket, and Laurie and I agreed on the dress that mom is going to be buried in, but I didn't know there had been any discussion about rings. I guess they think I'm too young for some things—they wouldn't let me see the car all battered up, even though I told them that I wanted to see it.

"I want to see the car."

"Oh, no. That would be a mistake," Aunt Maudie said in that way she has, and I swear she "furrowed" her brow.

"Why? I really want to go." I pressed the issue, getting all panicky and hot.

"Because it's...it's..." Aunt Maudie actually stammered! Then Jimmy said finally, "Beth, it would only upset you."

"I don't care," is all I could say, but they both just shook their heads.

What I really wanted to shout was, "You don't think I'm already upset?! WHERE IS MOM?! I WANT TO SEE HER! I NEED TO!" But I knew the answer would always be no: no to seeing the car, no to seeing Mom, who, since she died in that car, should really be a mess though Robert says she didn't have a mark on her. But I guess they decided I'm old enough for some things—like a ring—but not for others. It's so confusing! They seem to think they can protect me, no matter how hopeless and senseless that really is. But like I said, finally, I did talk them into letting me go to the mortuary to pick out the casket. My aunt didn't want me to go, but Jimmy said, "Yes, she can if she wants." Thank you very much, at least for that, I guess.

So here is this really weird situation. I took the ring, went into the house, lay down on my bed, crying a little and staring at the ring. It's way too small for me—Mom had such tiny fingers—so I can't wear it, even if I felt right about it. And neither of my sisters is petite like Mom, either. I hope when Dad comes home we can talk about it. Still, I kind of doubt we will because, like I said, he's hard for me to talk to under most circumstances. What would I say anyway? How would I bring it up? Maybe he will.

What's he going to be like when he comes home from the hospital with no wife? When I saw him right after the accident, he was so banged up. There he was, covered in bandages--and what wasn't bandaged looked raw and purply-bruised. I couldn't even really see his eyes, but he seemed so sad and kind of frantic, asking me about Mom. I could feel him trying not to ask, as if he didn't want to hear the answer. It was horrible. Funny, (not the right word!) how come, since Robert says mom was NOT all messed up, how come she's the one who didn't make it? How can this be? And Jimmy and Aunt Maudie insist the car is a mess. I'm just a kid, and I cannot believe this is all happening. I'm trying so hard to understand what God wants from me now.

Wasn't graduation just yesterday? Like I said, all this summer I have felt like such a child, a confused teenager, constantly asking Mom what I should do. I'm starting college, but not all that excited about it. I have a very cute sort of boyfriend, but not totally sure he's right for me. (Mom loved Robert! Not only is he handsome and smart, he's Catholic!)

Now, here I am. I don't look any different on the outside, but I feel so strange on the inside. Maybe God is telling me it's time to grow up. I'm not sure how, but I don't think I have a choice. It's so weird. I'm not walking around crying constantly; in fact, I have a hard time crying at all– but when I do, the tears seem to come mostly when I'm in bed at night. Yet, I feel this weight, like an enormous bomb waiting to explode, sitting on my chest most of the time. I can't even see how I'm able to get out of bed or move around; it just feels so massive and heavy.

And I tend to need to be with someone else, someone I can talk to, mostly Allie, who's trying so hard to understand. And anyway, she'll listen and talk to me about anything; right now, it's mostly about God and why this is His will. That's what we always say about things we don't understand:

"It's God's will." She doesn't pretend to have the answers, but she's somehow able to make me feel less lonely. I also need someone who can make me laugh for a while here and there, like Robert, the one I thought I was broken up with, but who decided to surprise me by coming with my parents to visit me and then ended up being the hero of The Accident! Now, he thinks I'm all strong like Jackie Kennedy, and yet, I just want to cling to him.

I'm looking at the ring: it's so very tiny and pretty in an old, kind of tarnished way. I can see it on Mom's strong hand. This was the hand that held my head to see if I had a temperature, the hand that shook a finger at me when I was snotty, the hand that patted my back when I was crying. I could go on, but then I WILL cry, and I can't do that right now. It scares me too much. What if I can't stop? Laurie will walk in and get even more upset. If I keep the ring in my underwear drawer, I won't have to keep looking at it, but also I won't lose it. It's such a big responsibility.

Margaret and I are pretty crammed in here as it is. And now Aunt Maudie says Laurie's going to move into the room with us. How's that supposed to work? We don't have a jewelry box, and the dresser we share has stuff all over the top of it, so a little ring like this would probably just disappear. I guess I'll just have to figure it out later. (Like I think I can really do that!) I wish I was really writing this to someone who could help me. I have never felt so alone. I never knew it was even possible to feel so alone, so incredibly, amazingly alone. God, where are you? And what I really want to know is...where is my mother?

Beth

5 PICK UP THE PIECES

I can't forget you
I've got these memories of you
Once we were happy; we were so carefree and gay
Then something happened, and you went away

~Patsy Cline

Jack stared at the newspaper spread in front of him. The familiar sound of the coffee percolating, and its rich, full fragrance, comforted him. A few minutes before, he had assembled the coffee pot guts and scooped the earthy-brown granules into the top strainer and inhaled deeply—though it hurt him to do it—the sweet, dark aroma that had begun his day for the past 45 years. He'd been making and drinking coffee since he was thirteen and his parents split up. Becoming the man of the family overnight taught him to do more than a few things back in those uncertain days in Minneapolis.

Anna liked the way he heaped in the coffee grounds—none of this weak-as-tea coffee for him—or her either. It was his habit to make it in the morning; over the years, she had become more and more of a night-owl—making lunches for the next day, waiting up for teenagers—and so she rarely rose when he climbed out of bed to get an early start on his day. No wasting a minute for Jack, though. Anna usually murmured to him that she was right behind him, but he would hush her, smooth her hair and urge her to get a little more sleep until their kids got up and needed her. He knew well that Anna's days presented their own special challenges. Although his days were their own particular kind of busy, he knew that every single day, without fail, she tended to the incessant needs of five kids in varying stages of growing up. One of them, though, Margaret, never would really grow up. And the boys, like the gangly, glorious wildflowers that arrived in Anna's yard each spring, resisted Jack's efforts to contain them. All through the summer, no matter what he did, his "boys," grew up—and out: Frank was almost through college now, and Jimmy had graduated and wanted nothing more than to fly the coop, to Anna's enduring dismay.

Why? Jack had asked her again and again. Hadn't Jimmy done all they asked of him: finishing school, working hard, helping out whenever they asked. "A fine young man!" their friends all said. With swelling pride, Jack and Anna gratefully thanked these people of their community who had witnessed Jimmy's metamorphosis from ball player to altar boy, to Sister Superior's little darling...to delivery boy, then high school scholar and, finally, college graduate. Perhaps the only time Jimmy had disappointed anyone was when Sister Superior had thought she'd convinced him to enter the priesthood. When Jimmy made it clear that was not his path, Jack's sigh was relief; Anna's sigh was disappointment.

It had all gone so fast. Too fast. One moment, their friends were congratulating Jack and Anna on Jimmy's college graduation, and the next, they were shaking their heads in sympathy: Jimmy was going to basic training with the Army to prepare for war. Oh, those were cold, cold days for Jack, walking in the door after work each day to Anna's somber face, resigned to catastrophe; he was reminded of the way she had been when she received the telegram about her brother those long years ago.

After all that, Jimmy hadn't been sent overseas—first, the Army toughened him up, then they threw him, with his college education, into some top-secret training. But when the training was done, so was Jimmy. He came home and, by God, he was a man! But maybe that was Anna's sore spot all along: Jimmy, her first, had gone and grown into manhood before she was ready.

Well, everything had changed again, and Jimmy was back, living at home. It was Jack's turn to be disappointed—not at Jimmy, but at what had brought him here. Disappointed? Strange little word for the big, monstrous feeling that Jack white-knuckled all day, every day, to fend off. Ever independent and determined to defy whatever quagmire, dilemma, or conundrum confronted him, Jack's confidence had always told him he could fare well no matter the circumstance. He'd acquired this trait long ago, and it had stuck with him.

Now, he faced something new, a bewildering loss that seemed to have him in a vise, and the more he resisted, the tighter it twisted. He felt like his gut was on fire most of the time. How the hell was he supposed to pick up his life and go on? His wife of twenty-five years was no longer beside him; his helpmate, his quiet, steadfast anchor was gone.

Today, after a month in a sick bed—actually, a recliner—he had decided to shake himself out of it all: his sister doting on him, his children tiptoeing around him, everyone hanging their heads. The house had become cold and heavy with something he couldn't and didn't want to name. He only knew he needed to escape or go mad. And, here he was, in his kitchen, doing what he had always done, acting as if things were...ordinary. For a moment, he stood at the kitchen sink, looking through the pretty little window whose overhead light bulb he had changed innumerable times. A sharp pain shot through him, and he clutched his ribs. Dr. Klein had said, "No, Jack, you can't go back to work yet. It's too soon. You need more time to recover."

"Listen, Doc, I've got a business to run."

"And you've got a partner and several employees. What's the rush?"

"What's the rush? What's the rush?!! You don't understand."

"I do understand."

"No. Listen. Do you know what it's like to wander around your home when the heart of it is missing? This entire month, I haven't slept in my bed. Doctor's orders. YOUR orders, because I had to sleep at an extreme angle, with the damned clot in my lung."

"Jack—"

"No. Let me finish. That wasn't a problem. In fact, it was a relief for me, to tell you the truth. That chair is my home, as much as ANY thing is. It's where I read every night after work, after dinner. It's hard to explain. I'm alone, but at the same time, I'm in the middle of everything in my big red chair in the living room, and every member of my family knows where to find me. Hell, they can't miss me –they know that's Dad's space. My space. Mine. But now you say the clot has broken up and is no longer a danger. So, now I'm supposed to go back to my bed in THAT room, where she is no longer. I can't do it. I just can't do it."

"Hmm. I see—or at least, I THINK I see."

"So, I'm going to switch rooms with my daughters—my kids will help me—and I'm going back to work, by God. I don't care how much pain there is; in fact, the more the better as far as I'm concerned. Gives me something else to think about."

"OK, Jack, OK. I'll prescribe something for pain, just in case you want it. At least it should help you sleep, which I imagine you're not doing much of."

"You're right about that."

Snapping out of his reverie, Jack squared his broad shoulders, looked at his bruised reflection in the shiny, chrome coffee pot, carefully picked it up and poured himself a cup of steaming black coffee, popped two pieces of bread in the toaster, and opened up the daily newspaper. It was a start.

"Jack. Hi, it's me, Maudie," came the strong voice on the other end of the phone.

"Hi, Maudie. How's everything?" said Jack, glad to hear his sister's voice.

"We're fine over here. Ralph's over whatever bug got the better of him the past few days. I couldn't get him to go to the doctor. You know

Ralph—he's so stubborn. Even when I warned him that people die all the time—and in awful pain—of illnesses that didn't get diagnosed. Oh, well, I guess he was lucky."

"That's good news. Poor guy, he works hard and he's been darn good to us. You both have." Jack knew better than to take the bait of criticizing his brother-in-law.

"How's everything over there? You feeling any better? Gettin' any sleep?"

"Oh, a fair amount. I went back to work on Monday."

"Jack, why would you do that?!" she scolded. "You know you aren't ready for that! Your ribs aren't healed, and you look like hell, with all the bruises and contusions on your face and body. You're probably scaring your customers! What does Dr. Klein say?"

"Hey, just hold on a cotton-pickin' minute. I've been sleeping in the damn chair for the past month, so, no, I'm not getting a world of sleep. But, during the day, I ain't doing nothing but staring at the walls. Doc Klein understood. I told him I'd come home if it got to be too much for me. But that damn Danny, he's got things in a mess at the store. It's good that I go back before all our customers are bent out of shape. Don't worry. I'm a grown man. I know what I'm doing."

"Okay. It's your life. I'm just worried about you is all."

"I know it, and I appreciate it. I do," Jack said, calming down. "I appreciate all you've done for us. I don't know what we would've done without you and Ralph."

"Jack, how's Beth doing? I know school started for her. How does she like it? Is she getting by okay with college studies added to everything else she's doing?"

"How cow! I don't know what you mean, Maudie, by "everything else." Beth's doing fine, considering the circumstances. She's riding to the college with a friend until we get a new car to replace the Mercury. I told her to ask Frank or Jimmy if she has any problems with classes or her schedule in general. So far, she seems fine."

"C'mon Jack, by everything else, I just meant the shopping and cooking, ya know, all the household responsibilities. How's she doing with that? She's barely eighteen."

"Goddammit, Maudie! How do I know? She's doing the best she can, just like the rest of us. I need her; we all do, if that's what you're getting at. She's the only one who can really keep things running around here right now. You know Margaret can't do it, and Laurie's just a kid—and a pretty sad one, as far as I can tell. Beth says Laurie's okay, but she also says she's not talking much. I think that's to be expected. They all just lost their mother. How do you expect her to be?"

"I understand Jack, but I think you should consider hiring a housekeeper. That's all I'm saying. From where I stand, it looks like it's too much for Beth. How's she supposed to concentrate on school? I was thinking about having her live with me and Ralph, at least during the week. We live so close to the college, and it's quiet here. She wouldn't have to cook and clean. She could focus on school."

"Judas Priest, Maudie, I don't know where this is coming from. Beth hasn't said a word about this to me. Has she talked to you?"

"Not exactly. But she's stopped by a couple of times after classes, just to talk. She seems lost. Just think about it, Jack. There are probably people from the church who might like to help out right now, make a little extra money at the same time. In the meantime, Beth could relax a little. You know me and Ralph would love to have her."

"Yeah, well…I don't know. Maybe you're right, but what in hell am I supposed to do without Beth? She's been the bright light for me since Anna…I don't know…."

"It would be temporary, until everything was under control over there, until she got adjusted to school. You wouldn't be losing your daughter, just giving her a break."

"Say, Jimmy, can you sit down here and talk to me for a minute?"

Jack took off his glasses and rubbed his eyes, then pulled a handkerchief out of his shirt pocket and began cleaning them. Jimmy had seen his father perform this ritual countless times over the years.

"Of course, Dad. Is everything all right?"

Jimmy sat on the couch across from his father who was, as always, in his easy chair.

"Well, I don't know. It depends. Has Beth said anything to you about her being overworked around here? Is she complaining that it's too much for her? That Margaret and Laurie aren't helping? That helping out around here is too much, ya know, with school?"

"No, she hasn't. Why?"

"Maudie told me she wants Beth to live with her and Ralph. Says she thinks Beth's doing too much around here. Maybe she thinks I'm relying too much on Beth, with the cooking and shopping and all. I don't know what to make of it, is all."

"Hmm. I don't know. I've been pretty preoccupied with finding a job. Sometimes, I don't see her all day. Other times, she's in her room studying, I guess."

"But she does do all the shopping that your mother and I used to do. And I haven't been able to make dinner or even help her with it. Poor kid."

"Dad, none of us thinks you should be doing that stuff. It's enough that you've gone back to work."

"Now, don't get started on that! I've already had an earful from Maudie.

God almighty, she thinks she's queen of the world or something! Anyway, I know she means well. But you think Beth's okay? Do you think you could talk to her about it? No, I should do it. But what if she says it is too much? I don't know. I don't know what we'd do without her…I don't know what I'd do without her around here."

Jack sighed deeply and slouched into his chair, his shoulders hunched over like a boxer waiting for the final blow, or the ref's whistle signaling his defeat.

"I don't think she would want to live with Maudie, Dad. This is her home. And she wouldn't want to leave you—I'm sure of that. But maybe we could get someone to come in and help with the housework or cooking. That would relieve Beth. Maybe it's hard for her to get Margaret and Laurie to help her. They're her sisters; she's not their mom…I mean, boss."

"That's what Maudie implied. Jesus, I don't know what's happening to me!"

And then Jack started to cry, his head in his hands. "I'm sorry, I'm sorry," Jack said, trying unsuccessfully to pull himself together. Instinctively, Jimmy bent over him, his hand on his father's back.

"Dad, please, don't, just don't be sorry for crying." Jimmy fought hard for control. "You're crying for your wife of 25 years…my mother. You have nothing to apologize for."

"She was my Annie, my…my…my darling, my heart," Jack sobbed. "I can't lose Bethie, too. What am I going to do, Jimmy?"

"We'll work it out, Dad. We'll work it out together. You're not going to lose Beth. We're all going to figure this out." After several minutes, Jimmy finally lifted his hand from his father's back, as he sensed Jack's composure return.

"Thanks, Jimmy. You're a good son." With that, Jack took off his glasses, wiped them, then used the handkerchief to blow his nose. At this last, occasional part of Jack's ritual, Jimmy winced.

6 RIDE ON THE BRINK OF DESTRUCTION

The eastern world, it is explodin'
Violence flarin', 'bullets loadin'
You're old enough to kill, but not for votin'
You don't believe in war, but what's that gun you're totin'?
And even the Jordan River has bodies floatin'?

~P.F. Sloan

Though dinner was over and it was time to clean up the kitchen, Beth, who had spent the last thirty minutes silently pushing roast beef and potatoes around her plate, rose from her chair and headed to her bedroom. There, she closed the door behind her and flung herself on the bed. Not for the first time in the last few months, she questioned herself, her decisions, her actions, her very instincts. On one hand, she'd been feeling powerless to make sensible choices, while, on the other hand, she felt compelled to do just that: change her circumstances, in doing so, reveal—or create!—some meaning, some purpose, that would move her forward from one day to the next. Instead of the girl in the snow globe, perpetually turned upside down, she yearned to be the girl confidently driving down the road, sure of where she was going and why.

The popular music of the day suggested that momentous changes were taking place all around her. On the news that her father and brothers watched every night, she saw images of soldiers fighting for their lives in Vietnam, as well as images of angry students protesting passionately against that same war. A few months after his college graduation—during Beth's senior year—her brother Jimmy had begun a yearlong stint in the Army. Maybe because it was early in the war, Jimmy had been fortunate to stay in the U.S. One of her friends from school, though, had joined the Marines the next summer, right after their high school graduation, and within a few months had shipped out to Southeast Asia. His letters home described jungles, mosquitoes and suffocating heat. Other classmates had already joined the Reserves or ROTC as a response to the growing draft, despite rumored promises of deferments for college students. And she knew the older brothers of two girlfriends who had gotten drafted and sent overseas in just the last six months. She didn't know what to make01 of any of it.

In one of her classes, her English professor lectured engagingly about the "Beat Generation" of the '50s, about authors who questioned the values she had grown up with and promoted experimentation with drugs and casual sex. And on the radio, she listened to music that described scenes of "violence flarin" and "bullets explodin'" and expressed bitter cynicism about love: "I'm not the one you want, babe/I'm not the one you need." This music only added to the alienation she felt increasing each day—but she couldn't help singing along with Linda Ronstadt as she firmly rejected any notion of commitment, "Now I ain't sayin' you ain't pretty/All I'm sayin's I'm not ready/for any person, place or thing/to try and pull the reins in on me."

Fragile and vulnerable, Beth felt fear and a desire for flight reverberating through her body with every bar and note. A world of dazzling possibilities was supposed to be opening up for her, but, instead, Beth saw herself adrift in a world of conflict and ambiguity. While she wasn't looking, it seemed young people her age had gotten locked in a struggle of competing values: either accept the rules of society or rebel against them; either follow their parents' choices or head for the hills as fast as possible; either go to school and keep their noses to the grindstone or take up picket signs and demonstrate. One song declared the world was heading for annihilation; another derided the notions of love and marriage. Somehow, the train she'd been on most of her life had veered off the tracks.

More than anything else, Beth sought relief from the agonizing confusion that had come to occupy every cell of her being. She desperately needed order restored in her world, and so she had considered what was immediate and taken action.

Tonight, her head ached as though it'd been hit with a two by four. The weekend before, she had told Robert—home for a break from school and football—that she was confused and not sure how she felt about anything, including them as a couple. For a moment, he was speechless with disbelief, but when he recovered, Robert insisted that they loved each other, needed each other, belonged together. Beth could dispute none of this; her only reply was tears.

Within his first few days back at school, Robert had written her, expressing again how he couldn't make sense of her decision to break up; he knew she still loved him. In fact, Beth agreed that she loved him. Still, her nagging inner voice insisted that her relationship with Robert was merely a byproduct of the still-fresh tragedy…which only increased her tension. It seemed to Beth that a break-up would somehow relieve the feeling that she was riding a dizzying Ferris wheel that never stopped. Since she could see no other option, dispensing with her romance with Robert seemed the logical choice.

In the days that followed, though, instead of relief, Beth felt only dread. It wasn't that she knew she'd made a mistake; rather, the relief she'd longed for had failed to materialize. Tonight, disappointment made her heart hurt. It was as if she'd eaten something rotten that was causing her heart to pound until she could no longer think of anything else. When she could endure no more, she'd fled the subdued family dinner. And now, here she was, staring at the ceiling, not sure what to do next.

"Beth!" she heard Laurie call. "The phone's for you. Are you okay? Can you answer it?" Bolting upright, Beth carefully asked, "Is it Robert?" Laurie seemed perplexed. "No. I thought you and Robert broke up." Automatically, Beth got up to do what she thought she should do: answer the phone. Still half hopeful and half fearful that Robert would be on the other end, Beth was surprised to hear a familiar female voice.

"Bethie, hi, it's me, Linda Sue—your old next-door neighbor? How are you?"

And just like that, Beth's spirits lifted at the smooth, velvety voice.

"Oh, my gosh, Linda Sue! How're YOU? It's so great to hear from you. I mean, we didn't really get to talk the last time…you know what I mean." Inside, Beth cringed at the memory, remembering Linda's beautifully sad face when she hugged Beth warmly at the funeral. She couldn't recall what she had said to Linda, but she did remember the zombie-like behavior that had overwhelmed her at the time. But Linda Sue had cried and spoken about Anna's sweet, motherly kindness to her.

"Of course, I know what you mean. I'm still so shocked about your mom. You know how I loved her. Everyone did. How's your dad doing? And all your family?" Linda had grown up with Anna, too, a quasi-sixth child in the Lawrence household for years. Linda was the only child of two working parents and under the purview of her cranky grandma most of the time. She seemed to thrive in the noise and confusion of the big family next door. Likewise, Beth enjoyed Linda's spacious, orderly house, with the perfect little girl bedroom. Little Linda Sue even had her own bathroom, which was, in Beth's eyes, green from top to bottom: not only green walls, floor and counter top, but also sink, tub and toilet! After Linda's parents had done some remodeling, eight-year-old Beth had walked into it and just marveled. It was probably true that each little girl had envied the other.

"Oh, you know. It's not easy, but Dad's doing okay." Now, Beth's voice broke. "We're…all doing okay, I guess."

"Please tell him and everyone else that we're all so sorry."

"Thanks. The card and flowers you all sent were so nice."

"My parents and I wish we could do something to help, anything…somehow…I don't know. We just live so far from you, now."

"Don't worry, Linda. We're fine, really. So…what's up with you?" Beth needed to change the subject—fast! "I'm really happy to hear your voice."

"Well, like I said at your house after the funeral, I'm in school. But what I didn't tell you is that I have a boyfriend. Well, now he's my fiancé! In fact, we set a date, and I'm planning the wedding. I've chosen my bridesmaids, and I want you to be one of them! I hope you'll say you'll do it."

"Wow, Linda! Tell me about him, the wedding, everything."

"Well, his name is George. He's a year older. We actually met last year at a fraternity party that one of my friends talked me into crashing. He's kind of a big man on campus, very cute, lots of fun. We started dating right away even though he knew I was still in high school. My parents weren't too happy at first, but they like him now. Anyway, it all moved really fast, and last weekend he proposed."

"Wow, again! When's the wedding?

"In January, four months from now. So, what do you say? You were my first real friend. I feel like I've known you forever. I have to have you in my wedding."

"Of course, I'd love to."

"Now, I don't mean to be insensitive if you're too sad for this. But you know, maybe it'll cheer you up. Is that stupid of me to say?"

"No, Linda. I'm excited for you. I'll be fine."

After the call, Beth, stunned, sat silent at the table in the entry, just staring at the phone. Then, suddenly, she was stumbling back down the hall, gasping through her tears. Safely inside the bathroom, door locked, she stood at the sink, hot water faucet on full bore until it steamed. Painfully, she splashed the scalding water on her face. Then, smearing the mirror with her hand until she saw her reflection, she stared at the girl standing there.

God, you are so UGLY! Why would she want YOU in her wedding? Doesn't she have eyes?! She's so pretty. You're going to RUIN it for her. Look at your straggly hair and that pimply face. Didn't she see your zits at the funeral? You pop them, but WHAT'S THE POINT?! They just come back, and you can't really cover them up with make-up—IT JUST DOESN'T DO THE TRICK! Maybe she just felt sorry for you. Poor Bethie! Boo hoo! You have to call her right back and tell her no. Make up something. She'll understand. She was so sweet! Good Grief.

Even if you do it, you won't know anybody there. Sure, she said you could bring a date, but who would want to go with YOU? Robert's probably not even talking to you. God. You must be crazy to break up with him. You were so lucky to have him, and you went and broke his heart anyway! The nicest, sweetest guy, and he said he thought he loved you. You! Oh, my God! What is WRONG with you? Why do you get so nervous all the time? Why did you have to tell Robert you had to take some time apart? WHAT DOES THAT MEAN ANYWAY? He was so confused. Poor guy! You've probably lost him forever. When are you going to calm down and be normal? You have to tell Robert you were wrong. But how can you? You're still a total mess! You can't figure out WHAT you want. You're flunking out of school. And you're A BIG, FAT FRAUD! THAT'S YOU, BETHIE. YOU ACT LIKE YOU'RE HAPPY AND WISE, NOT A CARE IN THE WORLD. WHAT A JOKE YOU ARE. AND YOU'RE SO DAMN SKINNY! You look like you did in SEVENTH GRADE! You have no boobs. You have NO FRIENDS. And now, you DON'T EVEN HAVE ROBERT!! She covered her face with the rough washcloth, trying to choke back the sobs.

"Bethie, hey! Is that you in there?" came Frankie's voice suddenly from the other side of the door as he jiggled the handle. "Let me in. I have to take a leak."

"Frankie, I was just going to get in the shower. Give me a few minutes, can't you?"

"C'mon Beth. It'll only take me a minute."

"I'm naked, Frankie, Geez!"

"Wrap up in a towel. I'll be fast. C'mon, hurry up. I gotta go!"

"Frank. Go outside, if you gotta go so bad. I'm upset and I need to get in the shower!"

"C'mon, I mean it. I don't want to go outside. Right now, Beth," he ordered firmly. And then, nicer, calmer, "Please."

Beth reluctantly unlocked the door and her brother walked into the little toilet stall that their father had built years before, anticipating the need in a big family of both sexes.

"I thought you said you were naked."

"I just about was. God, it's gross listening to you pee. You sound like a horse!"

"I didn't say you had to stick around. There. I'm done. See? Quick. Just like I said." A flush of the toilet, and out he strode.

Quickly, Beth re-closed and re-locked the door, turned on the shower and began to get undressed. Then she heard a new voice at the door, "Bethie, can you hear me?"

"Yeah."

"I just wanted to let you know, me and Margaret, uh…I mean Margaret and I cleared the table and did the dishes."

"Thanks, Laurie. I owe you."

"No, you don't. I just wanted you to know."

"Okay. Laurie? You still there?"

"Yeah?"

"If Robert calls, can you come and get me? Pound on the door if you have to."

"Okay, but…no offense… but I thought you broke up."

"Yeah, well, it's complicated. Just get me, in case, okay?"

"Sure."

7 REALITY BITES, HARD

Monday, Monday, so good to me
Monday morning, it was all I hoped it would be
Oh, Monday morning, Monday morning couldn't guarantee
That Monday evening you would still be here with me
Monday, Monday can't trust that day…

~John Phillips

November 7, 1965

Beth awoke early that morning to sounds and smells coming from the kitchen. They were familiar and comforting, and she had awakened to them most mornings of her life: bowls and utensils clattering as they came out of cupboards and drawers, and the aroma of coffee wafting through the house. She pictured her parents—each with their jobs: Dad at the counter, making the morning Yuban, and Mom in her silky flowered housedress, getting juice and the fixings for cereal or eggs from the refrigerator. She would rinse the rich red strawberries and hull them expertly into the hand-painted ceramic bowl that was a part of every family meal, and then set the bowl on the shiny white Formica table next to the bright yellow bananas. Next, she would turn her attention to a small basket of dark red cherries, rinse them and, with pits still intact, set them in the little glass bowl next to the bananas. Last came the juicy green grapes—yum-yum!

When else did you get such delicious fruit except in summer, Beth wondered to herself as Anna deftly removed the grapes from their gnarled stems and dropped them into their own red metal bowl. After she had put the bowls in their places on the table, Anna would stand back to admire the colorful bounty waiting for her family—but just for just a moment; then she would pour herself some coffee and seat herself next to Jack. Between the clatter of silverware and the clank of bowls, Beth could hear her parents chatting, discussing their plans for the day and what would transpire that evening. More than likely, they had a church event—a meeting, or bible study, or even something to do with the upcoming school year for one of their children.

For the first time in months, Beth allowed herself to settle into her pillow and soft, cozy blanket and drift back into her reverie. Everything was okay. There was nothing for her to do, just lie back and enjoy the blessed peace of the moment, with her mother in harmony with the household—no, providing the harmony for her household. Beth knew if she walked into the kitchen now, her mother would greet her with a cheery "Good morning, Bethie B., my sleepyhead! How are you today, honey?" as she got up to hug her. Jack would also rise, remarking, "Well, looks like it's time to go, time's flyin'! The store won't open itself, so I'll say goodbye to my two girls," and, at that, he'd give each of them a quick kiss. Then, Beth would be alone with her mother for a while until her siblings joined them. For that brief respite, Beth would sip orange juice or milky coffee in Anna's sanctuary, her heart safe.

She remembered sitting just this way with Anna on a summer morning when she was almost 10. Her Aunt Maudie had invited her to spend a week at a university summer camp for journalism students run by Beth's Uncle Ralph. Beth's younger cousin would love having Beth for company! And Maudie just knew Beth would enjoy the activities offered to the instructors' kids: swimming, going to the movies, eating in the school cafeteria…where you could have any food your heart desired at any time, even cantaloupe with ice cream at midnight!

It had sounded so exciting, particularly since Beth's family lacked the means for any kind of summer vacation other than a random day at the beach. Anna had stayed neutral in Beth's debate with herself, while Beth had worried aloud that she might miss her mother too much. She'd never been away from her mother except for one or two sleepovers with neighborhood pals. Anna had assured her that she would write to her every day and that the week would pass quickly. Still, she hadn't pushed; she'd given Beth the room to decide for herself, conveying her confidence that Beth was growing up.

So Beth had gone with her Aunt Maudie and, a few days into the trip, had grown homesick. When her aunt found her crying on her bed one afternoon, she came down hard on Beth, scolding her for her "silliness." "You're getting to be a big girl, too big to miss your mommy." At that, what might have been temporary sadness had turned into all-out misery, and Beth's parents had to come up to get her after the fifth day. Beth remembered how relief had rushed through her body at the sight of her mother! For what seemed like a long time after that, Beth had stayed in close proximity to Anna. Or had Anna kept her in close proximity, Beth now wondered; Anna could be subtle in her mothering.

In her world, Anna's presence, subtle or not, was the axis around which Beth moved. Beth took for granted it was the same with her friends and classmates. Yet, from time to time, she encountered situations wherein her friends' mothers didn't rub their daughter's shoulders when they sat down for a snack after a hard day of school, or give spontaneous hugs. With some moms, terms of endearment came seldom, if at all, whereas, Beth was always "honey" or "Bethie B" to Anna, and Anna was always "Mommy" to Beth. She loved her daddy as well, and delighted in his singing, laughter and boisterous ways almost as much as Anna's quiet softness. Actually, at ten, she'd found her parents to be the perfect pair. Now, looking back from her current "young adult" vantage point, the rest of that summer had passed happily as she skipped through carefree days, her mother at her side.

In her snug bed, adrift in sleepy memories, Beth had never heard of an actual Indian reservation, let alone pushed her parents to allow her to go to work on one; in this hazy state, life was as it should be: Anna was in her kitchen, with her family.

Suddenly, Beth floated above herself. She saw that she was shouting, though her mouth hardly moved. Then, she began to sob and tear at her face and hair, but no one seemed notice—no one, that is, except for a boy who gently took her hand. Now, she watched as, in her agitation, she shrugged him off and prepared to bolt. He didn't try to subdue her physically, but spoke to her earnestly, although, in her distressed state, she couldn't hear him. Her eyes were locked onto something off in the distance, and he could see that she was searching—left to right, then back again. He scanned the area with her, but indicated he saw nothing out of the ordinary.

Her eyes remained focused on a distant point, but to no avail; something—someone—was missing.

Had he clicked off her vision, she wondered, the way one turned off a light, so that she stumbled blindly in a thick fog? No. He searched with her, she realized. Though she felt his intense effort, his determination was wasted, for this was her life's course, her search. For what? Her legs flung her body forward into something hard and rough like a wall. Over and over, she threw herself at it. I'm numb, yet everything hurts so badly. Why don't I stop? Something's stabbing my chest; I can't breathe. I need to slow down. No. I'll know when I can stop. But my body's on fire. I must put the fire out. Now I'm on the ground rolling, squelching the flames. Where am I? Where is she, the ESSENTIAL ONE! Why doesn't she come to me? I just HAVE to find her, to get to her. Beth saw that she was wailing now. I HAVE TO FIND HER!

"Beth! Beth, honey. What's wrong? Are you okay?"

"Dad... What? What? I…I was asleep."

"Yeah, you must've been having a nightmare."

"Oh. Yeah. It was awful. I was…well, I guess I was lost, although I was also on fire and looking for someone to put it out. Or something. I don't know now." Still lying down, Beth struggled with the tangled blankets, then pulled herself up on one elbow. Jack sat down on the bed next to her.

"Pretty bad dream, huh? Poor kid." He felt her forehead for a fever.

Beth rubbed her eyes. What she couldn't say was how much worse it was to wake up and discover the harsh reality that replaced her early morning drowsiness…her former life with its beautiful Kodachrome quality. "Could you hear me from the kitchen? I thought I heard you in there with someone else, talking."

"That was Jimmy, having a bite to eat with his old man before going to sign some papers for his new job. I was getting ready to leave for the store, but I wanted to square some things with you first. I heard you as I was coming down the hall."

"Oh." Beth felt sick with disappointment. "Do you need something?"

Jack patted her covers, then said, "Just relax. It's nothing urgent. I need you to take Margaret and a couple of the workshop kids to bowling this morning. I can pick them up, but the timing's not working for me to drop them off before work today. Damned Danny!" Jack muttered the last under his breath. "Anyway, I need you to do it."

"What time? Laurie's got guitar at—what time, Laurie?"

Laurie was lying quietly in her bed, her big eyes taking in the interaction before her. "Nine o'clock," she murmured.

"Well, Margaret needs to be at the bowling alley at 11:30. You should be able to get Laurie to guitar and back and still have time to get Margaret and the others there. Okay? It's settled?"

"Sure, Dad." Beth hated it when her father threw her schedule off with no warning. Why couldn't he have told her this last night?

"Okay, honey. Bye, girls. I guess Daddy's gotta go make some money to pay the bills. Margaret, I'll see you at the bowling alley later," Jack said to the lumpy covers now stirring in the third bed. And off he went.

"You have bad dream, Beth?" croaked Margaret in her barely-awake voice.

"Yeah, I did. Really bad. Oh, God…Somehow, it was good, then terrible."

"'Bout Mom?"

"I'm not sure. Yeah, at first. I thought I heard her talking." Beth's voice broke as she struggled for control. "But then…somehow, I was looking for someone. It has to have been her."

"Know what today is?" Margaret asked.

"No. Not sure. What?"

"Day…er…date our mother die, the 7th. Three months ago. Today."
Now, Beth saw Laurie kick her feet and pull the covers over her face.
"Oh, God. You're right. No wonder."
It was quiet for a moment, then Margaret spoke again. "I have 'em too."
"Really? You mean you have dreams about Mom? All the time?"
"Mm, they come and go. It varies," Margaret said matter-of-factly.
"Well, I guess we just miss her. We miss her…." Beth choked, coughed, finally calmed into sniffles.
"Mm hm. You think Dad miss her?"
The question caught Beth by surprise. "Oh, yeah. For sure. Why?" she asked, wiping her face with her covers.
"Oh, no reason. I just wonder. That all. Well, better get up, right?"
"Ugh! I guess you're right. Got lots to do today!" Beth made her voice upbeat; it was a cheer she didn't feel.
"Grocery shopping, right? I goin' bowlin'!"
"So, you're saying you're getting out of the shopping today, huh? Lucky duck!"
"Yep, that me," Margaret giggled.
Beth heard a small giggle from Laurie's covers as well.
"You mean you'd rather bowl than go to the meat market with Laurie and me? You want to miss all that fun?"
"Oh, Beth, you teasin' me!"

8 DRIVE THE FREEWAY OF NO EXITS

They killed my mother
At the door of my room…
a voice full of harmony and it says
you're not alone…

~Umberto Giordano

December 15, 1965

Beth Lawrence
Creative Writing I
Prof. Michaels
Due: Jan 8

Semester Final Assignment, Take Home Essay: Write an account of a significant event and explain its importance in your life. Discuss its impact and how it has changed you in a particular way or caused you to look at life differently from before. Do not merely describe the incident. As far as possible, make use of literary devices studied in this course. You may use first- or third-person point of view. There is no required length. Write enough to complete the assignment.

Dear Professor Michaels,

I really appreciate this assignment, especially since you're counting it as our final exam. I know what I've written is really long, but once I got started, I couldn't stop. Besides, you always tell us to "Let the juices flow!" I hope it's okay.

A Life-Changing Event

They say you're an adult when you turn eighteen. Well, I just turned eighteen, and my mother's dead. Just like that. No warning. I don't mean to sound melodramatic. I know I'm not the first to travel this territory, this freeway with no exits. But I think this story could easily be described as a significant event in my life. Life can be so strange. I was a cheerleader just last year and such a child. I thought my big heartbreaks were over: not making Homecoming Court and having a "serious" boyfriend break up with me for his first love, basketball. I felt so mature. I was graduating from high school, finally coming face to face with "Sweet Sophistication"; she would introduce me to interesting people with interesting thoughts. I was excited about taking an English class that studied poems like William Blake's "The Tiger," which my older brother loves to quote dramatically: "What immortal hand or eye/Dare (his emphasis) frame his fearful symmetry?"

While many of my friends were going off to the security of Catholic colleges, my path would take me to State—big, anonymous, public, State. I was tired of having everyone know my business and tired of the safe, protected cocoon of Catholic school. Twelve years of nuns and priests in their all-black uniforms, with their holier-than-thou attitudes and their guilt-tripping lectures was enough. (It wasn't that bad, but you get my point!) Time for me to face non-Catholics and maybe even an atheist or two.

I have two brothers and two sisters; both brothers are older, and one sister is younger. Technically, my other sister is older, but she's "exceptional" and hard to categorize. While my younger sister, Laurie, was recently knocked into "muteness," except for her lonely singing and guitar playing, my "special" sister, Margaret, has never had many words. Sometimes, when I look at her, I think I see agony in her eyes, and I imagine that what she wants to say is locked tight in her throat. If she could, she would just vomit it up.

I'm a very visual person.

My oldest brother, Jimmy, is fresh out of the Army and grimly in mourning. He's moved back in with us to help get our father through his grief. Is that even possible? It's not like Dad has the chicken pox. Actually, I don't question Jimmy's motives. I'm glad he's here. He searches daily for a fulfilling job worthy of his college-educated attention, I guess. When he comes home in the evening from the search or a temporary job, he wears his disappointment like a shroud. My other brother, Frankie, in his fifth and final year of engineering at State is all white-faced silence; he speaks little, but somehow emits a sense of wondrous rage at the mystery of life and the cruelty of death. At least, that's my interpretation.

Rarely, do any of us talk about IT. Although Jimmy and I do talk some, it's different than it used to be. Here's an example:

Jimmy: How's school going, Beth?

Me: Ok. It's really a long walk from that crowded parking lot to my classes!

Sometimes, though, we take on a more serious tone:

Me: Jimmy, what's the point, really, of life? (I'm taking Intro to Philosophy.)

Jimmy: I don't know Beth. I'm trying to figure that out.

Me: Me, too. Let me know if you find any answers.

Jimmy: Yeah, you too.

In my household, the males dominate. By that, I mean their conversations about politics, school, and sports have always dominated the dinner table talk. And the household chores break down to the boys emptying the trash, garbage can detail and lawn-mowing; the girls help our mom with the laundry, cleaning, shopping and cooking. When you consider what's involved in the girls' vs the boys' jobs, doesn't anyone besides me see how off-balance and unfair it is?

I guess my parents decided that the boys were destined for more serious endeavors, so they had to have more freedom for study and outside jobs—like paper routes when they were younger, and helping my dad at his store as they got older. Anyway, now, in our new reality, I think my father thinks he's showing great confidence in me by getting me a checkbook and a gas card and turning over all the other "female" work and errands to me. This seems to include most anything involving either sister. I suppose he thinks I should be proud that he thinks I'm up to the job. I guess I am.

I remember how he had us all go with him to the car dealer to check out the sporty blue Pontiac—the replacement for the solid white family car, the Mercury, that was gnarled in The Accident that took my mother forever, put my father and sisters in the hospital for a time, and elevated me to my position of Queen Household Drudge. My brothers expressed surprise and interest at our father's choice, while the salesman described the pick up and go of this feisty, sassy machine. I suppose even my sisters and I admired the shiny, sleek design—clearly, unlike anything this family had ever owned. Dad seemed more enthusiastic than he'd been for a while, but it seemed strange that he had us all go to see the car. He'd never done that before. Maybe it was meant to be a pretty distraction for us all. But he shocked me when we got home. First, he said he wanted to talk to me. His voice went all deep in his throat; the way it does when he gets really serious. And he loses most of his slang talk for an almost professorial attitude. None of his normal "ain'ts" or double negatives pepper this kind of talk.

Dad: Bethie…now that your mother's gone, I'm going to need your help.

Me: I know. (Wasn't that what I'd been doing for the past month or so?)

Dad: Laurie needs looking after. She's almost a teenager. Although she usually walks to and from school, sometimes she's going to want or need a ride.

Me: I don't mind helping with that.

Dad: Then there's Margaret's car-pool to the training center and her bowling; I can get her to the workshop and bowling most of the time. When I can't, though, I'll need your help.

Me: Sure. (I silently cringe at the thought of a car full of "special" kids—the only word we ever use for her and "kids" in her condition. With their hugs and their frequent repetitions of "You're pretty" and "I love you," I get very uncomfortable, to say the least.)

Dad: (Looking at me intently.) I don't want this to change your life. I want you to go to college just like your brothers. I want you to have a social life, go to dances, join a sorority if you want.

Me: I've been looking over the…uh, school catalogue at, you know, activities on campus. (I lie.)

Dad: Good. I'm sure Jimmy or Frankie will be glad to take a look with you.

Me: (I want to laugh in his face at this statement.) Uh huh.

Dad: I plan to do the grocery shopping when I can, but you know your mother and I always liked to do it together.

Me: (Did he want me to now join him in this parental Saturday afternoon ritual that I'd always equated with freedom from my mom's endless list of weekend chores? Every Saturday since I can remember, my mother locked me indoors with "jobs." Incredibly, she was never hard-pressed to find another "job" and another until an enticing Saturday was just a memory. Then Dad would call her after lunch from his store so they could synchronize their "date" time for grocery shopping, and I would count down the minutes until she finally drove off, setting me free to grab the phone and attempt to salvage the afternoon with my best friend, Grace. My parents spent the rest of the day shopping for the perfect produce and cuts of meat—at bargain prices, of course. Blissful hours later, whoever of us was home was summoned to help bring in and put away groceries especially chosen for a large Catholic family: lettuce, tomatoes and other garden goodies, clam chowder, fish sticks…not to mention pounds of ground beef bleeding in its white-paper wrap.) Yeah. (I nod my head.)

Dad: I want you to go with me a few times, but I'm ordering a checkbook for you from the bank, so you can go by yourself when I can't. Of course, I expect Margaret and Laurie to help you as much as they can. (He looks at me meaningfully.) And that goes for the cooking and cleaning too.

Me: (I know what that "help" will entail. Does he?) Okay.

Dad: (He's on a roll, now, and seems to forget that I'm standing there, probably beet red. I feel hot. I need to open a window or maybe jump out of one. Then came the shocker!) I've ordered you your own Shell card, and these keys are your own set. (He hands me two keys on a little circular holder!) You can use the new car for school and your sisters. I can drive the store's truck most of the time. (My dad owns an auto parts business. He puts in a lot of hours for a modest living, but one of his benefits—his only one, I think—is a store truck, nothing fancy mind you, at his disposal. I learned to drive stick shift on one of these clunkers. He didn't teach me, Frankie did—back when Frankie used to be fun.) Now, I want you to tell me if this gets to be too much for you. I just don't know how we're going to get along. Your mother always…. (His voice faded away and his eyes glossed over, and I felt my stomach clench.)

Me: Okay, Dad. Okay. I know. (I mumble, waiting to be dismissed or interrupted. Thankfully, Jimmy comes in just then, and I make a fast exit.)

This is my "young adulthood," right here, right now. Honestly, I'm not embellishing. I remember, though it seems a lifetime ago, reading "Valediction Forbidding Mourning" in my senior English class. I was so moved by the author's claim that love surpasses time and space. And I cried real tears for the lost romance of the young family in James Agee's Death in the Family. The way these works got to me! And how troubling, but noble—and distant—all this truth seemed to me. But the "truth" is, I had plans for this time in my life, and they didn't include death. And, by the way, so far, I haven't found anything noble or romantic about it.

I used to be very social. My mom always complained that I was far nicer to any friend on the phone with a problem than I was to her or my sisters. And I constantly nagged her to let me spend the night or at least go out with my friends. I wanted my independence from her, from home. Now, I don't know how to respond to one girlfriend's curiosity, "Why don't you cry? I sure would." Does she think I don't—or didn't—love my mother?

And what do I say to another friend's insistence that I "Get out of the house. Come cruising" with her to the hot hamburger hangout. This will cheer me up, for sure. How do I tell one friend that Grief claims you in a way that can defy tears, that you walk with panic and dread, and, when you're really lucky, numbness? But she doesn't want to hear this, even if I could say it. She wants the sad details, the dramatic fireworks that must be unfolding in my house. The other friend tempts you, teases you with the promise of renewed girlhood, and you try the cruising scene. But the laughter and cheerful chatter leave you colder and emptier than you were.

I remember one such "adventure" with Molly—sparkling, spunky, cute Molly. We'd been friends all through St. Mary's, and then taken the bus together to St. Joe's for four years of high school. She was so thrilled with her "new" used VW bug, so persistent in her encouragement, in her confidence that getting out would do me good. I had made one excuse after another, but, finally, I decided to give it a try.

Me: Ok. You're probably right. Let's go.

Molly: Really? When? Tonight?

Me: Tonight? Wow! I guess. Sure.

A few hours later, she arrives, with her dark, shiny, shoulder-length hair, hip-hugging jeans, and bright blue eyes. She's giggling and revving her engine, raring to go. Me, I drag myself across the porch, down the red concrete steps, feeling nothing but dull and dowdy, longing to stay and play hopscotch with Laurie, but attempting a nonchalant and carefree air as I move my queasy, achy body into the passenger seat.

Molly: Hey Lizbeth! (Only Molly and Mom call me that.) Wipe that frown off your face! This is going to be fun! Wait'll you meet Paul. He's so fine! He's called me every day for two weeks. I guess I'm just gonna have to break up with Philip. Paul won't leave me alone. He says he goes crazy over my eyes, but I think these tight jeans will really drive him wild tonight.

Me: But I thought it was just going to be us going out. Ya know, a girl thing.

Molly: Well, it is. But he'll be down at Pop's. He hangs out there. Besides, lots of cute guys hang out there. Just wait. You'll have a blast.

(My silence only prods her on.)

Molly: Isn't my car neat? I can't believe my dad helped me buy it. He says it's so I can get to and from my job without buggin' my mom. I have to pay the insurance, and he'll buy the gas. The thing is—now I have wheels! Aren't you jealous? (I can hardly stop from smirking. I think of the brand-new, "neat" car my dad's driving home from work that day, the very car that will be mine for all my new adult responsibilities. How could I tell Molly about that car and how I really did envy her this little VW that would not be invaded by sisters and endless chores?)

Me: Yeah. It's really cute. Paul sounds great, too. But I'm not so sure about Pop's tonight. I'm not into the guy thing right now.

Molly: You? Who're you kidding? Little Miss Cheerleader. Little Miss Popular. I remember how you stole Nicky Reyes from me not so long ago. Right when I know he was getting ready to ask me out.

Me: You must have me confused with someone else. You're the flirt. (Which she was; still is, as far as I know.) But I did remember the Nicky mess. It wasn't one of my better moments. Truth be told, Molly had annoyed me with her cute, giggly ways more than once in our many years of friendship. Still, I could hardly recognize the Beth she was describing now.

Molly: My point is you have no problem with boys. It'll do you good to practice your heart-breaking skills again. I'm gonna make sure you lighten up a little tonight. And don't forget Pop's has the best burgers and fries.

Me: (I knew she meant well. A loyal friend, she had called me every few days since the accident and never acted offended when I didn't call her back. Just kept stopping by or calling.) I'm sure you're right about it all. To be honest, I'm not all that hungry. My stomach's really been bugging me lately. And don't forget about Robert. He's been so good to me.

Molly: I know. But he's away at school for football, right? I didn't think he'd been home for a few weeks, at least.

Me: Yeah. But we're still a "thing." I'm not sure what kind of a thing. But you know, with him being in the accident and all, we're definitely some kind of something. (Clearly, I had no words to describe this crazy, extreme relationship.)

Molly: Well, not to worry. You're only going to talk and laugh tonight, so quit being so serious!!

Poor thing! She was determined to cheer me up, so when we got to Pop's, I put on a smile, ordered a hamburger and fries, and tried my best to chat with the boys who buzzed around us. Pop's has a pool table, so a couple of boys asked us to play pool with them. "Sure," we said. The boys seemed nice enough—I didn't know them, but Molly had met them through her new love interest. About half way through the game, Molly spots Paul walking through the door. Nonchalantly, she whispers, "There's Paul. My God, Lizzie, isn't he just the cutest thing?" I glanced over; I had to admit he was good looking, a big guy in faded jeans and a tight, white t-shirt. "I'm going to pretend that I don't see him. Find out how long it takes him to come over here." Well, it was all of a few minutes. Once the game was over, he started a new one, and the other boys disappeared. After that, I didn't have to work so hard at conversation, and Paul was really nice. I was relieved when he said he had to go pick up his sister; that meant Molly was happy to go home, too.

Back in her car, Molly prattled away cheerfully, and the more I listened and made dumb, empty-headed responses, the less I felt like myself. No talk that night about my life, as it was now. I think Molly offered her brand of solace. And while I was grateful that she didn't ask searching questions, I remember feeling a million years older than Molly, and fighting an impulse to leap out of the car at every stop. Just my luck, her VW seemed to crawl its way home. Since that incident, I've remembered how Molly loved my mom. I'm guessing this whole thing has been hard on her, too.

The fact is, I was discovering that no friend, fresh out of the neurotic pressure cooker of high school concerns and on the threshold of college or work, wants to hear about the meat market and the grocery store, buying my sisters new shoes and the constant dumbfounder: what do I fix for dinner tonight? Fact is, I don't want to hear about that either.

Sure, I always helped with the family meals; I had to. And I used to go with my mom to the butcher shop, but I had not even a vague interest in cuts of meat and prices. Now, here I am, supposedly planning menus for six—three of them hungry men—on a weekly basis and attempting to purchase just the right amount of ingredients, always mindful of the cost. And then there's the butcher with his brisk questions:

Him: Ok, now, do you want six stuffed pork chops or ten regular chops? It's up to you, but the regular tend to shrivel up some when they get cooked. 'Course, it depends on how you cook 'em. How're you going to cook 'em?

Me: I don't know. I guess…broil them?

Him: Well, they're going to shrivel up for sure if you do that. You're better off getting the stuffed and baking 'em. So what do ya' want? Stuffed or regular?

Me: (If he only knew. It definitely made no difference to me!) Whatever. I guess the stuffed. I also need hamburger meat.

Him: What kind? Ground chuck? Ground beef? Regular? Lean? Extra lean?

Me: Huh?

And, of course, this is separate from the grocery store where I do the BIG shopping, which my sisters have no choice but to help with. Here, the decisions seem to involve which cereals to buy, which cookies look good, how many boxes of crackers do we need…. And my dad is really adamant about the produce: it has to be fresh and there has to be enough! Problem is, I'm not really sure how to figure all this out.

The worst part is at the checkout. My cart is always piled high. Without fail, someone pulls up behind me with just a few items in their cart. Am I imagining their eyes boring through me angrily? By the time I start writing the check, I'm just about hyperventilating. For some reason, I think I'm going to get caught doing something really wrong, I guess because it seems like I'm the youngest person in the store with her own checkbook. I AM getting used to this though, the way you get used to monthly cramps and diarrhea. These Saturday excursions so propel me into stomach-ache regions that I have taken to popping Rolaids the way my uncle used to pop life-savers.

I've done some thinking recently, and I'm seriously wondering if I should become a nun. I never thought I would say this, and my historic reason against it still stands: how can anyone live without romance? But now I wonder if God isn't calling me anyway. Maybe I haven't been listening well enough, and this latest turn in my life is His way of knocking me on the head with his invitation. I mean, those nuns always seemed so serene and wise. There's no hint that they eat Rolaids like lifesavers. Sure, there were a few we didn't like much in school, but on the whole, they were cool, much more like real people than the priests, who always seem to occupy some lofty, superior plane.

When I was little, I was in awe of the sisters and their body-enveloping black habits (I always wondered if they had any hair on their heads and if and how they went to the bathroom). They didn't really look like any woman I knew, but they seemed genuinely holy. I guess in some ways, I'm still in awe of them, but after my high school experience, I mostly see them as real people.

Take that time in Sister Agnes' Biology class when she caught me passing a note about my then-boyfriend, my first true love. Since having a boyfriend was strictly forbidden at our school, I knew I was in for trouble after she read the note. It was her duty to report me to the girls' dean. My punishment would include telling my parents, after I had so creatively kept my mom in the dark. So, of course, I lied to Sister. Ridiculously, I vehemently insisted that the note was about another friend's boyfriend, a friend who didn't go to St. Joe's. This friend's name: Beth!! I knew how clumsy my story was—yet, Sister Agnes smiled, dropped the note in the trashcan and proceeded with her explanation of mitosis or some such thing.

Then there was Sister Gertrude Joseph—Gertie Joe for short. Our entire school loved her. She had a great sense of humor and an amazing ability to throw hook shots and outplay many boys on the basketball court. I've begun to ponder these and a few others, wondering what I would be like as a nun. Could I be cool like Sister Agnes or Sister Gertie Joe? But every time I seriously consider this idea, I see the accusing faces of my two sisters and my boyfriend and think "Okay, okay. I won't leave you."

Another problem is that the thought of actually becoming a nun, for some reason, makes me cry. For the life of me, I don't know why. Nuns seem to have it made. Every night's a slumber party. Always someone to talk problems with. No worry about pleasing a man, cooking and cleaning for a man. I've been to convents—for piano lessons and a few times when I helped a teacher cart sports stuff from the park back to the convent. I found out that they had a housekeeper!

What a life! Oh, I know they work hard teaching and grading papers. And I'm sure they have to comfort people with problems, like bad marriages, or "bad" children. Whatever. Still, they have each other to share all that with, and they have God. After all, they're brides of Christ! They know where they fit. I guess my main problem is that it seems unnatural to live without a man by your side, going with you through life. Somehow, I can't see that having a parish priest nearby is anywhere near the same as talking over your day with your husband, figuring out what's wrong with the washing machine or making plans for the church dance on the weekend. So, my idea to try a convent is on hold for now.

Anyway, even though I seem to have this newly-won respect from my father, what I really have achieved is the privilege to cook, clean, wash and sometimes iron, and see to every one's needs, though, to be fair, it's not so much about my brothers. I don't actually see too much of them even though we all live in a pretty small house. Of course, my dad says my pre-teen and "special" sisters are supposed to help me. Gee, thanks, Dad.

I'm not a prisoner or a slave. My dad wants me to visit my boyfriend at his college—I can take the sporty car—and go to dances and such with girlfriends. But my life and theirs just do not match anymore. It seems that every time I visit my boyfriend, I'm plagued with horrible stomachaches. (I always bring plenty of Rolaids.) I pass into a reverie when we go to a football game, wondering what planet all these happy, carefree young adults are from. While they're drinking beer, hooting and hollering for their team, danger is lurking, just waiting for them...they just don't know it. It seems the only time I'm comfortable visiting him is when we're doing his grocery shopping or laundry or something. At least then I'm in my element.

Robert: How much spaghetti should I get for me and my roommates? One package?

Me: For four guys? Are you kidding? You need at least two packages and at least a pound of ground beef!

Robert: For real? Unbelievable!

And, not too long ago, I stayed overnight with a girlfriend in her dorm at St. Lawrence's, and went with her to a couple of classes. The handsome, young professor was teaching Catch-22 and talking about the meaning of life. Boy, the students were really eating it up; how funny that Joseph Heller was, how absurd death can be.

It was all so ironic and abstract, and I wanted to shake Heller and the professor and all the naïve students. I, who had thrived on "deep" discussions in high school, who had been in every honors English course, who led discussions in religion class and took pride in impressing my classmates with my high-level, complex thinking—I could make no sense of this discussion that maintained that the author was right on when he satirized the brutality of death so effectively. From where I sat, if he or they really got it, they wouldn't be so glib. They would realize how meaningless and hollow their parties and plans are.

I stumbled through the rest of that visit, eager to find my way back to my comfortable domestic dreariness.

Of course, as soon as I got back from that little vacation, I saw how sorely I had been missed. First, my waifish sister Laurie gave me those soulful brown eyes as I walked up the steps to our front porch where she sat, as usual, tuning strings or strumming chords or belting out her latest tune about trains carrying her "where I used to live a long time ago." She really has a great voice. I'm amazed at the solid, strong sound that emerges from this wordless, downcast kid who doesn't seem to know what to make of the woman's body she's got at twelve. I used to try to tell her to be glad she's going through puberty early.

Me: Trust me Laurie, the boys will love you in high school. You already wear a bigger bra size than I ever have. All the girls will be jealous.

Laurie: (In tears) Leave me alone. You don't understand.

Me: I do! Trust me. You'll be so popular. I'd give anything to have your problem.

Laurie: Oh, why don't you just go rat your hair?

Me: Fine. I'm just trying to help.

Clearly, all Laurie wants to do is cover up her "endowment" in big, sloppy shirts. Anyway, she always hated my erratic attempts at sisterly advice. My mother even told me once that Laurie did not want to grow up to be like me, so I gave up. She liked me much better when I played jacks with her on the linoleum in our entry. That was back when I started to realize it might be nice to have a little sister who was almost a teenager. Maybe, finally, there would be someone in my house who could understand, at least a little, what I was all about, and who didn't think I was too social and shallow (my oldest brother), sarcastic and self-absorbed (my mother), or unworthy of any kind of notice at all.

Next, Margaret appeared, all fluttering hands and stutters, and attempted to fill me in on the weekend's bowling scores and the latest indignity her boyfriend Larry has foisted on her. Now a somewhat frumpy 23-year-old, Margaret had once been quite pretty. I remember how my mother would brush and arrange her naturally curly golden hair into long, thick ringlets every morning while I, with my short, straight, Dutch-boy haircut, would watch, envious.

My father only recently told me the story of her birth and "exceptionalism." He said she doesn't have Downs or anything genetic, in case I was worried about my future babies. (As if!!) Margaret's oxygen was cut off during her 24-hour-long delivery, which he considers brutal incompetence on the part of the doctor, who is no longer in business. When I think that, except for those circumstances, I could have had a normal big sister and normal family, I want to explode. But what's the use? Anyway, her attractiveness has pretty well been done away with by the scars from the accident and the subsequent surgeries. Luckily, she's never seemed too concerned about her looks. I've been thinking lately how my sisters are a lot alike. Both are "women" in some ways; at least, they look like women because they have the necessary "parts," but both are still just kids.

I made my way through the living room where Dad sat in his red recliner, deep in his latest Hornblower adventure. Ever since I can remember, Dad's always had his head buried in a book. When I was small, he used to invite me to the library with him. I loved that. Anyway, he looked up long enough to greet me with a quick question about my weekend, which didn't require more than an amiable answer.

I have to wonder what he'd have thought if he knew that, all the way home, I'd considered why in the world I—or anyone else, for that matter—should want to go on living. It was pretty hypothetical. I wouldn't even know how to slit my wrists. And I have a special aversion to automobile accidents lately. But it strikes me that, six months ago, I would never have been allowed such a trip, or, at the least, it would have been the subject of some searching conversations:

Mom: Where exactly are you going to stay, Bethie?

Mom: Who will be going with you? Will any parents be going?

Mom: You say you'll be in a girl's dorm? There won't be any boys there, right?

Mom: You won't forget to call as soon as you arrive, will you?

Mom: I don't know. Let me talk to your dad and we'll see.

My mom was the world's biggest worrywart. I'm not sure this is better. When I poked my head in the kitchen and saw my brother Frank rummaging through the refrigerator, I knew that, next, he'd be asking if I was going to cook. Quickly, I headed for my room, threw my bag down, and plopped onto my bed. I was home.

Honestly, things really aren't that bad. I like school when I can force my body to sit through ninety minutes of lecture about native Africans (Anthro) or the life of a rock (Geology). (I really like my writing class, though!) Seriously, I do mostly enjoy my English classes. I have always been pretty good at literature; I love the vicarious experiences that come with reading fiction. I remember reading Cry, the Beloved Country by Alan Paton last year, and knowing then and there that I would one day see a South African township in person. Not long after, I struck up a friendship with a transfer student, Bruce, who had lived in Africa as an Army brat. We spent hours one Sunday afternoon on a "date," discussing his experiences in the country. I was enthralled—not by him, but about the possibilities of life. What a blast to talk with him about things not in my little world.

I had loved my senior religion teacher, Father Wade, for the same reason. He'd delighted in throwing controversial ideas at our class of girls. He'd said he wanted us to think about issues beyond our boyfriends or the next big date. This tactic had never failed to distract me from the note or poem I was discreetly writing, and soon he'd engaged me in a heated discussion on civil rights or young marriage or whether or not Mass should be said in English instead of Latin. He used to bait us with the topic of kissing: how long a kiss could be before it qualified as a mortal instead of a venial sin. (Venial sins mean purgatory; mortal sins get you thrown into the fires of hell!) But then he would laugh and ask how we could stand having another person's tongue in our mouths. This always elicited a ton of loud groans!

He was the only priest—up to that time—that I'd ever related to on human terms. And he'd seemed to see something in me, too. He'd seemed to value me for qualities other than—or in spite of—my carefully curled ponytail or short uniform skirts. He'd dared me to think and talk in a real way that I never did at home. Oh, I'd heard these kinds of conversations between my father and brothers; it's just that I was never included in them. In fact, Father Wade is the one who'd gotten me the scholarship to take a college seminar on Social Justice last summer at St. Clare's, a Catholic college. My egghead friend Barb, also recommended by Father Wade, audited the class with me. We bonded on our drives to and from. That's when she decided to join me on the Indian reservation later in the summer. Imagine that.

Being around so many adults, and religious ones at that, seemed otherworldly at first. I felt like a kindergartener trying to discuss the Beatles with a teenager. I can't say that I ever came close to understanding some of the topics, but I did find the discussions fun in a mental sort of way. I worried before every meeting. What if I said something totally ridiculous? What if I couldn't think of anything to say at all? I literally perspired all the way to class, and giggled and re-lived each conversation with Barb all the way home.

Father Wade had also been the one to suggest that I talk to our high school counselor, Father Rex, about volunteering on the reservation for two weeks after graduation. Of course, I did, and, of course, I went, and, of course, that started the chain of events that changed my life forever. (The topic of this paper.)

I've asked myself many times why my family had to drive up to blistering hot Bakersfield in the summer to visit me. I was going to be home in a week. Weekends away from his auto parts store were so rare for my dad, but I'm sure my mom talked him into going because she was worried about me—the irony of the trip's outcome is pretty obvious, right? So anyway, they came, and, unfortunately, a badly-loaded pick-up truck on a two-lane highway rammed into them, mangling them and the car.

Now, Father Rex and I are best buds.

Clearly, I do rely on him, definitely more than I rely on anyone else these days, but, if truth be told, I'm not sure I really want to rely on anyone anymore. What's the point? Just the other day, before my English Lit class, I got to talking to another girl around my age who's engaged—I can't understand why—to an older guy in the Army. She's having second thoughts, which her boyfriend doesn't like. She started telling me how she's been seeing a counselor at school—for free!—and how nice he is and how he's helping her. All through class, I was thinking maybe I should talk to someone here, too. But I'm not sure what I'd talk about. I don't know if I really need that, although things do seem to creep up on me unexpectedly.

I'll never forget the first day in this class when you had us do what you called an ice-breaker. You had us pair up and talk about ourselves with our partner. You gave us some questions, for what you called "guided discussion." Then you had some of us come to the front of the room and talk about ourselves. Again, you asked us some questions. I don't remember what the question was, but when it was my turn, I started bawling that my mother was recently killed in a car accident while visiting me on an Indian reservation! Instantly, humiliation had flooded through me! I cannot describe how much I hated myself at that moment. If I hadn't felt frozen, I would've run out of the room! I had just been talking to a nice, cute, blonde guy sitting next to me, and now it seemed the room had become a library with "No Talking" signs everywhere. Everyone just stared at me. You tried to say something to help me, and I ran to my seat. Why did I feel compelled to spill my guts to you and a class full of strangers? I never do that! Is it something about you?

Anyway, maybe this explains why a counselor seemed kind of appealing. Maybe she could help me sort things out, make them a little more manageable. Finally, though, I decided no. I have to handle this on my own. I wouldn't have a clue what to say. I've never been much good at telling my feelings to adults, except my mom, and even with her, I could get frustrated. I admit, Father Rex is a pretty good listener, but, like most people, he's better at talking. Still, he always makes me feel he cares. No, I have to do what people say I'm good at and be strong.

My best friend, Alison —"Allie" for short—was a big help when IT first happened. I think my whole family leaned on her, not just my sisters and me, but my brothers, too, in a strange way. After my first phone call home—the one where I got to tell my brothers all the gory details about what happened and who survived and who didn't, and what kind of shape the rest were in, I really haven't had that much to say to them—my family—about what's really going on in my head. Jimmy, the oldest kid in the family, in his quest to make me more enlightened, used to come at me from time to time with comments about things like Vietnam or existentialism. But now, once in a while, he pops off with something I can actually relate to. A few weeks ago, we're driving to pick up some fast food for lunch and he says, "Man, Bethie, I can't believe how unfair life can be. I just don't know if I can believe in God after this. I mean, do you think there's really a place called heaven? Maybe it's a state of mind. I just don't know."

And another time, I was in the kitchen, cleaning up after dinner, and he comes home late after his job as a juvenile detention officer—which did not last—and he's clearly brooding. He shakes his head. Then he says, "How do you do it, Beth? How do any of us do it?"

Me: Do what?

Jimmy: Why'd it have to be Mom? God, how are we going to make it? Look at Dad. Look at Margaret! And what about Laurie? And you, you shouldn't be doing this.

Me: Doing what?

Jimmy: This! Cooking and cleaning and shopping for us. Taking care of Margaret and Laurie. You're just a kid.

Well, I wanted to throw my arms around him at that last comment!

Finally, somebody understood! But I didn't tell him that. I don't know why. I'm often at a loss for words with him. I think it's because I admire him so much. My mouth just feels all tongue-tied. Even if I have a comment that makes sense, I can't seem to spit out the right words. Sometimes, I ask questions in my journal or in a poem I'm writing like, "God is love, ISN'T He?" and "If He is, then why is life so cruel?" I know, though, if I said it out loud, most people would tell me I'm weird. Not Jimmy, though. He'd probably just nod his head. Maybe try to answer, or at least say, "I don't know."

Anyway, back to Alison, or Allie. She walks into our kitchen bringing the sunshine with her. She's got silky blonde hair, laughing blue eyes, and a round mischievous face; she's a magnet we're all attracted to. And she seems to have no fear, to feel no intimidation about anything, even death. The night I made the phone call home to deliver my present of horrors to Jimmy and Frankie, Jimmy must have gone straight out of the house to one of the neighbors. Well, being a close-knit neighborhood, these people have known our family for years, and because of how soft and gentle she is—or was—they loved my mother. The news traveled down the block to Allie's house. It was eight o'clock at night, she said, but she just came running to our house to find both of my brothers devastated. She said Jimmy cried and shook his head; Frankie just stared at her, white-faced, mute.

What could she say? She probably asked what she could do. Frankie had always joked around and teased with her, which she loved. And Jimmy—well, she idolized Jimmy as much as I did. She loved talking to him, hearing his latest insight into a social problem, and he listened to her ideas, too. He also liked to make us laugh with stupid jokes. When she came back the next morning, she said Frankie just sat, silently looking at the newspaper, never turning a page. Jimmy mumbled about a fight he'd had with our mom. I don't know the details, but I heard him saying he'd finished college and the Army Reserves, and, at twenty-something, he needed his independence. I don't think Mom wanted to let go of him. I wondered about that, but, not too long ago, Jimmy told me they had made up before she went to see me. Thank you, God.

Over that first, horrible month, Allie was the lifeline for all of us, truly. She stayed home from the funeral with Laurie, who had silently let her know she couldn't face the church, the crowd, the coffin. I didn't really mind, because I had Robert and Frankie with me.

For the next few weeks, Allie had bopped into our house with jokes, teasing, and laughter, until she'd almost filled some of the black void. She even got Jimmy laughing at some really stupid elephant jokes, mostly because she made such a big deal out of cracking herself up. Frankie also talked to her, sort of. At least, he didn't ignore her. Of course, she and I had endless conversations during this time. She always understood me, or pretended to, anyway. I think I glommed on to her, probably sucked her dry, now that I look back. But she always kept her cool, breezing in any time I called her, and often when I didn't.

Then September came, and school started. Allie and I no longer shared that safe, zany world of high school. She's a senior now, one year behind me. I guess we've drifted. How could we not? At first, I picked her up from school once in a while, and we do still call each other sometimes, but it's different.

I know it's me. I can't imagine filling her in on my daily routine after she's just told me about the latest colleges she's considering or her world of Advanced Placement classes and Junior Achievement activities. I can't bear to tell her that I skipped my Anthropology final…just…didn't get up from my chair in the student lounge. I'll get an F. Be on academic probation, for sure. How could Allie, with her straight-A average, understand? I know I don't. No…I think I'm flying solo for now.

Anyway, Father Rex does his best for my family and for me, especially. He calls at least once a week to chat or invite me to have a hamburger or a piece of pie. He even addresses my nun obsession patiently, explaining that this is no escape hatch. It's a Serious Life Choice, like getting married. God forbid. One afternoon, he called, so cheerful and nice, like he always is. I was experiencing a big Rolaids day. My stomach was clenched as if Mr. Clean's fist had hold of it and refused to let go. I began talking about God calling me, about my possible vocation. I pictured myself dressed all in black, with this white poster board-like thing across my chest and forehead, and rosary beads at my side. I must have communicated my dread pretty well, or maybe he was just sick of my whining because he said, "I'll be right over." He must have dropped everything he was doing because he was there in ten minutes, I swear. First thing he does is take me by the shoulders, look me right in the eyes:

Father Rex: Beth, is this what you really want?

Me: I don't know. I'm so confused.

Father Rex: What do you feel when you talk about it?

Me: Petrified! What if God wants me to do this and I don't do it?

Father Rex: Listen to me. Do you think Sister Gertie Joe and the other sisters would want someone to join them who's confused, scared, and miserable?

This was an entirely new take on the topic. I never considered how they might feel about me, just me about them.

Me: I don't know. You think not?

Father Rex: I know not. They don't want you unless you want them. You do this only if it makes you happy, gives you peace.

Me: What about God?

Father Rex was finally exasperated with me. He just shook his head.

Father Rex: Don't you think you have enough to worry about right here? God's just fine, believe me!

With that, I started to cry, one of the few times in front of him, or, lately, anybody. I couldn't believe how much better I felt, at least right then. It's just that I think 18-year-olds are supposed to be figuring out their future vocations, aren't we? This is the way I was taught to think in my Catholic world, although most of my friends seem more concerned about sororities and mixers and cars and looking for boyfriends.

I, on the other hand, feel like a big washout in all those areas except the boy area. Robert has been a perfectly adorable boyfriend, smart and sweet, who sees me as Jackie Kennedy strong; you know—when her husband died, and she walked with her little kids in the funeral procession, holding their hands, looking straight ahead, stoic. Anyway, Robert's never really believed the nun thing. And not too long ago, I told him I thought we should date other people. He was shocked. I couldn't explain it, but I'd been worrying constantly that we should break up. I only made things worse. Now, we're at least talking again.

This proves my insanity. The guy got in a car accident, coming with my parents and sisters to visit me on an Indian reservation. Then he stayed by me night and day for the next two weeks, insisting on sleeping on our couch. Amazingly, his very strict parents understood—or just couldn't talk him out of it. The afternoon of the funeral, with my house filled with people paying their respects (which means eating, talking, and even laughing), a church friend of my mom's scolded me for not serving and making nice with these people, saying I wasn't behaving properly, as my mother would want. Well, Robert and Allie and her boyfriend kidnapped me. He drove us to the beach, just to get me out of that morbid scene. (Actually, I think my Aunt Maudie had a part in it, also.)

I felt kind of bad, leaving my brothers and Laurie—my father and Margaret were still in the hospital—but, on the funny side, as I passed through the kitchen, I saw Molly, my girlfriend of the "new" old VW, cleaning out our kitchen cupboards. I swear! She had emptied one entire cupboard onto the drain board, and she was scrutinizing each item, which she either put aside or back onto the shelf. When she asked me what to do with the half-used baking soda in the dingy orange box, I beat it out of there. I guess the awkwardness of death can make you do silly things. Allie couldn't stop cracking jokes at the entire scene. I just about wet my pants. (Excuse me!) Now, I think we should have kidnapped Molly, too.

Anyway, Robert and I have certainly bonded, but, weirdly, being a couple made me feel trapped. I thought if we were too close, it would mean this is it for me, for boyfriends and rollercoaster romances and fantasy men. He told me he wished I were at his college, so we could meet in the cafeteria for lunch and walk around holding hands. I couldn't have wished for anything less. I swear, when I made that two-hour drive to visit him, the closer I got, the tighter my chest got. And when we went out, just the two of us, and he wanted to be sweet and romantic, I almost gagged. I thought about breaking up when he first left for school. I mean, I went with his parents to move him in, and I cried all the way home. Then, just two weeks later, I went up with them again, for his first football game, and I thought I would crawl out of my skin. I don't know if this makes any sense. I'm definitely not normal.

This is the same guy who knocked on the motel door where I was staying with my Aunt Maudie the afternoon of the accident. I guess she and my uncle left the room, because the next thing I know, Robert and I are sitting on the bed, holding hands. I don't remember what we said, but he was there in a big way. It was eerie. Then, the next morning, at Sunday mass, I think I started to faint—it's still a blur—but there was Robert, his arm around me, leading me outside for fresh air. I felt married to this marvel who just instinctively knew what I needed. Then after a month of this, I said we needed to split up. He didn't understand, and neither did I. I don't know why, but I just wanted to tell him "Go away already!! I can't say 'I love you' back, even though I know I probably do." He wrote me a sad letter and then we didn't talk for a while. Now, we're talking again. I'm still so confused. I just don't know how or what I feel!" I kinda hope I get to see him over Christmas vacation. It might sound weird, but I miss him a lot.

But I can see my domestic days stretching endlessly before me. I, who was going to finish college, do the Europe thing, lead a carefree life until age 25, at least. I'm not so sure any of this will happen now. Robert talked about our being married someday, us pushing around a shopping cart at the grocery store with a baby or two in tow. In fact, he wants to have NINE KIDS! Enough for a baseball team, he says. At the time, I couldn't believe this was me he was talking to. He made me laugh, but then I thought, "Wait, there's already too much grocery shopping, too many guitar lessons, and cooking and cleaning."

On the flip side, my aunt Maudie wants me to move in with her and my Uncle Ralph. I think it was really Jimmy's idea, but she suggested it to my dad. She says I have too much to do, and it's not right. I think my dad felt guilty, because he asked me about it and said he would hire someone from the church to help out, which he did. That lasted about a month.

The thing is, as much as I love my feisty aunt, she's the polar opposite of my soft-spoken, mostly-gentle mother. Living with Aunt Maudie would be like being in the Army: commands, orders, no voice but hers. She means well, and I don't know what we all would've done without her these past months. In fact, I've always looked forward to her visits, her invitations for Margaret and me to spend the night after a family gathering, which usually resulted in a trip to buy new pjs or lunch out. When I was little, she taught me to play Canasta and let me watch TV in bed. But I never liked the harsh tone she can get, especially when she's criticizing my mother or father. She gets really frustrated with my father (her brother).

A few weeks ago, she was over, checking to see how we were getting along. Was I having any problems with grocery shopping, doing the laundry or anything? I mean, c'mon, I've been doing all these things with my mom for years. Anyway, my dad called from his store, I think, to talk to me. They got to talking, and then he got another call, cut her off and hung up. He's done this to my mom, my siblings, and me since I can remember, but she ranted for what seemed like an hour.

Aunt Maudie: He doesn't make time for us, Beth! He puts that store before his family—you know he does. How can he be so rude?

Me: I don't know. I don't think he means to be.

Aunt Maudie: After all I do for him! He never listens! I don't know how your mother stood it all these years. He didn't appreciate her. You know that, don't you?

Me: Umm…

What I know from Mom is that it's just part of Dad's business: he has to be available to his customers. But Aunt Maudie's wounded pride, close-up and aimed at me, caused me all kinds of consternation, and her tirade against Dad steamed me up almost to boiling-over.

But then, I kind of agreed with her, too. I wanted to burst out, "Yeah, he never listens to me! You know that! Right? I have to answer his questions about my sisters, then listen to him go on and on about the stupid store! And you should see what I do around here! I hear you, loud and clear!"

I could also hear myself yelling, "Don't you know how hard he works for us?! Don't you know how hard it is to run a store and juggle two or three phones and all those customers?! This is our house, not yours, so just get out!" Of course, never in a million years could I ever come close to using those words or that tone with an adult, especially Aunt Maudie.

No, thanks…no living with Aunt Maudie for me. My father asked me what I thought of the idea—he was using his serious down-deep voice at the time. Anyway, I got a big lump in my throat for some reason. I tried to hide how I felt, but then I spat out something like, "No, Dad. Laurie and Margaret need me. And I love Aunt Maudie, but she scares me sometimes."

"Yeah," he agreed. "She scares me sometimes, too."

I could tell he was relieved, and he went back to reading his paper.

Not that I really have much of a voice around here. What I have are ears: for Laurie's folk songs—which I really do love, and which she teaches me when I ask; for Margaret's woes about the workshop; but, mostly, for my dad. Until the accident, we seemed to be in different orbits. Now, I feel like his listener-in-chief. Since I became a teenager, we've had what I think is a pretty typical daughter/father relationship. We say good morning and good night, discuss what needs to be discussed—I mean, if Mom isn't or wasn't around.

But if I ever had a question about anything I was learning in school—and I mean anything! —he could answer it. I'm totally serious. If I didn't understand something in any class, I asked him, and he explained it with no problem. That goes for history, math, English, even geology. Mostly though, I did my business with my mom. She was just always there, available. Oh, there were a few years when I got too mature and sarcastic for my own good, but before that—and lately, too—it never would have occurred to me to go anywhere else.

Anyway, to go from being a non-entity to being center stage is weird. Somehow, I look forward to and dread the little evening one-on-one chats Dad and I have been having. They seem to be turning into a daily ritual. Dad gets home from work, looks through the mail, then goes to clean up and change out of his work clothes. Then he comes to find me. We go into his bedroom. I sit on his bed; he sits on his chair, and we talk. While I feel kind of important, I also feel strange. I don't know how to respond when he talks about his day or asks me if there's anything I need. I mean…like what?

Once, I tried to tell him about my confusion over Robert and how he'd talk about "us." To Dad and my brothers, Robert's conduct at The Accident has earned him eternal worship, although, when we first dated, my father and brothers couldn't even look up from their cribbage game long enough to say, "Have a seat while you wait for Beth." Anyway, Dad couldn't really hear what I was saying. How could I ever be this lucky twice? Needless to say, my dad wasn't a whole lot of help. But then, I've never seen him as the psychological type. He's strictly meat and potatoes, if you know what I mean.

Usually, in these little twilight chats, he asks me about my sisters. I want to tell him to pay attention to them, but I don't know how. So I talk about them, what they're doing, what they're saying. He seems interested, but it doesn't seem to go very far. Mostly, he wants to know how the car's working out, or about house business. He tells me about his day at the store. I don't say much about mine.

I think I'm a phony with my dad. When I was little, I was his princess. I sat on his lap to watch Engineer Bill, and sang songs with him when he took me for a ride in the car. Then—I don't know exactly when—things changed. I didn't want to hold his hand anymore. I waited to see if he would ask me to kiss him goodnight, and when he didn't, I quit. Did he get too tired to see me? Did I get less me around him? Maybe he just saw me growing up and tried to give me breathing room. I still admired him from a distance and, once in a while, we came together. In 7th grade, I got asked to write a speech about the United Nations for a contest, and he helped me with it. When I won, I had to present it at a Knights of Columbus meeting. He helped me until I could stand at the microphone and say it clearly. When the time came to give the speech to a room full of people, I was so nervous that I had no idea what I was saying. Anyway, now I look back and see the self-centered teenager who didn't appreciate how hard her parents worked for her. For our family.

For the first couple months after the accident, it seemed to me that we all tiptoed around Dad. This naturally exuberant man who had filled our house with "Jackie Begorry" stories and one-finger-plunked-out songs on the piano—this man who was rarely quiet, except when engrossed in a book or newspaper—now brooded and stared silently into space most of the time. Because of a blood clot in his lung, he had to sleep sitting in his red chair…probably a blessing when I think of his going into that room, that bed, alone.

With our small house and the cluster of bedrooms at one end, I grew up familiar and comfortable with the soft sounds of nighttime murmurings coming from their room. And many nights in my younger, fretful days, I made my way to my maternal safety net, only to find her entwined with my father. I never minded intruding into the middle of that benign web. I remember that sometimes, I coaxed her into a web in which I was her exclusive partner. Finally, as a proud pre-adolescent, I tossed and turned in the moonlight rather than ask for her soothing. Why did I waste such an opportunity?

Still, it's eerie, getting up every morning, finding that this man that I've had so little interaction with for the last couple of years is suddenly unavoidable.

But Dad has returned to some kind of normal. I give my brother Jimmy credit for taking Dad to bridge games, especially since Jimmy dislikes how nonchalantly Dad approaches games—he's always in them more for fun than competition, which probably drives Jimmy crazy. Jimmy has also encouraged Dad to start square dancing again, an activity we all consider a pretty primitive form of entertainment. I have to hand it to Jimmy that, even though he would never "twirl his partner" to the hillbilly music those people dance to, he knew getting out and doing something he and our mom enjoyed would be good for Dad.

I can't get over how my brother thinks of subtle ways to get Dad back into the traffic of life. In the past, I thought Jimmy found Dad, with his army-style khaki pants, boisterous laugh, and war books, something of an embarrassment. Once, I heard him suggest to Dad that he change some element of his lifestyle, but Dad just shrugged, muttering, "Don't see the problem. It's my life, goddam it!" (Sorry) Now, I can see how much he cares about Dad. And they always seem to be discussing sports, politics, or some esoteric subject like math. I, on the other hand, must admit I have a running commentary on my father. It's internal, and I do try to squelch that voice. Sometimes, though, she just won't shut up.

In high school, I was jealous of my brothers. Animated conversations between Dad and the boys dominated every dinner while we girls sat, just eating. Most meals, my mom spent almost the entire time cutting and serving tomatoes, cucumbers with vinegar, and more of this or that. Once in a while, Dad would look up at her and impatiently urge her to sit down. After dinner, though, the two of them lingered over a cup of coffee, talking quietly. When I look back, it seems that they would sit there together for so long…until the girls were called back in to do dishes, and Mom got started on the next day's lunches. While we washed, dried, and clattered the dishes away, Mom sat at the table, assembling bags of sandwiches and apples and cookies.

Unlike my brothers, my conversations at home mostly took place on the phone to somewhere else. I have always been a good listener. In fact, my mom often accused me of using my nice, patient voice on the phone with friends and then turning all cranky when I got off the phone. She would say, "Lizbeth, why can't you be as sweet when you're off the phone as you are when you're on it? Your friends seem to think you're Dear Abby! I need you to come peel these potatoes. Can you just please be nice about it?" I have to admit there was some truth to this. These days, though, the phone doesn't ring as much, at least, not for me. But I don't mind. I guess I'm getting a little too mature for endless conversations over what outfit I plan to wear tomorrow or what to do on Saturday night.

Sometimes, I think I'll just let loose and scream to my father, "Enough! I can't do this anymore! I miss her too, but I'm not your wife, I'm your daughter, and I need her so desperately! My heart hurts every second of the day and night! I don't want to hear about your business. I don't want to think about Margaret's bowling or Laurie's schedule. I don't want to wonder what to fix for dinner. I don't want to get up Saturday mornings and drag out to the butcher shop and the grocery, and do the cleaning and laundry and errands."

Mostly, though, I don't want to be so confused.

Where is my mother? The one who always cooked me tomato soup and rubbed my feet and cut my hair and seemed to worry about me constantly…the one who tried to protect me from the big, bad world. It's still here, but she isn't.

I look for her on every street corner, at every bus stop, in every crowd. I catch glimpses of her hurrying away. I dream she's living somewhere else, that she's forgotten me. I cry out, "How could you? Don't you know I need you?" She just smiles patiently.

And I know—though I can't really believe—I'll never see her again, and I wonder how I will ever endure it. I will never feel her hand on my forehead again, never smell her scent again, never hear her murmuring endearments when I'm sick, or have a bad sunburn, or am just plain sad. And I can never, ever, tell my father or brothers or sisters or anyone else in my family any of this. I'm the oldest (functional) girl, Miss Responsible, and I hate it.

I think this qualifies as a significant event in my life, one that has definitely changed me. I'm sure I went (a lot!) overboard in describing it. I guess once I got started, I couldn't stop. I'm sorry about that! I don't even know if you could endure reading the entire thing. If you did, then I'll end by saying I suppose, for now, I'm marking time.

It's been six months. If I've learned anything, it's that life, in some form or fashion, goes on. People think I'm strong, and I do believe I've found ways to get through the days, but I prefer the nights, the cool, dark nights, when I can finally perch on my bed, reading and writing, and looking out the window into the black void. Sometimes—often—I imagine her approaching. She's walking up the street…to our house…up the steps…across the porch and through the door. And then I can sleep.

9 THE SUN PEEKS OUT

Good morning star shine, the earth says hello
You twinkle above us, we twinkle below
Good morning star shine, you lead us along
My love and me as we sing our early morning singing song

~James Rado, Gerome Ragni, Galt MacDermot

Dec. 20, 1965

Oh, man! This is unbelievable! How could I be so down one minute and sky high the next?! Rolling around in a dark pit, then at the top of a Ferris wheel.

Robert came home yesterday for Xmas break. He called and asked me to go to a party at Tony R's house that night. He sounded happy, joking and all flirty-like. When I got off the phone, I actually ran outside and did cartwheels. Laurie and Margaret followed me, laughing and asking me what was going on. Somehow, though, it turned into déjà vu all over again.

When Robert got to my house, he came in with Freddy and Kris and Joe. They were all riding in Freddy's car, but they had gone by Robert's house first, so he told them just to follow him to my house to get me. Okay. Fine. Freddy was sweet and complimented me on my dress—the one I was supposed to wear to Linda Sue's wedding, which got called off because of her cheating fiancé, unfortunately for Linda!

Anyway, per instructions from Linda, I had made my bridesmaid dress out of a pretty pink velvet. It was long, though, so I thought I'd just cut it short and hem it for the party. Unfortunately, I made the dress pretty short, and, because I've gotten so skinny, I kept taking it in. I guess it's probably a little too tight now. I mean, the boys seemed to give me the once over. I felt kinda funny—and good, too, for a change. I mean, my anxious heart may not make appearances for all to see, but it prevents me from doing much flirting with boys and that sort of thing. I guess that's where the trouble started, only I didn't know it then.

On the way over to Tony's, Robert hardly talked to me. He hadn't kissed me, and he didn't hold my hand as we walked up to the door. But we were officially seeing other people, so what did I expect? I guess I hoped this would turn out to be something more. It turned out to be a pretty small party but nice, with a bunch of kids from last year all catching up and everything. But any time I said anything, Robert said something sarcastic and gave me a weird look—or ignored me altogether. It was really embarrassing.

He never asked me if I wanted anything to eat or drink. In fact, he acted just like he did last summer at that beach party. I finally got him to a quiet spot and said, "Robert, I want you to take me home." He looked really frustrated and mad and said, "What? Why? We just got here."

I told him, "Look, you're being really rude and mean to me. I don't know why. It doesn't matter. I'm just not going to pretend everything's fine. If you're mad at me about something, you should've just told me before we got here."

He stood there, just staring at me, with his jaw almost on the floor. I wasn't yelling. I was very calm. I repeated "Just take me home, please," and I started walking toward the door. He followed me outside.

I didn't look at him when we got into his car, just stared straight ahead. Finally, I said, "Listen Robert, this Christmas is hard enough for me. I definitely do not want to spend any time with someone who's going to be mean and rude and jerky. If you like someone else, and that's what this is about, just tell me. Maybe you regret taking me with you tonight, but even if we are just friends, you asked me to this party. You can still be nice." I was steaming mad and almost crying, but I hated myself because I didn't want him to think it was because I liked him. And, really, I kinda hated him at that moment.

First, he sorta huffed and puffed, and I thought he was gonna erupt. But he shocked me by saying, "Beth, believe me, I'm not mad, and I don't like anyone else. This is really hard for me to say, but the reason I've been acting weird…uh, I mean, the thing is, I'm jealous."

I was so confused at that! I was just looking at him, and then I asked "Jealous of who? Why? About something I did?" Robert had his head down, but then he looked at me and sort of whispered, "The thing is, you look really, really good tonight. Sexy. All the guys noticed, I could tell. You know I'm not good at compliments, but I wanted to tell you, In fact, I was going to tell you in the car, but then Freddy said it first. I knew you liked the compliment, and I thought maybe you and Freddy had something going. You know, you went home with him from the beach party last summer."

Well, all my anger just melted away. "Good grief!"

Yes, I actually said 'good grief'—what a weirdo I am! Anyway, I told him, "Me? Like Freddy? Heck, no! He is absolutely the last thing on my mind! Yes, of course, I liked the compliment, but I would've—and do—like it much better coming from you."

Robert said he was sorry for being a jerk, that I didn't deserve that, and he still really likes me. Then, we started really talking, and I told him I regretted the break up; I didn't know what I was doing…I thought he knew that by some of our phone conversations and letters. I even hoped that, when he asked me to the party, we would get back together. Well, we did!! And we talked for hours. We never went back into the party. I am just so relieved and happy (as I can be for now).

Dec. 22, 1965

He's home
I only know
I'm emotional about him at the present

He is one of the finest boys I know
If he turns out to also be one of the finest men I know
I will not let him get away

He has made me happy
as only he is allowed to do
    considering the position in my heart he holds

The sky is blue today
    and the sun is shining
Of this I am sure,
    (though I haven't yet been outside)

Dec. 27, 1965

Although the sun is hiding behind stormy-looking clouds, life has been somewhat sunny for the past few days with Robert here. How is it that it makes SUCH a difference when he's home and around? (And being nice, of course!) He calls me and we make plans, or talk forever about nothing. It's such a luxury! When he's at school, we have to keep our conversations short because of the cost. It's so frustrating; sometimes, it's just not worth it. It seems like, when I call him, we just get started, and I hear my father's voice: "Hey, Bethie—don't forget that's long distance." So Dad is at least half-listening to my conversation and he didn't really mean it when he told me not to worry about calling Robert long distance. But when Robert calls me, he has to watch the clock because he REALLY can't afford the long-distance calls.

Anyway, Robert's home for another week. Yay! I thought we could do some things with Laurie and Patty—good old Patty, Laurie's lifelong friend. I'm so glad they're still friends. Laurie needs her.

Anyway, we're going to the park to shoot baskets and maybe try flying kites. I don't care. I know Robert will make it fun. He just always does. Even doing the grocery shopping is fun with Robert. What an improvement over my regular life these days.

10 CLIMB OUT OF THE DARKNESS

If you're going to San Francisco
Be sure to wear some flowers in your hair
If you go to San Francisco,
You're gonna meet some gentle people there..

~John Phillips

Christmas was over. Robert had gone back to school, and Beth lolled on her bed, re-reading the paper on a "life-altering event" that she had written for Professor Michaels' class. She had poured her soul into this final term paper, as if, by recounting the events of the disaster that had thrown her life into such chaos, she might somehow get some control back. Though she'd never have admitted it, somewhere deep within her, Beth clung to the belief that she could change the outcome of that "event."

At first, she let anger steer her narrative. Her life had been on a course—now, it wasn't. To believe such a thing was unalterable, that something this devastating was permanent, just couldn't stand. Beth was determined to expunge her current situation and, instead, hang onto the pre-accident time that now seemed a lovely fantasy.

However imperfect that life might have appeared to her adolescent self, Beth saw it all through new eyes that startled her with their clarity and depth perception. Words had poured onto the pages as if her story, required—demanded! —a raw, honest narrative, and so Beth had written fast and feverishly, using this vantage point that forced her to face the girl she had been: self-centered, stubborn, unappreciative. Immersed in her story, this freedom to tell the truth had allowed her to peel away layers of the anger in which she had wrapped herself months earlier.

Where did she go from here? Could she get back that angry armor that had helped her resist the truth? Should she even try?

And why had she trusted this teacher, this man, with her story? Simply because she needed to trust someone? Well…so, now I've done it. I gave him the truth. It's too late to take it back. It's time to move on. Somehow.

Beth closed her eyes, picturing her mother near, stroking her hair, murmuring softly as she rustled quietly around her.

In her daily life, when anyone asked her how she was doing, Beth usually replied, "Fine." "Okay." "Pretty good." There was no confiding in anyone outside of her family these days, not that there were many opportunities for that. She didn't have the energy for trust, let alone the right words for her feelings.

This inability filled her with frustration, causing her to turn to her journal.

Jan. 6 1968

Why don't I try and open up to someone? Call a girlfriend, or even Aunt Maudie? No, I just…they couldn't possibly understand. Even if they did, I just can't talk about it. It was hard enough to write about it. Anyway, I'm getting by. Aren't I? Things aren't so bad, are they? Well, yeah, they are! They stink! But I'm moving on…and that's that.

When I look back—before the accident—it's like my world consisted of colorful birds chirping in harmony, or white foamy waves rolling on an undulating ocean with bright green palm trees swaying against the azure sky. Families walked along the beach on its bright, warm sand, parents holding hands, while children scampered ahead or dawdled behind—all clearly bound to one another, secure in who they were. I was part of all of that not so long ago! Now, though, in this life—in my life now—dull black crows screech their jarring caws; angry waves roil and crash, angrily pounding and slashing at a jagged, rocky shore, tossing lonely girls here and there. There are no shapely green palms…only bare, lonely trees. No children scamper around parents. No families bound by their own indefinable glue decorate the picture I see now."

There, Beth had thrown down her pen. What a load of crap! she castigated herself. What would Allie think if she saw this? What would she say? She'd tell me to shake it off. She'd say, "You miss your mom. Okay. So, now what? Get yourself in gear!

With that, Beth had picked her pen up again.

My words just can't express what I'm trying to say, but, hopefully, Dr. Michaels will get the idea of the before and after of it—the event that changed my life forever. And anyway, it's all I've got. If it's too long or not really what he was looking for, that's too bad. I definitely poured on the literary techniques. And no one could argue that I didn't write about a significant event in my life. So that's that.

The next few weeks passed in a blur for Beth. She turned her paper in to

Dr. Michaels and prepared for her remaining final exams. For two of those tests, she worked hard; she succeeded in making note cards for them, and spent a few hours studying for each. She thought she had done fairly well in one, and she was guardedly optimistic about the other. Now, lying on her bed in the early afternoon, she stared at the open Anthropology textbook.

This was the class she'd thought would introduce foreign countries, peoples, and cultures to her eager mind. Well, something had very definitely gone wrong. For any number of reasons, she just hadn't cared much about those "foreign peoples and cultures." She'd tried to read this text and given up, and, just as before, she found her mind wandering aimlessly as she turned the pages, occasionally reading the captions under the pictures. "Oh, well. I already failed this one," she reminded herself. Just then, the phone rang, and Beth, relieved at the interruption, decided to let the worry about this subject wait till later.

It was Joe, calling to remind Beth that he was picking her up the next day.

"I didn't forget. I'll be ready. At 9, right? For our 10 o'clock finals?"

"Sounds about right. How've you been, Bethie?"

"Pretty good. As good as anyone can be studying for finals. How about you?"

"Yeah. I feel pretty good about my classes. I think I'm gonna do all right. You feeling confident about your classes?"

Beth took a breath. "I don't know, honestly. I just hope my grades are decent. I think…uh…I was at least somewhat ready for history, and the Comp final was a paper, and that's done, thank God. It's been a pretty hard semester for me."

Beth didn't want Joe to know how much she was hoping just for passing grades. Images of F's or D's on the school reports due a few weeks after finals marched across her mind, growing bigger and blacker and bigger and blacker until Joe said, "Yeah, I know." Beth wondered if he actually did know.

"Well," he broke into her thoughts, "I'm looking forward to seeing you. It's been couple of weeks, Bethie."

Joe sounded excited, and Beth realized how much she had missed him.

"Hey, I don't have all my books for next semester. Do you mind, tomorrow, waiting for me to go to the bookstore?"

"Of course not, Joey. Why would I mind? Just go after your final. I'll see you in the student union—where we usually sit."

"Okay. Hey, how 'bout we grab a burger there to celebrate the end of finals?"

"Sounds good."

Now, though happy at the thought of being with Joe, the idea of having to ask her father for money immediately hit Beth. She hated it. Years of hearing her parents talk about money problems had gotten under her skin. Money, money, money…never enough, it seemed. How could she forget whining about not being able to buy her lunch at St. Joe's, instead of taking the "brown bag" lunches her mother put together every school night? Get over yourself, Beth, she thought. Of course Dad'll be fine. He always says I should have cash when I'm driving all around. He just forgets to give it to me. I should ask for an allowance!

"It'll be good to see you, Bethie," Joe repeated.

"Definitely," Beth returned, not knowing what else to say. That's Joe, always upbeat and enthusiastic. Thank God for him. He's the best guy friend I've ever had, and also the only one who doesn't mind saying it and showing it. I should appreciate him more.

Beth hung up the phone, aware that she had put on a bit of an act for Joe. She would be humiliated if he knew she was failing one class. How hard she'd studied for the other finals in the hopes of passing those classes with Cs! As a kid, she had done well in school, taking good grades for granted—at least through the eighth grade, there'd been only As and a few B's for her. In high school, though she knew she needed to work harder than she had in elementary school, she had left academics somewhere on a back burner. Generally, she had liked her teachers and classes, but she found she focused more on the fascinating world of first love, new friends, and the psychosocial games played every day at school. Somehow, learning French from a little Irish nun and studying American heroes and wars simply didn't motivate her to exert much effort.

The exception, however, was any class that involved a novel or an essay. In fact, she rarely worried about her English classes. Sure, she'd had a few tough teachers who didn't let her slide by with her usual casual approach. These teachers admonished Beth and challenged her to think harder. "Dig deeper, Beth. You say you understand Ethan Frome's feelings for young Mattie; you feel sorry for him. Isn't that a little too easy? Don't you think he tramples on his wedding vows to take the ride with Mattie?" When Beth defended the actions of the young protagonist, Sister Teresa probed, "Okay, so it's difficult for him. He has a moral dilemma. What choices does he have? What could or should he have done?" When Beth answered dubiously, "Well, I suppose he could have considered Zeena's feelings more." "Why?" her teacher demanded. With every answer that Beth gave, there came a new question: "Remember, Beth, I asked if Ethan is true to his moral responsibility. What drives him? What about the results, the ultimate consequences? Could they have been avoided?"

Beth dug in, rallying to these questions, feeling for this character, trying hard to make a case for his actions, and reluctant to admit the duplicity of his choices. Her teacher had squelched her romantic sympathy, instead demanding that Beth think of the big picture and apply it to her own world, her own life. Eventually, she had to confront the crushing truth: romantic love might not be enough in certain circumstances. Married love came with responsibilities and obligations. And sacrifices.

While these academic episodes stimulated and engaged her, the social scene of high school piqued Beth's interest more. Ultimately, it seduced her. Besides navigating the culture of high school girlfriends, the world of boys distracted her as well, though during the first year or so, that part of things came alive mostly after school.

Beth had met John the summer before high school at the local park. On a lazy summer day, one of her friends had suggested they check out the rec program at Pop Luter's for something to do. With no ride to the beach in sight, Beth and Kathy had wandered over to Pop's gym a few blocks from Beth's house. Kathy had walked into the gym first and started laughing, "Oh, man, Bethie. Look at this!" Scattered in front of them were kids of all ages playing volleyball, ping-pong and pool; some were even doing crafts. When a friendly girl asked them if they wanted to join the volleyball game—they were short a couple of players—they eagerly agreed, and just like that, Beth and Kathy had met a new group of kids, boys and girls from the nearby public school. After a few games, the group broke up and the two girls started for home, talking excitedly.

"Can you believe it? We actually just played volleyball with boys, cute boys!"

"Yeah, and boys who aren't our brothers!" Beth agreed.

"What a difference from boring St. Mary's where we were never allowed to play sports with the boys!"

"Or have mixed parties or dances! You name it!"

"Wow! I'm calling Sandy and Terry. They need to come over here," Kathy said.

"That's for sure. I'm gonna call Grace. She might know some of these kids because of her next-door neighbor. She'll want to come. Do you want to go tomorrow? I hope my mom will let me go." Beth worried about the chores Anna might cook up to keep her home; though, since eighth grade graduation, Beth noticed her mother giving her more freedom. Was this her imagination?

"Me, too. Just don't focus on the boys when you talk to her."

"Don't worry, I won't. And I'll try to get my chores done early."

A rec center, close to home where Beth went with other kids Anna knew, seemed acceptable. Anyway, she told Beth she could go. Beth and Kathy spread the word among their girlfriends, and before long, lots of familiar faces were showing up at Pop's for volleyball and so much more. If there wasn't a game of some sort going on or getting started, the vending machine area always had plenty of teens clustered around, chatting and flirting.

Just as Beth surmised, Grace knew some of the kids, including one boy in particular, John. A year older than Beth and Grace, John attended the public high school where, instead of St. Joe's, Grace would be starting her freshman year. Before long, they found themselves laughing and chatting in a game that included John. Grace introduced Beth to John, and later, John asked Grace about Beth.

"What do you mean, he asked about me? You're kidding, right?"

"He wanted to know if you have a boyfriend."

"Really? What'd you say?"

"I told him you didn't—because you don't!" Grace replied testily.

What it was about her that attracted John, Beth couldn't fathom. While her mother called her "boy crazy" from time to time, she'd never had a boyfriend or even kissed a boy. John, on the other hand, had a reputation of "getting around," according to Grace. From what Beth could tell, he represented a foreign world of fast boys and fast cars. The clean-cut Catholic schoolboys she knew, including her brothers, wore loose-fitting chinos and striped t-shirts. In contrast, John and his friends wore tight Levis with narrow cuffs that they carefully turned, and white t-shirts with the sleeves rolled up to show off biceps, or hold a pack of cigarettes. In her world, boys sported short, neat haircuts, parted on the side. John slicked his hair back into a sort of long-ish ducktail. Everything about him shouted, "Danger!" Why in the world is John interested in me? Beth wondered. More importantly, was she interested in him?

Still thirteen—she wouldn't be fourteen until the end of the summer—and clueless of where she fit in the world of boys and high school life, Beth couldn't picture herself with any boys who looked like John. She saw herself as a late bloomer who had only recently started her period and begun developing. Nevertheless, rumor had it—particularly from Grace—that John liked Beth. "He said something about your dimples and blue eyes," Grace remarked. Surprise aside, Beth discovered that she was both terrified and excited. With Grace encouraging her and acting as a go between, Beth accepted a secret daytime date with John—on certain conditions.

"Grace, you have to go with us. His friend can go, too."

"Beth, you're kidding, right? Okay, I'll go, but only because Kenny's a nice guy. Maybe it'll be fun."

"And tell John I'm only going to get to know him. That's all it is."

"Good grief, Beth! I can't say that. I feel stupid enough just being your go-between."

"Okay. But I'm really scared."

"Don't worry so much. He's really nice, and he likes you! It's gonna be fine!"

A few days later, the foursome met at Pop's, then went in Kenny's car to A&W for hamburgers and root beer floats. Awkward at first, Beth relaxed as she sat by John's side in the back seat, chatting and laughing along with the group. With Grace in the front seat, what could go wrong? But on the way back to the gym, John casually put his arm around her and soon bent over to kiss her. She'd been practicing with her sister's Patty Playpal doll, just in case, and Grace had assured her she was ready, that kissing was not that big a deal. Beth closed her eyes, slightly parted her lips as Grace had instructed, and then boom! Alarms bells rang, and it was all Beth could do not to scream "Stop! Let me out of the car!"

It was awful. If kissing meant slobbery, mouth-open, tongue intrusion, she didn't want it! Where was the nice, soft, gentle meeting of the lips? When she got back to Pop's, Beth barely said goodbye to John; she just grabbed Grace and rushed out of there. On the way home, Beth described the backseat events, squealing in disgust, shaking her head and shoulders, and repeating, "Yuck! Yuck! Yuck!" Grace laughed so hard she doubled over and had to stop walking to catch her breath.

"C'mon Beth, it couldn't have been that bad," Grace said through her giggles.

"Yes, it was! What's with the tongue thing, Grace? Am I supposed to like that?"

"It's called 'French kissing'. It can be good, but it can be bad. Maybe John's just not good at it. What am I supposed to say when he asks me if you had a good time?"

"I don't know! He seems nice, and he's really cute, and I was starting to like him, but I don't want to do that tongue thing again. Am I just a big baby, Grace? What do you think?"

"Yes, you are! You're a big baby. Can't you just tell him not to French?"

"Oh, my God—me tell him?! No way! Could you tell him for me?"

"Really, Beth? Are you serious? That's so weird. Oh, my God!!"

The next two days, Beth stayed home from Pop's, but Grace went. Just as she'd predicted, John asked about Beth. Where was she? Did Grace think Beth liked him? As calmly as she could, Grace explained Beth was new at the boyfriend thing, and while she liked John, he was different from the boys she knew—from the way he dressed to the way he wore his hair…and she definitely didn't like French kissing. That's all she could tell him. Both Grace and Beth figured that would be the end of John's attraction to Beth.

The next day, though, when Beth went to Pop's, she joined a group starting up a volleyball game, and there came John, walking through the door in bermuda shorts, with white tennis shoes and sox and a short, flat-top haircut. Beth did a double take. Did he do all that for me? she wondered.

When he joined the next game, Beth noticed how athletic he was. After the game, John talked to Beth, clearly still interested, and she took a fresh look at him, seeing a boy who didn't really fit the stereotype she had attributed to him, after all. He seemed nice and cute, just like the boys she knew and chatted with from school and her neighborhood. He asked to walk her home, and she said yes, so he and Kenny walked with her and Grace. At some point, he took her hand, and she found she liked that, too. But when they got close to her house, she shooed him away, saying her mom wouldn't like the surprise of boys she didn't know; really, though, Beth wanted to avoid any possibility of kissing.

However, she soon realized she could talk naturally to John, and in his new style, he fit in with her friends and with her idea of a boyfriend. Most importantly, when he kissed her again, it was tentative and gentle. Soon, Beth looked for John whenever she went to the gym. And, just like that, they were a couple. For well over a year, thoughts of John absorbed her. Her mother, though…her mother didn't like the idea of Beth having a boyfriend at 14.

"You shouldn't tie yourself down, Bethie. You just started high school. I didn't have boyfriends until I was much older."

"But that was you, Mom, a very long time ago. Things are different now."

"But he's not Catholic. He goes to a public school. What's wrong with the boys at your school?"

"Aw, Mom! John's a really nice boy. You can see that, can't you?"

"I suppose he is. But why do you have to see him every day? He's practically a fixture on our front porch. I wouldn't mind if you came in and helped me some of the time after school."

"Oh, Mom. Come on! I help you plenty. And aren't you glad we're here where you can see us? You know, so you can see we're not doing anything bad?"

"Bethie, you have an answer to everything."

Nice and polite, John always said hello and asked Anna how she was. What's more, he always smiled and talked to Margaret, and Anna couldn't find fault with that. Beth was smitten. When she took the bus home from school, John met her at the corner, took her books and walked her home. Then they sat on the porch by the hour, talking about school, friends, and their families. It turned out John also had an "exceptional" sister and understood Beth's ambivalent feelings towards Margaret.

Growing up, Beth had been embarrassed by the teenagers in her neighborhood who occasionally made jokes about Margaret being a "ree-tard." Once, walking with a friend to the nearby shopping center, Beth had been shocked and shamed by graffiti mocking her sister. But with John by her side, Beth never worried. In fact, she felt proud. John not only accepted Beth as she was, he shared his feelings with her: distressed feelings about his sister, the conflicts he had with his parents, and his confused feelings about the future.

On the phone, in person, and in long letters, John spoke to Beth intimately, the way no boy ever had before. He would never let her read his letters in his presence, though, so Beth saved them for nighttime when she went to bed. Sometimes, after reading one, with his last few paragraphs so loving, so passionate, she couldn't sleep. She would hug her pillow and kiss the teddy bear he'd given her, wishing for him to appear. Thoughts of him often distracted her in class, where she often re-read his letters and tried to match his passion in her letters back to him.

For a good part of her freshman year, Beth didn't think she could ever feel this way about another boy. Eventually, however, she found her feelings for John ebbing and flowing. For one thing, her brother Frankie, now a senior at St. Joe's, had some cute and funny friends who began paying attention to Beth when they came over. And, since John didn't go to her school, once in a while, she found herself considering her options there as well—which stirred feelings that embarrassed her and made her feel guilty.

She tried to put other boys out of her mind, but once or twice, Beth shocked herself when she found John too charmed by her: at a summer party at her house, watching the other girls around the stereo choosing records to play as they gossiped and giggled, she felt the desire to un-peel John's arm from around her shoulder. She just wanted to join them…and be boyfriend-less for a while. This feeling didn't last, though. A day or so later, he appeared a little earlier than she expected at Pop's. Tall and lanky, he strode over to her, all wide blue eyes, full pink lips, and perfect blond flat top. And she was smitten all over again.

Then, one day, Beth realized that John's urgings that she demonstrate her love physically were becoming more insistent.

"But, Beth, I don't understand. I love you. You know that."

"I know."

"Well, don't you love me?"

"You know I do. But I've told you before, I just can't."

"I don't understand. I won't think less of you. I just want to be closer to you. It feels so right to me. It will to you, too, Beth. Let me show you. Come on. I don't understand why this isn't the same for you." Beth would get angry and shrug him off, confusion and doubt washing over her.

She valued their closeness, the special bond of what had knit between them after being together over a year. And she felt John knew her so well, in so many ways. But in this way, she felt she had only begun to know herself, her body. She was not ready for him—or any boy—to explore this private part of her. Besides, she'd been taught a moral code, and, for now, that was enough. She had heard that some of their friends assumed she and John were physically close; kids thought any couple dating for more than a few months had to be. For Beth, however, knowing she and John had spent this time getting to know each other without moving to sex had made her feel proud.

Now, his pressure caused her to see their relationship differently. In his world, if kids were going together, they got physical, especially kids who really liked each other. He couldn't see how Beth could listen to the priests who weren't even interested in the opposite sex. How could they know what was right between a boy and girl in love? In this area, though, Beth believed what the nuns and priests said: sex belonged in the marriage bed. What boy would respect a girl who gave herself to him before that commitment? It didn't matter what he said. The "If you really loved me" fights grew until Beth knew John would no longer be content with kissing.

For a while, confusion roiled Beth's world. John had served as her mentor into adolescent romance, holding her hand, dancing with his arms around her at parties, showing their society of fickle teenagers, that they belonged to each other, and what they had together would last, no matter what anyone thought. More than that, however, he had been her friend as she entered the tangled and tricky world of high school adolescence. Younger than most of her peers, she had gained confidence and a sense of herself through John's unwavering regard for her, and from their mutual trust and easy confidences. The idea of leaving him caused her tearful nights and unsettled days. Over the next month, they exchanged letters full of their regrets, their confusion. They agreed to meet halfway. Try again. Twice.

The first time, Beth went to a school football game with Molly, whose parents picked them and some of their friends up after and took them back to Molly's. John met Beth there, and Beth told Molly's parents he would walk her home. On the walk, he had stopped her under the cover of a big tree near her house and begun to kiss her, the way they had done so many times before. This time, though, John's kisses were insistent, almost angry, and Beth had pushed him away, hurt at the rough treatment. They walked the rest of the way in silence.

He called the next day and apologized for his behavior, and Beth again thought she could compromise with him, show him she did love him. This time, now with a driver's license and his dad's car, John took Beth out for a burger, to their hangout, A&W. Afterwards, he parked down the street from her house. Soon, they were kissing, and reaching the inevitable point where Beth always balked. She tried to allow him more freedom with his hands this time, but, after a few minutes, he stopped and held her face in his hands,

"Bethie, are you okay? Do you like this? I can tell you're tense. Are you okay, really?"

"I want to be, John, for you." But she couldn't relax, and eventually, she stopped his hands and looked down. He moved away from her.

"You can't, can you? Even for me." Again, John's questions came from frustration.

"I'm sorry. I'm just too…I don't know." Beth melted into tears.

This time, she saw clearly that this struggle couldn't go on, and when John dropped her off at home, Beth knew her first romance was over. She would no longer be seeing the boy who had occupied her dreams for over a year.

A few days later, John dropped off a long goodbye letter. She cried on and off for the next few days at his last few words, "I'll always love you and think of you. Stay good. You have to be you, true to yourself. Thanks for loving me the way you have."

It took her a while to shake off her sadness, but soon Beth's life resumed, with all of its responsibilities and distractions. It wasn't long before, Beth put her energies to playing the popularity game. Since the boys and girls were segregated in her Catholic high school, the boy thing was tricky, but not impossible. She threw herself into the drama of the dating scene, setting her sights on this guy or that, while keeping up to date on the current romantic crises with her girlfriends, always keeping one eye on being popular.

Then, in her junior year, Beth began to see her high school world as an exhausting game. She felt herself changing. In the journal part of her notebook, one day, Beth began writing:

What am I doing? I'm trying too hard to be popular. Talking to Will on the phone last night kinda made me think. I mean, he was really putting down the girls who are pressuring him to ask this popular senior to the upcoming dance. When he asked me "Why should I ask her? Just because she's popular?" I told him I didn't know. Then he said, "I could care less about that. I guess she's cute, but that's it. So what if she's popular? There's not much more to her that I can see."

I had no real comment. When he asked me what I thought he should do, it made me think. I'm trying out for cheerleader. Do I know why? I guess it would make me more popular, but that's a shallow reason. I need to care more about my classes, my grades, especially English and Religion. We have some really good talks in those classes. It's so interesting to hear what Karla has to say in English. She seems to like the same books and poetry I like. Actually, I'm pretty sure I've heard her and a few of her friends discussing the stuff we read for class even after class. I love that. And they tease and joke around with each other as much as any girls, but I haven't heard them gossip about other people. I should get to know them better. They seem really fun.

I'm so glad Karla lives near me. It was neat to ride home with her and her older sister and listen to their conversation. Karla has a great voice and is in the glee club. Her sister kept asking her about a part she wants in the spring musical. I could tell she was pretending not to care that much, but I think she does. How could she NOT get the part? I can't imagine having such a beautiful voice. But she's not stuck up about it at all. I'm so glad I'm getting to know her. It's also great that she's got some cute guy friends who are also in the glee club. Wow. I had no idea. I thought about trying out when I was a freshman. What happened? I guess I thought I wouldn't make it. I was also too consumed by John and trying to be popular. Stupid me! Oh well. Too late now. I thought only athletic boys were neat, but now I'm meeting all kinds of cute guys in this group; some of them are athletic like my brothers, but not all of them. Hmm.

Beth found herself moving into this group, joining in their conversations, wondering why she hadn't noticed them before. And this is how Beth came to know Joe and Robert, smart boys who were friends with her new, smart, and interesting girlfriends, like Karla.

One day, a few of these friends saw Beth with her "Odds" notebook—the notebook where she wrote her some of her daily musings and favorite poetry, poems newly "discovered" as well as those from her own heart. She and Allie had conceived the idea one day as a place to give voice to the sweet, sometimes harrowing moments in the vibrant, swirling, events that propelled them forward, sometimes with feet dragging, sometimes with eyes wide and eager.

It was a journal of sorts, but more than that. Here, they put down lines that struck them, poetry that they, in their youthful "sophistication," described as "deep." Here were works that amused, touched, or informed them. Wasn't e.e. cummings clever? And Robert Frost…how profound he was! Gwendolyn Brooks…what a truth teller!

During sleepovers, they took turns reading poetry to each other, often writing and talking late into the night. Sometimes, their poems included variations of prayers proclaiming that, instead of being angry or stern, "God is love, and he who abides in love, abides in God!" They reveled at being "modern" Catholics. In different grades and groups of friends, Beth and Allie shared their ideas and thoughts with like-minded friends. Soon, a little sisterhood of aspiring poets passed around their own cherished lines or poetic contemplations. One day, Joe, a boy Beth barely knew, asked a mutual friend about the "Odds" books he heard girls discussing. She had pointed to Beth. The friend made sure Beth knew about Joe's interest. Beth had mentally filed it away for later.

Beth first got to really know Joe in the school library, second semester senior year. Both were filling a gap in their schedules by working as Library

Aids. Sitting down at a table across from Joe, Beth had introduced herself,

"Hi. I'm Beth. I had an empty spot in my schedule, so I thought this could be good for getting some of my homework done."

With a smile, Joe had teased her knowingly, "Of course, I know you. You're the girl I've heard about. The one who writes more than history notes in her spiral notebook."

Recognizing the tease, Beth shot back, "I have no idea what you're talking about, but I'll never tell what I've heard about you."

"Me? I bet you didn't know I existed before now."

"How could that be true with the reputation you've got?"

Unsure if Beth's comment was still a joke, he maintained a half-smile anyway, and replied, "Well, that's interesting. I'm pretty sure we don't travel in the same circles."

"It doesn't matter where romance is concerned."

"Ah, but the girls I date never kiss and tell."

"So you think!" Beth quipped.

Joe was ready to concede defeat to Beth when Sister Carmela walked over to meet her new students. The next day, Beth got to the library first, having decided to start over with Joe. Her repartee of the day before had been her way of putting up her guard where boys were concerned, especially nice-looking boys who teased her. Growing up with two older brothers, Beth learned the power of this tactic, and she utilized it as an automatic defense. Looking back that night, she decided to re-meet Joe with an open mind. Her reward: finding in Joe an affable boy with many appealing qualities.

Talkative and enthusiastic about books—Beth's first love—Joe also charmed her with what he had to say about poetry. She had never known a boy who enjoyed reading books and poetry, certainly not one who said he liked to discuss them as well. He piqued her interest when he said he had some definite opinions where poetry was concerned. He thought some of what people called poetry was anything but the soaring verse he preferred.

Time and again, Sister Carmela shushed them as their conversations grew more animated, and their friendship grew as well. Eventually, they resorted to notes in which they shared who they were:

—she, fourth in a line of five kids; he, the only child.

—she, the daughter of a dad who worked long hours at his auto parts store and a mom who kept a close eye on those she called her "kiddies."

—he, the son of a dad who worked long hours at his butcher shop and a mom who also kept a very close eye on her kid.

After establishing favorite subjects and teachers, their written correspondence led them back to poetry: Joe couldn't stand e.e. cummings…one of Beth's favorites. Beth wasn't sure about Emily Dickinson; Joe wasn't either. He couldn't stand Kahlil Gibran—she exulted in him; after all, her brother Jimmy quoted Gibran to her and Allie. This had to mean Jimmy appreciated this author and thought they could, too. Eventually, the subject turned to Beth and Joe's own forays into the genre. Beth talked about her "Odds" books; Joe described his writing experiments. Soon, their notes consisted of silly and serious lines and stanzas back and forth.

All this coincided with Beth's blossoming romance with Robert, a casual friend of Joe's and also part of Beth's new world of friends. While she felt some definite chemistry with Joe, and excitement at their common interests, Beth had already moved toward smart, handsome, football player Robert. Both boys were so different from other boys she dated in high school. Qualities that Beth equated with maturity seemed to emanate from both Joe and Robert.

A casual comment by Robert caused Joe to go to Beth. Had he misread their chemistry? Her attention to him? She told him, no, not at all. Then came a heated note from Joe: "I like you. But from what I'm hearing, you're not being honest with me. If you're serious about Robert, say the word, and we'll be friends. Choose!"

"Joe, I have been on a few dates with Robert, and I do like him, but I don't know any more than that. I like you, too, Joe. I like how many interests we have in common, and how easy it is to talk to you." This evasion didn't satisfy Joe, so he chose for her.

"I have no interest in being in the middle of a drama. I like you, but I like Robert, too, Bethie. Pursue your relationship with him, see how it goes, and, in the meantime, we'll be friends." And she had, with some regret…but in no time, Robert won her heart. She couldn't deny it.

Still, they all remained friends, and the friendship among the three continued to grow. Joe met a girl who became a girlfriend that summer, but stayed in close touch with Beth and Robert. After the accident, he couldn't quit talking about Robert's heroic part in it. Once classes started at State, carpooling afforded Beth and Joe time for deepening their friendship.

These days, Beth could think of very few people who mattered to her the way that Joe did. Passionate about learning and eager to share his discoveries, Joe's take on life offered a welcome counterpoint to her confusion. His eagerness to share his thoughts became a balm for her loneliness, and she gladly let him take the lead in responding to the college world they had just entered.

Joe provided Beth with vicarious experiences. He loved the campus. "Isn't the quad cool?" He embraced his courses. "Do you mind waiting while I meet with Prof Thompson during office hours? Are you sure you don't want to see any of your professors? Office hours are a great opportunity to tell the professor how interested and serious a student you are."

Though she nodded her assent that Joe was right, Beth imagined how she would stutter, her brain blank as she tried to converse with one of these adults who stood in front of her day after day, talking for hours on end while she scribbled in her notebooks and chewed her nails.

But where Joe was concerned, it made little difference to Beth what he wanted to talk about during their commute to and from the University. With his open enthusiasm for their friendship propelling her, as well as his obvious expectation that she shared his eagerness to embrace this newfound freedom, Joe dropped breadcrumbs for Beth to follow. He reminded her that she was a friend and college student, nothing else. Still, no matter what stirring topics they might discuss going to or from school—from hippies and free love to the Beatles and Dylan—once Beth reached home, her world changed.

She figured her priorities were so different from Joe's that it was fruitless to try to explain them to him. How could he relate? What would he think of her other life? She didn't dare wander too far down this road with her best friend; she needed him in her life, sharing his dreams and his feelings. And she knew—or, at least, thought at times—if she gave him the word, he would want her as more than a friend.

But, she thought, if she left Robert, if she gave in to the sporadic temptation to tell Joe maybe she liked him romantically, she always reached the same conclusion: my life is so messed up!! If he really knew me, he might not even want me as a friend. And if we wound up dating, what would happen when we broke up? I would lose two very important people in my life, Joe and Robert. No, thanks.

So, if she found herself fantasizing about a different relationship with Joe, she shut her thoughts down. Fast.

11 TIME TO BUCK UP, YOU OLD BASTARD

You'd never know it
But buddy, I'm a kind of poet
And I've got a lot of things I want to say
And when I'm gloomy, won't you listen to me
Till it's all, all talked away…

~ Johnny Mercer and Harold Arlen

January 1966

Jack drove purposefully. He was doing something he had never done before: getting help…psychological or, perhaps, emotional help.

Can't believe I'm doing this. But something's eating at my gut. What else can I do? Gotta get these thoughts out of my system. Damn Rolaids ain't doin' much good. Know that drinking's not the answer either, not for me with my history. No way around it, gotta give this a try. What else can I do?

Lately, Jack had been asking himself questions non-stop. Something had been nagging at him, much like the itchy rash he had recently developed, only he couldn't doctor this away. There was no paste of baking soda and water like Anna used to make to ease bee stings, cooking burns or pesky sores—not for this. No, whatever this was, it affected his insides, keeping him awake at night when he sorely needed to sleep, and distracted him at work during the day when he needed to pay attention to his customers. After a month of this, he'd decided to take action.

At first, he thought he would consult Beth; she'd understand. But that just didn't sit right. What could she say? And worst of all—what if she agreed with him? Though she would never come out and say so, he would be able to tell by her face. Same thing with Jimmy. And Frankie, well, my God, Frankie had practically turned into a walking ghost. He never mentioned his mother or the accident, but Jack figured it lurked inside him, possibly eating him up. But Jack knew better than to bring that subject up with his son. Jack remembered all too well how he'd reacted when anyone brought up his mother's death all those years ago.

To this day, he could barely talk about it. It couldn't help but summon up so many painful feelings—sad, guilty feelings. He'd told Anna about it, of course…how his strong-willed, vibrant, and beloved mother had died suddenly of a cerebral hemorrhage when he was a young man. Only Anna knew the wrenching sorrow of that loss. And Jack had confided in her, and only her, throughout their marriage. When they were younger, sometimes they'd talk away half the night, drinking coffee at the kitchen table long after their children had gone to bed.

Well, Jack, those days are definitely over. My darling Anna…after so much living, the long days apart during the war, facing the facts about Margaret, struggling with the business, the ups and downs with the kids…those crazy, hard, wonderful days are long gone. I've got to quit acting like such a bastard—snapping at the guys at work, clamming up at home with the kids, crying in bed at night. What a baby! Oh, God, I hope Father can help me.

He pulled into a parking space in front of the rectory where Father Rex lived. "I've got an appointment with Father Rex. Don't hold dinner," he'd told Beth. "I'll heat it up when I get home." She knows I have an appointment with the priest, but she doesn't know why. She doesn't need to. Poor kid has enough on her plate, crazy with grief and somehow thinkin' that losing Anna was her fault. She never says much, but I know.

In Father's office, they shook hands, exchanged pleasantries…and then Jack came out with the reason for the visit:

"Father, I need to ask you about something that…well, it's been eating me up."

"Sure, Jack. That's what I'm here for. If I can help, you know I will. Does this involve Beth, or the rest of the family?"

"Well, indirectly, I guess. Maybe directly. I don't know. But it's mostly about me, something I'm trying to come to terms with." Jack leaned forward, his arms on the desk. "I've gone over the accident a hundred times, and I can't quit dissecting the way it happened."

"What do you mean, Jack?"

"Well, the other driver, the screwball who had his goddam head up his—sorry, Father—his trailer loaded so unevenly, I could see him starting to swerve back and forth as his truck was approaching my car. I mean, it didn't seem too bad at the time, but when I think about it now, I wonder why I didn't pull off the road when he got close to my car."

"But, Jack, I don't know what you mean. That was a two-lane road. Where could you have pulled off to?"

"Well, there wasn't any shoulder to the road, I know. But if I had at least tried, even if it meant we went into the gulley on the side, maybe the accident wouldn't have been so bad." Jack shifted in his chair.

"Jack, what is it? Do you honestly think you could've avoided the crash? Because I'm here to tell you, there's no way. I went out to the site the next day after, and that gulley you're talking about, it's pretty darn steep!"

"I don't know. But it wasn't a cliff or anything! I just wonder why I let the cotton-pickin' truck slam into us like I did. If I'd swung to the right away from it, maybe I could've made everything less severe. I keep worrying that maybe Anna—oh, my God—I keep wondering...would she have survived if I had just reacted different, or quicker. Maybe I...maybe I didn't handle it the right way. It just happened so damn fast! I didn't have time to think. But maybe I just didn't THINK—period!"

"Jack. You're grieving for your wife! It's natural that you would question—"

"I know, I know. You don't have to tell me. It's just that...it's more than that. My God! My kids lost their mother. I'm trying to figure out why...you know, make some sense...outta things. For over ten years, I've been running a store. For the first few years, I worked seven days a week, then six. I was finally getting to a point where I could be home more. Lately, Anna seemed depressed all the time; she hated that the kids were getting older, Jimmy planning to move out and all, and Frankie right behind him. I told her, just before this trip, to buck up, that soon I'd be able to take off more weekends, that she and I, just the two of us, would be able to go places, spend some time alone for a change, start seeing the world. We had so much to look forward to. Father, how do I...I mean, I'm tryin', but I can't seem to get any peace over this. I just...my God, it's been six months."

"Listen Jack. What you and your wife shared was precious, blessed by God. She was your angel on earth."

"Yes, she was. She surely was that, all right."

"Well, now, she's your angel in heaven. You've got to know she's watching and helping you in her own way, just as God is giving you extra blessings right now. I know it doesn't feel like it, but He's with you now, and so is Anna, in her own, new way. And Jack...you couldn't have prevented what happened."

"But why did it have to be her? My sister Maudie said she didn't have a mark on her, and you saw me—I was so banged up! I looked like raw hamburger meat, and I felt like it, too. Why would God take her instead of me? When you get right down to it, I can be a lousy bastard." Jack didn't apologize this time, just sat there glumly. "What I was saying before, I meant that...our kids need her, especially Margaret and Laurie. And Beth, though she's acting so strong, I know she's broken-hearted. It's not fair."

"I agree, Jack. It's not fair. And your family—your children and you, too—you need her and you miss her. It's a heavy burden to bear for all of you."

"Yeah, but I'm tough; they're not, especially the girls. I had to be. Depression, my parents' break-up, my younger sister—I had to start earning money to help my mother feed the family when I was 13. I had part-time jobs all through school from then on, even picked peaches one summer. I'm not complaining. What good's in that? There was no time to be down. Wouldn't have helped anyway. My mother needed me. That was that. But boy, was she strong! Made of steel, I used to think. Never let on if she was bitter, though she did have a temper."

"Jack, I think I know what you're saying. Your life, like most people's, has been mixed—happiness and hardship. That's just the way it was and still is. And you're not perfect, Jack—but no one is. So, what else is new? You've still got your five kids. And two are young men, just finding their way, starting their adult lives. Am I right?"

"Yes, Father. That IS right."

"And your daughters. Of course, they're grieving. Beth's the reason you were going on that trip, so she's got questions, too. And another daughter is still very young, and one's got her own, very special, needs."

"Yes, of course, she loved them all, but Anna was especially devoted to Margaret…so devoted. You can't imagine how much love and attention Anna gave to her." He looked Father Rex straight into his eyes. "Anna had endless patience. Boy, she was a saint!"

"I believe you. Anna was a tireless wife and mother. You're all 'broken-hearted' as you said. But Jack, who can say why it was Anna that God called and not you? Nobody knows. Nobody can decipher God's ways, no matter how much we want to make some kind of sense out of it."

Jack sighed, but Father Rex continued.

"As you said, you're tough. You've had to be. If you had been taken, how do you know how Anna would have fared? Yes, your family needs her, but they also need you. You have provided for them all this time. Trust God—and your angel, Anna—that you'll find a way to use the toughness you've developed to help them all through this. And Jack, you can count on me. It's not just Beth I'm here for; I'm here for you all. And six months, with a loss like this under these circumstances, well, six months might seem to you like yesterday…and rightfully so."

"So much of the time, Father, it does feel like yesterday. And I know what you say is probably right. God knows, you've been great, coming by to visit and all. And especially visiting and calling Beth. She needs someone, and I'm just not…I can't…I need her…but I'm not much good for her, if you know what I mean. She keeps talking to me about Laurie. I know she thinks I need to spend time with her—Laurie's her little sister, and she's lost. Beth thinks I can talk to her, offer her some comfort. Of course, she's right—but then I see the poor kid walking with her head hanging down. I hear her sad songs on her guitar. It kills me, but I just don't know what to do. It seems simple to Beth, because she's like her mother in that regard—a good listener. How could you know what I mean? You're there for people, you're special—not like me—I'm not good at listening. I'm better at talking. I guess I'm saying that I'm not that great in the emotions department. But my kids need more. They deserve more. I'm a broken down old man."

"Jack, are you broken right now? Yes, you're right. You are. You're broken, your heart is broken, maybe your spirit is broken, but that doesn't mean…it doesn't have to mean you won't heal. Don't look at me like that. I don't mean you're going to get over Anna or that 'time heals all wounds.' I know you won't agree with either of those things. But I do believe—and I've seen this happen, trust me—people get through tough times.

"You said yourself that your parents went through some really tough times, and your entire family suffered. You had to start working when you were just a kid, for heaven's sake. You endured though, didn't you? You came through it. You'll come through this too, Jack. And so will your family. Give yourself some credit, you can provide more for them than you think. And, Jack, you can grow as a listener. None of us is perfect. We all have room to grow until the day we die."

"What about the rotting I have in my gut? Most of the time it feels like it's on fire. I can't seem to shake the questions I have about the accident, the idea that it should've been me and not Anna who died that day."

"Jack. No matter what I say or what anyone says, you'll probably continue to replay those terrible moments in your mind and second guess your actions until you just can't anymore, because the truth is, no one knows if one little move on your part might have changed the outcome.

"And that's just it—no one knows! No one is ever going to know! My advice: pray. Pray for acceptance, pray that you can have the humility to accept what is and move forward the way you have before. Anna's not coming back, Jack. But you can talk to her; you can listen to her when you pray, when you're quiet, when you're troubled. And listen to your kids—really listen. Try to do this for them and for you."

"Okay. I'll try. I will try to pray and listen, though it's not in my nature. At least I did listen to Anna. We had that kind of marriage. We talked to each other, and never went to bed mad. I've always known life is hard. But I also know that my life, especially with Anna, has been good, until now." Jack looked away for a few seconds, shrugged his shoulders, then looked back at the priest. "Will you bless me, Father?"

"I will, Jack. And I'll pray for you that God will show you the way through this just the way He's helped you through other difficulties. I know He has faith in you. Now, you must have faith in Him. Let's pray together, Our Father, who art in heaven …."

Jack bowed his head in prayer as images of Anna floated through his mind.

12 "YES!" WHAT ELSE?

When I'm feeling blue, all I have to do
Is take a look at you, then I'm not so blue
When you're close to me, I can feel your heart beat
I can hear you breathing near my ear
Wouldn't you agree, baby, you and me got a groovy kind of love

~Toni Wine and Carole Bayer Sager

The end of the first day of second semester found Beth lying on her bed looking out the window. Journal in front of her, open with "January 5, 1966" written at the top, she let her eyes rest on the trees, rustling their leaves and standing sentinel proudly over her street. Beth searched for the right words.

She wanted to see this time as a new beginning for her, a second chance. She wanted to be a girl preparing herself for the intellectual challenges awaiting her. Once, she had thought college would be a thrilling world, a place where students and professors presented her with exhilarating new ways of thinking, and learning. So, the questions she put to herself now were: Could she do this? Could she view the future as an eighteen-year old college girl with a life full of possibilities in front of her? Could she shake off the choke chain of sadness and anger? Would she finally be able to push the tragedy of last summer, which had demanded center stage, to the side, and at least attempt to lead the life of a young adult?

Beth closed her journal. Instead of always spewing my thoughts into this journal, I'm going to call Molly or Karla. I haven't talked to either one of them for a while. I wonder how it's going for Karla. It must be weird to live with an older lady who's not your mom or a friend of your mom's. Anyway, I'll try to make some plans with one of them to do something. Just as she started out of her room, she heard a knock on the door and went to answer it. There stood Allie.

"Allie! Hey!" Beth exclaimed, surprised and happy to see her old friend. "Come in. What're you doing here? I'm so glad to see you!" Beth grabbed her in a big bear hug.

"I was just driving down the street and had the urge to check to see if you were home. That's all there is to it. Lots of times I drive by and your house looks empty or I see Robert's car, so I don't stop. This time I saw the family car and didn't think…just stopped. You know me…impulsive. How are you, honey?"

"Good! I'm good! Second semester started today. How about for you? How's senior year going? Has your second semester started yet?"

"Just finished finals. Senior year is, you know, Beth, senior year, fraught with drama," Allie said, smirking. "What can I say? I've got one foot out the door."

"Have you chosen a college yet, or is it too early for that?"

"Oh, I don't know, I have a few in mind, but it depends on what my parents decide. They might move. What am I saying? They are going to move. Not yet, but probably in the next six months to a year."

At this news, Beth felt her heart crack. "Good grief! Why, Allie? That's awful! Isn't it? Did something happen that I don't know about?" The warmth that had flowed through Beth at seeing her friend had suddenly cooled.

"Nothing terrible. My dad's going to make a job change, and he's thinking about his options. But Beth, I'll be off to college anyway—maybe northern California—I'm looking at Santa Clara. Or maybe somewhere close to wherever my parents land. There's talk of Hawaii."

"Yeah? Really? I didn't know about your dad, but for some reason, I always saw you as living down the block from me. I guess I wasn't thinking realistically." Beth looked down. She tried to hide the pain in her eyes.

"Oh, honey, you know I would love to live close to you, be close to you, but it's time to grow up, experience the real world. You know it's just waiting for us. Right, Beth? Are you running into some crazy characters—atheists and hippies, at least?"

"I was just thinking about doing some of that this semester…ya know, try to start fresh? Give the college world more of a chance than I have so far." Beth felt her optimism ebbing. Where were the drugs that could ease this ever-flowing malaise?

"Oh, Beth, I'm sorry. For a minute there, I forgot…I can't…I haven't seen you in a few months, have I? What a bad friend. I'm just so busy. It's crazy."

"Don't you ever say that or even think it! I could never think of you as a bad friend. When I think about you last summer…I just…I don't know." Again, Beth looked away, perplexed by her confusion as two feelings fought for control: her love for Allie and her inability to separate that from the gnawing in her stomach.

Allie took Beth's hands, "How have you been, really? Has life gotten any easier? Tell me the truth!" Allie's whole demeanor radiated concern.

"Well, yeah. I mean—I think so. I'm not looking forward to getting my grades…I know they're going to be pretty bad. But I think I'm doing a little better, otherwise."

"Come on, you know you can tell me. Are you still running the house? Doing the shopping and cooking and all? Is your dad doing better?"

Beth felt her guard go down in the safety of her friend's love. "Well, yeah and yeah. I'm still the household drudge—cooking, cleaning. Same old thing in that department. But I'm kinda used to it. Dad's definitely better. I mean—still sad, but…different. He's trying to be cheerful. Jimmy's got him doing things at church again—playing bridge and poker with his Knights of Columbus friends. But Allie, I really want to start over this semester. At least in the ways that I can. I need to study more and maybe get involved in something—if I can just figure out what that would be—and then, how to do it!" They both chuckled. "I checked out the Newman Center, where you can meet other Catholics on campus, but I nixed it. I mean, I still love God and all, but I'm not planning to be a holy roller any longer. I've been questioning Him a lot lately. Is that bad of me? I find myself questioning so many things lately. I just feel a little crazy…ya know, mad and confused."

"I totally get it, Beth! It had to happen, honey, especially in your case. I'm pretty sure I'm not far behind you. What about Robert? He's in school in Santa Barbara, right?"

"Yeah, I baffle myself. In fact, I make myself sick! Poor guy. I broke up with him a while back, thinking I'd feel I don't know…relieved or something. Wrong! I went on a few dates, but I was miserable. We got back together just before Christmas. I don't know how he can stand me most of the time. But then, I try not to tell him all the crazy things I think about."

"Like what Bethie?" Allie asked softly.

"Well, first—I did tell Robert this one—I thought God wanted me to be a nun."

"Seriously, Beth? I didn't know that you…." Allie smiled at her friend.

"Yeah, I know. Only, here's the really crazy part: the whole idea really made me miserable, sick to my stomach. I mean literally. Finally, Father Rex put the thing to rest. He said, in no uncertain terms—I mean, he was adamant!—No order of nuns would want me unless joining them made me happy!"

Beth shrugged her shoulders and looked straight at Allie. "Another thing I think about? I didn't tell Robert this one. Why don't more people commit…you know…?" Beth drew a line across her throat for emphasis. "I mean, once they figure out they're really going to die. If they don't believe in God, why go through life? Life is just plain hard, Allie. I'm sorry to sound dramatic, but…it's so full of suffering, ya know? And even if we do believe in God, why would God care if we end it all? He's going to have us all die one day, anyway. I actually asked my dad about this not too long ago. I can't believe I did this, with Mom and everything. Anyway, you know what he said? He's sitting in his red chair, right over there, reading, as always, and I say, "Dad, I have a question." When he looks up, I say, "Why do we human beings keep going when things get so tough, knowing that we're going to die anyway?" He puts his book down, and he says, very calmly, "Well, honey, I don't think too much about this kind of thing, but I will tell you this. Sure, life can be hard, but I've had a good life, an interesting life. I know I'm going to die someday, so if I died tomorrow, it would be okay with me. I'm not going to rush it, but I'm ready to go when the big man calls me."

Beth looked at Allie squarely in the eyes for a long moment. Finally, Allie spoke. "Wow, honey. Wow. That is crazy, but good crazy. I mean, we should think about this kind of stuff. Even the nun stuff. You know? I absolutely love that you asked your dad about that. I mean, look at him, at his life…the Depression…the war…your mom. All of it. I think he's pretty wise, Beth. Even though it's tough and nutty and awful and horrible, life is also good and beautiful and exciting. And, in some ways, the best part is that you don't know how it's going to turn out. So, you get to just keep on going and see what happens. Right?" With that, she grabbed Beth's hands again and held them tightly. "You know what, Bethie? You look so pretty right now. You're thinking, and questioning. It looks so good on you! I love you, honey."

Beth laughed, blinking away tears. "You're my only friend that would say what you just said to me. Heck, you're probably the only friend I would even tell any of this stuff to. And I love you, too! Even though I still think it's weird that you call someone your own age 'honey'!" And they both started belly laughing until they had to stop to catch their breaths.

"Crap-sakes, I miss you Allie. I need you just to keep me from feeling like such a weirdo. I feel sorry for myself way too much." Beth shook her head, then said solemnly, "What great conversations we've had!"

"Hey, they're not over, either. They never will be!"

For the next few weeks, Beth tried harder to engage in discussions with Joe and to listen more attentively to what he had to say. He seemed to notice everything and get excited, even passionate, about what was happening around him. One afternoon, on the way home from school, "When A Man Loves A Woman" came on the radio. Joe turned up the volume and started singing along. "He'd give up all his comfort…if she said that's the way it ought to be…" When it ended, he looked over at Beth, who had been content to listen to him in the moment.

"Don't you love that song, Bethie? I mean, doesn't it just capture something really profound about love?"

"I don't know," Beth hedged. "I like it. But…I mean—what's so great about it?"

"Seriously, Beth? It's so intense. The guy singing it, Percy Sledge, he sounds so in love, and he tells it from a guy's point of view. You hear in his voice that his heart's broken. But he can't leave his woman. He just can't lose her. He's helpless."

"I understand that. But it's so darn sad. It sounds like he's having such a hard time, like he's in so much pain, he can hardly control himself."

"Exactly. He is. It's the blues, Beth, but a modern rendition. Do you know the blues?"

Beth heard condescension in Joe's tone, and she resented it.

"I might not know an exact definition, but I know generally. This is about a guy who is…well, he says himself that he's in misery. There's no happy ending."

"That's the great thing about the song: he's hurting in such a beautiful way. It's not only the words, but the way the singer expresses it that's so incredible."

Joe's words stung Beth. Tears sprang to her eyes. How could anyone say something so stupid? You lose someone and sing about it, and although you're dying inside, it's "incredible" because someone decides the way you're feeling miserable is profound. And this coming from her best friend Joe, of all people! She turned her head and looked out the window, willing her tears to stop. She felt a few slide down her cheeks, letting them go, not wanting Joe to see her wiping her eyes. But he noticed anyway.

"What is it, Beth? Are you crying? I didn't mean anything by what I said. It was just an opinion. I just want you to like the song because I like it. That's dumb, I guess. But I'm not sure why you're upset."

"Joe, I'm just being silly. I'm sorry. Let's talk about something else. It's not you, at all. I do like the song. It's just something about the way he's expressing his pain. He's so sad. I guess it hits a little close to home. Sorry."

"Did something happen with Robert?"

"No, it's not Robert. It's me."

"What? What is it? You know you can tell me anything, Beth."

"I—my life is kind of…a muddle these days. But don't worry. I'm working on it, and I'm lucky to have you as my friend. Really." And she smiled at him reassuringly.

"Is it your mom?"

"Yeah, but don't worry. I'm okay, I promise."

Soon enough, Joe pulled up in front of Beth's house, put the car into park and turned and looked at her. Beth's feelings confused her. While she still felt a bit angry at Joe, she also regretted making a scene. What did he do wrong, anyway? Shared his admiration of a beautiful song with her. Excitedly. She had vowed that she would allow herself to enjoy being a college girl. Wasn't listening to new—or, in this case, old—music and being open to its virtues part of that? The least she could do is keep an open mind. Looking at Joe now, she decided to try again.

"Hey, do you want to come in? I'll make you a sandwich, and we can eat some lunch. I'm hungry, aren't you?"

"Are you sure, Bethie? You really want me to come in?"

"Of course, I do. Come on. I'll see what's in the fridge. I'm sure there's something to make a sandwich with. We might even have some Cokes from my dad's store."

"Can't say no to that." Joe smiled at Beth and turned the engine off.

Jan. 11, 1966

Okay, I re-read what I wrote the other day about turning over a new leaf and all. And, yes, that's how I felt then; now, I feel like a failure. For the past few weeks, I've felt almost normal. I don't know what changed, but it doesn't matter. Today, I'm stumped. How can it be, this life that finds me walking around campus, just smiling away at people? I mean—actually smiling! Or chatting with friends in the campus lounge while eating donuts or french fries? I guess I look like a normal girl, but I'm really just a façade—I think that's the word—dressed up to look like a college girl.

I'm trying so hard to be interested in my classes. I'm already on academic probation from last semester. Quit going to Anthro class, then didn't show up for the final. Just skipped it. Didn't tell anyone; just didn't go. And it was actually a subject I would've been excited about last year. Oh, yeah—but last year was different. When life was normal, when I always knew, no matter what, I would be okay.

No, Beth! Stop! What is wrong with me?! Why do I do this to myself? I made a vow that I was not going to feel sorry for myself this semester. I need to look ahead, or at least put some effort into what I'm doing now. School is the only "normal" thing I do right now, something most of my friends from high school are doing, too. I've got to keep myself together. I guess I'm having an attack of the "lonelies." I need to go out and do something fun for a change. Maybe get a burger with Molly. But, then...who would make dinner?

I'll take a walk, clear my head, come back and get started on the poetry I've got to read. More Emily Dickinson. I'm liking her much more than I did in high school. I just need to read a little about her time period. What Dr. Coleman had to say in class interested me, surprisingly. Don't know if I'm going to be crazy about the history class, though. At least the reading is going to be familiar. More American history. Better that I get going on it now, while it's daytime and I'm awake. Maybe I'll call Robert later, see if he can come home this weekend. Maybe I can get some money from Dad, and we can go to a movie and at least study some together. That should make me feel better. Mom, look out for me. I need you.

Jan. 13, 1966

Okay, I'm glad to say I got myself together the other day. I'll have to remember to take a walk the next time I'm feeling so ridiculously down. And I had a good afternoon with Joe today. I met him after my last class at the usual spot; he was with Mike and they were talking a mile a minute. So, I asked them what's up, and Joe said, "Hi Beth. Hey—do you know who Timothy Leary is?" And I had to say no because I didn't know who he is. Never heard of him. Sometimes, I feel like I live on another planet. How come Joe knows so much about so much more than me? Anyway, he said, "He's this professor who's been experimenting with LSD—this psychedelic drug. He says it opens up the mind to new experiences. What was it, 'Tune in, turn on—with LSD—drop out.'"

I couldn't help it—I had to fight the urge to be annoyed. I took a deep breath and asked him, "Joe, what does that even mean? I'm sorry. I guess I'm just dumb, but I have no idea what you're saying."

But Joe ignored my sarcasm. He just calmed me down. "You're not dumb Beth. That's what we want to find out, too. Professor Miller told us about Dr. Leary at the end of class and said we should hear what he has to say. He's going to be speaking here in an hour or so. We want to stick around for it. What do you think? You're driving, so if you can't stay, Mike'll give me a ride home."

Joe's comment made me waver. Part of me wanted to say, "Yeah, I'd better get home." In other words, "I'd better just stick to my little routine." But another part said, "Come on, Beth. Relax. What are you so afraid of? Listen to Joe. Be a college kid. Follow Joe's—and Mike's—example. It's not like you have to do anything dangerous. Just hear what the guy has to say." I mean, what's wrong with me that I don't jump at the chance to listen to a doctor talking about drugs and getting your mind "expanded"? Not that I know anyone who actually smokes pot, let alone takes LSD—unless I'm completely ignorant.

Anyway, I decided not to waste this opportunity to try to open my mind. So, I said, "Hmmm, actually, I could stay, but I don't think I have enough money for lunch. I guess I can get some fries to tide me over. Maybe I can learn something useful from this guy. Maybe I don't have to be 'Miss Goody Two-Shoes' forever! Maybe I'll do some mind expanding of my own." I laughed and smiled, not sure why I said that.

Mike cracked up, "Is she for real, Joe?" Joe looked at me, smiling with his mouth, but not with the rest of his face. I could tell. Anyway, he said, "Ya never know, do ya, Beth? I think I have enough cash for both of us to get something besides fries. Anyway, it should be really interesting to hear why a Ph.D. thinks anybody should take drugs. I mean, when they don't need them." Mike agreed. I took a deep breath and looked at them.

"Okay, you guys. I'm game. Let's do it. But I am hungry, Joe. So, let's go get some food!" and I picked up my pace, and headed toward the student lounge.

Anyway, I'm glad I decided to stay. The guy was pretty interesting, but, mainly, I'm glad I can say I know who Timothy Leary is and kinda what he has to say. Joe and I talked about it on the way home. He asked me if I thought I really would ever try LSD. I asked him to tell me first if he would. I was so glad when he said he didn't think so. But then, he surprised me, saying "It was kinda weird to hear you talking the way you did today. Ya know, kinda reckless. Was I imagining that, Bethie?"

"No, but I was just joking around. I guess I do sometimes wonder what if I were some other girl, someone who would take a risk now and then, live a little dangerously…but I AM a goody two-shoes!"

"Yeah, well, I like you just the way you are. I'm glad you're not some other kind of girl." It's eerie that he read my mind like that. Because Dr. Leary did make me wonder about myself. Not taking LSD—which sounds very crazy—but just doing something a little crazy. Amazing that I actually thought about this today!

Anyway, Joe and I talked about the whole idea all the way home. I mean, Dr. Leary said LSD was legal, and that in his experience the drug really "expands the mind." We both wondered what that really means. Would we get some great insight about the meaning of life? Would we have some great kind of God experience? What if whatever we saw went against everything we think we know: that God doesn't exist, or—for me—that I should forget about Robert…forget about my family, and just "drop out" of it all. I guess that's the word. Anyway, I'm glad Joe's not saying, "Come on, Beth! Let's try this stuff! You only live once!" And, really, Dr. Leary didn't push us to do anything other than listen, and, I have to admit, that didn't hurt me.

January 30, 1966

It's Laurie's birthday today. It's Sunday, and all we had planned today was church, so I decided to do for Laurie what Mom always did for each of us: cook our favorite meal and make our favorite birthday cake. I made a mental note to get ice cream. On the way to church, I asked Laurie what she would like to have for dinner and she said, "I don't know." So, I said, "Just think for a minute. Is there anything particular you'd like me to fix for you? It's a special day—you're turning 13. You're a full-fledged teenager!"

Then Dad joined in. "That's right, Laurie. We have to celebrate this day. C'mon, I seem to remember you like fried chicken. Beth, let's you and me go to the store after mass and get the fixings for a nice meal for our new teenager. Margaret, I bet you could make a swell chocolate cake—if that's the flavor you want, Laurie."

Laurie shrugged, but the conversation sparked Margaret's attention. "Umm, uh-huh! I can. I make a nice one."

Finally, Laurie said, "I don't care what I eat. Whatever you all want to make."

"All right," I said, maybe a bit too brightly. "Dad and I'll come up with something we think you'll like. How about a chocolate cake with chocolate ice cream?"

"Okay."

"Hey—why don't you invite Patty over to eat with us?" I thought maybe that would cheer her up.

"Yeah. I'll call her and see if she can come." Laurie's voice seemed brighter.

"Okay, then, it's set. We'll have a special dinner for you 'cause it's your special day!" Dad said cheerfully.

There was a pause—just a little one—then Laurie said, "You guys…don't make a big deal about me. I mean, I don't care about being a teenager. I sure don't feel like one. Today doesn't feel any different than any other day."

Dad spoke first. "Oh, c'mon honey. It's gonna be fine, just wait and see."

I think we both knew we were all talking about more than just her birthday.

So, Dad and I made fried chicken, mashed potatoes, canned corn and fresh green salad. I thought she'd like that. I know I had Mom make it plenty of times for me. Margaret made a chocolate cake and put candles on it. I reminded the boys about Laurie's birthday. Of course, Dad told me he hadn't forgotten, and he had a present: a check with a dollar for each year. I said that was nice, but maybe he could also get her some candy or something a little bit more…I was tongue-tied! I didn't know exactly how to say what I meant. I just wanted her to have something to unwrap. Anyway, he gave me his credit card and told me to go to Sears and pick out whatever I thought she'd like.

While Margaret made the cake, I went to Sears and got her a sweater from Dad and a book of poetry from me. Patty came over, and she and Laurie talked and laughed on the front porch for a while. Later, when I came to check on them, they were shooting baskets. Laurie's actually pretty good—she's definitely more coordinated than I've ever been. I think the dinner went fine; at least, Laurie got through it.

I guess we were all pretending, but what else could we do? We've been living with the empty space at the table for six months, now. It's always hard, but it had to be doubly hard for Laurie today.

After dinner, Margaret brought the cake to the table, and we sang "Happy Birthday." Laurie opened the few gifts from all of us. She read Frankie and Jimmy's funny cards and laughed out loud. When we finished the cake and ice cream, she retreated with Patty to our bedroom while Margaret and I did the dishes and then watched TV. I thought we should give her and Patty some time alone. I know she was sad, thinking of Mom. I can only guess how I'll feel on my next birthday.

Feb 13, 1966

Robert finally came home for the weekend! We hadn't seen each other in three weeks. I really missed him. But what made it so special is that when we talked on the phone the other night, he seemed to understand how I was feeling. I mean, he said he knew because he was feeling the same way. He knows I'm trying really hard to like my classes and be more light-hearted. He says college is hard for him too, not because of the classes so much—he got pretty good grades last quarter, especially considering he was on the football team—no, he just knew what I meant about feeling lonely. To him, that means not being with me, except when I go there or he comes here.

He doesn't really like his roommates, or, at least he only says, "They're okay." He says besides having a part-time job and working out for football, he just studies. Though it's what we're supposed to be doing, he wishes I was going to his school so we could spend all our time together. That's hard for me to imagine, since I spend so much time with my family. I mean—I am trying to study more, and I do like my classes better, but my reality is pretty different from his. I'm working on being more fun!!

Anyway, since his VW is on the fritz, he got a ride from a kid who posted an ad for someone who would share the gas with him. But that only got him to Hollywood, so he started hitchhiking. The awful thing is, he got picked up by a pervert who wanted Robert to go to a motel with him. When he realized what the man was really saying, he told him to pull over and practically jumped out of the car.

Poor Robert!! He called me from a phone booth all freaked out and tells me where he is. He was going to surprise me by just arriving at my front door, but that plan got totally blown to pieces. He was so freaked out! He wanted me to pick him up at this place near the freeway. I got the number of the phone booth and told him I'd call him right back. Then, I ran and asked Dad. He didn't think I could do it—thought I'd get lost—but I begged him. He hemmed and hawed, said he didn't really want me to go looking for Robert in a crummy part of L.A. Finally, I guess because he also felt bad for Robert, he told me to get REALLY specific information for where Robert's was.

It took forever, but when I finally got to the gas station where Robert was, he was standing with his arms crossed. He looked so serious. Then he saw me and came running. He didn't want to talk about the weirdo right away. When we got home though, we talked and talked about it. It just sounded so crazy! I mean, the man just assumed Robert had run away from home or something. Why would he think that? How awful for Robert! Anyway, he finally said to please change the subject, and pretty soon, we were talking about other things we've been realizing.

I don't think I could explain to any friend how all this made me feel. Yes, I love him and worry about him, but this was more about being really, really close friends who can share what's happening to us as individuals. Life can be crazy for both of us. Does everyone else our age feel like this but just hide it? I definitely do! What I'm realizing is that what matters is how we handle things, and also that we have each other to talk to about them. I'm also realizing that this is what it means to grow up. Like it or not.

Feb 14, 1966

Okay, this weird thing happened today at school. There's this guy who's a year or two older than me. He hangs around the quad a lot between classes, etc, and he's been talking to me about his family in Austria and Germany. His parents were born in Austria, and he still has relatives there. When he talks about it, it seems so romantic and beautiful. I picture the hills in the "The Sound of Music." He's thinking about living there after medical school. I like him to talk so I can at least picture it all. Also, he's very handsome and has quite a big vocabulary.

So, today, he says something like, "Austrians are much more intellectual than Americans. Americans are so frivolous and materialistic. In Austria, people know what's important. They care more about what really matters in life than Americans."

I really wasn't trying to pick a fight—I mean, Herb is smart!—but that bugged me, so, I asked him "What do you mean by that? I know some pretty smart people who care about more than just material things—people who aren't entirely shallow."

"That's not exactly what I'm talking about, Beth. Yes, there are smart people, but, for the most part, people here care more about making money than anything else. No one really wants to discuss how to get out of Viet Nam. I mean—why are we there in the first place? I can't say one critical word about JFK without getting my head chopped off—but if I want to talk about something related to money? Oh, yeah, that's fine. How many friends do you have who listen to classical music or discuss philosophy?"

Stupidly, I'm not sure why, I said, "I don't know, Herb, I think you're wrong. I'm taking a philosophy class. (I am! but so what?) And my brother and his friends love to talk politics and to discuss current events and social issues. I bet he'd be open to hearing whatever you have to say about JFK. Anyway, I think you're being unfair about Americans—pretty dogmatic." (NEW WORD FOR BETH!!)

"Dogmatic!? Is that what you call it when I try to have a conversation with you? You call me names! What about what I said about culture? You know—art…music? Gonna call me names if I say something you don't like? I bet you'd react differently if I talked to you about how much I'm going to make when I become a doctor!!"

He was so indignant and heated up! I didn't know how to back out. I just wanted to try out a new word, I didn't know it was an insult. Finally, I said, "Sorry, Herb. I really don't care about making money and getting rich. I mean, my family doesn't…."

He surprised me when he said, "Don't worry about it. Oh, I gotta go. My class is coming up pretty soon." He got up and left.

Stupid, stupid Beth! And I like Herb. I normally like talking to him because he DOES talk about interesting things. Darn!

I miss the days when I had a best friend, a kind of soul sister. When I was ten, Grace moved into my neighborhood. We played football and baseball in the street with the boys. We called each other constantly to make plans for watching Dick Clark and practicing our dancing for the next all-girl party. We thought we were hot stuff because we won so many dance contests.

Then, Grace moved on to a new best friend in 7th grade—and Rosie rescued me. That's a weird way to put it, but I had never really noticed her before that day she sat down next me on the bench at lunchtime. She was so sweet and funny. She introduced me to tortillas and rice and beans. Her mom was always cooking! Rosie made me laugh and feel special. Then we were off to high school, and I hardly saw her. Not in the same classes, I guess. But weren't we on drill team together? Hmm.

Molly and I took the bus or rode with Dad to St Joe's and talked and did things all the time. She made me half-crazy, daring me to do things we could get into trouble for—running down the boys' hall at school between classes, or making up stupid excuses to get Sister Pat to let us out of French class. She'd take a safety pin, prick her finger, put a little blood on her skirt, then go to Sister's desk to show her, saying she started her period and needed me to go with her to the bathroom What a nut! And she put up with so much drama when John and I were a thing.

At some point, Allie and I discovered each other as similar people; even though she was a grade behind me, we carpooled to school and talked like crazy for those 30 or 40 minutes each way. Since she lives so close, we spent the night at each other's a lot, always debriefing after our dates. That's about the time I started learning about the real world. Besides boys, we talked about civil rights and politics—like who our parents were voting for and why. We talked forever about books and love and God. We were so in sync. We had (or have) the same funny bone, so, sometimes, we made each other laugh so hard that one of us wet our pants!

Then I discovered my Poetry Pals—girlfriends like Karla in my honors classes junior and senior year; we secretly wrote poetry while pretending to be listening to our teachers. And what about my buddies on the Cheer squad last year? I got pretty close to some of them—people like Carol, who liked to talk and figure things out, who understood me on some level, who knew what I meant.

Where are they all now? Off…being who they're supposed to be the year after high school, the first year of liberation. They've scattered. Poof! Though Allie's still in high school, she's looking forward, planning, preparing to fly the coop. Molly's working, enjoying being free and in love. Karla's living off campus with a woman she does work for to help with tuition. Grace lives at home, going to a nearby JC, making plans to transfer to Uni, to be with Tom. (I'm lucky Tom goes to school with Robert, so Grace and I can drive up together sometimes). The other girls are doing what they're doing—going to other colleges, living in the dorms or off campus. I talk to them now and then. Life isn't great for all of them either. But we're different now.

I wish someone wanted to be my friend right now, a REAL friend. Shit, shit, shit! Again, Miss Melodrama's on stage! It's not like I couldn't call any of my old girlfriends if I wanted to. And I have Joe and, of course, Robert. But who am I kidding? Right now, I need a girlfriend. It probably wouldn't work. I can't be the kind friend I want, anyway. I'm too confused, and I just don't think I could fake it any more than I'm faking it now.

Feb 14, 1966

I miss you tonight,
Not miserable, desperate—just
Warm, reminiscing sad.
You were so very loving—yes, but that's not quite it!
You were just so motherly—yes, but that's not quite it either!
You were…EVERYTHING! WRAP-YOUR-ARMS-AROUND-ME, MAKE-IT-BETTER EVERYTHING!
Sometimes…
When I'm content, with a fairly full heart
And a smidgen (your word) of peace in my soul
I still miss you...And I know I always will.

Goodbye: No! I howl in protest. How can I even think that word?
I know you will never really be gone. How CAN you be gone?
And though your spirit is all around me

I still need the you that I can see and whose arms I can melt into
I will always search for you and cry for you…and the past that was so secure.

Feb. 15, 1966

I'm actually happy today. This is the first Valentine's Day that has ever really meant something to me. I made Robert a "Valentine packet." Not that it was so great—I have no money, so I got creative. I didn't know he'd like it so much.

I took a manila envelope that I found in Dad's stuff and decorated it with hearts I cut from Laurie's construction paper. Inside, I put in a little book, kinda like the Odds books Allie and I started making ages ago. I used onionskin paper and a black Sharpie. I cut out pictures to represent R and me. I used some Peanuts characters I love and copied some silly love poems and goofy rhymes that I made up.

I mailed it a few days ago, hoping it would get there on time. And it did! He got it, and called me late last night. He told me how excited it made him that I would do something like that for him. No one's ever done anything like this for him. He thinks I'm the best "lover" ever, and he's coming home this weekend no matter what! He wants to do something really special for me, too.

Burning, burning, like a full force flame
That has matured from a cinder…To a spark…Then…pop!
Flaming orange-ly brilliant, pink—bright for a moment or two,
Bringing the smoke-black of night, and after it…the twilight sky

Feb. 19, 1966

Robert came home last night. I was excited all day because he said "I have something special planned for you, Beth. I sure hope you like it." He called it a late V's Day outing. He got home about 7 and said he was going to spend the evening with his family, and I should expect him late Sat. morning. Then he asked if he could talk to my dad! Of course, I asked him why, but he wouldn't tell me. He told me not to worry; it wasn't anything "too crazy."

So, I called Dad to the phone and they talked for a few minutes while I stood and waited. But Dad told me to wait in my bedroom. He called for me a few minutes later, and I got back on the phone. Robert said he just wanted to tell me goodnight. His mom had made him a late dinner, so he had to go, but he'd see me in the morning. Everything was set!!

I could hardy sleep that night, but the day of the big surprise finally arrived. Just as he said, Robert arrived at 11 with a big smile, all cute and secretive. He ushered me into my dad's car, and said, "Okay. I'm not telling you where we're going, but I think—I really hope—you're going to like this."

Next thing I know, we were driving on the freeway, heading to LA and eventually arrived at a very famous, fancy theatre—Grauman's Chinese! The marquee announced the movie: "The Sound of Music"! Oh, my God! I could hardly stand it! I just peppered Robert with questions. Q: Why did we take Dad's car? A: Robert was afraid his wouldn't make it, and then there was the matter of gas. Q: What made him pick this movie? Does he like musicals? A: He picked this movie because I told him several times that I really wanted to see it. He didn't know if he liked musicals because he'd never seen one! Finally, he said, "Well, this is your Valentine's present, Beth! It looks like you like it!" I grabbed his hand and squeezed hard. After the movie, neither of us could stop talking. We both loved it—the music, the characters, the scenery—all of it. It made me think of Mom, but in a good way. I don't know why.

Robert happens to be beautiful. I hope he thinks I'm beautiful
No one can make me happy…the way that he can make me happy

Feb. 21, 1966

A bad day…that's all I can say
I am so full of black, no one sees me and I see no one
I've spiraled down, down into a land of confusion, doubt, self-pity
Where armies of anger and misery clash and maim each other
I am wretched and wear a body of armor and a mask I call a face
I take this face through a world of anxiety called a day

When I rest, I am wondering yet.
He calls me, this figure of unreality—
A missionary to all that is poor and needy inside him—
He looks to me as a child, pure and innocent,
He sings my praises, says I am his happiness.
God alone could send a blind man to love an ugly woman.

Feb. 29, 1966

I re-read what I wrote a few days ago. I'm trying to figure out what was going on with me. I had such a great weekend with Robert, but when he left, I got an attack of loneliness. So that led me to thinking about Mom. I didn't feel like making dinner or eating. That wasn't a problem because Dad makes dinner on Sunday a lot, and when I didn't show up in the kitchen around six, I guess he just started doing it himself.

When he called everyone to dinner, I said I wasn't really hungry, that I'd get something later. There was a game on TV and it sounded like Dad, Jimmy and Frankie took their dinner into the den to watch it. I didn't pay much attention to Laurie and Margaret. I wasn't really doing anything, except moping, which I now gather sent Laurie into a funk. She comes in our room, flops onto her bed, and I eventually see she's crying. We have this very awful conversation. Kinda like this.

"What is it, Laurie? What's wrong?"

"Nothing."

"Come on. God, I can see better than that." I wasn't being very nice. If anything, I was annoyed to be interrupted in my own bad mood.

"Everything. Just everything."

"What does that mean? Just tell me. I'm not a mind reader!" Now, she's really crying, and I finally realize that this is bad. "Come on, Laurie. I want to know…really."

"No one—I mean NO ONE!—really cares about me. You're so lucky you have Robert. Who do I have? Dad and the boys don't care. When you didn't come to dinner, it was just me and Margaret, staring at each other. I miss Mom so much! Why did she have to die? I wish it had been me…or…anybody but her."

Now, she was sobbing, could hardly get the words out.

"God, Laurie. I'm so sorry. I understand. I do."

"NO, YOU DON'T! DON'T EVEN SAY THAT! YOU DON'T! AT ALL!"

"Of course, I do! You don't think I miss Mom, too?? That I would give anything if they hadn't come to see me at the reservation? I think and think about it, and I can't…I don't understand why they had to come. I was fine."

"But, Beth," Laurie said, still crying, but not as much, "I heard Mom and Dad talking. He knew she missed you and was worried about you."

"But why? Why?" I might've been crying, too, by now. But I know I said, "That's what I don't get. I talked to her on the phone. I told her I was having such a good time. I REALLY don't get why they had to come!" And I don't.

"Well, I don't know, but Dad said, 'Why don't we take a drive, see Bethie. It'll be great to see a real Indian reservation,' or something like that. And I was excited to go, to see you and to ride there with Robert and your friend—the big kids. But then…. In the hospital, I was so scared. And I was all alone. I don't think anyone even thought about me. If Mom had been there…." And now she was sobbing again.

"I'm sorry, Laurie, I was so shocked. They made me talk to Dad and then call Jimmy and Frankie. It's such a blur. I don't really remember half of what went on. I didn't mean to leave you alone. I didn't know what to say. I was so numb. I couldn't believe it. Any of it. Later, I don't even know what I did or what you did. Somehow, we were just home."

"Yeah, well, and now you have Robert. I like him, Bethie, but you're so lucky. I don't have anyone."

She has no idea how I torment myself with uncertainty. "You have me. You do. And you have Robert, too. He cares about you."

"Yeah…I know. I guess…I just…I miss Mom." Of course, I said I do, too. Then we both cried hard for a while.

After that, we got quiet. She still cried, but it just sorta calmed down, and she started playing her guitar. I couldn't get the whole thing out of my head the next day. Yesterday, when Dad got home from work, I asked him if I could talk to him. So, we went into his room, and I start telling him about Laurie. About how she feels like no one cares about her. How she misses Mom. I tell him I don't know what to do. How bad I feel for her.

He didn't get it. He tells me what a good job I'm doing, helping her and Margaret, being such a rock for them all, taking over for Mom. I didn't know WHAT to say to that. How could he get it so wrong? I was trying to talk about Laurie. She needs him now. And I do too, because I CANNOT "take over" for Mom. How could I ever do that? I don't think Laurie needs that or wants that. But I don't know what to do. It's all so crummy for her. She doesn't need anything as much as she needs her mom.

I just miss Mom so much, and I don't know how to say any of this to Dad. When I tried a second time to talk about how lost Laurie is, he misunderstood, I guess, and said, "Now, honey, don't beat yourself up. You're doing the best you know how. Laurie's had an awful blow. We all have. We're going to get through this somehow."

Nice, but not what I needed.

The thing is, I think it IS different for Laurie—somehow harder. I don't really know. I mean, her heart is broken, and she's also brave, trying to be as normal as possible. But she's still a little girl, really. And what do I know? I'm just glad she has her guitar, though what is that, really? Nothing compared to our mom. What must it feel like to be barely 13 and have your mother gone, just like that? And nobody in our family is really talking about it! God, please! help me to be a better sister. I need to quit obsessing over my own stupid problems, no matter how big I think they are.

March 15, 1966

Laurie and I have been talking more the past few weeks. I'm trying to be sure to ask her how her day was, about school, etc. It's amazing, but she's still a really good student. I don't know how she can concentrate on her work, but she does. I've talked to her teacher a few times, and I can see she cares about Laurie. She's really young and athletic, plays basketball with Laurie and her friends at lunch, and after school sometimes, too. That's how I met her—I was picking Laurie up, and Sister Marcia was practicing lay-ups and free throws with Laurie. I don't know for sure, but I don't think Laurie confides in her. I wish I could talk to her. I really wish I could, but that's selfish. Sister is Laurie's teacher, and if getting to know her might help Laurie, I should do it. Otherwise, forget it.

Anyway, I think Laurie's starting to believe that I know how she feels about Mom. I could be wrong though. I mean how can anyone really know that? Just like how can anyone really know how I feel? Anyway, I want to be a big sister who helps her little sister, even though I have no real idea how to do that. Yesterday afternoon, we played hopscotch on the porch with Patty. It cheered me up—and I hope Laurie, too.

March 17, 1966

Today was a pretty good day, overall. Nothing special really happened. It's just that I've been thinking, and everything that's gone on with Laurie lately has made me realize some stuff about myself. It's kinda weird, but, in a way, I—at least some of the time—I realize I feel a bit of relief lately.

I'm not sure how to put this. Ever since the accident, I've felt sick to my stomach most of the time. I know I've lost weight. I can now wear dresses that used to be so small on me that I had to suck in my stomach to wear them. And, once in a while, Dad tells me to come to his store and have lunch with him. I used to hate this, because I only ever ordered a grilled cheese sandwich, which I would barely touch. He would get all irritated…"For God's sake, Bethie, eat your lunch!" No way could I tell him I had stomachaches ALL the time, that, most days, I went into his room to steal Rolaids. I mean—where does he think they go? Seriously. Anyway, now I can eat most of that sandwich.

Lately, I've started to get a bit of my appetite back. And I don't feel quite so crazy. I guess I'm getting used to the fact that my life has changed in a big way.

Without Mom, our family is so different. We don't have the same order. The routine we had when I was a kid, I mean—then, I never paid any attention to it. Now, I miss it. I try to put it back in by having dinner ready around a certain time each night—even though, most of the time, it's just Dad and the girls and me eating. I stick to Saturdays for grocery shopping and cleaning the house. These things seem empty, in a way. But the purpose is still there. The need to keep the household running, to try to keep everyone secure and calm. With her gone, that stuff is missing, and I'm realizing why I've felt so adrift. I mean, I knew it was because Mom's gone, but now I really see that she was our glue, our safe place—the heart of our home! I see it so clearly, now.

In some strange way, I'm feeling closer to Jimmy and Frankie. I guess that we're all going through the same thing, even though it's in our own ways. I mean.

I have always really admired Frankie, but now I talk a lot more to Jimmy than I ever did. Allie and I have tried so hard to impress him the last year or so. He just seems so smart and wise. He was pretty neat about it. When I graduated last year, he was gone on some army thing, so he missed it, but he sent me a long letter and a really pretty watch. He's been on a pedestal for me, but now, he talks to me on almost an equal level. I think it's because we both went through this terrible, awful thing, and we both know it.

I guess my point is that I look at our family as kind of special in a weird way…different from other families.

Another thing: I always thought I was a nice kind of girl, but now I know that I really only thought about myself. I fought with Mom about stupid stuff, and I got so annoyed with Laurie—if I even thought about her at all.

Starting college was a BIG shock, and, all year, I've felt sorta invisible. But, at least now, I don't worry constantly about what will happen next. I don't feel so panicky.

I'm still not sure how I feel about God. I mean, I don't blame Him for taking Mom. Not sure why. But I don't really know where He fits in my world anymore. Without Mom, things still seem upside down—though they're starting to seem less upside down. Last semester, I wondered why I shouldn't just go ahead and die. Without Mom, nothing made any sense. I still miss her so much. And I still don't feel like a normal college freshman, but it's not as bad as it was.

Having Joe to ride to school with helps a lot. Thank God for him, but for some reason, I still don't feel like I can share everything with him…and yet, I know he knows me anyway. Crazy! I'm glad he likes school and talks about it. I'm starting to like school more, and I'm glad I have him to talk to about that.

And Robert, too.

Well, I'm getting tired. I guess that's enough of my philosophizing for tonight. Only one more thing to add—

The smile-traced mouth… After a belly-aching joke session

The ocean-quenched body… Following a day of beach-baking

The lumpy, luxurious couch… After a tense ride in a stiff-seated car

The liltingly slow instrumental… Following the ligament-tearing jazz session

The sun-stroked day…in conclusion. Night.

March 20, 1966

Just a few months ago, I had a really hard time going to Santa Barbara to visit Robert and to St. Mary's to visit Karla and Mary Ann. I hated being away from home. The whole time I felt like I was going to throw up, especially that first football game with Robert. All those screaming kids! And sometimes I did—at least I got the dry heaves!!! Even staying with Mary Ann in her dorm—the farther I got from home, the less tethered I felt. It's as if I might float right out into space. Still, I know I can't lock myself up in my room. Lately, I've found that I can tell Robert how I feel, and he doesn't make me feel like a total weirdo.

So now, I'm taking on a challenge. I'm going with Jan, Karla and Jill on a road trip to the Bay Area to visit a new friend, Robin! With spring break coming up, they thought it'd be neat to go somewhere. I guess I saw an opportunity. When Karla mentioned it, I took a breath and said, "Hey, that sounds like fun. I'll drive if everyone will help pay for the gas." Then we started talking about where to go.

Later, I was talking to Robert about it, and he said, "Why don't you go visit Robin? She lives in the Bay Area. You really liked her when she came to visit Mike." I told him to get Mike to ask Robin what she thought—and now it's all working out! I can't believe I'm doing this. I think it helps that I'm driving. It's going to be hard, but I need to do it anyway. It's all about taking one little step at a time. San Francisco, here we come!

March 30, 1966

I'm not completely sure how I feel about Robert. Of course, I KNOW I really like/love him—whatever the heck that means. He acts like such a kid sometimes, which I love. He's always coming up with these crazy ideas. Last night, we were kind of goofing around on the phone—that is, the most we can really goof around with only about three minutes to talk!

"Hey, Beth," he said, "let's go to the park when I come home this weekend. I want to fly a kite." I said that sounds like fun. And he said, "Do you like to fish? I think there's a lake not too far from your house. If I don't tell my parents I'm coming home, I could spend the night on your couch, and we could fly kites on Saturday, then get up early Sunday and fish. What do ya' think?"

I think I have NEVER been fishing or even wanted to. The last time Robert came home, he challenged me to ping-pong. His parents' neighbors have a ping-pong table in their garage. He bet he'd beat me in five minutes or less. He didn't know I used to play with Frankie! He beat me, but it was close.

April 10, 1966

Lying on my bed, my head at the foot, is my favorite of all past-times
Here, my window opens up to me all of the world that I care to see
(Which is NOT extremely narrow)

The rustling trees, chirping birds, fluttering butterflies on the bushes…they sing their life's song. The cars and the motorcycles…all warble their life's tune.

But the children coming home from school…tall and small
Now running or skipping…

screaming or laughing…
teasing or whispering
Lingering here or rushing…somewhere…
Those children perform the greatest concert of all
They tell me all my heart wants to know
about the world, right here
From the foot of my bed….
as I gaze out my window.

April 26, 1966

Friday, I went to see Robert. I called Grace a week ago, and she wanted to go up to see Tom, too. She agrees that these long-distance romances are frustrating, but she's planning to transfer after next year, so she figures it's just a waiting game. Anyway, it's Robert's 19th birthday, and I wanted to celebrate ON his birthday, rather than wait until he comes home in a week or two. Spring football is pretty demanding, so I told him I'd come there.
I was nervous—anxious stomach, Rolaids, the whole bit—but going with Grace helped. She always makes me laugh.

She's so blunt about everything, like when I asked her about Tom and marriage, she said to me, "We aren't talking about that yet. Ya' know, Beth, my mother told me, don't be in a hurry to get engaged. Keep your options open. It's just as easy to love a rich man as a poor man." We both giggled at that. "I think she's right. I might as well wait and see what Tom's going to do after college."

"Are you serious?" I asked. "Isn't it about how you feel? Wouldn't you feel guilty if you met some rich guy, and broke up with Tom because the other guy had money?"

"Probably. But I'm not really thinking about any of that yet. We're so young. What about you and Robert? Are you thinking about getting engaged anytime soon?"

I didn't really know what to say. "For sure, I'm not. But I get kinda worried about Robert. Sometimes, he talks about us being married. I mean, he's mostly goofing around, joking about me being pregnant with a watermelon-like belly or about us having a bunch of kids who are athletes. He's just joking, though."

"Really? Are you guys having sex?"

"Yikes!" I thought, but I didn't say that. I tried to sound calm when I replied "No way! I'm too confused about it. I still think about the stuff the nuns and priests said about waiting 'til you're married. 'Once you've had sex with a boy, he'll think you're used goods.' I guess I'm still such a good Catholic girl."

I was kinda embarrassed, but this was Grace.

"You're not silly, Beth, but I don't think all boys feel that way. I just think it's a natural thing. Not that I know that much about it, but—do you remember when I went to Truman for 9th grade? And I told you about kids bragging about doing all kinds of sexual stuff we thought was weird? You were always so shocked. " She giggled again.

"Yeah, I remember. I was shocked! Is that why you told me that stuff?"

Why'd she have to laugh at me? So, then she said, "Yeah. I couldn't help it. You'd get this disgusted look on your face—like when John tried to French kiss with you when you were 13!"

"I was almost 14!" I would've hit her, but she was driving. But I had to admit—she was right. "Oh, man, Grace. Poor Robert, I guess, 'cause I'm pretty much the same prude now as I was then. But look at John now! I mean, he got that girl pregnant and got married before he finished high school. I'm glad that wasn't me. I remember when I went to visit him in his dinky apartment when I was dating Mike in senior year."

"I know. Are you worried you won't like sex?"

Grace gets to the point!

"No, it's not that! It's more that I think Robert or whoever won't like me, my body. I'm not exactly big on top. And now that I've gotten so skinny, I don't look like much without my clothes on. I guess I'm insecure."

"Oh, Bethie. Who isn't, really? Maybe not about sex, but still insecure. You just need to lighten up…I mean…relax about the way you think about sex. And the way your body looks, too. Boys don't think so much about all of that. I don't think it's really as big a deal as you make it. Do you love Robert?"

I was afraid she'd ask me that.

"I do. At least, I think I do. No…I know I do. But how do I know what kind of love it is? I mean—for sure? Before the accident, we weren't even a "thing." Then, suddenly, we're glued to each other. I mean—Robert's great, but I get so confused. It's not fair to him."

"What are you confused about?"

"Oh, it's hard to say. So many things," I told her. "I've just gotten very weird, and I question everything. He's a good listener, but, even more, he makes me have fun. I can't really imagine NOT having him around. But—like you said—we're so young…."

"Yeah, just remember that. We're all young, so have fun now. If it doesn't bother him that you have questions and stuff, try not to worry, at least about him."

It was great talking like that with Grace. It seemed like a long time since we'd had that great a conversation. I felt really close to her.

It turned out that two of Robert's roommates were gone for the weekend, and we hardly saw the other one. That night, Robert and I made dinner together, watched TV, and fooled around. I slept in Robert's twin bed with him. We behaved, but we snuggled, and I fell asleep with his arm around me.

Before we went to bed, I told him what I had planned for the next day—his actual birthday. Since I didn't have any money except the ten dollars Dad gave me, I told him my low-cost ideas: a picnic lunch at a nearby park, a walk at the beach and the surprise of it all, a game of Horse—I had brought Laurie's basketball. He said it all sounded great…but when I woke up, I heard him on the phone.

When he got off the phone, he told me, instead of the long walk on the beach, we were going for a long ride on his friend's motorcycle! What a blast! We rode up into the hills where we could look down at the ocean. We stopped at a grassy spot and ate the picnic lunch I'd made that morning. It was so darn beautiful! We stayed there for a long while, lying on the grass, talking.

I told him about Laurie missing Mom, and about Dad not understanding. Robert talked about how disillusioned he is with school, but how much he loves his part-time coaching job. And we were quiet for a time.

Eventually, I reminded him about Horse, so we rode back to his room and got the basketball. We went to St. James, where he normally coaches on the weekends, and played Horse for an hour or so. Somehow, I managed to hold the ball while holding on to him. Of course, he wiped me out—but at least I made some baskets! It was just carefree and fun. Finally, at some point, we went back to get ready for dinner.

Robert said he wanted to go to a place where he'd been with his parents, "…but it's a little pricey."

I reminded him "I only have ten dollars." He said, "I know. It's okay. It's my birthday. I'm so glad you're here that I want to celebrate! You chip in your ten dollars, and I'll pay the rest."

That was so unlike Robert! When I saw the menu, the prices shocked me--my family NEVER goes out to dinner. Then, I saw Robert gulp. We decided to share a steak and baked potato dinner, and then we went into the bar to listen to music.

Amazingly, the group was playing "You're my soul and my heart's inspiration," our new favorite song. We both love the Righteous Brothers! Then, a waiter came over and asked Robert if he wanted a drink! He didn't hesitate, just said, "I'll take a seven and seven, and she'll have the same."

He pretty much shocked me, but we had SO MUCH FUN, just kept cracking up at everything! Anyway, Sunday morning, while he was scrambling eggs, I decided to put the weekend into words.

May 17, 1966

Why do I love him? What is he to me?

We're not always laughing or kissing or talking.

Sometimes we're frowning or fighting or silent
But we're both after the same things in life.
And we are each other's ideal.
We will have 9 kids (boys?) who will grow to be honest football players.

They will love God and appreciate the blue of the day and the black of the night.

June 14, 1966

Robert is coming home from school for the summer! Finally! Some wonderful miracle has occurred, making the course of my life beautiful and fantastic: my love and I have met and are traveling our courses. Together!

June 16, 1966

Three giggling teenagers are washing and splashing the car and themselves while I
await my dearheart.

Hello, Robert, the tenderhearted! You are the Spring in my soul and the grace in my heart.

What alternative do I have? You were made for me and I for you.
Our minds complement each other.
Our hearts bind to each other.
Our bodies sing to each other. We must love one another and—we do.

July 5, 1966

One simple question—FOUR LITTLE WORDS--can make such a difference: Will you MARRY me?? Those were his words.

But first, he whisked me up in his arms, carried me to the middle of the bridge—our bridge at our park, our special, fun and romantic park, the place where we play and talk and make out and run around in our bare feet and quack at the ducks. This is the place where he picked me up, carried me to the middle of our bridge…and then what did he do, you ask?

He PROPOSED!!

What did I say, you ask?
What would I say—except YES! This feels right, so right—
And I will always see the image of the oh-so-handsome, shorts-clad boy holding the delighted, very smitten, shorts-clad girl in his arms
on this warm, wonderful, summer night as he declared his eternal love…
…to me... to me... to me!

July 9, 1966

Two thousand years with a pencil in hand would not be enough time. Two words must suffice:

Robert Dolan.

Now…Elizabeth Virginia Dolan AND Robert Thomas Dolan. Dearheart, you are my purpose. I love you always. God bless and keep you safe forever.

August 7, 1966

A few weeks of utter bliss and then this. I woke up with a feeling of dread, as if an announcement was about to be made that I didn't want to hear. I felt like I should put my hands over my ears—but why? What is it? I went into the kitchen for breakfast, and Frankie was there, reading the sports page, and he looked up and said, "Hey, what's up? Still on Cloud 9?"

I said, "I don't know. Is something going on? I have this uneasy feeling, like something's really wrong."

Frankie looked at me funny for a moment and said, "Something like what? Seems to me, you've been walking around in the clouds. Am I wrong? Are you having some kind of premonition?"

"More like something's on the tip of my brain that's like deja vu. Like it's happened, only I don't know what IT is. Weird, right?"

"No weirder than a lot of things."

Sometimes, Frankie kids me in that "big brother" way. This wasn't one of those times. He looked away for a second, then looked back. "I'm having…I don't know…the same kind of weird feeling. You know what, I…."

And he just went silent.

"Frank! Finish what you were going to say! Come on."

"I shouldn't've said anything. I don't want to bring you down. 'Bout time we had something to be happy about."

"C'mon! You're not bringing me down. Please! I'm goin' nuts!"

"Okay, Beth—but remember, you asked me."

"Okay, I asked! Now tell me!"

"Okay, it's just…when I walked out here this morning, I felt something was off. I thought, what's wrong? What's missing? Am I forgetting something? I stood here a minute, ya know? Then I spotted the calendar. I walked over to it."

Frankie paused and took a deep breath. Finally, he went on. "You know what today is, Beth?" He looked away, then back right at me. "It's…it's …uh… August 7th."

Of course. It's that day,
when she left…
one solid year ago.

She is gone. Still.
And, she's never coming back.
We can't un-know that.
As I face this truth with my brother, I realize
SHE is my truth.
Always.
I won't ever forget that.
Ever.

13 TOO LATE TO WORRY

Goin' to the chapel
And we're gonna get married. . .
Gee, I really love you and we're going to get married
Goin' to the chapel of love…

~Jeff Barry, Ellie Greenwich, Phil Spector

November 25, 1966

Struggling with her oversized school bag—which also served as her purse—and two heavy grocery bags overflowing with chicken, tomatoes, onions, bread, salad ingredients, and a bottle of cream sherry, Beth walked through the garage and up the back steps to the kitchen. When she heard the commotion—doors squeaking and slamming, and a loud "Ow! Watch where you're going!"— she put it all down and hurried into the living room to find her brother, Jimmy, and sisters Margaret and Laurie, moving the table in from the patio.

It took Beth a moment to figure out that they were heading toward the den, but when she peeked in, it was clear they were in the midst of transforming the space from a cluttered depository for people's everyday lives to a neat, somewhat respectable dining room. Since the room had never been used for family meals, it had no actual dining room furniture. Beth's brother appeared intent on fixing this problem by getting the patio table and benches inside the room with help from his reluctant sisters.

Beth felt a slight twinge of panic as she assessed the situation. "What's up, Jimmy? What's going on? Where's Dad's chair? And the trunk and TV? What are you trying to do?"

"What does it look like?" Jimmy stopped what he was doing, and glared at Beth.

"I don't know. It kinda looks you're trying to make our TV room into a dining room. Am I right?" Why is he doing this? Is he mad at me? God, what'd I do?

"Beth, aren't the Dolans coming for dinner?" Jimmy's voice contained a note of barely-concealed annoyance. "Isn't this the night when the families are supposed to…uh…celebrate that you and Robert are getting married? Where were you expecting this significant meal to take place? The kitchen? The room that hardly holds the seven—I mean six—of us. We are entertaining Robert's family tonight, right?"

"Well, yeah. I was at the store getting the food. I guess—I mean, I assumed—I thought we'd eat outside on the patio. Dad said he was coming home early to help me. Why? What's going on? What are you trying to do?" Why is Jimmy like this? I have this planned out. At least, I thought I did. Now, I feel stupid, but I'm not sure why.

"I'm trying to figure out a place for us to eat, a realistic place. C'mon Beth, you know it's too cold outside. Besides, the patio would need some serious cleaning. And you should know by now that Dad never knows what's going to come up at the store for him. How many times have you known him to come home early? And anyway, I doubt that he'd be too concerned about where we eat or what anything looks like—those are not things he normally worries about. But Beth, these people have a nice house, with nice things, right? Don't they live in the North Springs neighborhood? Isn't Robert's dad an engineer? You've been to their place enough; how does it compare to ours? Really."

Jimmy's voice rose and fell in a crescendo, while his face grimaced and his hands gestured at their surroundings. With the last question, his voice grew almost quiet, and his hands landed on his hips.

"Yes, yes, and yes! I guess their house is nicer. But geez—do you think Robert's going to be ashamed of my house? He doesn't care about that. Do you think his family is going to care because our house isn't as nice as theirs?" Beth fought tears. Am I all wrong about Robert and his parents? Should I have been more worried about this?

"I have no idea. But I care and you should, too! You should have given this a little thought. Did you forget about the stack of clean laundry that was still behind the door over there until I moved it into your room a few minutes ago? This is not the way you entertain adults, especially your almost in-laws, and especially those with means."

"I didn't think about any of that. I just thought…I mean, I didn't think…." Beth stood there, avoiding Jimmy's gaze, and wondering how she could have been so stupid.

"I know you didn't think about it, Beth, let's face it, you've got too much on your plate for this, and I mean all of this." Jimmy softened his voice as he looked at his sister.

"Are you saying I shouldn't be having the Dolans over? Or that I shouldn't be marrying Robert? Or what, Jimmy?"

"I'm just worried about you. To me, this is one reason why. You're so young, Beth. Maybe you don't realize what a big deal all of this is."

"I don't get you, Jimmy. Do you mean that you think that because I don't have the dinner all sorted out it means I'm just young and immature? Are you worried that I'm making dinner for my future in-laws and it's going to flop? Or is it because we don't have a regular dining room to impress them? Or…just that I shouldn't marry Robert?"

Exasperated, Beth dropped onto the couch with her arms folded. She asked herself if Jimmy was right—was she pretending to be a grown up when she knew, without a doubt, that she wasn't even close.

"I don't know, Beth. I just hope you've had the chance to really think about what you're doing, and, in terms of tonight, what you're trying to do, you know…" Jimmy hesitated, then held his arms out in a shrug and continued "…to entertain your future husband's family. This needed careful planning. It's not just a casual dinner. It's an important night for the two families to discuss and celebrate their kids' future. At least, that's what I think, anyway. Did you even talk about this with Aunt Maudie?"

"No, Jimmy, I didn't. Why? I make dinner every night. I've eaten with Robert's family lots of times. They have a dining area just off their kitchen. It's nothing fancy—actually, it's pretty much like our dining area in our kitchen. And I did try to plan carefully, because I know it's a special dinner. And I know what I'm about to do—I know you mean me getting married to Robert—is a big deal!"

"Okay. Look. I'm not trying to upset you, Beth." Jimmy met Beth's gaze and held it. After a few seconds, he said, "Come on. Help me get the benches in here. How many Dolans are there?" Beth stood up.

"Oh, God. Eight, I guess. But I don't even know if they're all coming. Scratch the eight! Robert's older brother is staying at school over the break, and I have no idea if all his other brothers and sisters are coming."

"Ok. Then call him. You've got to find out from him right away. It's going to be tight; we'll have to bring the best of the chairs from the kitchen in here. Do we have any tablecloths? We'll use Mom's china. What are you cooking?" Jimmy sounded like the army officer he had recently trained to be.

"Dad wants me to make chicken cacciatore. Something different from turkey. I bought everything on his list, but I don't really know how to make it. Shoot! Oh, man." Beth's hands reached to hold her head. "Robert's mom is Italian. She's probably going to hate our idea of chicken cacciatore! Dad suggested this, said it would be a good idea, and he would help me, but it isn't. It just isn't! Where is he? Oh, God. Why DID I think I could do this?"

"Too late to worry about that. Let's just get going. We've got, what, two hours?"

Beth clutched her belly. "Yeah. I feel sick to my stomach."

"Come on, Beth," Jimmy said, his voice even now. "Let's all work together and hope Dad gets here soon to help with things. Laurie and Margaret—you finish carrying the benches in. Beth, help me with the table. We can do this if we all pitch in."

Now, Beth took note of her sisters, who stood staring at their siblings; Margaret had crossed her arms over her chest and tucked her hands under her armpits, while Laurie alternately shifted her eyes from Beth, out the door, to the floor. When Beth's eyes met hers, she smiled weakly as if to offer support. Beth offered a worried smile back, then helped Jimmy move the table. With that done, she headed to the kitchen, asking frantically of no one in particular, "Where's Frankie? Why isn't he helping?"

"Heck if I know where he is," Jimmy called as the screen door to the patio screeched. "We can't worry about that now."

Three hours later, eleven members of the two families sat, squeezed onto the patio benches and kitchen chairs around the redwood patio table that was Jack's pride and joy. Every summer since Beth could remember, Jack had found time to sand and re-stain this table and its matching benches a glossy cherry color. And tonight, here it sat, in the center of the quasi-dining-room, the very table that had set the scene for so many Lawrence gatherings. There were the obvious summer meals and parties, but, many times over the years, it had also served as a tent for sleepovers, or as a short ping-pong table on a family game day. Tonight, two mismatched and stained tablecloths that Beth and Jimmy had tried to disguise with strategically placed dishes and trivets covered it.

Beth took a moment to look around and realized that Jimmy was right. The room's paint was a faded pea green. The area rug on which her dad's easy chair usually sat in front of the big console television was spotted and frayed. The trunk with the laundry piled on top of it was gone, but now the room seemed devoid of life. In fact, it screamed "tawdry!" Thankfully, Jimmy hadn't moved the one nice piece of furniture—their mother's antique sewing machine—out of the room.

Beth's eyes lingered on the compact oak cabinet and the machine it housed. With its small drawers delicately carved in circular flower patterns, and the word SINGER painted in gold across the front, this machine had played a key role in Beth's girlhood. How many times had Anna made use of it? In Beth's earliest memories, she saw Anna sewing her ballet costumes—and Margaret's too—for the lessons at Dora May's. How she had transformed those yards of pink tulle into dainty little skirts! To the very young Beth, it had seemed magical. And Anna had also made the rips and tears of Beth's school uniforms disappear —uniforms that, as a kid, Beth never seemed to change out of before playing hopscotch or baseball or climbing their pine tree after school.

When Beth was approaching her senior year in high school—the one year girls were allowed "free dress"— and fretting that her parents couldn't afford the kinds of clothes her friends wore, her mother had come to the rescue. She had augmented what sewing skills Beth learned in her Home Ec class, and got Beth her own portable Singer. Beth remembered lugging the heavy white machine to the living room coffee table to fashion many inexpensive, A-line skirts. Though plainer than the skirts from Judy's Department Store that lots of the girls wore, these skirts freed up money for Beth's shoes and blouses. And, somehow, Anna still found ways to outfit Beth for special dances and events. As she stared at the pretty, honey-brown machine in front of her, she saw only the back of her petite mother, with the little light on and the machine whirring away as the rest of them watched Ed Sullivan. And just like that, into Beth's reverie burst Mr. Dolan's intimidating voice.

"Yes, Beth, what do you plan to do after you two get married?"

"Huh? I'm sorry. I mean…umm, what did you say?"

"Well, Robert has to finish school. And he just said he plans to get a part-time job while doing that. You must know he's thinking about coaching in a high school. My wife just asked what you plan to do. So, what about it?"

Beth glanced around to see everyone looking at her, as if she were about to reveal a juicy secret or a sensible plan. For the last hour, she hadn't said more than "pass the potatoes, please" or "thanks." She had tuned out of the conversation as soon as Jimmy engaged Mr. Dolan with questions about his job as an engineer. At first, it seemed her dad was going to do all the talking as he lavishly praised Beth's cooking skills, causing her to flush with embarrassment. But he had moved on to the wonders of his soon-to-be son-in-law and finally to his auto parts and paint business. To Beth's great relief, Jimmy had steered the conversation to the space program and the part Robert's dad was playing as an electrical engineer. She hadn't noticed the shift that moved the subject to the topic of the hour: her and Robert's engagement and the issues surrounding it.

"Well, uh, I'll get a job, too."

"Oh? And what will you do?" Mr. Dolan asked, looking intently at her.

"I'm not exactly sure, I, uh…well, I'm so busy, you know, busy planning uh…."

"Her Uncle Ralph's a journalist," Jack offered. "He writes for The Examiner. He knows all kinds of people in all kinds of jobs in the area. He's looking out for a job that Beth—and Robert, too, if he wants—can start next summer. That is, until Robert's coaching job starts in the fall. She'll still go to school part-time, like Robert will. Of course, I want her to finish college, just like we all expect Robert to do. Anyway, Ralph thinks soon there will be openings in Parks and Recreation. Isn't that right, honey?"

Beth smiled at her father, nodding.

With that, Jack was off about his brother-in-law and all the interesting people he'd met through his job, how many truly exciting stories he'd covered as a reporter, and what a rock Ralph had been since Beth's mom had died.

There was little talk after that about the impending wedding—just that it would take place the following summer —in six to seven months—but the undercurrent was strong. Robert's mother after trying and failing to bring the conversation around to Robert and Beth's engagement and wedding plans, had said very little about anything, mostly directing her conversation to her younger children. As Beth and Laurie began clearing the table, her future mother-in-law offered to help with the dishes. Beth, though, sensed her insincerity and replied "No, thank you, Mrs. Dolan. Margaret, Laurie and I can do them later, in a jiffy."

Beth wasn't surprised when Robert's mother did not insist.

Robert's parents were against the marriage. They had said as much to him, urging him to wait until he had finished school. After all, he was attending a good university, and had kept up his grades for the past year and a half while playing football and navigating life away from home. His parents had great expectations for Robert's future. He had gotten into West Point, but then had chosen a state university and a pre-med major. Now, with this wedding talk, they didn't see how he could do even that. They were angry and disappointed, mostly—it seemed to Beth—with her. Do they think I pressured him into this? Beth wondered. If they only knew.

When Robert first mentioned the idea of getting married, declaring, "I hate this long-distance romance stuff. We should just run off and get married!" Beth had responded sarcastically, "Yeah, sure. Or, we could just buy a plane and fly back and forth every other day to see each other!" She had resisted the idea as ludicrous, hoping he was joking. But the more he brought it up, the more serious he seemed. She had begun to wonder: Could they actually do this? Could she? Was this really love? Was it a lasting, marriage kind of love? How could she know? At first, she had decided, no. No way. This was just too much for her to consider. Already she had too much confusion careening through her. Certainly, it was reassuring to see the flickering light where, before, there had been only darkness, but, still, she wondered: How does anyone decide the time's right to get married?

The night he proposed, he was so sweet and charming he'd disarmed her, and "Yes!" had tumbled out of her mouth as effortlessly as her giggles. At that moment, nothing had ever seemed so right. Beth had thrown anxiety, uncertainly and fear in the air, feeling, for that moment, pure joy at this boy-man who wanted her, who pledged his love and life wholeheartedly to her. She felt, for the first time in a long time, that she had something to look forward to.

Robert had said that, instead of Beth transferring to Santa Barbara and leaving her family behind, he would transfer to her school. Now, the whole idea of classes was more fun, more exciting. They would go together! Beth could still help her family because she and Robert would live close to them. Though part of her knew that, considering their ages and their individual circumstances, they weren't thinking clearly, she felt her optimistic spirit awakening from its long hibernation.

Beth needed to believe in Robert's youthful optimism. A shell-shocked survivor, she needed to attach herself to his lifeline, and to his promise that went well beyond just bringing her to safety. For Beth, in those early days after the proposal, she believed Robert would lead her through the suffocating fog of the past year and into the bright light of love and happiness that was her prize for the trust she'd placed in him…and them.

Now, despite the weaknesses that were becoming increasingly obvious to her, Beth was determined to follow through with this plan. It was clear that first year of college had been tumultuous for her and Robert for many reasons. They'd both needed to work through the events of the previous summer, adjusting to the changes in their lives, and moving forward as young adults. In spite of the formidable obstacles they'd faced, they had shared a moment in their young lives that had fostered a deep bond between them. In spite of the trauma—and because of it—their relationship had grown into something neither could quite describe. They just knew they had to be together.

That night, after she and her family had said goodbye to the Dolans and restored the house to some semblance of its old order, Beth retreated to her bedroom and eagerly reached for her journal.

Nov. 25, 1966

I'm not sure what to make of tonight's dinner. Was it a disaster? Thanks to Jim, we ate in an actual "dining room" instead of the kitchen or the freezing patio. And—also thanks to Jim—we ate on Mom and Dad's china, which I didn't realize was so nice. Thanks to Dad, who DID get home early, the food was pretty darn good.

But when Mr. Dolan pounced on me with a million questions, my head just went completely blank. WHY? I'm so glad Dad let Mr. D know Uncle Ralph is pretty sure he can get Robert and me rec jobs, at least for the summer. Hopefully, I'll keep mine even after school starts with the park's fall after-school program. I'm sure I could handle that—even with school. Robert wants to coach. But he's still planning on going to school full time. At least, I think he is.

Wow. Is everybody worried about us finishing school, or what? What do they think? We know we need to do this. I don't know why he didn't speak up, but Robert has plenty of ideas about all of this. I guess he really is a little bit afraid of his dad. Now, I see why. He can be kinda scary.

I guess the whole evening rattled me.

First, Jimmy with the dinner. I felt so embarrassed that I didn't think everything through. And he pretty much came out and said I'm not ready for marriage. AS IF I DON'T KNOW THIS! But what am I gonna do? I love Robert, don't I? And I know he loves me. I'd be lost without him. I know I have a lot of growing up to do.

I remember when Jimmy first found out about the engagement; he said he guessed a girl might say yes because she didn't know if or when she'd get asked again. I guess he was trying to understand why I'd do this when I'm so young. But geez! He has no idea who I am or WHAT I'M FEELING! But am I really that immature? Dad doesn't seem to think so. Anyway, Jim DID help me so much tonight. I could not have pulled off anything as nice as tonight without my brother.

And I thank God for Dad, tonight. He really stuck up for me. He seems to understand about my getting married to Robert now. When I told him I had a few doubts about stuff, like not getting to travel or finish college beforehand, he really listened. He asked me: if I pictured myself doing these things without Robert, how did that seem? I said the thought of doing those things without Robert seemed like a rainy day with no fire, no warmth…just cold and lonely. He got a big smile on his face, and said that's how he felt about Mom before they got married. He said that was my answer.

I'm definitely scared about getting married, but I'm also excited. I need someone in my life who really knows me, someone I can pour my heart out to. Robert is becoming that person for me. People say we're too young and should wait. I know they're right, but I just don't feel that I can go on waiting, and neither does Robert. Why should we have to?

Being without Mom has been torture. I now know the true meaning of the word "lonely"!! Sometimes, I tell Laurie about my problems with Robert and my worries about the future. But what can she say? She has her own worries. Once in a while, we talk about missing Mom or we gripe about Dad. But even then, she thinks I don't understand her feelings about Mom. She thinks it's easier for me because I have Robert. It's probably a little easier, but he can't really understand it. He has both of his parents!

And Dad! Laurie has no idea how it makes me feel when Dad singles me out to talk to. How can she know how much I hate it when he ignores her? It's not fair and it's not her fault. With Robert, I can talk it out, and he can sort of understand. Even though he loves Dad, he sees that Dad favors me. And he really cares about Laurie. He sees her as another little sister. Oh, well, I just want to feel excited again about June and being with my darling Robert all the time.

The next morning, Beth sat cross-legged on her bed, going through the box she kept tucked under it. This box held all her mementoes of high school: her yearbooks, Robert's last Track and Field letter, both of their class rings, pictures of her with different high school boyfriends, as well as pictures of her going to fancy dances. When her eyes rested on the collection of notes and letters with a big rubber band around it, she stopped. She lay back onto her pillow, took the rubber band off and sorted through them until she found the bunch of letters from Robert. Mixed in with these were also some she had never sent to him. She began reading one from Robert.

10/10/65
Dear Beth,

I can't believe how busy I've been these past two weeks! Football is harder than I ever expected. We have our first game coming up. Are you coming with my parents? I hope so. I don't know if I'll get to play. All the guys on the team are so good. I'm not sure I'm good enough to get a chance on the field. I'll just have to wait and see. And my classes are killers. I'm so tired after practice, but I still have to hit the books for at least three hours. I barely have time to eat.

Anyway, I was glad to get your letter. It sounds like your not liking school too much. I'm glad you and Joe are carpooling. That must make going to school better. I wish I had someone here that I knew to hang out with. I know Tom, but not that well. I've really only met him through Gracie, and now I know him through football. I like seeing him at practice. He is a REALLY good player. He'll probably get to play in the game Saturday, maybe even in my position.

My roommates seem like nice guys, but I don't really have much time to get to know them. I'm not worried about it. They'll be fine.

Well, say hi to Laurie and your dad. I hope you can come to the football game. I really want you to watch me play. I know you have alot to do on the weekend. Just try, okay? I'll try to call you this week.

Love, Robert

Nov. 26, 1966

I'm going through my letters from Robert since we started college. I just read the very first letter that he sent, which was all about him and football. Ugh! I remember reading it, and thinking, "Wow! Is this really from Robert? That's what he was thinking about after everything that'd been going on? And "alot" and "your"! Will he ever learn that the word is actually two words —a lot? and then "your"? Hello!! It's a contraction: "you're"!!

I remember going up to that football game. Robert had no idea I'm not really into football, etc., but I tried to act excited, although I really thought I was going to throw up. I knew I wasn't sick, but my stomach was queasy the whole time. After the game, the Dolans took us to lunch, and then we headed back home, without Robert. It was such a relief to leave. Wow. Hard to look back on.

I just found one from a month later. This is going to be bad.

10/23/65
Dear Beth,

I still can't believe what happened to me two days ago. I just don't understand how you could break up with me. I still feel like someone hit me in the stomach with a baseball bat. I want to punch a wall or else cry. I haven't cried since I was a little kid. I thought things were so great between us. We had so much fun together and talked so much. I have never talked so much to a girl or anyone else in my life. I can't stop thinking about you and all we've gone through together. You were my Jackie Kennedy, so strong and beautiful. I thought I knew how you felt about me. I still think I know. You know how I feel. I love you. But now you say we should see other people. Beth, do you like someone else? You say you don't, but what other reason could there be? I'm having a hard time studying or concentrating. I have to figure this out. I still love you.

Robert

Nov. 25, '66 continuing

Oh, man! How could I do that to my Robert?? I feel like crying. That was such a rough time. I had no idea what I was doing or why I needed to break up with him. Now, when I look back, it had been only a little over a month since the accident. How could I even have a boyfriend then? And we hardly even knew each other. But then, since he'd been in the accident, everything was all jumbled up. Poor him. Poor me. He said I was strong like Jackie Kennedy. What a laugh!

I remember how Jan paid me a back-handed compliment. "Beth, I can't believe you. You're acting so strong and brave. I always thought you were emotionally weak!" I didn't know what to say. I wanted to tell her that strength and courage did not apply here, at least not to me. Whatever attributes she was thinking I had, I didn't. It was more like an act…one big act. I just wasn't capable of showing her or anybody what was really going on inside me.

Maybe that's how Jackie did it. You seem courageous, but all it is, is you being stoic because you don't know what else to do. It wasn't like someone had confronted me with a life or death decision, and I had thought carefully, then figured it out and made the right choice. I hadn't gone to an Indian yogi and come away with insight and wisdom, like the Beatles. No way. I just felt like a little kid, wandering around blindly. I was definitely lost. I went along, pretending I belonged, but the secret I carried around of being a misfit dogged me, kept me off balance. And I kept looking for Mom. Even if I wanted to tell someone that, I didn't have the words. And really, I thought they'd all think I was crazy…'cause I kinda was.

Oh, here's a letter to Robert. What is it? Wonder why I never sent it.

11/7/65

Dear Robert,

I'm glad you're doing better and that you're dating. It's kind of weird that her name is Elizabeth. Oh, well. I tried to go out on a date with this guy, Ken. But I didn't have any fun. He's a nice guy, but I have a strange problem. Please don't laugh, but...I REALLY THINK I NEED TO BECOME A NUN!!! I'm just so preoccupied, thinking about it. I'm not sure why I think this. At least, it's hard to explain. But here goes. You know I think about God a lot, and I feel like He's calling me, that I'm SUPPOSED to be a nun and serve Him and only Him. I question this all the time, and the thought of it makes me feel so weird. I think about the sisters I had in grammar school and some of them in high school, too. I wonder if God really wants me to be like them, dressing in a habit with a rosary always at my waist. I guess after reading this, you're REALLY going to think I'm nuts and be glad you're dating someone else. But I hope not, because I think about you a lot too, Robert. I want you to be happy. I'm thinking I'll talk to Fr. Rex about this nun thing the next time he calls.

Beth

Nov 25, '66 continuing

Wow! I'm glad I didn't send that! I was trying to sound so brave "I'm glad you're dating"!! How RIDICULOUS! Then, the nun thing, I sounded like someone who's lost her marbles! But I know we did talk about me being a nun at some point. I think he just ignored me whenever I tried to bring it up.

I'm sure I never told him about my very strange experience right after the accident either. I felt Mom in my room, actually in my room, and I asked her to PLEASE not show herself to me. I had the feeling she was about to, and I didn't think I could handle it. Now, I wish I had let her. I could hold onto that for the rest of my life. I'm pretty sure I only told Allie. She probably didn't know what to make of it, but I know she at least listened and didn't act shocked. If anyone I know would trust me that this really happened, it would be Allie.

I know I told Robert that I talked to God a lot though. He never has told me how he feels about God, come to think of it. Hmm.

11/7/65
Dear Beth,

It was great to talk to you on the phone the other night. I was kinda shocked that you were really thinking you might want to be a nun. I'm so glad Fr Rex talked you out of it. You're a good Catholic girl, and I knew you thought about God alot, so I'm not surprised about that part—you know, that you pray to God all the time. I mean, especially after the accident and your mom and all that. But to be a nun? No way, Beth! That's nuts. What a waste!

In your last letter, you talked about writing prayers and asked me if I would like to read a few of them. Well, sure I will if you want me to. But I'm not sure what you want me to do with them. I can tell you what I think. I guess that's probably what you want, right? But mainly, I think if it makes you happy, that's what matters. Of course, you also said God makes you mad, too. At least you have said that. So, I'm confused. Why would you write Him prayers about loving Him and also being mad at Him? But then, I guess that's possible. When you broke up with me, I was mad, but still cared about you. Kinda the same thing, right? Anyway, I guess I'll see when I read a few. I have to tell you that this kind of scares me.

Well, I have to go to class.

Robert

Nov 25, '66 continuing

I so remember this! He did not get my God stuff at all. I didn't understand. I guess I still don't. I remember putting in a letter to Robert what I always thought and wrote about and sang about—that "God IS love, and he who abides in love abides in God, and God in him." I learned that on my senior retreat and it stuck with me.

But, I was still mad at God. I needed Him, and I prayed to Him constantly, but I couldn't understand how He could take Mom away from me. Still, every prayer ended in a plea. I wrote a prayer once, telling God I needed some Pepto Bismol for my heart! How corny! But man, some of the things Robert said back then made me think he was so shallow. I remember wondering how could I be in a serious relationship with a boy like him? He didn't even know who Kahlil Gibran was. Never heard of "The Prophet."

Oh, here's one from him last V's Day.

2/21/66
Dear Beth,

I know I just left you, but I have to tell you what a great time I had with you this weekend, going to see "The Sound of Music" and all. You made me so happy on Valentine's Day, and then I got to make you happy a week later. I loved surprising you. I've never felt this way before. You make me want to be unselfish, to do things for you. When I'm with you, I don't care if we're talking. I know how we feel. I'm just happy being with you. I don't need anyone else around. I know I'll miss you tomorrow or the next day, but right now I'm just so happy.

Love, Robert

Nov 25, '66 continuing

I love that letter! I have never felt that way about a boy, either. I was starting to realize how bonded we were. At the same time, he kinda scared me with his feelings. He could be so intense. I really remember, though, how I ached for him when we were apart. (I still feel that way.) I ached for his arms around me, telling me how much he missed me and wanted me.

I also missed all his teasing and light-heartedness, and how he came up with so many silly, adventurous plans. There was that time he insisted we get up really early to go fishing. He slept on our couch the night before, then tiptoed into my room to wake me up, then drove me an hour away to the lake with the funny name and "taught" me how to fish. It was so goofy, but so fun. I think we threw back anything we caught. When had I ever done anything like that before? Never! The other day, when he went grocery shopping with me, I thought I'd wet my pants when he put a watermelon under his t-shirt and started waddling around the aisle, mimicking what I'll look like when I get pregnant. Clearly, I HAVE to marry this crazy guy. Gotta go. Laurie's got guitar lessons!

Beth knew most of her college friends thought she and Robert were foolish to be engaged. After all, they'd spent hours together, talking over coffee about traveling through Europe during the summers. They'd even made tentative plans to go to San Francisco's Haight Ashbury for a few months after graduation to check out the "flower children."

At one time, this excited Beth, but now she had no curiosity for adventure. Here she was, planning a wedding—her wedding. What did that mean for her life? The sad truth, she had begun to realize, was that she no longer knew what she wanted to do with her life. She found it next to impossible to look to the future at all. That is, beyond a few months. For now, that meant thinking about Robert and planning a wedding.

Once, she had considered a psychology major or, possibly, sociology. She thought back to some of her high school classmates that she had found fascinating and funny…like Barb, a pear-shaped girl with white cat-eye glasses who joined the band just for something to do. And what did she do? She sounded the gong once or twice when the band performed.

She'd laughed loud and long when she described this to Beth, whose curiosity had nudged her to ask: "But Barb—you play the piano, don't you?"

"Yeah, but, kiddo, I'm not trying to be some virtuoso. I just want to have fun. You have no idea how crazy it is to watch everyone else working so hard with their instrument, and then when it's time, I just have to hit a gong with a mallet." Then she'd laughed as she made a funny face and called out, "GONG!" which made Beth laugh with her. "I've never been accepted by the popular kids," she'd said. "I don't know why you're even talking to me now. But I have fun anyway. I make my own way." And Beth had been charmed. Someone her friends thought "weird" lived a life parallel to that crowd, and Beth had been awakened to someone who'd previously been invisible to her.

Then there'd been the very pretty, very hard-talking, hard-acting girl in her 11th grade P.E. class. Other girls had gossiped that Carolyn smoked, and was easy with boys. The way these girls had told it, outside of school, Carolyn had hung out with tough kids inclined to find themselves in trouble. But Beth, who'd talked to Carolyn in the locker room from time to time, had found her sarcastic perspective on high school society hilarious, and her mockery of all the cliques intriguing. Carolyn had seemed like someone above all the nonsense of mainstream high school. Both Barb and Carolyn had inhabited their high school worlds in a way that Beth still admired: determined not to allow others to define them. Beth had realized that these girls had detached themselves from the everyday gossip that, until then, Beth had not resisted. She'd found them compelling.

At the beginning of their senior year, Beth's class had spent a day listening to speakers representing different fields that the students might pursue. Afterwards, she'd found herself in a discussion about the day with Barb. Both girls had been moved.

"What'd you think, Barb? About the day, I mean? Did this help you know what you want to do after college?"

"Ya know, I'm not sure. I thought what the police detective had to say was pretty interesting. I could do that. But I really liked what the guy from the Catholic Worker down on Skid Row had to say. Beth, I want to change the world! Work for justice and peace!"

Beth had been bowled over. Barb had sounded so independent and passionate. "What about you, kiddo?" Barb had asked.

"I listened to both the psychologist and the social worker. I found myself really interested in what they do. I mean, I've just begun to realize how interesting and unique people can be. Wouldn't it be neat to be able to help people who are trying to be...I don't know...I guess who are having problems trying to be true to themselves? I mean, to do that as my job? Ya know?" Beth had asked Barb.

"Like people who think they're crazy? Or can't get along with other people?"

"I don't know for sure. But I think I'd probably more want to help little kids or teens who get labeled as "weird" or "different," who have problems fitting in. Something like that. I don't know for sure. I'd like to find out more. But what you're interested in seems really interesting to me, too. I just don't know if I'm gutsy enough to try and change the world—although I did go door to door, working for Kennedy with my friend, ya know, Molly."

"You guys did that? So did I."

Beth asked herself what had happened to the girl she had been. Life, apparently…because here she was, planning her wedding—and after all her assertions that she would not marry young and not have kids young. She had so many memories of Anna at the clothesline or stove, and fretting, always fretting, about "the money." Later that night, she tried to get ahold of her feelings.

I probably haven't been concerned enough about my actual life after the wedding. I let myself get too caught up with house stuff. And school…I'm doing better so far. I'm so determined to do better this semester! Then I start looking through these stupid magazines! I start worrying about the food, or the flowers, things involving the wedding.

Am I just a silly girl in dreamland? Am I really going to have to drop out of school for a while? It's not as if I love school anyway. NO. I should and I will finish school. But everyone says it's more important that Robert finishes, so he can get a good job. Of course, that's because the man is supposed to be the "breadwinner." Do I really believe that? But then, I certainly don't want to be the breadwinner!

And then, what if I get pregnant right away? When I have a baby, I'll be taking care of him or her, won't I? Oh, man! A baby?! I am NOT ready for that. We haven't talked about any of this. Robert says we'll work all of this out. Don't worry. But being so far apart, we have very little time to talk. That can't be a good thing. We HAVE to talk before he goes back to school. Is this really going to work?

14 DARKNESS CREEPS IN, AGAIN

What becomes of the brokenhearted
Full of love that's now departed
I know I've got to find some kind of peace of mind
Maybe....

~William Weatherspoon, Paul Riser, James Dean

November 1966, on your engagement to Robert

Dear Bethie,

Congratulations! It's official that you and Robert are getting married now that the Dolans came over and everything went OK. (At least it looked like it to me.) I know you were nervous about the Dolans, but the main thing is you and Robert. He asked you and you said yes. Besides, how could his parents not like you and want you in their family?

Anyways, I wrote this song, and, although it's not a love song, I still wanted to tell you that I thought of you when I wrote it. So, it's kinda for you. (Hope you don't think this is too weird!) You always compliment me on my songs and guitar playing, and I really appreciate the encouragement. So, this is a thank you. (I plan to try to write a real love song for you guys.) This song is not really about anything, just a guy who feels he has to leave the people he loves to do his music.

Love, Laurie

PS I don't think I'll EVER have to leave the people I love to do my music!

Hello darkness, of course, you've come again
I'm not sure why or even where you been
Is it 'cause I left my life; why–I up and left 'em?
And now I'm lost, just lost and driftin'?
I didn't want to, but my life keeps on shiftin'
Oh, yeah, it does, it does

Don't know why I did it, but something made me go
Here I am; once again, I've sunk so low
But I had to do it; something called to me
I know I've done it before, don't you see?
It's something in me, I've got to run, be free
Free, free, free

I know I need some help, but I don't ask
I couldn't do it, it's too big a task
I know I caused them pain; that's nothing new
Sure, it haunts me, knowin' I can't be true
They deserve my heart; hey, I know they're due
They're due, it's true

But the road, she calls, oh, she calls to me
To sing and play and wonder; why can't I let things be?
I have to go, it's my shame, it's my used-up story
It's my life; it'll bring me no glory
Leavin' my people, they don't know I'm just so sorry
I am so sorry

Well, here I go, heartless me, I'm off again
I know it's bad; Yeah, it's a blessed sin
To cause you pain, heartache and more
But, honey, I got to go like I done many times before
It's my cursed calling and honey I'm cursed to the core
You know I am, I am

I have to hit the road and cry out those blues
for those that listen, I know it's only the poor, sad few
Still I know to you it sounds so vain
But I just sing my story; you know I'm not searching for fame
But I hurt you so, please know you're never to blame
I miss you, I do. I do.

~ Laurie Lawrence

.

15 WHO'S REALLY READY?

It's a sign of the times,
That your love for me is getting so much stronger…
Now I know that I won't have to wait much longer…
For when you hold me now, I feel like you never want to let me go…

~Tony Hatch and Jackie Trent

When Jack came home from work the night after the engagement dinner, he found Jim already home and, uncharacteristically, sitting in the kitchen with a cup of coffee, going over some papers. He looked up as Jack walked through the door with the mail.

"Hey, Dad."

"Hey-y-y-y, Jim!" Jack said, voice singing in pleased surprise at seeing his oldest child sitting at the kitchen table. Did you get off work early today?"

"Actually, today was my last day at the bank. I gave notice a week ago. They let me off early. I guess I forgot to tell you. There's been a lot going on around here lately."

"Did I miss something? I don't remember this news. Another job you couldn't stomach?"

"It wasn't that, Dad. Far from it. No, the fact is, I finally got the results of my civil service test. I passed with high marks, so I'll be interviewing for what I think will be a much better administrative position. Decided that, uh, I, well, I wanted to get myself ready. Take a few days, get some new clothes—you know."

"Well, Jim, what good news! Congratulations! God knows, you've earned this. I couldn't be more proud! I knew, sooner or later, the breaks would fall FOR you for a change. This is gonna be the start of some good things for you…I just know it, Jim."

"Thanks, Dad. I know you've been rooting for me. I'm not really sure about what comes next. This letter said they'd keep me informed. Anyway,

I wanted to talk to you about some other things, too," Jimmy said tentatively.

"Sure. Shoot!" Something in Jimmy's tone warned Jack to come back to earth. He'd worried so much about this son struggling to find his niche in the working world. Jim had no interest in Jack's business. He'd even told Jack a few years before that he wasn't working so hard in college to end up in a "garage." Although Jimmy's approach at first disappointed—even inflamed—Jack, his business was far from a mere garage, and, by the way, hadn't this same "garage" paid Jimmy's way through school? In the end, though, Jack was relieved; he wanted more for his first-born child than the insecure business that he'd inhabited.

"Are you concerned about Beth getting married? Because I am."

After a moment, Jack looked up at Jimmy. "No, I'm not. And I'll tell you why. Robert is a fine young man from a good family. They love each other, and, what's more, I can't keep Beth here taking care of all of us. She's got to have her own life."

"Okay, okay. I know what you say is true. Robert has been great, and they do seem to love each other, but what about how young she is—they are? She's barely 19, and she's engaged! Why?! What's the rush? Why don't they finish college first? And what about Laurie and Margaret?"

"I'll grant you that they're young, but, so what? That doesn't hafta' mean anything. And they went through something horrific. Together. That has a way of growing a person up! As for the other girls, well…I have a pretty good routine going with Margaret, with her workshop and bowling. Laurie will be in high school next fall. She's growing up—"

"But, Dad—good grief! She's only 14. It's pretty obvious she's still going through a hard time, and she depends on Beth. I remember Beth at 14, and she had Mom. I remember Mom talking to me about her worries about Beth back then. Beth was a handful…so rebellious. Hardly listened to a word Mom said! That wasn't all that long ago, you know? How can Beth know what she's getting into?"

Jack looked down, then shook his head as he faced Jimmy, "I don't know what you mean, Jim. Beth's always been a great kid. Yes, she went through the same things a lot of teenage girls go through. Yes, she had a boyfriend that she mooned over. That passed. If memory serves, she had a few more after that. So what?"

"I didn't mean to say she was a bad kid…or girl. I just remember some of the trouble Mom had with her. I remember that first boyfriend—the public-school boy, John. Mom was so worried. Beth thought he was the love of her life. Mom was sure Beth would get into trouble, but she wouldn't listen to Mom. She wasn't easy for Mom to deal with."

"God knows, your mother was about as good as you can get, Jim, but if you ask me, she was always a little tough on Beth. Treated her like a baby, and tried to keep her by her side long after most kids Beth's age had spread their wings. Of course, Beth wanted to grow up! Besides, look at the way she handles herself now—going to college, managing the house, helping her sisters, and shopping and making dinner for all of us."

"All I'm saying is that last night showed me just how young Beth still is, even though she's been great in this crisis. I'm just trying to think of her well-being, her future."

"And I'm not?? Judas Priest, I'm her father! Don't tell me I'm not thinking of her well-being, for God's sake! She's not a little girl. You should see that. I can't just tell her what she can and can't do. What was wrong with her last night, anyway? I was so proud of her. Look at the dinner she made for all those people. And she just sparkled."

"Calm down, Dad. I'm not criticizing her. I'm concerned about her. You know this is a big decision. How can she make it right now? Did you see her when Mr. Dolan asked her what she planned to do after she and Robert get married? You can sure see he's not happy about what his son's about to do."

"Yeah. He put her on the spot. Poor kid."

"But—that's just it, Dad. If she were really ready for this, thinking it through, she would have had an answer, a plan. Robert, at least, seems to have given some thought to graduating and working in the near future. I just don't think Beth's considered what she's about to do…I mean, beyond the wedding. What kind of a future do they have this way? She seems to think everything will just fall in place."

"Look, Jim…some people are better at thinking—or maybe at doing—on their feet. Not everyone has everything completely planned out. Maybe Beth's a lot like me, which is not the worst thing in the world. I've managed to raise five kids and put them through twelve years of Catholic education, except, of course, Margaret."

"Times are different, Dad. I think a lot of Robert and give him credit for how he took charge at the accident. I think he's smart and should have a future ahead of him. And Beth's my little sister. I want the best for her. I guess I just…I see signs that she's got a lot of growing up to do before she tackles marriage, although I will admit I don't know a lot about it. I can't imagine myself at 19 thinking about something like this."

"And yet, when you were only a little older than Beth, off you went into the army. You weren't ready for that, but you survived. Hell, maybe you did some growing up, going through whatever they threw at you. Anyway, I have faith in Beth. And if she says Robert makes her happy and she wants to be with him, and he says the same about her, then that's that. Don't you think it's gonna be hard on me? She's been my…she's done one helluva job, helping out around here, doing a lot of things your mother would do if…."

"I know, Dad…I know she does. And I have faith in her. I'm not concerned about that." Jack and Jimmy sat in a silence for a moment. "Look, Dad, this may not be a good time, but I actually have something else to talk to you about—about me, I mean."

"More serious than this? Go ahead, Jimmy. I can take it." Jack rubbed his eyes, then replaced his glasses and looked at Jimmy.

"Well, I met someone…someone I really like."

"Wow! You had me worried there for a minute! How could I find fault with that? Man, oh, man!"

"The thing is, I'm looking for a place—you know, a place of my own. I think it might get serious, and I think I should have…uh, my own place."

"Of course, you should! You scuttled your plans for this once, for me. Don't think I don't appreciate it. You're a young man. You need your independence. You've been great to me, Jim, to all of us. You gonna tell me about this girl?"

"I met her—her name's Janie—several months ago, and we started dating right off the bat. We seem to have a lot in common. She's Catholic, a nurse…and just a nice girl. Besides that, she has a great sense of humor. And—the best part—she laughs at my jokes! Only real problem I see, so far, is that she doesn't care much for baseball. Could be a deal breaker…I'll have to wait and see." Jimmy and Jack chuckled. "Anyway, we've been seeing each other a lot, lately, and, like I said, it's going pretty well. Don't make any announcements, though; I'm not ready for that."

Jack grinned. "Don't worry, I won't jump the gun, but, you know, when the time is right, I'd like to meet her." After witnessing the confrontations between Anna and Jim over what Jim had pronounced his private life, Jack knew better than to push.

"One of these Sundays, I'll bring her around for dinner." Jim paused. "You going to be okay with me moving out, especially now that Beth's getting married next summer?"

"Oh, my God! Now don't go treating me like I'm some little boy you have to coddle. I can take care of myself. You should know that by now. Criminetly! You worry just like your mother used to!"

Jimmy shrugged, then raised his hands in a gesture of resignation. "Okay, Dad. I imagine it's gonna take me a little while to find a place, anyway. And I want to know for sure what I'm going to be doing, job-wise."

Jack nodded, then said "And leave Beth to me. I know my daughter; she's my responsibility if she's anybody's…that is, besides Robert's pretty soon."

A little later, Jack sat in his red recliner, reading his crime novel, when Beth came through the front door. "Sorry I'm late, Dad. I had to hunt for a book at the school library for a research paper. Did Laurie get home yet? She said this morning she would probably go over to Patty's for a while. I told her I wasn't coming right home from class."

"I just got home a while ago. I haven't heard any mice stirring, so I assume I'm home alone. Margaret was going on an outing after the workshop today. The Bakers will bring her home after dinner.

"Ok. I'll put my books down and start dinner. I don't really have anything planned. I can probably make some spaghetti. Does that sound all right?"

"Sure. That sounds just fine."

Jack's mind raced.

How do I bring up the wedding to her? Or should I? Do I really believe all that I said to Jimmy? Is he right—that she's not ready? She seems so excited. 'Course, now that Robert's back at school, she's on her own again. But, pretty soon, she'll be making plans. Or is she already? I'm just gonna let her come to me if she wants to talk. I think she'd let me know if she was in over her head. Besides, she's the one who said "yes" to Robert...said that she'd be so lonely without him.

Jimmy does worry...he's so much like Anna, brooding about things. But when has he had time to notice what goes on with Beth? I don't think she confides in him. Come to think of it, does she confide in anyone? She doesn't really run around with any of her old girlfriends, at least not that I know of. She's not hanging on the phone for hours with anyone like she used to. But she's got Robert. That's the point. He's the one she wants to talk to. Look at how they were over the summer. Together constantly. He must have spent part of everyday here when he wasn't working or checking in with his folks. Come to think of it, his folks did seem a little cool the other night. But what of it? Maybe that's just the way they are. How do I know?

"Uh, Dad...Oh, wait, that's the phone. I'll get it. Hello. Hi. No, I just got home. Barely put my books down. Yeah. Okay. I have to stop at the store, though—tomato sauce... Yep! Okay.... I'll honk. Bye."

"Who was that?"

"Laurie. She wants a ride from Patty's. I was just gonna say we need some tomato sauce, so I'll get Laurie on my way to the store. But I put some onions in a pan to sauté, and I have the hamburger meat defrosting. Do you want me to turn off the stove?"

"No. I'll watch it. Don't worry. Take your time. Both of your brothers are out right now, and, as I said, Margaret's on an outing."

"Okay, Dad."

Jack watched Beth walk out the door, thinking about how she had just taken on picking up Laurie and making dinner...just assumed it was her job.

He wrestled with himself, wondering why...*Why did I let that happen?*

Why didn't I say I would pick up Laurie—or at least go to the store? Why did I assume it was Beth's job to make dinner?

Maybe, there is something to Jimmy's concern. Is she getting married just to get out from under these responsibilities?

Jack sighed, watching Beth walk out the front door, then wiped his glasses with his handkerchief and returned to his book.

16 SILVER FOUNTAIN, PINK CHAMPAGNE

Here comes the bride,
all dressed in white
Sweetly serene, in the soft,
glowing light

~Richard Wagner

She had done it! Or rather, they had done it. They were hitched. Two were now one. They were married. "What God has joined together, let no man tear asunder!" No going back. No "If it doesn't work out, I can always... "Beth wouldn't even entertain that idea. No, it had to be forever. This was it. It hadn't been perfect. None of it had been exactly what she wanted, but it didn't matter now. Through all the objections, the nay-saying, the doubts, she and Robert had held each other's hands, leaned into the blustery wind, and run. The hurdles had come at them—some rather high—but they hadn't wavered, racing straight toward, then over, and, finally, beyond them.

Beth beamed at the shiny little rings gleaming in the sunlight. Could this really be her finger wearing these solemn symbols of adult life? When was someone going to confront her and tell her,

"No, siree! You didn't really do this. You couldn't and you can't! Look in the mirror! You're still a child. And besides, you've got responsibilities! You've got commitments, Missy, commitments! You can't just go gallivanting off into marriage! What are you thinking?"

Yet, here she was, outside the church, with Robert kissing her. She kept giggling. Her bridesmaids hugged her. People congratulated them. The men patted Robert on the back. Somehow, they had made it and grabbed the golden ring! ..though they'd had some rocky moments, a few setbacks, and the inevitable reality checks.

Robert had choked with shock at the cost of wedding rings. He'd said they should save their money, and forego the engagement ring. Stunned, Beth had momentarily recoiled from him. Was this love? Romance? Maybe not romance, he had argued, but it was love—of the obvious, common sense variety. Consequently, at first, he would not be moved. Taurus—the bull—he knew he was right. Could her practical side not see it?

For the past few months, Beth had shared her excitement with Robert—the wonderful wedding day she was planning, and her dreams for their future. She'd included him in the myriad details—asking his opinion about pictures, flowers, invitations—though, by virtue of their still-long-distance relationship, he could play no substantial role in these decisions. No doubt relieved to be spared these responsibilities, he had, nevertheless, listened attentively on the phone, weighing in on money matters and visiting vendors with her when he was home for the weekend.

They weathered the periodic storms, including the inevitable:

"What's wrong with sex now? After all, we're engaged."

"Robert, is this what the engagement is really about to you? I thought it was about deepening our love, sharing ideas for the future. You can't wait a few more months for sex?"

"Are you kidding me? Isn't making love a "deepening" way to share our love?"

"You're changing your major to Phys Ed? What happened to you being pre-med? My uncle says there aren't good jobs for teachers these days, let alone PE teachers."

"The pre-med classes are so darned hard! You know I had to pull all-nighters just to pass a couple of my classes. And I love sports. I love working with kids. What's wrong with that?"

"But are you thinking you can be a full-time coach?"

"I don't know yet. Sounds like you don't think I can do it. Why not?"

"How can I move to Santa Barbara? I have to live near Dad and my sisters.

"Won't you at least look at the married student housing? I met a couple who live there, and they love it. It's so beautiful here. All the open space, and the ocean so close."

"I have looked. I know it's beautiful and great there, but I just can't be that far away from my family. I thought we already talked about this."

Every argument had presented frustration and unvoiced questions about their relationship. They knew they were taking a big step; the big question was: should they? Invariably, the doubts melted into reassurances as each quickly reminded the other that soon they would be together full time. No more lingering on the phone, reluctant to say goodbye. No more tears when Robert left Beth to go back to school. Their problems had solutions, and they would work things out together. That's all that really mattered.

What Beth had excluded Robert from were the issues that—like distant thunder rumbling closer and closer—had begun nagging at her soon after her "Yes!" to his proposal. These were issues that gripped her heart and preyed on it with sharp, painful doubts. But, worst of all, were the answers she feared were true.

Am I deserting my sisters and father? (Yes!)

Laurie will be starting high school next year. Who will help her with her questions, problems? (I don't know. Dad? No one?)

Will Margaret be okay without me there every day? (Maybe….)

Will Laurie? (No, probably not. She'll miss Mom more and soon hate me!)

How can I, of all people, do this to them? (I'm selfish. I'm just thinking of myself as usual!)

How will Dad be, with Laurie and Margaret to himself? Will he begin talking to them more? Try to understand and reach out to Laurie in her silent spells? (Hopefully. Maybe? Probably not.)

Why don't I call the wedding off? At least, postpone it? (I can't do that to Robert. We would break up for good. I would miss him too much. I have to go through with this! I'm really so selfish, selfish.)

Ultimately, why is it up to me to make things okay? (I know why, but I can't stand to think about it!)

Why don't I act like a grownup and face facts? (If I let myself, I might as well plan never to be happy again.)

But, really…do I deserve to be happy, especially at the expense of my family? (No, probably not.)

Then, the same maddening questions and answers would begin again…and repeat…in an endless cycle. Beth worked hard to bury this side of the impending marriage. If she didn't give voice to the unanswerable, maybe, just maybe, she could eventually banish them. After all, she, alone, knew the distress the decision to get married at this time cost her. She didn't allow herself to talk about it to anyone or even to write about it in her journal.

In the first few months after the initial surprise of Robert's proposal, Beth's delight with him had filled her with a feeling she had forgotten: hope. Suddenly, she'd felt flooded with hope—hope for a new life that would ground her, secure her, embrace her with Robert's love and affection. For the first time in so very, very long, she'd thought about the future. The wedding plans were one thing—and they were wonderful! —but what would come after had teased her with possibilities: picking out their first apartment together, going to school together, coming home in the evening—just the two of them. Their life together now stretched out before them. Beth had even found herself picturing a baby and thinking to herself, I've got to start eating better…a baby will need its nourishment from my body. My! body!

When her delighted whirl slowed down, however, the hard questions had come crashing in, all boiling down to the big, unavoidable one: how could she walk out on her family like this? It'd been just one year since Anna's violent death…coming to visit her on the Indian reservation. Robert's plan had been to marry early the next summer. But her father, her sisters, even her brothers—none of them had really recovered from their shock at the accident and its aftermath. For that matter, have I? Beth had wondered. Would ten months change that to any significant degree? Did doing this make sense?

Together—at least Beth, her father, and sisters—they'd managed to establish some kind of routine, such that a modicum of calm had begun to settle on the household. While her dad rarely walked in from work whistling as he used to, Jimmy had begun telling silly jokes that got Beth, and even Laurie, giggling. Laurie's guitar lessons were going well, and she had grown to really like her teacher, Brian. Lately, he'd tasked her with ever more complicated pieces, which she gladly and devotedly practiced; in return, Brian complimented her diligence and praised her improvement. Beth thought Laurie's confidence was growing with this steady development.

Margaret…was anyone's guess. She'd reestablished her old routine: she went to the workshop every day, watched TV, and talked on the phone. She helped with the dinner dishes, and went bowling on the weekends. She took pictures and catalogued them. Beth hadn't worried that much about Margaret…she seemed okay. Best of all, the more time had passed, the more she'd talked the way she always had to Laurie and Beth, which brought a sense of normalcy to the cozy bedroom they shared.

In those early days of mourning, Beth had recognized that Margaret also played a big part in why the sisters still prayed before bed. This was something Anna had always done with her older girls when it was just the two of them in their bedroom. It was a soothing mantra learned with their mother, and sweet reminder of precious days now past. Oh, I'm going to miss this!, Beth had thought wistfully.

But as much as her anxiety had dogged Beth, her joy and excitement had matched it. Robert—for better or worse, she smiled to herself—had taken to filling her thoughts and dreams. Manly practicality, boyish playfulness, and handsome sexuality—he exuded all these qualities and more, bowling her over time and again over the rest of the summer.

When the time had drawn near for Robert to go back to school in the fall, he and Beth had decided to shop for rings. Excited, but having no idea how to start the process, they'd gone to a jewelry store they found in the phone book. While Beth had gasped at the brilliant and beautiful rings, Robert had looked for the prices. "Beth, where are the price tags?" he'd whispered loudly to her. Seeing them deliberating, heads together at the glass cases, a sales clerk had come over and asked if he could help them. When Robert had said they were looking for wedding bands, and maybe an engagement ring, too, the man had brought out a tray of wedding and engagement ring sets. Robert had watched in silence while Beth had asked a few questions and hesitantly tried two or three rings on her finger. She'd looked at Robert quizzically. Facing the sales clerk squarely, he had asked about the cost. Beth had held her breath, but, with the clerk's answer, she'd let the air out as she'd met Robert's eyes. The shopping trip was over.

They hadn't talked on the way back to Beth's house, but when Robert stopped the car in the driveway, he'd turned to Beth with his practical opinion. "No way, Beth! I'm sorry, but that was way out of our league. I mean, even just the wedding bands alone, I couldn't believe it. You have to see that I—or even we—cannot even think about a diamond engagement ring." He shook his head imploringly at her.

Meanwhile, in her silence, Beth had been trying to remain calm. Unprepared for both the cost and the sophistication of the gold and silver ring sets—the ones that included an engagement ring—she had realized only one thing: that she lacked the sophistication and style to wear anything so beautiful. Though she didn't have words to express her feelings, she knew her simple upbringing, with its dearth of material things, meant she would never be comfortable wearing anything so elegant. Then and there, Beth felt she had just failed the grown-up test. Other girls her age wore nice jewelry, but they also wore nice clothes. In high school, when she had gone shopping with some of her friends, and they'd started trying on skirts and tops, she just watched. Unless, that is, she happened to be in Sears, where her mother had done most of her shopping for household appliances and sundry items, as well as clothes for the family.

When Robert had expressed his dismay at this financial development, and strongly suggested that they forego the diamond engagement ring, she didn't immediately disagree. Still, she decided, this first look would not be their last where rings were concerned.

"I don't know what to do!" Beth had said to Molly on the phone that evening. Molly was newly married herself. "What is a girl like me doing, trying on such dazzling things? I would feel stupid wearing them! I know the rings would look silly on me.

"Lizzy, first of all, you do deserve a nice set of rings, but you don't have to go to that store. It is pretty expensive. We found ours at Seymour's. And I love my diamond. I know Paul and I both work full time, but you and Robert should look there. What's your budget?"

"I don't know. Not that much. We just started talking about it. Did you guys talk about it together? I mean, Robert's proposal was so romantic. But this was….well, not what I pictured." Beth had hated admitting all this to Molly, who'd seemed so far ahead of her in this department.

"Yeah, we looked together after he proposed, but then he went back and bought what he knew I liked, and surprised me with it. I couldn't believe he got this one. Every time I look at it, I love it more."

"Wow. That's great. You're lucky, Molly."

"You'll get there, Lizzie. Just keep looking."

Beth had kept her friend's words in mind. She hadn't expected to get a ring like Molly's, which though simple, held a pretty, prominent, shiny diamond. But she had to have something on that finger which represented the import of the promise she and Robert had made. Somehow, Beth intuited that having this little symbol of her own would keep her calm as she made the plans that meant leaving her father and sisters. The engagement ring would be her talisman; it would keep her focused on herself and the future she hoped would bring an end to her anxious stomach and wildly fluctuating emotions.

So, instead of tears, she'd worked hard to persuade Robert with her own brand of logic. It was no easy task for her to squelch her disappointment, her anger at him. How close she had come to "You can't really love me!" After all, where was the adoring fiancé who would put the beautiful diamond on his beloved's finger and swear that her love is worth any amount of money? Though she had again questioned their compatibility and, thus, the wisdom of their wedding plans, ultimately, Beth had accepted that Robert's forthright practicality, though frustrating at times, was part of what she loved about him. She'd decided that the convincing would have to come from emotion and logic.

"Look at our parents. Your mom has an engagement ring. Mine had one. (Beth couldn't bear the thought of wearing her mom's as her own, and Robert never suggested it.) It's a tradition that says our love will stand the test of time."

"C'mon Beth. Of course, we'll have wedding bands, but can't you see, I need to save every penny I can make to get through this school year. How do you expect me to come up with hundreds of dollars for a diamond ring? What's the point of it anyway? It's just a way for stores to make more money off of weddings!"

"No, Robert. I don't look at it like that. That diamond on my finger tells the world that we're in love. That you asked me to marry you! AND I SAID YES! It says we're promised to each other forever! Think about that. Why else did our parents get them? Why else do all engaged couples get them?"

"Why does it matter so much what other people think? We know we love each other."

"It matters to me. I care what my friends think. I want them to know the boy I said yes to—the boy I'm promising myself to, who I'm going to MARRY—loves me enough to find a way to buy me a diamond ring."

"But, Beth…"

"Robert, I don't think I would ever get over this. To me, this is about our…your commitment." He had met her burning blue eyes for a long moment, shaken his head, and, finally, shrugged and agreed to look again. She assured him she would be happy with something very modest.

Beth's intuitive and passionate belief that giving in to Robert on this issue would bode ominously for their early marriage, had resulted in a shopping trip to a few more stores and, ultimately, Sears, where, to Robert's great relief, they found simple, matching bands and an engagement ring that they could put on lay-away. Between their part-time jobs, they had paid off the diamond ring in time for Beth to show it off at Christmas parties. They had kept the bands on a lay-away plan until May, a month before the wedding day.

Now, she looked at the sweet little diamond ring with matching white gold wedding band, and thought about her happiness—and relief—at putting the very significant wedding band on Robert's finger just an hour earlier. Looking up at her new husband, Beth noted, not for the first time, Robert's athletic form and rugged handsomeness. Maybe that gold band would keep some of those flirtatious girls away.

Beth had, over the past few weeks, repeatedly ordered herself to put the nerves away for this—her—very special day. It was only a week ago that Robert, upset and angry, had confided to her that his mother had told him to rethink his decision; it wasn't too late, she'd said, to change his mind. Hiding her hurt, Beth had asked as calmly and steadily as she could muster, "What did you say?" "I told her I didn't need to think about it. I knew what I wanted to do," he said with a sigh. "How could she even say such a thing? I just can't believe it!" Beth had reached for his hand and said, "I'm glad." But, truth be told, the surprising question, coming from the mother he practically adored, had left Robert shaken; meanwhile, Beth's determination not to let anyone or anything stand in the way of a wonderful, carefree day only grew as the wedding approached.

Now, the deed done, Beth acknowledged they were a little crazy—even a lot crazy—but they were in love, and it was their day and no one else's. Robert had clasped her hand after she left her father and joined him in front of the altar, whispering that he had been sick in the bathroom right before coming into the church, but now that she was with him, he knew he would be okay. They had laughed and whispered throughout the long service, and gazed deeply into each other's eyes when they said their vows. Beth wondered what her new in-laws thought when she chuckled out loud as Father Flynn read the gospel, admonishing Beth and Robert in his thick

Irish accent to "be fruitful and multiply!" In other words, they should have sex, sex, and more sex! —the very activity good Catholic kids were supposed to avoid until marriage. Now, all bets were off! Finally!

Earlier in the day, Beth's determined optimism had faltered as clouds gathered for morning showers. Then, she found herself pacing around the house, regretting that she had allowed Aunt Maudie to convince her to let her teenaged cousin do her hair. Maudie had insisted that Lily did all her friends' hair, so why not Beth's? It would save money, and Beth would love it. But there hadn't been any practice sessions. May and Maudie had been late, and May had forgotten to bring her new, heated curlers, the ones her aunt had bragged would do as good or better a job than any professional stylist's.

Fighting nausea, Beth considered her options. She knew her own curlers, designed to be worn overnight on damp hair, couldn't do the job now. They would never create the special style she had planned for her thick, shoulder length hair—certainly not in the hour remaining before they left for the church. Often, for special occasions, she wore the curlers to bed the night before, then spent over an hour teasing and spraying until she had her hair the way she wanted. Otherwise, she just put it in a ponytail, a style perfect for her everyday life.

Today, however, she wanted her hair flipped like Jackie Kennedy's—for Robert. But May couldn't manage that without the special curlers. Why hadn't she gone to the stylist in town? The biggest day in a girl's life—her life! Spilt milk now. In the end, Beth took over, got her hair flipping gently, and then sprayed and sprayed it. Then she tucked it behind her ears and let the little pill-box hat and veil do the rest.

Fortunately, the heavy clouds that had threatened rain, had produced nothing more than a light drizzle, and when she and Jack got to the church, the drizzle, along with hairstyle worries, were long gone.

Jack held Beth's arm protectively as she lightly clutched the long, dainty lace train, the treasure of expensive material that Aunt Maudie had magically put together as a finishing touch to the simple satin gown that Beth had chosen. And before she could take a moment to catch her breath, gulp, or hesitate, Beth and Jack had made their way up the church steps and into the vestibule.

Now, with teary eyes, Beth took in the magical scene before her. Whispering, preening in compact mirrors, and admiring each other, were her specially-chosen friends, cherished by Beth for the important part each had played in her life. How beautiful they all looked, arrayed in their knee-length aqua dresses with dyed-to-match pumps and hand-made gauzy rosettes in their hair!

In the front, looking solemn, stood her maid-of-honor, Laurie. Though once dismissed by Beth as an annoyance, Laurie had been Beth's lifeline these past two years, and had come to symbolize both the crushing pain of their past and their search for happier tomorrows. Laurie, though she seemed pensive, looked beautiful...all grown up.

Just then, Beth saw Laurie's face break into a smile as Allie, next in line, giggled something into her ear.

Beth gazed now at Allie, her sister-friend. Allie was particularly striking in the soft aqua, what with her golden skin and shoulder length blonde hair. Good friends and neighbors, they had grown closer through high school as they shared similar values and an easy understanding of each other. Would Allie ever understand the gift she had given Beth when her body and soul cried in despair? For what had seemed like an interminable time, Allie had offered whatever strength she could muster to be on call to Beth. Day or night, Allie had talked, listened, prayed—whatever she could pull out of her invisible bag of tricks. Even Beth's siblings had been benefactors of Allie's warm spirit as she laughed at Jimmy's witty stories and gave sincere consideration to anything Beth's sisters had to say. Beth could find no words for the gratitude she felt to this remarkable friend.

Next was Grace, her first best friend at age 10. Grace had made an indelible mark on Beth at that innocent age when, as girls sharing the freedom of childhood, they had unabashedly declared their bond and sealed it with a blood sister ceremony. A year later, they'd even celebrated with an anniversary lunch. Now, here they were—apart due to life's developments, but with their childhood bond intact.

It was from Grace that Beth had learned that, while it was okay to be a "tomboy," it was a blast to be a girl. Grace had taught her that she could play street baseball all summer with the boys and then, after school, learn how to dance like the teenagers on "American Bandstand." In those days, they had roamed the neighborhood, putting on backyard carnivals and trekking to and from school. They were inseparable for a couple of years, until whatever it is that often afflicts girls' friendships had crept in. They had moved on to find new best friends, but Beth never forgot their early friendship.

Finally, there was Robert's sister, Agnes. Elegant with her black, shiny curls piled on top of her head, she smoothed the front of her dress and tugged at her white kid gloves. Looking at her, Beth felt the young woman was fast becoming another sister. Younger by a few years, Agnes had let Beth know that while she welcomed her into her family, she expected Beth to accept that Agnes' siblings had a shared history and nearly impenetrable inner circle. Beth fully appreciated that she would have to work hard to be part of that. Agnes would play an important role in her future, Beth knew.

Just then, breaking into her thoughts, Larry, one of Robert's groomsmen poked his head through the door, asking, "Has anyone seen Robert? He seems to have disappeared!"

"Oh, no!" Beth had cried to Jack, "Where could he be? Did he get cold feet?" But Jack gently patted her hand, assuring her there was a logical explanation. Sure enough, the same groomsman reappeared a few minutes later, laughing when he told them that Robert had been holed up in the bathroom with a nervous stomach but was better now, and on his way. Jack had soothed, "There, I told you. Who could resist my beautiful girl?"

Told that Robert had taken his place at the front of the church, one of the priests officiating had flung the big doors open. The music started, and the bridesmaids began their slow march down the center aisle.

"Dad, where's the white carpet that I'm supposed to walk on?" Beth had murmured. "Don't all brides walk on that? What could have happened?"

Beth's Aunt Maudie, who was adjusting Beth's train, spoke up. "Jack, I told you I should have been in charge of this. Beth had too much on her plate! The runner should have been ordered with the flowers. Did you do that Beth?" Beth couldn't remember.

"Now, Maudie, hush! Don't upset Beth. Honey, everything's so beautiful. Look at the flowers and candles. And just listen to Karla's voice! It is truly beautiful. I just know your mother is smiling on you today."

And, with that, Beth focused, realizing that, yes, her friend's singing was enchanting. How could all this be in her honor? Bridesmaid after bridesmaid made her way down the aisle. Finally, it was Beth and Jack's turn down the aisle, but Beth hesitated. "Wait, Dad! The organist is supposed to be playing 'Here Comes the Bride.' Why isn't he?" The heavenly music had changed, but, to Beth's consternation, though still beautiful, it was nothing she recognized.

"I don't know, honey, but don't worry. Everything is absolutely perfect, just as it should be. Enjoy it. Father's motioning for us." And with that, Jack started to walk…as did Beth. As she took her third step, Beth remembered that Karla had said that she had a special surprise for her. She knew this was it, special and beautiful. So, no white runner, no "Here Comes the Bride." But Robert was waiting for her, and she intended to go to him, marry him, and have a fantastic day. Love, life, her future with Robert—awaited her.

Later, Beth's mind was a blur as Allie shooed her and Robert into the car, then climbed into the front seat next to Robert's older brother, who had taken command of Jack's Pontiac. Beth smiled when she saw the family car had been festively decorated with the puffy, white, tissue paper flowers that her bridesmaids had made, and she laughed with delight as the streams of paper flowers flowed out behind the navy-blue car.

Best of all, everyone had joked and laughed as they exclaimed over the fact that Beth and Robert were really married.

"Unbelievable! I cannot believe you two actually did this!"

"Every time I looked at you two, you were laughing. Were you laughing at Father Flynn? You were making us all laugh, too."

"Are you going to stop kissing any time soon? You're making us both sick!"

But Robert couldn't help himself. A moment later, he broke off a kiss with "You just don't know how relieved I am. Oh, man, what a morning! The electricity isn't on at our new apartment yet, so I couldn't really see when I was getting ready. I can't believe that everybody—including you, big brother! — could tell that one of my sox is blue and the other's black! And we didn't have any food there, either. So, when we got to the church about 8:30, I started getting hungry. Someone offered to get me something, but I figured it was too late. So, instead, I got sick! Man! And, Connor…hey, man, thanks for paying the priest. When he came over to me, I thought he was just congratulating me. Then I realized he was expecting something from me. But I didn't bring any money today. I didn't know I was supposed to pay him. Geez!"

"Don't thank me. Jim handed me the envelope when he saw the priest going to you. He motioned for me to give it to you to give to him," Connor emphasized. But it was too late for that, so I just hurried over and gave it to—What's his name? Father Flynn?"

"Yeah, he's the pastor. I wonder how much Jim gave him. I'll have to thank him."

"Robert, you poor baby. We gotta get you some food soon," Beth interjected.

"It's okay, Beth. I was so darn nervous, I couldn't really have eaten anyway. But, Beth! Baby! WE DID IT! We're married!" With that, he started kissing her again and everyone started laughing.

The rest of the day passed in a blur; Beth wondered if, in the future, she would remember all the details that she had chosen so very carefully, hoping somehow, some way, they would blend together to make the special party that she had hoped would celebrate this unforgettable day.

But what if they didn't? What did she know about planning a wedding? The bridal magazines with their dazzling brides, resplendent in their stunning gowns, walking down church or garden aisles adorned in tulle and flowers of every imaginable color and variety; handsome grooms in their tuxes and tails—some even had top hats— these magazines might as well have been depicting brides and weddings on Mars. Her father had given her a modest budget, and Robert's parents had offered their backyard for the reception site. That was what she had worked with.

A few months before, when she had gone to pick Laurie up from school, Beth had walked over to the church hall and peeked in. Cavernous and dark, the room had seemed tired and…sad. Beth took a moment, and fantasized how, after the wedding ceremony in the adjacent church, she and Robert would walk into this room. What would she see?

Not the bride, all dressed in white…but little Bethie who had eaten pancake breakfasts here with her family as Jack cooked with the other dads and Anna chatted with the other moms. Bethie who'd gobbled down glazed donuts and watery hot chocolate after attending First Friday Mass each month. Bethie…who'd tap-danced with Grace for Knights of Columbus socials after Jack had coerced them with his profuse compliments and Anna had pledged pretty costumes….

In that moment, Beth had wrestled with herself: How am I doing this without her? How can I look forward to a day this special, knowing she won't be there? I don't see how…. Think Beth, what are my guts telling me? Yes, my body and soul ache, but what can I do? I have to move forward. I feel like Sisyphus—now I'M pushing this boulder up an impossibly steep hill. I think I can't do it, but I try anyway…and it rolls back down. My body cries, "No! Don't make me take another step! I can't, I just can't!" but, despite the tears streaming down my cheeks and the gaping hole in my heart, I get behind the boulder and push again…and again. I AM going to do this, but I know now I'm not going to do it here, surrounded by memories of my childhood…and HER.

Right then, Beth had made up her mind: the church hall represented childhood and her primary family, with her mother at the center. With Anna gone, Beth needed a place free of so many painful, poignant memories. And so, Beth had agreed to the Dolans' offer of their backyard.

Bursting with all kinds of flowers in myriad hues of pink and coral, the back yard and its immaculately sparkling pool set the stage for a brilliant, sunny afternoon. And the Dolans' den—which opened onto the patio—welcomed the wedding party and their guests with its warm and cheery ambiance. The caterer had set up tables draped in festive pastel tablecloths; one held trays of finger sandwiches, chosen by Beth because they reminded her of those her mother had made for the church's women's club. Another table held a shiny silver fountain serving pink champagne—an extravagance, particularly since the wedding couple and all of their party were under age for alcohol.

On this, though, the Dolans had insisted: a little alcohol would only enhance the party, and Beth and Robert had happily conceded. Now, toasting to their future, Robert's arm crossing Beth's arm, the photographer memorialized the moment. A little later, he caught them laughing as they fed each other bites of wedding cake, strawberry filling oozing out between the layers. And, in a heart-rending moment, Jack held Beth's hand in a family photo with the Dolans on Robert's side and Aunt Maudie next to Jack. Then, there they were, in an unguarded moment, shoes off, sitting together, newlyweds smiling into each other's eyes. Finally, in one last moment, Beth played the diva, vamping in her honeymoon clothes, ready to dash off with her leading man.

Beth waved at their friends and family who'd gathered on the Dolans' lawn, as Robert drove Jack's car, white streamers flying from the bumper, "Just Married!" written in shaving cream on their back window. "Now what?" Beth wondered out loud. And Robert had put his arm around her and smiled at her. "Now, we get the heck out of Dodge, Bethie. The wedding day is over. We're married. WE ARE MARRIED!" A few blocks away from his parents' house, he pulled the car over.

"Oh, man! I can't believe that is finally over!" He slumped a little in his seat, sighing and looking straight ahead.

"Robert, what do you mean? Didn't you enjoy our wedding day?"

"It's not that, Beth. I've been so nervous since I woke up this morning. I haven't been able to eat much of anything all day. I've just been so glad you were with me."

"It's our wedding day!! Where else would I be?" She laughed. "Oh, I feel so bad for you. I loved almost every minute of the whole day. I told myself that I wasn't going to let anything stop me from enjoying everything! We're going to remember this all our lives, Robert. Wow." Beth looked out the front window, too.

"I know. I can't exactly describe it. I'm so happy we finally did this. And everything was perfect...because of you. You did all this, Beth, you planned it, made it happen...along with everything else you do. And your dad and brothers brought all those chairs from your church over. Wow! It was so great of them! "

"Thanks for the credit, honey, but remember: your parents gave us their home for the reception. Everything was beautiful. I'm so glad they wanted the champagne fountain! What a treat that was! Oh, Robert, it was a perfect day." Beth leaned into Robert and snuggled her head into his shoulder, as he squeezed her tightly. Then he kissed her head, straightened up, and looked down at her. Sensing a change in mood, she looked up expectantly.

"Yeah, and it's going to be a perfect night. Let's go get our honeymoon started." With that, Robert put the car into gear and eased into traffic.

17 CALL IT MARRIAGE…

Take me home, country roads,
To the place I belong
West Virginia, Mountain Mama
Take me home,
Country roads…

~Bill Danoff, Taffy Nivert and John Denver

Beth walked through the darkening campus. Fall seemed to be arriving early—it was only mid-October, but, already, the breeze cut through her light jacket.

She pulled her books tightly to her chest, trying to hide behind them. Walking down the narrow concrete path that led to the parking lot, she smiled at the hues of brilliant oranges, fierce pinks and opulent purples that filled the sky. She had recently learned that beautiful sunsets are usually the result of smog. She didn't care. It was beautiful, and mirrored her delight as she scanned the parking lot for her car. Almost there. Then she spotted it. Yes! The '57 Chevy's bronze gleamed in the midst of all the ordinary cars. With relief, Beth climbed in. Books and purse on the passenger seat, she drew a satisfied breath and started the engine.

On the freeway, she adjusted the radio dial to their usual station—usual that is, if a ball game wasn't intruding—and soon, she was crooning along with John Denver: "…And driving down the road I get a feeling that I should have been home yesterday, yesterday…."

At last, she could leave behind thoughts of snooty professors and upcoming papers. She was heading to her home and her man. She loved their tiny, furnished, one-bedroom apartment. And, if she arrived before Robert got home from his coaching job, Beth would turn on the stereo and put on a couple of their favorite albums—maybe Smokey Robinson and Carlos Santana. Friday night. No studying tonight for either of them. They had made that deal: unless it was finals or some other impending disaster time, Friday night was date night: play music, eat dinner, play Scrabble or another game, then watch "Mission: Impossible" and "I Spy," followed by love-making. Yes! Fun, freedom!

The months since their wedding had flown by, and, to Beth, being married already felt so right. She knew most of her close friends did not envy her—even the ones in serious relationships. They'd said they'd rather wait until they graduated college to get married, so that, at the least, their husbands would have good jobs, and they wouldn't have to sacrifice nice things. Mary Ann had said straight out, "I plan on having an airy, unfurnished apartment with modern appliances. I already know what kind of furniture I want—something modern, completely different from my parents' heavy, dark set with the plastic coverings." Others, including a couple of her closest girlfriends, had asked why marry—even after graduation? They didn't want to get tied down for at least a few years. What's the rush? We'll have degrees. I want to see what's out there for me. It was the '60's, after all. Beth remembered feeling much the same way once upon a time.

Joe had tried more than once to convince Beth and Robert to join him on a trip through Italy and France, where they would stay in hostels and travel for a month. In a letter, he'd urged Robert to consider it. "Don't you realize we're living in an exciting time of change? Did Beth tell you about Timothy Leary? We need to 'Seize the day! Carpe Diem!' You and Beth should get married next summer. Come with me this summer; we can pool our money, live on the cheap. You can come home and work after that. You'll never regret seeing Europe while you're young and carefree!"

So, Robert had half-heartedly talked to Beth. "I suppose it would be fun, especially traveling around with Joe. But how is he doing it financially? My parents have told me they're not giving me any more money for college. Their deal is we get the first year of school paid for and, after that, we work for it. If you and I postpone the wedding and go to Europe, I'd have to transfer schools, which means I'd be going to school with you. That's good, but Beth, I'd have to live with my parents! I can NOT do that. No way! But, without doing that, I'd never be able to make enough money after the trip to go back to Santa Barbara. Anyway, with our part-time jobs, I don't see how we'd have much of anything for the plane over there and then hostels and trains. Oh, man, Bethie. What do you think?"

When Robert read Joe's letter to Beth over the phone, she had quietly asked him what he thought about postponing the wedding to travel with Joe. She hadn't voiced any reaction. Now, with Robert's comments and question, she tried to maintain control.

"Well, the fact is, I can't go, and unless that's where you are, I don't even want to go. Anyway, I still have to think of my family. Joe doesn't get that."

"You don't think your dad would let you go?"

"It's not that. He'd probably want me to go—with you, that is. Dad and I talked about this, and I said going to Europe wouldn't excite me unless I went with you. He understood. But the only way that can happen is if we postpone the wedding for a year. What do you think of that?"

"I don't like it. We have a plan for the summer, and it includes getting married. That's what I want. What's the big deal about going to Europe, anyway?"

"I know! And I'm glad you said that about getting married. I mean, in a way, postponing the wedding would make me feel better about—not better, but, well, not so guilty about—Laurie and Margaret…but it's hard being far away from you during the school year."

"Okay, then. It's settled. The wedding is still on!"

Beth and Robert had gotten married without Joe, and he'd followed through and gone to Europe. He'd returned with colorful stories spilling into every conversation it seemed. How he'd shared a hostel room with a 70-year-old woman. How it seemed like "everyone" had smoked pot. How he'd been in the Pantheon during a thunderstorm. Did we know there's a 30-foot opening at the top of it? But he didn't get wet, even though the rain poured down. And had we ever eaten gelato? He had the most deliciously creamy gelato while admiring the Trevi Fountain. He'd pretended to be a poor, starving artist as he sipped coffee while sitting at an outdoor Parisian cafe. And on and on. He had asked about the wedding, but Beth knew Joe well enough to see he'd only been half-listening. As far as Beth was concerned, Joe had had his exciting adventure, and that had ended, while, for her and Robert, the adventures had only just begun.

October 15, 1967

Waiting for Robert to get home. Already changed my clothes and looked in the fridge for something for dinner and came up with fish sticks and french fries, and maybe some cottage cheese and pineapple. I've got Smokey on the record player, so here I am, looking forward to relaxing together, a married couple on a Friday night. I was just thinking about Joe going to Europe last summer. He seemed to think R and I would regret getting married instead of going traveling, but I don't at all. Though he couldn't have understood, I didn't want to go. I just know I would have been homesick, missing my family and worrying up a storm!

Instead of telling amusing stories about gelato, my husband (!!!) and I are living in a little apartment with no dishwasher. But, you know what? Big deal. Robert and I get to be together all the time, come and go as we want, and very importantly, make love when we want. Robert can be so silly and sweet. He carried me over the threshold the day we actually moved in here, after our honeymoon. He said the hotel of our first night together counted in its own way, but everyone did that. This is our first real home; and it blew him away. He just had to carry me into the place where we would begin to be a family!

Yes, I do still cook and clean for Dad and the others, but I don't do it every day and night. Dad does much more of the grocery shopping, too. Last year, at this time, I would've driven home to Dad's house, in Dad's car, to talk to Dad about what Dad wanted to talk about. I love Dad, but I really love that I just drove home from school in our car—Robert's and mine—to our apartment, thinking about our plans!

For the last two years, thoughts of my family flooded my head all the time, drowning out MY life—MY plans, MY dreams, MY future…just ME, period! Now, with Robert, I feel like I have that. Do I still worry about them? Yes! But now, I can breathe a little...maybe even a lot!

As muddled and confused as I was last year, I knew I had to DO something—make some kind of change—to survive, to move forward. It was clear—if only to me! —that the options some friends were choosing weren't really options for me, what with my complicated situation. Instead, I gave myself a different choice: make a life with Robert now or say goodbye to him forever, and stay home with Dad and the girls. I could help them live their lives, or I could live mine. How sad! How gloomy! I know I did this for me, and I will live with that choice, trying not to hate myself for choosing something fun, frivolous…something for me. I guess to other people marriage is anything but a fun and frivolous choice. But to me, it was, and I'm glad and relieved, at least for now. Just so long as I can keep from feeling guilty. And just so long as I can still be there for the others—especially Laurie—when they need me.

A few months earlier, on the summer morning Beth and Robert had driven to their in-service training for their jobs at Parks and Recreation, Beth's nerves roiled her stomach. The third time she said maybe she should go to the bathroom one more time before they left, Robert said, "No! You're just nervous, Beth! They'll have bathrooms there. We don't want to be late for this meeting. I want to get a seat."

"Of course, you're right, Mr. Maturity, but what am I supposed to do with this stomach?"

"Where are your Rolaids?"

"I never buy my own. I steal them from Dad's dresser. Guess that's gonna change." I am nervous, Robert. I wish we could have a park together."

"I'm just glad they're letting us both work in the same department."

"I know you're right. I wonder how much Uncle Ralph had to do with us even getting these jobs."

It wasn't lost on Beth that Robert had repeatedly been through the processes of applying, interviewing, and actually starting a job. And what jobs had she gotten on her own? None. There had been one, right after she turned 16; her mom had seen a sign in a cafe window, saying "Help Wanted" and made Beth inquire about it. That had lasted just a few weeks. Then there'd been another job, during the summer between her junior and senior years. This time, thanks to her mom and dad, there'd been no application to fill out, no interview—Beth had known and liked Mr. Chapman all her life. There'd also been no pressure to perform; she'd gone into his insurance office periodically throughout the summer and done a little filing. Then, right after senior year, she'd done some bookkeeping for her dad's accountant, Betty Gross. Beth had hated that job, and had known immediately that she was awful at it. Betty had snickered about her for a week or so, then told Jack she was out of work for Beth.

This time, though, Beth wanted to be different. She knew her uncle had made inquiries for her and Robert, but it was clear they still had to earn the jobs. That had meant applications and interviews. When she'd gotten the phone call telling her when to report for "duty," Beth had been relieved and happy. So, in mid-June, the young married couple had driven to their first team meeting, where they would get their park assignments.

Arriving on time, Beth had made one last run to the bathroom. On her way back into the main room, she'd grabbed a donut and sat down next to Robert just as the Director of Recreation had formally called the new recreation leaders to order. He'd begun by welcoming everyone, and then immediately had got down to business, calling out names of the new employees who would work together throughout the city.

Beth had felt her body flush with an inner fire when she saw the pretty blonde, Ruth, who would be Robert's partner at his park. As he'd taken his place at Ruth's side, Beth had seen them smile at each other, whispering a little. Then, she'd heard her name called to come forward to meet her partner, Gary, and it was her turn to take her place beside a handsome guy who grinned hello. Let Robert ponder that for a while!

Immediately, however, Beth had reminded herself that the game of jealousy she had sometimes played in the past must be held in check, no matter how difficult that might prove to be. As a married couple entering the world of work together, they must leave behind adolescent possessiveness and jealousy. Can I do it? Beth had asked herself. Self-confident Robert surely could—if he even felt any threat.

But now, in their apartment, just the two of them for their Friday night date—well, who cared about jobs, school, other boys, other girls?

Early the next morning, Robert had practically jumped out of bed, declaring, "I need to shower and get going!"

"Why? What's the rush?" Beth stretched and smiled at Robert, "Don't you want to stay in bed and snuggle?"

"Can't. It's Saturday, sleepyhead! I've got to open the facilities at Wilderness Park by 9 for the youth basketball program. Don't you have to take your sister to her lessons?"

Beth groaned. "Of course, I do. And Dad'll probably want me to do the grocery shopping for him, too. I just hope I can get Margaret and Laurie to do some vacuuming and dishes. Oh! And Margaret's got bowling today. Oh, well! I guess I'll join you in the shower." Robert shot her a smile as he dropped his pajama bottoms.

A few hours later, Beth walked up the steps of the big, red porch and through the door of her family home. "Laurie!" she called, "I'm here to take you to your lesson! Are you ready?" When she got no response, she walked back to the bedroom that, until recently, she'd shared with her sisters. There sat Laurie, on her unmade bed, strumming away on her guitar and singing earnestly. When she saw Beth, she stopped abruptly.

"Oh, is it time?" Clearly, Laurie had been crying.

"What is it? Did something happen?"

"I don't know. Everything. Why does everybody around here ignore me? And now Chili hasn't called. Even he's ignoring me," she sobbed. "I miss Mom!"

Beth, unsure what to do, made her way to Margaret's bed, directly opposite Laurie's. She sat down, leaning in to where Laurie sat. "I know. I do, too. But what about what we talked about? She's always with us, watching over us." Beth found herself gulping out words that she wanted so badly to believe. "Have you been talking to her, asking her to help? I know Dad's probably not much help—"

"Dad? You must be joking or crazy. I can't talk to him! I don't even know what I'd say. The only thing we ever talk about—and I mean ever!—is what we should fix for dinner, and that's only if you're not doing it! He doesn't care about me."

"I know that's how it seems, but he always asks me about you, and—"

"Why doesn't he ask ME about me?"

"I guess he's just too wrapped up in his own worries—"

"You don't have to defend him."

"I'm not trying to, it's just that I don't want you to have the wrong idea—"

"Beth, you don't get it. Let's just get going." Laurie stood up, stuffing her guitar into its case. She grabbed some tissue from the nightstand. "These lessons are the only thing I have."

As Beth drove, she tried to get Laurie talking again. It had been just over two years since their mother had died. During that time, Laurie had let her hair grow long and straight, like Mia Farrow on "Peyton Place." Also, like the show's protagonist, Laurie at first had seemed to hide behind it, so that she looked perpetually downcast. But, then slowly, it had become clear that

Laurie was warming to the nun who taught her seventh grade class, and that she was responding to her friends. Little by little, she'd even started doing things Beth considered normal for 13-year-old girls, like talking on the phone.

The next year, when Laurie was in the eighth grade, her school had needed a coach to field the girls' athletic program, and Laurie's teacher had asked Beth. "I'm not an athlete," she'd told Robert. "I wasn't any good at sports when I was in 7th and 8th grade. I just played to be with the other girls. As I remember, it was a pretty miserable time."

"C'mon, Beth, It'll be something fun for you to do with Laurie. I'll help you," he'd insisted. I have some books I used when I started coaching the boys at St. Paul's. You'll get to be outside, and make a little money for the wedding,"

With that, Robert had convinced her.

"Yeah, and I guess it'll give Laurie and me something fun to talk about. I can get to know some of her classmates, or at least listen to them talk, and learn a little about what's going on in her world." As luck would have it, Laurie had enjoyed and even excelled at the CYO sports.

Then, in the middle of eighth grade, a crush of Laurie's—Carlos, nicknamed Chili—had turned into a boyfriend.

Now, a month into high school, Laurie already had an older boy interested in her as well. Beth saw these as good signs for Laurie and wanted to cheer her on, but Laurie seemed to resent Beth's obvious interest. Once again, Beth found herself confused by Laurie. How could she be so different from the young teen that Beth had been—boy crazy and eager to talk about it?! Beth reminded herself to tread cautiously.

"So, what's up with Chili? Are you guys having a fight?"

"I didn't think so, but now I'm not sure. It's hard having him go to a different school. The other day I told him that Alex had helped me with my locker. So, then he wanted to know who Alex is, how I know him, what I think of him, and on, and on. Maybe he was mad—I'm not sure."

"What did you tell him?"

"I told him the truth! Alex is just a friend that I talk to sometimes. His older brother is a friend of my sister—you know, you."

Beth thought briefly about the boy whom she had dated a few times in junior year. As Beth recalled, everyone loved George, a fun, friendly guy. But though they liked each other, she and George as a couple never materialized. For Beth, George was definitely not boyfriend material. "Yeah, I know. Does he know Alex is older than you?"

"He does now. I don't know why that seems to make a difference. It's crazy. I'm so confused."

"So…does that mean maybe you do like Alex as more than a friend?"

"I don't know! I still like Chili. I don't want him to think anything's wrong. What should I do?"

"Welcome to the world of boys! Chili's your first boyfriend; there will be others. Do you think Alex likes you?"

"I don't know. He's a year older than me."

"So? He's paying you a lot of attention lately if he doesn't like you. But you are just a freshman…and since he's a sophomore and might be driving soon, you should really take it slow, if you know what I mean. You're very mature looking for your age."

"Oh, Beth, God! I know what you're thinking. Just don't go there. Please! I'm not you. And don't say anything to Dad, whatever you do! I mean it."

"I won't. Oh. We're almost there. Okay, quick—should I go in or wait in the car for you?"

"You always go in. What's different?"

"Well, it's different now that I'm married. You know Don was pretty flirty with me, asked me to go hear him play that gig last spring. When I told him I was getting married, he acted all weird, and now, at the last few lessons, he seems aloof."

"I don't know! Just pretend everything's fine and read your book. You're married. What do you care?" Then, Laurie slammed the car door and stomped up the steps.

"Wait, I'm coming!" Beth grabbed her purse and book and rushed after her sister.

After the usual pleasantries, Laurie focused on Don's directions, carefully following his fingers as he strummed on his guitar. Watching her sister mimic her teacher almost flawlessly, Beth took note of Laurie's delicate beauty. Her hair, brushing her shoulders in silky straight lines, framed Laurie's face. Was it just a year ago her face had been round, babyish? -- because it sure had softened into a gentle oval. It suddenly struck Beth that, Laurie resembled the Ivory Girl from the TV commercials: young and energetic, with clear skin, and a smile that could bewitch anyone.

Beth knew she drove Laurie crazy with her constant questions. She also knew, married or not, she was still just a kid herself—so how could she help Laurie through her adolescent confusion? She loved her so much, and worried about her constantly.

Still, Beth had to admit that, along with pride in her little sister's confidence and beauty, there was a little seed of jealousy. She hoped Laurie would never see it. Beth wanted nothing more than for her sister to bloom and be happy. Fortunately, Beth thought, the pride she felt in her sister overshadowed any envy.

On the way home, Laurie strummed her guitar awkwardly in the front seat. Clearly in a better mood, she bubbled to Beth, "Did you hear Don play **'Malagueña'**—wasn't that awesome? He thinks I can pick it up quickly, but I can't see ever being able to play it as well as he does. Still, isn't it neat that he thinks that?"

"You're right. He does play it beautifully, but I couldn't get over how carefully you were following him. I think you WILL have it down in a short time."

"I'm going to start practicing on it right away. Oh, heck! I promised Patty I'd come over this afternoon. I haven't seen her in a while."

"How does she like the teachers at Roosevelt? Is everything going okay for her?"

"I think school's okay, but she said her parents are fighting again. I think that's what she wants to talk about."

"That's too bad. You think you'll go over there then?"

"Is it okay? I mean, do you need me to help you shop? I'll vacuum later."

"No problem. I think Dad's going to do the shopping on his way home from work today, although he's supposed to pick Margaret up from bowling. I'll see what's going on. When you go to Patty's, I might head on over to the park where Robert's working today."

"Are you guys going to eat with us tonight? I hope so."

"Sure. I'll ask Dad to pick up some burgers to barbecue. What do ya think?"

"Yeah. That'd be great! I'll ask Patty to come. Maybe we can hit the volleyball around later with Robert."

"Far out, Laurie! I love that idea!"

Later that evening, after the burgers and volleyball and coaxing Laurie into playing her guitar for them, Beth and Robert settled into their apartment. After a few moments' silence, Beth shyly broached a new topic for them: her health.

"Robert, honey, I'm kinda worried about something."

"Something new?" he teased.

"Yeah, when you touch my body, sometimes, it hurts."

"Really? Since when? Where?"

"Well, right here," and Beth touched her breast. "I've noticed it for the past few days, maybe a week."

"Is it in just that one spot?"

"Now that you mention it, I guess they both hurt. Not hurt, exactly—it's…they feel tender. Do you think I should go to the doctor? I haven't had my period in a while."

"Maybe I should call my mom and ask her what she thinks."

Inwardly, Beth cringed.

Mrs. Dolan has been so frosty to me ever since the engagement dinner. Why? Even with the wedding, she never once called to ask how the plans were going, or if she could help. She even backed out of hosting the rehearsal dinner. She said it wasn't proper wedding etiquette to invite Aunt Maudie's family—but that was so mean! How could I not invite my aunt?!

She has to see how much Aunt Maudie loves Robert *and has helped us…especially me—for sure, after the accident, then, with the wedding. She asked me again and again what she could do, I kept saying "nothing." I didn't really know what I was doing. So stupid of me to put her off, thinking I could pull it all off alone. I thought she'd be bossy, and I wouldn't know how to handle it. Turns out, I could have used her help—bossiness or not.*

At least I let her take me shopping for wedding dresses. Good thing! I know she thought some of them were so pretty—and I know some were—but they were so expensive. And I just felt ridiculous in how big and full they were. I felt kind of swallowed up. I guess they didn't make me feel like me.

But then, Aunt Maudie said that, if I wanted, she would make my dress. Wow! Helping me find a pattern and material that I liked. How sweet she was during all those fittings. I couldn't believe that was me looking so sophisticated in the simple, soft satin that draped snugly on my body, especially when she got the train done.

I remember the first time I saw all those yards of beautiful lace trailing that slim, elegant gown! That was a moment I won't forget.

And then she helped me find the rich aqua crepe for the bridesmaid dresses. My favorite color! And that material…it just made those dresses…and, of course, her idea for my "Jackie" style hat with the veil, especially for Robert*—and the girls' veils as well.*

Aunt Maudie just thought of everything! I would never have thought of a "going away" outfit, and nighties for the honeymoon, either. Oh, and the corset-thingie! I'm so skinny and flat, and that thing made me look like I had at least a bit of a figure.

I know Robert *said his mom thought Susie should be the flower girl. I just love that little girl. I already feel like she's another little sister. In a way, I wish I had chosen her. But I had to choose Sophia because I was her mom's flower girl. I still remember when Millie and Bud asked me to be in their wedding. I was so excited!*

Aunt Maudie smiled the biggest smile when she heard me say I wanted her granddaughter to be in my wedding, creating a family circle. I felt Mom smiling at that, too. We needed a bit of family significance, what with our main member missing. At least, I know I did, and I think Dad felt the same way. After all, he paid for the wedding—and ended up hosting the rehearsal dinner, too. Oh, well…Mrs. Dolan is my mother in law, now, and, like it or not, I'll just have to hope things improve over time.

"Sure, it couldn't hurt to ask."

When he got off the phone, Robert told Beth his mom was going to make an appointment for Beth—with Mrs. Dolan's doctor. "Guess what she thinks?"

"What? Tell me!"

"She thinks you might be pregnant!"

"Oh, my gosh! Did she really say that? Oh Robert, what do you think?" At that, Robert raised his eyebrows, smiled and shrugged his shoulders, "What do I think? I think it would be great! Just think, we might be having a baby!" And he held out his arms to Beth.

Later, in the shower, Beth tried to fathom what Robert's mother had actually said about her symptoms. "How did your mom really sound about us possibly having a baby?"

Robert replied that she sounded "fine."

Beth had pressed him. "Yeah, but did she sound excited?"

"No," he said, "but nobody knows anything yet." Beth thought he sounded irritated. His voice had that, "I called for advice. She gave it to me, even promised to get us into her doctor. What more do you want?" tone to it. He had been grateful for his mother's help. He left it at that.

Beth let her mind wander back to her earlier train of thought. For a while, after the accident, Mrs. Dolan had called Beth to ask how she was doing. She had seemed genuinely interested. Once, she had asked Beth to drive her to the airport, and they had talked and laughed non-stop. Grateful for the attention, Beth's ease had grown, and she'd looked forward to the invitations for dinner or the occasional drive to visit Robert. It had seemed Mrs. Dolan enjoyed her company, and Beth had responded with enthusiasm.

When her confusion about her life had begun to affect Robert, however, Beth had noticed a shift in his mother's attitude toward her. And when he'd told his mother about their engagement, the "Ice Age" had set in. Though they had offered their home for the reception, Robert's parents had still made it clear they were less than eager for the upcoming wedding.

For Beth, her relationship with the Dolans presented a new set of challenges. As Robert's parents, they would, she'd assumed, treat her as someone special; somewhat like her dad treated Robert. But, so far, at least, they hadn't. Instead, Beth felt a decided chill from both of them. And so, when Robert had recently announced, "They want you to call them Mom and Dad," Beth had been flabbergasted.

"Really? How do you know? I don't think they even like me."

"My dad told me the other day. I guess they see you as another daughter now."

"But Robert, I just told you, they don't seem to even like me, let alone see me as a daughter. Maybe your father wasn't serious."

"No, Beth, he meant it. He said they had called their in-laws Mom and Dad—so you should, too."

"Does that mean you're going to start calling my dad…DAD?!"

"It would be kind of weird, since I worked for him and already call him by his name. But, if he wants me to, I will."

Robert got them some cookies; then turned on the TV. Beth felt distracted, her mind a whirl of confusion.

Oh, good little Robert, who always does everything right. I just want to scream, "Your parents are nothing like mine! My mom would never have ignored or been cold to ANYONE, let alone someone married to her daughter. All my friends and boyfriends over the years loved Mom!"
And Dad! Good grief! He thinks Robert walks on water.

I don't see why Robert is so close to his parents. I can't believe how his mom treated him the day we came over after our honeymoon. As soon as he'd let us into the house with his key, there she was, all righteous, saying, "What are you doing, Robert? This is no longer your home. You have your own home. Give me back your key." Poor Robert! He was stunned! We didn't stay long, and he just about cried on the way home. I said maybe she was just in a bad mood, but that didn't help, because he'd thought she'd be happy to see him.

For Pete's sake! The night before, when I couldn't find my key, I'd climbed through the living room window, then unlocked the front door for Robert. We'd pulled out the couch and slept on it. In the morning, as Dad had walked through the living room on his way to the kitchen, I heard him say, "Oh! The kids are back. Isn't that swell!"

What a difference! I don't think I'll ever be able to call the Dolans "Mom and Dad." And how would Dad feel to hear me say those words to people who're not my real mom and dad? I just won't talk to them unless they're looking at me.

October 23, 1967

Could it really be? So soon? We just got married a few months ago, didn't we? What if it's not true, and something is really wrong with me? I could have cancer. That would just be great! First, I do something so terrible and marry her son; then, I get a really terrible sickness and screw up his life but good. The Dolans would really hate me then. And what about my poor family? What if I died, too? First Mom. Then me.

But what if Mrs. D's right and I am going to have a baby? Should I be happy? I think I'm too young for this! Who would I turn to for advice? I can't think of anyone I go to school with that's got a baby.

Well, wait. I do have Molly. Toby must be six months or so by now. I could probably ask her about it. Man, I have no idea what I'd do or feel. I can't imagine asking Aunt Maudie a bunch of questions. How embarrassing! And Mrs. D? No way!

Oh, Mom, I need you so much. If I am pregnant, I pray you'll be with me. How will I do it without you? I can only imagine how you would be with a little grandbaby. It makes me cry to picture it, but I've seen pictures of you holding one of your babies, one of us, and I know if that was your grandbaby, your smile would light up the universe. Oh, man…

Robert really was so sweet about it. I'm sure he would be a great dad. But I just didn't expect it so soon. Maybe I'm not pg, but, if not, then what's wrong with me? Oh, this is plain weird. This appointment is going to be embarrassing. I've never been to a doctor for anything serious without Mom. Is Mrs. D going to be there too??!!

Oh, holy hell!

18 TURMOIL ANEW

To everything (turn, turn, turn)
There is a season (turn, turn, turn)
And a time to every purpose under Heaven…

The Book of Ecclesiastes; adapted by Pete Seeger

Beth awoke in a sweat, heart pounding. She sat up, her hands to her face wet with tears. Moments before, she had been hysterical as she watched her mother, dressed in heels, a hat and a long, beige coat, move quickly away from her,. She'd gotten a glimpse of Anna in a crowd. "Mom?" she had murmured. Anna turned toward her and cocked her head, a little smile on her face, but as Beth had tried to run after her, Anna moved further away. Beth found herself held back by throngs of people as she cried out "Mom! Mom! Wait! Wait for me!" And just like that, her mother was gone. That's when she opened her eyes and realized that she had been dreaming. But it felt so real. Beth gasped for air. Why? Why did she leave me? And why was she smiling? Was she glad to leave me? No! How could that be?

"What's wrong, Beth? Are you okay? Bad dream?"

Robert's voice brought her fully back to her present, and anchored her there, with him. "Yes." Beth fell into the comfort of his arms and, for a while, lay there, afraid of sleep, afraid to dream. Slowly, the soft rhythm of Robert's breathing soothed her, and she found herself releasing the paralyzing fear.

The next morning, she awoke to what had to be the stirrings of the little being inside of her. Beth laughed, expecting to see alien bumps move across her stomach. This morning's movements gave her the distinct impression of a baby yawning into a great big stretch.

"Robert! Honey! You've got to feel this! I think I can feel our little one's hand or foot. Here, right here. And she took his hand, placing it on her stomach. "Can you feel it?

"Are you kidding? This kid is strong! I don't know if that's a foot or a fist, but whatever, this is one solid kid!" And he sat down on the bed, his face half-full of shaving cream. Clearly, he didn't mind the interruption from his morning ablutions before school. "All I want to do right now is watch this little guy make his moves."

"Now, c'mon, what if this little guy is a little girl?"

"That's fine. But I just have a feeling that it's a boy and a very coordinated boy at that. I can just see him now. He'll be the best at everything!"

Beth didn't really care if she had a boy or a girl…or, for that matter, if he or she turned out to be "coordinated." All she cared about was that her baby arrived in this world healthy and happy. As she moved to pull herself up, Robert put his arm around her for support.

"You're starting to look like you're carrying a baby watermelon inside, for real," he laughed.

"I know. Jeez, I definitely don't look like myself anymore." At that, the phone rang, and Robert moved toward the dresser to answer it; after a quick hello, he handed it to Beth.

"Hi, Laurie. No, I was awake. The baby's making some big moves this morning. No ignoring this kid. Sure. I'll pick you up. I don't have class today. Where, exactly? When? Good, I was wondering what I was going to do all day—it's so boring, just waiting for the baby. No, I don't mind. We can stop on our way home to give Barb her homework. Then, maybe you can help me make dinner. Of course, after you do your homework. Good grief! I'll peel the potatoes! No big deal. I'll see you at three by the flagpole in front."

"What's up with Laurie? Carpool problems?"

"Yeah, Barb's sick; her mom's not driving today. Dad's going to drop our little high-schooler off on his way to work now, and she wants me to pick her up after school. Geez, I ask her to help with dinner, you'd think I was a slave driver. Will I see you, maybe? I'll be there about three."

"Maybe. But I'll probably be hustling to get out to practice. I'll see if I can run out front for a minute. Don't be mad if I don't make it."

"Okay. But you better not be flirting with any of those cute high school girls!"

"Give me a break. I have no idea what you're talking about. What're you going to do today?"

"I'm going to Aunt Maudie's. She's got some baby stuff she wants to give me. I guess they're hand-me-downs from my cousin's kids. She says they're neutral, but, just like you, she's sure I'm going to have a boy. I'll probably have lunch with her and stick around and talk, then head over to school for Laurie. You're meeting me at Dad's for dinner, right?"

"Wouldn't miss it! But we can't stay too late. I've got homework for college classes and planning work for teaching classes!"

Later, driving over to her aunt's, Beth remembered her dream. Her mother—was she going to haunt Beth? Not for the first time, she awoke in tears, feeling abandoned. In this dream, she recalled how Anna had smiled at her but had moved away from her in the crowd. Was she being pulled away by the crowd? No, Beth knew in her gut that Anna had deliberately moved away from her. Why was she smiling? Nausea seized Beth—or was it morning sickness—and she fought for control. A horn honked, and, realizing the red light had turned green, she lurched forward. Now dizzy, Beth gritted her teeth and tried to take a few deep breaths. Stop. Pull the car over. Up ahead, she could make out a liquor store, and soon she was stopped in the parking lot. Moving the driver's seat back, she rolled the window down for a blast of fresh air, and plopped back, taking deep breaths. The baby pushed hard against her belly, but she didn't feel any pain.

Relieved, she started the car, eased out of the parking lot into the late morning traffic, and turned on the radio and, without thinking, sang along to the Byrds: "…and a time to every purpose under Heaven / A time to be born, a time to die / A time to plant, a time to reap / A time to kill, a time to heal / A time to laugh, a time to weep…."

With the first few lines of the second stanza, she began crying softly as she sang, but with the last line, she found her body shaking hard. She knew she had to pull herself together before she got to her aunt's. Aunt Maudie wasn't big on freely expressing emotions. Beth's stolid Midwestern father's stolid Midwestern sister was better with humor and an occasional outburst of temper than with tears. This time, Beth pulled over on a residential street, switched off the radio and again, rolled down the window.

Oh, God. What's wrong with me? My heart's racing. I feel like I'm about to jump out of my skin! It was just a dream. I need to shake it off. I should be so happy right now, not acting like a neurotic psycho. I am happy, gosh darn it! I'm so lucky—gorgeous husband, baby on the way. We are so excited! Well, Robert is, for sure. I'm excited but nervous, too. I know why I keep crying. It's the darn song. It just always reminds me of Mom. But it says, "There's a time for weeping." This isn't it. Yet, here I am.

Why do I keep thinking about why I got married so young? Did I really rush into marriage? I don't want to feel that way.

Every bride gets the jitters. I bet people wonder how I could leave Dad and my sisters. HOW COULD I? But they seem to be doing okay. Oh, man, I don't know what I did. I definitely made a big decision without even telling anyone my doubts. Is that why I keep getting choked up? Well…I did tell Laurie, but she didn't know what I was talking about any more than I did. But how can anyone be totally sure? And if I had told anyone I had doubts, they would have told me to wait.

People were saying that anyway. When I picture Robert, I realize how much I love him. I'm crazy about him! It seems I love him more every day. Doesn't that mean getting married was a *good thing for me?*

I couldn't have broken up with Robert; I just couldn't! So, what else could I do? Wait until we graduated—two more years of a long-distance romance. Two more years of confusion and sadness. Trying to write each other letters and talking on the phone for a few minutes once or twice a week. Getting scolded when we talked too long. Driving back and forth two hundred miles once in a while on weekends? That was all so crazy.

And what about two more years of cooking for six, making dollar-sized hamburgers and gross, sticky meat loaf and going to stupid meat markets and grocery stores?

And then there was lonely me, spending so much time with Joe, feeling feelings that seemed like more than just close friends. I knew I was lonely for Robert, then Joe would look at me a certain way that tempted me a few times. But besides being my best friend, he's one of Robert's best friends, too.

Why am I even thinking about that? What's wrong with me?! I love Robert. So much! Our relationship is so great, especially now that we're married and together. And we're going to have a baby. So, what's going on with me? And what does any of this have to do with the dream? I just need to snap out of it. It's probably my hormones going crazy. Isn't that what the book says happens to a woman's body when she's PG?

With that, Beth sat up, wiped her face with her sleeve, started the engine and continued on to her aunt's. Later that evening, Jack asked her, "Say, Beth, can you take Laurie to the doctor on Friday? She's been complaining of a sore throat for three or four days now, poor kid. It seems pretty bad. Wouldn't hurt to have Dr. Klein take a look."

"Sure. I have a doctor's appointment that day, too. What time is hers?"

"Let me see. I wrote it down here on the pad by the phone…it's at 11AM."

"Okay. As long as Dr. Klein says everything's looking good with this kid!" Beth said, patting her belly. Lately, she had found herself wondering what the whole thing would be like. Would the baby take right to her? Would she know what to do? Who could she ask about nursing? Aunt Maudie? Should she really even try to nurse?

She could just see herself getting home with the baby and not knowing what to do. She wanted written instructions! Robert insisted the hospital wouldn't let them take the baby home unless the doctor, or nurse, or someone was convinced they could do it. She was so glad he included himself in the situation. She knew he liked kids, but did that mean he would help her change diapers and figure out the feeding? She sure didn't feel comfortable asking her dad and maybe not Aunt Maudie—and certainly not Robert's mom.

"Well, of course, the baby comes first. Absolutely." Jack said.

Beth grimaced, hoping Laurie hadn't overheard that last remark. Laurie had been really sick, and she did need to see a doctor, in Beth's opinion. In fact, Beth had suggested to Jack that he call Dr. Klein for Laurie, but Laurie didn't know that, and she wanted to keep it that way.

"No, no, Dad. Laurie needs to have her throat checked out. I'm just joking. Nothing's going to be wrong with this baby. He—or she—is going to be strong and coordinated and very healthy…according to Robert, that is. And I feel great.

Beth and her dad were lingering over dinner, chatting. Or really, Jack lingered as he'd always done with Anna. And, as often was the case with Jack and Anna, he consulted with Beth about family matters. They'd become a pretty regular occurrence, these tête-à-têtes, even now that she was married.

Is he blind? Can't he see how sick Laurie is? He's her dad! Why doesn't he focus on her instead of me? Of course, he's excited about the baby. But what about Laurie? He has no idea how frustrated and angry she's getting at him….and at me, for always defending him. In fact, he makes me mad, too. Why doesn't he act like he cares about her? I mean, I know he really does—but it's weird. Wrong. When we had Mom, he acted like a father. At least in the important ways. But he mostly expected Mom to hug us and worry about us and stuff. And she did. But now, Laurie needs that. Why won't he see that? It's so crappy of him. But what can I do?

I remember when I complained about the rec job last summer. He just said, "Well, listen, that's why they call it work. Sometimes, it ain't fun!" So, it's not just Laurie. When I was little, though, he was so different. I was his little princess. Did he ever treat Laurie like that? She's starting to make snide comments under her breath. She calls our talks, "cozy father/daughter chats." And I know it makes her so, so mad! Not just at him, but at me! What can I do?

These days, Laurie's moods were a mystery to Beth. One day, she talked and smiled, asking Beth's advice on school or boys. The next, she might sulk and complain about their father, or let her guitar drown out any attempt Beth made at conversation. Beth talked about this with Robert all the time, but his advice ran from, "So, talk to your dad. Tell him that Laurie needs him," to "He's got enough to worry about. Laurie's just a moody kid. You can't change that. You're doing enough already!" Mostly, he tried to avoid talking about problems. Oh—and there was "Why don't you talk to Maddy about that? You guys love to dissect why people are the way they are or why they do what they do. You guys eat that stuff up. I sure don't know."

On the way home that evening, Robert asked her about her day.

"It was fine. You already know I went to Aunt Maudie's—which was good. She had lots of advice for me about my pregnancy, though."

"I'm sure she did. Anything to calm you down about the whole thing?"

"Kinda, I guess. But she laid a trip on me about working after. Questioned me about what I planned to do with the baby if I go back to work, not-so-subtly implying I shouldn't work."

"What'd you tell her? We don't know what we'll do. I can go over the bills again, see if you can stay home, but I know it's going to be tight. Do you want to stay home with the baby?"

"I don't know. I can't imagine being away from him or her. But what about school? I know we'll need any money I can make working. I might be bored if I don't do anything. Can we just look at things while I think about it?"

"Sure. You should still go to school, but I don't know about right after the baby's born. It's pretty expensive, especially with both of us going. All of the fees and the darned books. They cost a fortune! I don't see how we can afford for you to go right away."

"So, it's more important if you keep going until you graduate? But not me?" Beth asked, attempting to tease Robert. Somehow, her questions sounded sarcastic.

"What do you mean, Beth? It just makes sense right now. When you finish this semester, you'll only have a month or so until the baby's born. You're already starting to show, so you know you're going to lose your rec job before too long. You can't keep covering it up with your big jacket. We're going to lose that income. What do you expect me to do? Quit working? Quit going to school and watch the baby so you can go?"

"No, I didn't mean that."

"What then? I'm already busting my ass with school and teaching part-time. It'd be great if you could go back to school. But we'll have to wait and see."

Beth wanted to ward off a fight. She hadn't meant to get Robert riled up, especially when he did work so hard for them.

"But, you do think it's important for me to finish school?"

"Of course, I do. But c'mon, let's face it. I have to keep working and finish school as soon as I can so I can get a real teaching job. We're going to have another mouth to feed, and I'll be able to make more money than you would."

Beth looked out the window, silently seething. There was no getting around it; Robert was right. Though frustrated, she knew he was just being practical. Of course, he would find a teaching job that paid more than any job she could get. Besides, she had to admit she didn't love school and she didn't love her job. So why was she so annoyed? Why was he always so right?

Changing tacks, she said, "I had a really bad dream last night."

"Yeah. I remember that you kinda cried out. What was it about?"

"My mom. I saw her in a crowd of people, like in the middle of downtown when it's really busy, and she was in the middle of this crowd, and I tried to call to her. She turned her head toward me and smiled, but she kept going! She…she…uh…kept going away from me until she disappeared." Beth gulped out the last part.

"Oh, honey bun! I'm sorry. Come here," and he pulled her next to him until she could burrow her head into his shoulder.

"On my way to Aunt Maudie's I started crying just thinking about it."

"Did you talk to Aunt Maudie about it?"

"No. We don't talk like that. She's not much for sympathy. You know what she talked to me about besides what I plan to do when the baby's born?"

"What?"

"How much it's going to hurt when I go through labor and have the baby."

"Oh, man, she can be so comforting, can't she? Just what you wanted to hear, right?" While Beth joined Robert in laughing at Aunt Maudie's lack of tact, inside she felt her heart pounding and her stomach lurching.

19 BEAUTY EMERGES

What goes up must come down
Spinning wheel got to go 'round
Talking 'bout your troubles it's a crying sin
Ride a painted pony, let the spinning wheel spin…

~David Clayton-Thomas

"Laurie, are you ready for high school to start?" It was shortly before the start of the new school year. Laurie had just walked out of Sunday mass.

"I guess so." She'd giggled uncomfortably. "What do you mean, Mr. Chapman?"

"You know, looking forward to it? Some people say it's the best time in their lives: meeting new friends, dating, going to the dances, getting ready for college—does the prospect of all that make you excited?"

"Well, I'm not sure. Maybe. I hope that's right. I mean, I'll have to wait and see."

"Everybody's pulling for you!" She hadn't known what he meant by that, but rather than ask him, this friend of her parents with whom she'd never really shared a conversation, she just said, "Thanks."

No, the words "looking forward" and "ready" were not the words to describe Laurie's feelings about her impending high school years. Two years ago, before the accident, she might have felt different about a change like this. Now, she wasn't so sure. Then, she'd loved cuddling with her cat on her bed, playing jacks with her friend Patty, and talking to her mom. She had done well in school and had a fair number of friends. Laurie had felt comfortable in her life.

When her mother died, though, she'd lost interest, and found herself detached from most things. Like the bedraggled cats that Anna used to save, Laurie felt bereft, lacking that essential substance that made sense of everything. She found herself operating on instinct, like the cats that searched in the rain for a safe haven, until Anna heard their mews and came to the rescue.

Laurie had helped Anna do this very thing many times. A malnourished creature would cry at their back door pathetically, drenched from the rain or just mangy and scrawny from neglect or abandonment, and her mother would gently lift it with a towel, rubbing its mashed fur while Laurie went to the refrigerator for milk and an egg. Then, as Anna had taught her, she would pour some milk into a bowl, crack the egg into the milk, and beat it with a fork until it frothed. Next, Anna would tenderly set the kitten in front of the bowl, and she and Laurie would watch as it purred and licked up every last drop. If the cat decided to stay, with her mother's coaching, Laurie would feed it and pet it until it morphed into a filled out, healthy, shiny-coated cat, ready to face the world. Anna had been able to see the beauty waiting in every creature.

Sometime in the last six months or so, Laurie had begun to feel less like those bedraggled cats and more like her old self. It was like she was reconnecting with the world. But this Laurie was new, and changed; she was pretty, with straight, strawberry-blonde hair and a slender, swimmer's body. Classmates, neighbors—boys about whom Laurie had never given a second thought—had begun paying attention; now, she finally understood the fuss that her sister Beth had been making for the past several years. In the spring of Laurie's eighth grade, one boy in particular, Carlos—or, Chili, as his friends called him—had courted Laurie with phone calls and impromptu visits on his bike. At the end of one of these visits, Chili had said goodbye and quickly leaned in for a kiss before riding off on his bike. That kiss had sealed the deal; they were officially a couple!

Now, whenever Chili flashed his warm smile, Laurie felt her face turn red. At first, that had evoked subdued giggles, which had quickly turned into hearty laughter, and the phone calls that at first had consisted of hesitant murmurs on Laurie's part soon became boisterous chatter.

Having Chili's attention—teasing, joking, looking at her squarely when she talked—energized Laurie, and made her feel attractive. She had never experienced anything like this, and she struggled to put her feelings into a secret song or private poem. Then, one day, Beth put on pop music for the sisters to clean to, and Laurie found herself singing along: "I thought love was only true in fairy tales / Meant for someone else, but not for me / Love was out to get me / That's the way it seemed / Disappointment haunted all my dreams" and then, belting into the broomstick microphone "Then I saw his face / Now I'm a believer…."

Suddenly, she had Chili to think about. Just like that: life had gone along, moving in one direction, then bam! It was crazy, and breathtakingly foreign, and then somehow, after a while, her life settled into a weird, wonderful new kind of normalcy.

Chili started calling on a daily basis. He showed up at her house, shouting "Surprise! I got you a carton of rocky road ice cream. I hope you like chocolate!!" He told her he thought of her every time he heard the song "Sunny" on the radio…and so, it became "their" song. Laurie took a look at herself in a new way. Though she wouldn't say Chili rescued her, she found she was having fun, and looking forward. The blackness of the tornado that had upended her life had finally let a little light in, and Laurie asserted solemnly to herself that she would never be so shaken and shocked again. She had willed herself to develop something steely in her spine, some invisible core that would shatter-proof her in some way. She let herself enjoy having a boyfriend and decided it might not be so bad having a boy-crazy sister. To Laurie, Beth seemed so knowledgeable where boys were concerned, always ready with thoughts on what it meant when Chili said or did something that confused Laurie.

Four or five months later, navigating the beginning of high school and wondering if and where Chili fit in this world, Laurie had again asked Beth for advice. This time, though clearly Beth had tried to be helpful, she went overboard. Instead of stopping at a few suggestions and giving Laurie time to think and consider, Beth had bombarded her sister with a fusillade of talk, invading Laurie's inner privacy until, one day, she erupted at Beth, angrily telling her to "Just stop with the questions about Chili and stories about old boyfriends. Okay? I can't even think!"

Beth had clammed up after that, which made her sister even more miserable. Laurie found herself fretting and anxious. She hated the silent treatment and needed to fix things with Beth fast, and so, she decided to write Beth a letter; just to let Beth know she needed to work out her relationship with Chili in her own time, in her own way.

November 10, 1967
Dear Beth,

I'm sorry I got mad at you when you tried to talk to me about Chili. I know you were just trying to help me. You do a lot for me like picking me up from school and taking me to guitar lessons. (I know there's more.) I look up to you as my big sister, and I shouldn't get so snotty with you after all you do for me. I guess I'm just confused and was taking it out on you. I don't know if I still like Chili. No, I like him, but I don't know if I want him to be my boyfriend right now. I'm still trying to get used to high school.

I'm not even sure why I got so mad at you except sometimes when you talk to me, it gets me confused. You seem to go on and on. I know you know more about boys and you have good advice, so why can't I just listen? I guess that it's just hard for me even though I know you have a lot of experience with these things.

I know you won't like me saying this, but it's true. Now, that you're married, I don't see you as much, and I know I have to figure things out for myself. And I AM working on it. That doesn't mean I don't still need you to help me with things. I do. And I don't mean that you did anything wrong. I'm happy that you're married to Robert and having a baby.

I'll try not to be a brat with you when you talk to me because I really do know you're trying to look out for me. I appreciate you and look up to you. So, please, don't be mad at me.

Love, Laurie

PS I really am excited about the baby.

Laurie's note caused an immediate phone call from Beth.

"Hi, Laurie. It's Beth, I got your letter." Beth's tone said, "I'm trying hard to be calm."

"Okay. Are you still upset with me?" Laurie asked breathlessly.

"No. I appreciate the apology, but I am a little confused. I just want to understand what you mean when you say it's hard for you to listen to me. I don't want it to be hard. When you asked me those questions about Chili, did you really want my honest opinion?" Beth's voice barely masked her defensiveness.

"Yeah, I did. I really did…and I do. I mean, uh, I do want your advice."

"So, what did I do wrong?' Laurie heard the frustration in Beth's voice.

"I think since I don't know much about this boy stuff, I just need to take my time figuring it out. I don't know. I want to hear what you have to say, but I can't necessarily take your advice, at least right away. I guess I just need to let it sink in.

"That's fine. I still don't totally get why you got mad. Did I seem to be expecting you to say my advice was right and you should listen to everything I say?"

"Kinda. I like that you care about me, but if you could just answer my questions, then change the subject, that might be better. I don't really know. I'm just confused."

"Okay. I'll try to do that—not talk about whatever it is quite so much. It's a confusing for me, too, so you might have to tell me again." Beth seemed to relax.

"Thanks. I don't mean to make it so hard. I want your help, and I know I need it. I'll try to tell you next time if I need time to think. I'm glad you're not mad at me." Laurie prayed this would end well.

"I know. I'm not. I'm really not. And Laurie, I know we don't spend as much time together as we used to…uh…before I married Robert, but I want to spend time with you. It's just that I'm trying to juggle school and work and, well, everything, and I've been tired a lot lately, ya know with the baby coming and all."

"I know, Beth. I'm sorry I said that. I just get lonely. But I'm working on being more independent."

"That's good…I guess, if that's what you want, but you don't have to do that. I want to be here for you, you know. I really do."

"It's okay. Thanks for saying that. It's going to be great when you have the baby."

"Let's hope so. But you know I don't have much experience with babies. I'm kinda nervous. I'm sure I'll need your help."

"Sure. What does Robert say?"

"Oh, ya know, he says everything's gonna be fine. He can't wait."

"I'm sure he's right."

Though the letter had initially resulted in an uncomfortable conversation, Laurie thought maybe she and her sister had found their way to a positive conclusion. Maybe now Beth understood what Laurie needed when it came to advice. It had been really, really difficult to use the word "lonely" to describe herself, but Laurie was relieved that she had. She could see that she needed to work on being more honest with Beth, and more independent from her, too. Right now, she felt that she could. She knew, also, she needed to look to someone besides Beth as a confidante. The next day, Laurie did just that.

November 12, 1967
Dear Patty,

I'm so glad you wrote me a letter. I guess you were pretty bored in your English class the other day. I guess I'm kinda bored, too. We have a sub in religion class. She just told us to read a couple of chapters, but I can do that later. I'd much rather write to you!

You asked me if I'm enjoying school and also how some of our friends from last year are doing. Well, school is okay. It goes by pretty fast because we change teachers every 50 minutes. (So much better than elementary!) Is it the same for you? 'Course, I ride to school with my dad, and ya' know I've got nothing to say to him, so that 30 minutes actually seems like forever!

I don't have too many of our old friends in my classes. Jo Ann is in my PE class, and she seems to be doing great. You know how good she is at sports, and we're playing volleyball in our class, so she's doing good there. I like it, too. I'm glad I played last year, even if we didn't win too many games. Anyway, everybody likes Jo. She told me she has Cheryl, Diane and Tammy in some of her classes. So that's good for her. I see them at lunch, but I feel kinda funny going up to them when they're in a big group. I never really hung around with them outside of our CYO teams, so it's kinda hard. I haven't made any new friends yet, just hi and bye friends.

How about you? You know how I can be shy, so I'm telling myself I better start making friends or I'll just curl up in a ball and disappear. No, don't worry. I'm just being dramatic.

Remember I told you that an older boy started talking to me at my locker the first week of school? Well, I see him almost every day, and he always says hi and asks me something, or tells me a joke. That makes me feel good, but I don't know what it means. He's the younger brother of my sister's friend, so I think maybe he's just being nice.

How's Chili? I miss him, but he isn't calling me. I don't know if he likes someone else or what. Maybe you could find out—that is, if you see him around school and feel like it.

I know you're wondering if I've talked to Beth about any of this. You think I'm lucky to have an older sister like Beth, and I know you're right. I've talked to her a little, but I just wish she wouldn't keep nagging at me after I ask her something. She's a little too big on the advice sometimes.

But the biggest thing is, now that she's married, things are really different. She's going to have a baby for one thing! I'm pretty sure I told you that. She still comes over a lot and all, but it's not the same. She's still working at the park, so she usually gets here late, and then she's tired and making dinner or helping Dad do it. And then Robert comes, and they start talking with each other and with Dad. Anyway, I pretty much feel that I'm on my own. I wish we were still going to the same school. I kinda need someone to talk to, someone who understands me. Hopefully, going to different schools doesn't change you and me being friends.

Well, I hope you can write me back. Tell me how it's going at home and at school. I miss you!

Laurie

PS Here's my latest song. Tell me what you think it's about, besides loneliness!! I'll play it for you the next time we get together.

Loneliness—
Oh, I'm not crying, no, not me; I take the day as it comes
Once upon a time, I cried, well, nothing changed
So I put those tears away, I did.
I shook my mane, let my hair dance around my face.
I defied you. Might as well. I look around now with eyes wide open.
I'll stare you down. I can do it.
You think you've got the best of me. But you'll see.
I'm stronger than you—I have myself; that's enough. I know it now.
Just have to lift the weights. Stay strong. I'll do it.
Flex my muscles, get in my stance. Now, go! Go! Go! Go!
—Laurie

Laurie Lawrence
English I, period 4
November 12, 1967

I'm Sisyphus; I'm strong, but I used to be mighty. I know I did wrong. At least that's what they say about me. I guess they're right. So, I'm stuck here, pushing this darned heavy boulder up the hill. The crazy thing about this punishment is that when I get the boulder to the top of the hill, it's just going to roll back down. Then I push it up again. Over and over. Why? Was I so bad? A little horseplay, really. Trying to outsmart Death so that I wouldn't have to die. But they, and you, doom me for that. This boulder is my arrogance, thinking that I could be smarter than the gods who set my fate. Can I apologize? I would gladly die rather than this. Is there no one to hear my pleas? Really? To be in pain for all time. I could kill myself, but no. I'm immortal now, aren't I? I guess I'll take my punishment and suffer the agony no one should have to endure. What did I do again? And is there really no one to help me?

This myth relates to my life in a big way. Two years ago, my family was in a car accident, and my mother didn't make it. Since then, I have not been happy like I used to be. Like me, before I lost my mother, Sisyphus was probably happy before he realized he was going to die one day. That was his fate, and, according to his society, he did wrong when he tried to change that. In that boulder he endlessly pushes up and up are the unbreakable rules of the gods of his world—the rules he thought he could break, and, in doing so, outsmart his gods. I feel like Sisyphus sometimes because I feel I'm doomed to be sad forever. The boulder I push is my wish that if someone had to die in the car accident, it would have been someone else instead of my mom. It's also the way I feel about my family now, which is not very good. I worry that I'm going to always be pushing my boulder up my hill.

Sisyphus and I are different in a big way, though. I was just a little girl. I didn't try to change my fate. I mostly liked my world, and God and His rules. In fact, I can't figure out why I deserved to have this happen to me. Sisyphus tried to change his fate and this is what brought about his punishment. I still don't know what brought about mine.

Laurie had worked hard on her English assignment, enjoying the creative bent to it. When she was finished, and looked it over, she wondered if maybe she had been too personal in her paper. But she liked her teacher and, eager to do well, decided to take the chance. A few days later, Ms. Rigsby returned the papers. Laurie smiled to see a 48 out of 50 at the top. The note at the bottom said, "Good grasp of the meaning of the myth, Laurie! And excellent application to your own life. Please see me for a moment after class." Reading the note brought a blush to Laurie's face. *Why would she want to see me after class?* She wanted the young teacher's approval, but, nevertheless, felt awkward about talking to her.

When the bell rang, and the students started filing out of the room, Laurie approached Ms. Rigsby.

"Hi, Laurie," the teacher greeted her with a smile. "I wanted to talk to you about your homework assignment. I wanted to compliment you in person. You know, I almost gave you 50 out of 50. I probably should have. I only saw a few minor weaknesses. By the looks of it, you enjoy writing. Am I right?"

"Yeah, I've always enjoyed writing. In my elementary school, the teachers assigned lots of writing and encouraged creativity."

"Do you write a lot on your own, then?"

"Well, I play the guitar, so I mostly write songs, but, like I said, the nuns had us do a lot of writing, and I always enjoyed those assignments."

"Well, that explains a lot. Also, I wondered if, in comparing yourself with Sisyphus, you were talking about something that really happened to you."

"Uh, yeah. That really happened, unfortunately." Laurie put her head down as she answered.

"I'm so sorry. How are you doing now? Are you still pretty sad? That's a dumb question! How could you NOT still be sad?"

Laurie laughed a little with the teacher who had no problem making fun of herself. "You're not dumb, but you are right, I guess. I'm doing a lot better, but I am still kinda sad." Laurie felt the tears well up in her eyes, and Ms. Rigsby patted Laurie's arm.

Just then, both noticed that students were filing in for the next class. "Gosh, I'm going to make you late. I'm so sorry. Let me write you a tardy note. But Laurie, thanks for talking to me. I'm looking forward to getting to know you. You seem like a very nice and smart girl! I may have an idea for you about how you're feeling. I'll talk to you later, if you're okay with that." Laurie nodded to her teacher, took the note Ms. Rigsby handed to her and left for her next class.

At lunchtime, Laurie lingered at her locker just as she usually did. Today was the day she had promised herself that she would try to mingle outside in the yard by the cafeteria. She knew where Jo Ann and the others sat. *Why don't I sit down with them? I'll say hi to Jo Ann, say something about her volleyball skills. At least that'll get me started. I know a couple of the other girls, also. I mean, it's not like I have three heads or anything. Once I'm sitting, and they're okay with it, I can just be quiet. It'll be fine....*

"Hell—o-o! Hey, you! Laurie! Girl, with the goofy look on her face! I'm talkin' to you!" Suddenly, there stood Alex, grinning down on her as she knelt at her locker. "What's so interesting in your locker?"

"Alex! Hi, I—uh, I didn't see you standing there. I guess 'deep in thought' kinda covers where I was!" Alex dumped the rest of his stuff in his locker and slammed it shut, then folded his arms and smiled at her again.

"Really? No kidding! I've been standing here talking to you about my a-hole of a teacher, and you're just ignoring me, like I'm invisible. Thanks a lot!"

"Oh, Alex. I'm sorry. Were you really talking to me?" Laurie couldn't tell if he was serious.

"Don't worry your beautiful brain about it! I'll survive. So, what's up with you today?"

"Well, honestly, I'm trying to figure out how to go sit with a group of kids at lunch."

"Really? Well, listen, you've come to the right place for advice about lunch. After all, it's a jungle out there. So, where do you want to sit? Or who do you want to sit with? I have to warn you—if it involves a boy, I might not help you. I'm just saying…"

"Hmm. I don't know if I should trust you. You sure you want to hear my pathetic problem?" When he nodded, she took a deep breath and let the words tumble out. "I've been avoiding lunch because I don't have any real friends yet, but I decided that's really stupid, so I'm going to sit with someone today. I decided it would be a group of girls from my old school. We know each other, but we've never really hung out together, ya know?"

"Say no more. Here's the deal. And it works for me every time. The main thing is to be confident. Tell yourself they've been dying for you to eat with them, and you only now noticed them. So, you're going to try to set them at ease. With that as your backstory, it'll be easy. Ya know what a backstory is?"

"Can't say that I do. What is it?"

"I'm in drama—you might want to join—and our teacher, Ms. Rigsby, tells us there's always a story that's implied, not stated outright. It might be a conflict, something just lurking beneath the surface of the plot. So, here, you have a group of girls who look up to you, and they'd like nothing more than for you, Ms. Pretty and Charming Laurie Lawrence, to notice them and be friends with them. So, go—do this nice thing for them!"

Laurie found herself laughing at the charm of this older boy who had already spent the first 10 minutes of lunch on her, a measly freshman. Pretty soon, they would be kicked out of the hall by a passing teacher. It was now or never. Run to the bathroom to hide or head outside to the lunch area.

"Okay. Thanks for the advice. I'm going right now, and I'll grace them with my presence. Nicely, of course."

Later that night, as she started her homework, Laurie thought about the day.

Wow! That was something with Alex! He is so nice...and cute...and sweet! He had such a great idea. I mean, it's crazy! I tried, but I think I was a little too nervous to pull off thinking I was doing the girls a favor. Heck, who knows though? I have no idea how I came across, but the main thing is—I can't believe I sat with the girls at lunch! Today was so much better than last week. Whew! I think I might actually get some sleep tonight. And I'm looking forward to school tomorrow!

I kinda feel hopeful for a change. Maybe high school will turn out to be good, after all. But then, this is just one day. Still, I feel like I can talk to Alex—I mean, he teases me, and makes me laugh, but he gave me some good advice—like he understood! Maybe he's gonna be like the older brother who's so different from mine. I don't really think he could like me—I mean, LIKE me like me! And the girls couldn't have been nicer. I feel pretty sure it'll be fine if I start hanging out with them at break or lunch or something. And Ms. Rigsby. Hmmm... that was a little embarrassing, but I don't know. It seemed like she really did like my work. And she DID seem to care about me. I guess I'll see. I'm kinda nervous, but also kinda excited to go to English tomorrow. And she said she wants to talk to me again. When she said she might know how to help me...I wonder what she meant. And then... Alex—he is just so, so nice.

Nov. 18, 1967
Hi Patty,

I'm so glad we started writing letters. It's so awkward sometimes to talk on the phone at home. I never know who's listening, so I can't really say anything about Beth, my dad or brothers. I hope you'll be able to come over sometime during TG break, so we can really talk. I'll tell you basically what's been going on with me now, though.

First of all, I finally started eating lunch with Jo Ann and those guys. I'm so glad. They're nice, and make me feel welcome, and also now I've met some of their new friends. A few of the girls I have in classes. Anyway, it gives me people to say hi to in the halls and to talk to at different times. So that's good.

Also, I think I'm getting over Chili. I mean, he called me after you said you talked to him, and I told him Alex was just a friend, and that's all. But the thing is, it's been weird since then when he calls me. We're supposed to see each other this weekend, so I'll see how it is.

But it's turning out that now I kinda like Alex. He is so nice to me. Gives me all kinds of advice, and he compliments me a lot. He's probably just teasing me, but he's always saying things like "your beautiful brain" or "your pretty little self." I know he's goofing around, but it makes me feel kinda special. I don't know. Like I said, I'll see how it is with Chili this weekend. And it's not like Alex has asked me out. He probably likes me like a little sister. I mean, I'm just a little freshman. I guess I just have a crush on him. He also said I should join Drama. And he's in it!! The best thing is, Ms. Rigsby, my English teacher, is also the Drama teacher. I really, really like her.

Okay, now it's your turn to tell me how it's going at your school with you and everything.

Oh, and Beth is showing! She's got a really poochie tummy. And you can feel the baby moving inside her belly. It's like she gets these bumps that move, and then she yells for you to come feel it. You've got to come over when she's here. She'll let you feel the baby. I know she will. She's scared, but she's also excited, and so am I. I can't believe "we're" going to have a baby. We're getting along better since I wrote her a letter. She's trying not to be so nosy and bossy.

No change with my dad. Sigh!

Love ya,

Laurie

Something was definitely shifting for Laurie. She felt stronger—as if she'd been working out with weights and could finally see muscle where there had been flab. The first few weeks of high school, she'd been more than a little dazed, and she'd felt unfocused and lost in the sea of anonymous faces. She knew her way around the high school—she'd been there often enough with her sister and brother-in-law—but that was before she'd come to inhabit it for seven hours a day. She'd tried to be open to new friends, smiling at and saying hi to kids in the hall, like Beth had recommended, but she was less than thrilled with the results.

"I feel stupid!" she complained to Beth, on a recent car ride home from school. "I mean, I don't even know who I'm smiling at."

"It doesn't matter." Beth was in her optimistic "you can do this" cheerleader mode. "People like people who smile at them. Pretty soon, those people will start saying hi back. Some—probably a lot—of those kids, feel lost and stupid, too. Give them a little time—they'll appreciate the pretty girl who's being friendly."

Laurie changed the subject. "So, Chili and I are officially over."

"Oh. Did it go okay? Are you okay?"

"Yeah. He felt the same way. He agreed that we're at different schools with lots going on. He said something about going in different directions. He's playing football, and that takes a lot of time. But he called me 'Sunny' again and said he wanted to be friends. I agreed. It turned out good. Really, Beth."

"He's a good kid, Laurie. I'm glad he came along for you."

"Yeah, me too. I think he was kind of a good influence on me. He was so much fun. He made me laugh."

"I kept telling you, you were getting so pretty. And he wasn't the only boy who noticed."

"Oh, c'mon, Beth! Don't embarrass me."

"Well, I'm just saying it can be fun to be a girl."

"Okay, okay. Now, I need to focus on school. I'm making friends, talking to kids at lunch and all that. And I'm getting to know some of my teachers. I'm thinking about going out for Drama. My English teacher is the moderator."

"Wow, kiddo, that's great! Really cool! My little sister, the actress!"

"Yeah, I'm gonna talk to her about it after school, maybe tomorrow."

"Fantastic! I want to hear all about it. That will be s-o-o-o great for you."

Uh oh. What did I just do? Now, I have to follow through or she'll never let me forget it. I don't want to tell her about Alex being in Drama or she'll make a big deal out of that.

"My point is, I'm not so insecure lately. I mean, I don't feel as lost as I did the first month of school. I guess I have more self-confidence than I did. God, I sound like a stupid little kid. I know, I know—I'm not alone in thinking that way. But it doesn't seem like it when you watch some kids walk around school."

"Well, yeah…but don't believe everything you see. Some kids have a knack for seeming good no matter what." Beth leaned in to turn up the radio, then started singing along

"If you're going to San Francisco / Be sure to wear some flowers in your hair

If you're going to San Francisco / You're gonna meet some gentle people there…"

She sure is right about that. Alex seems to be one of those people. Thank goodness for me he is that way. He's helped me a lot already this year. I wonder why. I doubt that he likes me like that. Still, it's kinda like it was with Chili in the beginning.

I still don't know why Chili liked me and called me "Sunny" after the song came out on the radio. Boy, if he had only known how I felt inside when we first met…I was so sad and mixed up. Definitely not sunny! Maybe he thought I was stuck up. Beth says some boys like girls that are "hard to get." I don't know if that's what it was with Chili. He was so darn friendly and cute. I know I acted shy…I had no idea what to say to him or how to act the first time he talked to me. It was all I could do to try to look at him—which was hard—I'd never talked to a boy like that before. Oh, and then the first time he called me—I can't believe how embarrassed I got. My heart beat so hard, it almost hurt. I know when I got off the phone, I finally understood why Beth did so much to impress boys. I couldn't wait to tell her. And when I did, she looked like the Cheshire Cat, smiling ear to ear. I remember she told Margaret when she came into our bedroom, "Guess what? Laurie's got a boyfriend!" Margaret said very seriously, "Ooo-oh!" Then we all started laughing.

I guess I felt and acted the way I see Beth feel and act about Robert. I wonder how she was with her first boyfriend, John. I know Mom didn't like him. Seems like she argued with Beth about him so much…but they argued about everything then. And she warned me not to look up to Beth.

I remember how shocked I was when--out of nowhere--Mom said "Don't be like Beth!" What was that really about? I know she'd always gotten mad at Beth for her short skirts. Beth used to roll them up, and that had just driven Mom crazy. She'd also hated that Beth ratted her hair and then filled the bathroom with a choking fog of Aquanet. Well—who hadn't hated going in the bathroom after Beth fixed her hair? I'd known Beth had been wearing make-up to hide her pimples for a long time, but for some reason, it was more Beth's rolled up skirts and almost-white lipstick that they'd fought about. But when Beth met John—he was going to public school and wasn't Catholic—when they'd walked down the neighborhood streets together, I guess they'd put their arms around each other's waists—that really irked Mom.

"Beth, I was driving down Palmer, and I saw you and John with your arms around each other. I've told you not to do that." Mom had sounded so exasperated!

"Oh, Mom! What's so wrong about it? He's my boyfriend. We're not doing anything wrong. At least we're not standing around making out!" When Beth talked like that to Mom, it made me cringe. It embarrassed me to think of her and John doing that, for sure. It had hurt Mom's feelings, too…but I guess she couldn't give up, so she'd keep on arguing.

"Elizabeth Lawrence!" Mom had scolded her, "how can you say such things? What do you think our friends think when they see you on the street like that—short skirt, teased hair, your arms draped all over that boy in his jeans and flat top? If you don't care about your reputation, I, as your mother, most certainly do! You shouldn't have a steady boyfriend, anyway. You're too young."

"C'mon, Mom! You bug me about everything. I can't do anything right with you! Remember—I'm in high school. I'm not a little kid anymore."

"You watch your tone, young lady, or you won't be parading around with that boy at all."

Why hadn't Mom just told Beth to break up with John? She'd deserved it. For whatever reason, Beth had seemed to go out of her way to upset Mom. I don't get it.

To Laurie, Anna had represented a soothing ocean of calm and loving concern. Anna had anchored the family, kept them safe.

How could Beth have risked separating herself from that force in her life? Sure, Mom had made her mad, but so what?

Mom was Mom. I never would have fought her, not like Beth did. I never thought about it before, but I think I was Mom's favorite, at least over Beth. We kinda had a "Beth's Not Like Us" club of three: Mom, Margaret and me, though Margaret never really took sides against Beth; she just kept quiet. Come to think of it, Margaret and Beth had always shared a room, and they'd talk and laugh in there— just the two of them. I thought Beth hated me, thought I was a spoiled brat. I guess I kinda was, really. But, ever since we lost Mom—I hate the word "died"—Beth talks to me and Margaret all the time. I mean, I can see she cares about us.

The three sisters had started sharing a bedroom after the accident, and during that time, the three of them had woven a new bond that allowed them to comfort each other wordlessly. If Beth had been hurt by Anna's advice to Laurie, or by Laurie's close relationship with Anna, she hadn't mentioned it; certainly, Beth had never alluded to feeling second string to Laurie's star status.

Beth had cried into her pillow after bedtime prayers for weeks after the accident. Laurie knew Beth missed their mother. Too bad Mom hadn't see this side of Beth. Or had she? Beth seemed to think Anna practically sat on their shoulders. She expressed total confidence in Anna's protective spirit, contending "She's always with us." At times, she tried to comfort her sisters with, "She knows we miss her. Pray to her—or at least talk to her. She's listening."

She asks Margaret about her bowling and her boyfriends—Beth's favorite subject! She's always been interested in my guitar playing and new songs; I mean, she even tries to learn them on the piano...sometimes on the guitar too—that's always good for a laugh for both of us.

When I think about it, I guess I...I have to say I'm pretty much in Beth's inner circle of important people. I mean, we're closer than most sisters for sure. I suppose, after the accident, I was kind of floating, adrift in a...sea of confusion. Beth showed up in a little boat and pulled me in. Then, for a while, we drifted together ... until we finally figured out how to help each other paddle to shore.

It was so hard, but. somehow—maybe because she's older and everyone needed her—Beth began to adjust to the new terrain, the new life. I never talked. I just didn't know what to say—ever...at all. But Beth talked non-stop. It seemed like talking helped her with the pain that never ended. But I think I had just frozen up, solid and silent...and Beth reached out to me. I'm sure she was worried—I think I acted like a zombie or something—but I think she needed me, too. It took me a while, but we did get pretty close.

Looking back, it was like Beth looked at me with new eyes. She...kinda started to really see me, not just an annoying little kid. She had to drive me places, but I started feeling like she liked to be with me. And Robert—I liked to be with him, too. Maybe 'cause we shared something so big.

And Beth shared Robert with me. Whenever he appeared—home from school, or whatever—we all huddled together in our bedroom or living room, singing and even laughing. It was neat...or at least I felt less terrible. They liked hearing me sing, and they always wanted to learn my songs. I don't really know why. But I'm glad, because, when I sing, I express myself. Somehow, little by little, I've been able to talk again...which is good.

Then Beth got married. And, boy! Did everything change! She just disappeared from our sad house...leaving me and Margaret to fend for ourselves. One day, she was showing off her ring, sitting on her bed, looking through some magazines for brides' dresses and planning her big day. I can still see that so well. But what I didn't see was that...poof! Just like that, she'd be gone! After the honeymoon, she moved out. When she came for her stuff, she hugged me, promising to always "be there" for me. Now, only a few months later, she explodes a bomb on us: she's going to have a baby.

I guess she's moving on, too. She acts like she still cares about me. And she and Robert come around a lot. But she doesn't sleep in the bed across from me anymore. She isn't there at night, sitting there, humming to my music while she writes in her journal. No more bedtime prayers with me and Margaret before turning out our bedroom light.

Sure, she still cooks for us a lot, but is she going to do that with a baby? I'm trying to be excited at becoming an aunt. Maybe it'll be good. But why is it all happening now? So soon? I wish I could talk to her about it, but I wouldn't know what to say. I know about the birds and bees. Learned more than I wanted from her when I was 11. And how many times did she come home fuming after a date with Robert because he didn't understand her views about sex before marriage? She really used to give me an ear full. I hated that. What did I know? Funny, though. Beth really held on to Mom's morals. A few years ago, all Beth wanted to do was rebel against them. I guess Mom would be pretty surprised. Life is so weird.

I wonder if she thought about us missing her when she left. It seems like all Dad can talk about is "how great Bethie is." I understand. She took charge and everything after the accident—but in a way, it still bugs me that he goes on and on about that. How does he know I wouldn't have done the same thing if I had been in her shoes? I mean, it all happened on the way to visit her!

I know the accident wasn't her fault, but she said it herself—if Mom hadn't wanted to check on her, maybe we wouldn't have gone. I know Dad said he wanted to see a real Indian reservation, but he may have said that just for Mom. I mean, Beth said she had to go on this trip with Father Rex. Not only would she be doing something good, she'd be "going on an adventure."

Dad loved that. I just wonder if that's maybe why she's the goody-goody daughter now? If we hadn't gone, Mom would still be here doing what she always did—loving us, taking care of us. Beth could have gone off and gotten married—I wouldn't care a bit. I'd probably have been glad for her. I would have my MOM. God! No! I will not think about that!!

Anyway, Beth jumped into the role, got us all used to having her do…what she did. Then she left us. Now, here we are. I'm happy that she comes over and takes me to my lessons and all, but what's going to happen next? What if Dad starts to expect the same from me? And all those talks about Margaret and meals and the house? What if he wants me to follow in Beth's footsteps like that? I don't want to be that girl!

"What're you thinking about, Laurie? You seem a million miles away."

Laurie wanted nothing more than to tell her sister how hard life at home was with her gone, and to cry out about her relationship with their father. But what she said was "Oh, just about stuff, I guess…about the baby, ya know, what it'll be like when he or she comes. You're probably going to be pretty busy."

"Probably. But I'm going to need your help, you know. I'm going to be over here all the time."

"Are you still going to work? And go to school?" Laurie worried out loud.

"Gee, I don't know. Not for a while, for sure. I guess I'll have to wait and see."

"I hope you'll still come over," Laurie said quietly. "You know, you have to keep Margaret and me in line!"

"I know! You two are a real handful, all right. I'll be there so much, you'll get sick of me. You know me, Miss But-in-ski!" She looked at Laurie, who made a face. Beth smiled at her, and Laurie smiled back. "So…is that all you were thinking about?" She cringed, afraid Laurie would think she was prying.

"I guess…I was kinda thinking about a couple of years ago, ya know—after the accident?" Laurie wanted to be honest with Beth.

"Yeah. Awful, huh? What about those years? It's been a little over two," Beth said, her tone now subdued.

"Oh, I don't know. I guess about how you started getting Margaret and me to do work around the house, cooking and cleaning and all that. You still try to do it."

Laurie decided to keep it safe.

"Uh-oh, it sounds like it doesn't work anymore. You mean turn music on loud and sing and dance the work away?"

"You guessed it. We're on to you, now."

Beth laughed with her sister. "It still makes it easier for me. Hmm."

"Yeah, you got me singing to the Beatles —'She loves you, yeah, yeah, yeah / With a love like that, you know she can't be bad.'" Laurie sang. "And the Supremes. Remember this, 'Baby love, my baby love / Why must we se-e-par-ate my love? / Been missin' ya, Miss kissin' ya,'" Beth joined in.

"Oh, heck yeah! And don't forget the Beach Boys, 'Let's go surfin' now / Everybody's learnin' how / Come on a safari with me,'" Beth sang off-key. "We always get a lot done when we listen to that song. Right, Laurie?"

"Sorry to tell you, Beth. Me and Margaret are going on strike. Though I guess it's still better than working without the music!"

Later that night, Laurie did her homework with the radio on. When Bob Dylan came on, she chimed in, changing the words to fit the mood that had stayed with her since her earlier conversation with Beth:

"I'm not the one you want…Dad
I'm not the one you need
You say you're lookin' for someone
Who's never weak but always strong…
I'm not the one you need…Dad
I will only let you down…!"

When Beth wasn't there, Laurie never gave a thought to any chore—cooking, especially--she just waited until Jack got home at night, let him figure it out, ask her for help if he wanted it. He rarely asked her. And besides, she didn't know much about fixing a meal and didn't want to learn.

So, Laurie and her dad didn't talk much. From Laurie's point of view, Jack didn't seem to be much interested in her or Margaret.

Besides, when Jack returned from work, Frankie would emerge from his room, sit with Jack, and they'd sip drinks before dinner, a new ritual for them. Then, Frankie would return to his room, probably to bury himself in his studies. After Jack threw some kind of dinner together, Frankie might re-emerge, but there was no semblance of "the family evening meal," which had marked Laurie's childhood and that Beth had tried to re-create. Both men seemed preoccupied, and, anyway, Laurie didn't have much to say to either of them.

Almost nine years older than Laurie, Frankie remained a mystery to her. She knew Beth admired his brilliance and considered him the big brother with whom she shared good childhood memories. But Laurie couldn't say the same. To her, Frankie was just a moody recluse. In fact, besides the "cocktail hour" with Jack, Frankie hardly came out of his room.

Laurie couldn't really remember if Frankie had always been such a hermit. She had vague memories of dinnertime conversations—but that was when the kitchen was Anna's domain. In that memory, while Anna fussed over the meal, seeing that everyone had what they needed, her father had engaged her brothers in what seemed to be loud, opinionated man-talk. She didn't remember even wanting to be included—which she didn't think she ever was. Besides, she'd been busy engaged with "the girls" at their end of the table, by her mom.

Even when Jack did shine his light on Laurie, surprising her with questions from time to time, she had little to say to him.

"So, Laurie, how are you liking your algebra class? That used to be one that I found to be challenging at first."

"It's okay."

"Now, Beth tells me you're doing well. Just got an A on a test."

"Uh-huh."

"That's great, honey. Let me know if I can help you. I eventually got the hang of it and did well, if I do say so myself."

"Okay." With that, Jack turned back to his newspaper. Laurie shrugged her shoulders and headed back to her room. So many of their conversations started and ended this way. Sometimes, on the way to school, he'd give her an opening:

"So…Bethie says you've got an interesting English teacher."

"Yeah. I like her a lot."

"Well, that's swell, Laurie. What are you studying now?"

"We're working on Greek mythology. I just did an assignment on Sisyphus."

"Oh, good ole Sisyphus. Just rolling that rock up the mountain over and over for all eternity."

"Yep. That's the one."

"Did I ever tell you I read Sophocles in elementary school? Got my first library card when I was five. I loved reading all the classics."

"Oh, wow. I don't think we get to him this year." Laurie had no idea who Sophocles was. Character? Author? How should she respond? But Jack continued:

"The Oedipus Trilogy is some great reading, I'll tell you. Do you know about the Sphinx and the great riddle he posed to Oedipus? No? Well, when Oedipus…."

And off he would go, sometimes for the rest of the car ride. Laurie conceded that Jack could tell a good story, but what did that have to do with her—or her world? She wouldn't have minded having her dad offer fatherly advice or at least his shoulder to lean on. And when he finally finished one of his stories, she didn't know how to respond.

Other mornings, he seemed to be off entirely, somewhere in his own world. On those days, he might make a half-hearted attempt at an exchange, but Laurie rarely had much to say. She had no real experience in small talk with her father. Her mother had been her confidante, and that had been instinctive, the words unimportant.

With her father…not so. Often, Jack didn't seem inclined to keep the conversation going, at least as far as Laurie could tell. On those days, after the initial small talk, they would lapse into an awkward silence for the rest of the drive to school, the chasm between them growing deeper and wider by the mile.

20 DEEP JOY AND HIGH ANXIETY

The moment I wake up,
Before I put on my make up
I say a little prayer for you…
Forever and ever, you'll stay in my heart
Oh, how I love you…
To live without you would only mean heartbreak for me…

~Burt Bacharach and Hal David

April 11, 1968

He's two days old, and he is our miracle—a small, soft, bundle of drowsy sweetness. When the nurses bring him to me, I hold this little life in my arms and stare at him. His skin is so smooth; his little body is so perfect. I want to memorize every inch of him. My daytime nightmare is that someone will take him, and I won't be able to find him because I won't recognize him. This is my horror! I hate for him to be taken away, but the nurses take him anyway. They tell me I need my rest. That means I only get to see him for feeding—very awkward and painful—and a little cuddling…the best part, so far.

I can't believe I have a baby!

My body, on the other hand, totally knows it. I have never been so sore. And I haven't got one ounce of modesty left in me! I don't care who sees the stitches on my butt as long as they're bringing something to make the pain stop: cream, compresses, sprays. The best, though, is something called a "sits bath." The nurses (who are very nice!) help me carefully waddle to a little bathroom a few feet from my bed, where there is this thing that looks like a toilet, only it's not. It's a shallow porcelain bowl that I sit in, and warm water gushes over all my aching stitches! It is soooo great!

Anyway, Bobby is so beautiful! But when that boy wants to eat or be with his mommy, he screams louder than any baby in this hospital. The other moms in the room think this is very funny—but Robert is as proud as can be of his boy! (Bobby is—of course! — named after Robert. His middle name, "Anthony," is for our friend, Tony—Robert's best friend, and a really neat boy I've known forever, who is in Viet Nam.)

I'm so incredibly tired, but I'm also very lucky. My labor only lasted about two hours before I got a shot in my spine, which numbed me from the waist down, and, before long, Dr. K held him up to show me! Then the mean man handed him off to a nurse. Eons later, a little baby "burrito" snugly wrapped in a blanket was handed to me!

On Bobby's "birth" day, we went to the Dolans for Easter dinner. It was their turn on the holiday rotation. I felt so fat and uncomfortable! This was now day #8 past the due date. I prayed that Mrs. D would tell me not to help with the dishes…but no such luck. I could hardly get my fat self up and out of a chair. Still, I tried to clear some plates. Finally, R's aunt laughed at me. "Goodness gracious, Beth! Sit yourself down. We've got this!" I wanted to kiss her!

We left for home a little later, and then my dad called to ask how I was doing. I said "I feel so fat!" He told me not to be discouraged—I'll have my baby soon. Then Dad said, "Hey, how about I come over and take you two out for a drink?" This was a new one from my dad, but I asked Robert, and we both said, "Why not?" I mean, neither of us is 21 yet!

Dad drove us up to this great bar on Signal Hill where we could look down on the city lights. He ordered a grasshopper for me—this minty, creamy, totally yummy concoction. (Robert got a 7 and 7.) I slurped my drink down, which made Dad laugh and order me a second one! After our drinks and a little conversation, he took us home. It was about 10 by then so we got ready for bed and R went straight to sleep.

I wasn't so lucky. I just couldn't get comfortable, and tossed and turned for a few hours, then, about 1am, I woke R up. I said, "This might be it!" When he asked me what I felt like, I just said, "I hurt!" We debated for 15 minutes about calling Dr. K, but finally, he did.

Dr. K asked a few questions, then said, "Get to the hospital." I wonder if the drinks finally persuaded our baby into motion!

I think I get to go home tomorrow. I want to, but I'm so, so scared. The nursing is not easy. I mean, the nurses help me. What if I can't do it at all by myself? They say the milk should come in tomorrow. What does that mean?? And I haven't even changed Bobby's diaper yet. What if I don't know what to do? Robert keeps telling me not to worry, that it's all going to be fine. He's sure the hospital won't let us take Bobby home unless they trust us.

Oh, God. Please let me be a good mom! If only Mom were here. She was so good with babies—and all little kids, really. Please be with me, Mom—I need you badly!

April 9, 1968
Dear Beth,

Dad came into our room this morning before we were even up to tell Margaret and me we have a new baby in the family. I couldn't quit thinking about it. I mean, I couldn't concentrate at all on any subject. I wanted to forget school and come over to the hospital. Dad said he had to go to work, but we'd all go later. Darn! Anyway, if you couldn't already tell when we were there a little while ago, I am so excited!

This is a gift from me for my new nephew. I've been working on it since I got home from the hospital tonight. I composed it just for him, but, I have to say, I got the idea from the Simon and Garfunkel song "April, Come She Will." (Obviously, when I hear that song from now on, I'll think "he" instead of "she"!) Of course, it's not as good as that, but it comes from my heart. I hope you and Robert like it. There was such a crowd of us visiting, I didn't get to really talk to you. Just tell Robert I'll teach it to him on the guitar if he wants. I'll play it for you later so you'll know how it sounds, and maybe you can learn to play it on the piano. Anyway, here are the words:

Baby, oh, baby. Baby boy of my heart.
You're so fresh with wonder, wonder in your eyes
What do you see and where will you start
To see the beauty all around you, in the trees and in the skies?

Baby, oh baby, I only just met you, but I know who you are
By the way you gaze around you, already aware
Of adventure waiting for you, your own guiding star
That will take you to places, near and far, yes,
Wherever you dare, wherever you dare, baby, oh baby.

So, baby, oh baby, be the boy of my heart
And we'll wonder together, we'll gaze with our eyes
I'll help you see the beauty, we'll both be a part
Of all that surrounds us, the laughter and love
In God's beautiful work, in the trees and the skies
You'll help us all feel it, to know it for sure, 'cause you're our baby,
and baby, you're the boy of my heart.

Love,
Laurie

April 23, 1968

Bobby's two weeks old today!!! I can hardly believe the mystery that is this little being. He has made us the perfect little family. I admit—I felt pretty inadequate and insecure the first few days home from the hospital. R, however, took to his baby boy immediately, demonstrating with strong, confident hands that Bobby will not break, whether we're changing his diapers, dressing him or bouncing, patting and soothing him when he cries. Now, I hate to have him out of my arms, unless, of course, R's got him. Then, all I can do is look at them with wonder.

Otherwise, in my own personal real world, I hurt!! The "episiotomy" (stitches in the area where 9-pound Bobby came bursting into the world) hurts like hell-fire and brimstone! Still and all, I feel a little better each day. The milk—it arrived as the nurses said it would—so now my boobs hurt, too. Robert loves that they're "big and beautiful." To me, they're volcanoes that ooze and leak. I look at them, and I cannot believe they're attached to me! For the first time in my life, I am top heavy!!!

Bobby's feeding relieves them, except that it hurts when he sucks. Which is worse? Hmm. But this kid is non-stop hungry. Dr. K says to stick to a schedule. How? He cries, then he eats for 30 mins or so, falls asleep for what seems like just a few minutes, then he's up and boom—he's rooting around again, kinda like a little kitty, looking for Mommy's feeding machine. He could stay "latched on" all day, I swear. Other than that, and that I'm so unbelievably tired, I'm in a new world, consisting of baby, body and Daddy.

April 30, 1968

A week has made a huge difference! I feel much better. Bobby still eats non-stop, and my boobs are still very sore, but they're better. The idea of getting up to pee doesn't make me cringe like I'm about to hear fingernails on a blackboard anymore. Dr. K said to give Bobby a bottle of formula during the night to give me a break. That means that, for now, at least, R and I are taking turns with Bobby at night. I'm getting a little more rest and am not completely exhausted, so I'm back in the land of the living! R is working and going to school, so he needs his rest, too. It'll all work out. We both keep saying that.

Laurie has been very sweet, having whoever's on carpool duty drop her off here every day after school to help me. She wrote a beautiful song for Bobby. She hasn't had her guitar with her after school, so she just sings it to him. She has a great, strong voice. He loves it, I can tell…and so do I.

I hate to think this, but she brought up something that could be a problem between us. Alex asked her to go out with him on a double date. I guess he's been calling her a lot, and he's even gotten rides over to Dad's house some evenings. That's all well and good. I'm sure he's a nice kid, but I'm worried about them "going together."

I can see she really likes him. She's mature-looking on the outside, but she's such a kid on the inside. She's a little freshman still, inexperienced, just getting her bearings about boys. Alex is older, but more important, he seems much more experienced. If this gets to be a "thing" between them, can she handle it? I just want her to wait until she's older. No, that's not it. I want her to meet someone who's more on her level. I just worry about her. So far, I've just been listening, trying to be cautious and steer her to other boys…but that doesn't seem to be working!

May 15, 1968
Beth,

I'm excited about my date with Alex. I know that you're worried about me, but I think you'll see that it'll work out ok. I think I'm going to have fun with him. He's got a great sense of humor. You know he's had the locker next to mine all year. That's been good for me, because he's complimented me when I needed it and reassured me when I was worried about school or drama or something.

I'm glad Dad said yes, of course, but what's better is that he seems kinda excited. I can't believe he's interested in something I'm doing, but I think he actually likes Alex. He always says hello and asks Alex how he is when he comes over. You know Dad likes that I joined Drama, so I guess, that this date is to a Drama party, makes it better for Dad. I hope for you, too.

Anyway, I was thinking about all this in History today, so I thought I'd write a note to tell you how I'm glad you're not putting up a stink about my date. You're my big sister, and I want you to help me get ready for my first date. Will you?

Laurie

"Whew! That was some traffic!" Robert said, walking through the front door and into the kitchen to where Beth stood at the stove stirring tomato soup. After a quick kiss on Beth's lips, he bent over Bobby who lay cooing at his parents from his baby bassinet.

"Hello, my little man. You look awfully excited to see me. You must know that I got all the classes I need for summer quarter. I'm gonna be a full-fledged senior when August rolls around. And I brought home another catalogue for Mommy so she can find a few more classes she needs to take! What a relief to be off that freeway, Beth. Oh, man, I could use a cold beer!

"Hi hon'. I think we have one or two in the frig. You were gone a while. Were the lines long for registering?"

"That part wasn't too bad. You know me. I'm good at taking cuts. Naw, but the lines to get the professors' signatures were nutso! What were those people talking about? I just went in, smiled, gave whoever was at the desk a few short answers, showed him my paperwork and that was that! In and out!" The freeway! Now, that was crazy!" Robert popped open his can.

"Well, I'm scared about tomorrow. I can't get over how that advisor grilled me for being on academic probation. Made me feel like a friggin' idiot. Basically, told me she shouldn't let me into any upper division classes. Guess she thought I was some dumb airhead girl."

"What do you care? She did sign it, so we get to take the English class together. You're gonna have to help me with that long book on the syllabus...the one about a magic mountain!"

"Oh Robert, you'll be fine. The only other class I want to take is the one on educational psychology. I think it's about stages kids go through. It'll be good for me with a growing baby and a little sister who thinks she's grown up...that is if I can get in."

"Don't worry, Beth. That advisor was a jerk. She doesn't know what you've been doing the last few years. Considering that, you did great. So, what's up with Laurie, anyway?"

"Oh, I just talked to her. She's good. She said Alex got a summer job and is also going on a family vacation to Mexico. She seemed excited for him. Says he's a good friend. I don't know.

Anyway, she's gonna be helping us with Bobby, babysitting while I'm at school. So that's cool. I'm hoping she'll find things other than Alex to keep her occupied. I said Patty could help her babysit Bobby if she wants. She liked that idea. And she's going to do Drama camp in July."

"Sounds all right. So, what's the problem?"

"Oh, she just gets so annoyed with me sometimes. And I don't always get why. Basically, though, things are fine. She wants to help us paint the crib for Bobby, so that'll be fun."

Beth tried to tread lightly with Laurie when she sensed a mood or a tone that warned "Look out! Danger ahead!" Often, this happened when she broached the topic of Alex, though she tried hard to stay purely conversational. As far as Beth could tell, Laurie and Alex had stayed on a friendly level. They talked on the phone a few times during the week, and he came over once in a while.

Immersed in her own life of baby, husband and school, Beth tried not to fret too much over Laurie. At two months old, Bobby filled most of her thoughts, especially where nursing was concerned. In the last week, she had reluctantly decided that she couldn't keep it up.

A big, active baby, Bobby wanted to nurse constantly, so that her breasts were red and raw all the time. Recently, she had been on antibiotics for a breast infection. For over a week, she just about screamed when he sucked. She needed reassurance that things would improve, but she only had one girlfriend who even had a baby, and she hadn't nursed her baby. Beth's doctor was no help, saying, "It's not for everyone. It's no crime to give your baby formula. Look at him. He's the picture of health." Though Beth knew all this, she also knew what she read in her baby books: a baby's chances for future health and security had so much to do with mother's milk. Well, she told herself, in resignation, this was the way it had to be. And with her going to school this summer, it would be much easier to leave formula for Laurie to feed Bobby.

August 20, 1968

So, school's starting in a week. Robert will be coaching again at St. Joe's. And now, they want him to teach a couple of lower level science courses. They say his college transcript so far—not to mention his high school grades at SJ's-- shows him to be a good student. He'll still be carrying a full load at Cal State. I should be thrilled since it probably means I can stay home with Bobby or, at the most, work part-time. I'm just worried he's going to be so busy, he won't have time for Bobby and me. We've had such a good summer, going to school together and taking Bobby everywhere with us: Even when we play volleyball with our friends, we take him. He plays in his playpen, happy as can be. Now, R's going to be studying as well as preparing for classes. He's so nervous already. I'm going to have to work really hard to be "Ms. Good Wife"!

Oct 10, 1968

Well, I was right about R. He was and still is pretty nervous about teaching the science classes. I can hardly talk to him after dinner. Between him planning for the next day and studying for his college classes, he's a drag. I love my time with Bobby, and I have been hanging around with Maddy. We take Bobby and her Kyle to the park and stuff, but I have to admit, I still get bored. I feel so bad. It's not that Bobby's boring. I mean I love him so much. He's my darling boy. But he needs my attention constantly.

I'm pretty sure I'm going to apply to work at the drugstore at Xmas time. It'll give us money for presents and me something different to do. Hopefully, between Laurie and Agnes, babysitting will be covered.

Things are going good for Laurie this year. She loves drama, has lots of friends from drama, and is still Miss Smarty Pants. Bad news: Dad's social life is pretty active, which means he usually goes out a few nights a week. I mean, I guess he deserves to have fun. He works hard, but I hate it for Laurie and Margaret. Dad says L's a sophomore in HS and seems v mature to him. Are you kidding? I mean, she's 15 ½. Yes, she's mature in some ways. So what?! Does that mean she likes being alone in the house with Margaret night after night now that Frankie has a girlfriend.?

December 1, 1968

Dear Beth,

First of all, thanks for making my Winter Dreams dress. I think it's going to be really pretty. I know I'll love it. (I already do.) I have something else to say, and it's really hard for me to say it. I've put it in a letter because I know you're going to be hurt, even though I don't want that. I just really hope you can please try to understand. I really have to tell you this, and I don't know how to except in a letter, because if I try to talk to you, I'm pretty sure I'll end up feeling even guiltier than I already feel. So, here goes.

You're a good big sister, but sometimes I don't like your advice. I made my decision. I'm not going to go to the dance with my girlfriends like you want. I know I made plans with them and you and Robert, but now that Alex has asked me, I'm going to the dance with him.

My girlfriends understand. I need you to understand, too. I'm not backing down this time. I've thought about your advice, but you already know that I really like Alex. I like being around him. But it's more than that. He's the first person in so long to really care about how I feel and what I think. And I feel the same about him.

You know the last three years have been really hard for me. You have Robert, and now you have little Bobby, too. Who do I have? Dad? Margaret? You know that's not enough for me, not by a long shot. I just wish you could give Alex a chance. You think he's too old for me, too experienced. (I think that's what you're really worried about). But, with me, Alex is always sweet and gentle. I know I'm not just "any girl" to him.

I know you care about me, and worry about me, and I appreciate that. But I really just want you to trust and like him—at least, give him a chance.

So, please—back off about Alex and me seeing each other, and about how long we're going to stay out and everything you think you need to warn me about. I'm not really a little kid anymore. Not with what's happened to me and you and all our family.

I'm worried you're going to be hurt and upset about this letter, but I hope you can think about yourself at my age and how much you hated it when Mom tried to get you to do something you didn't want to do, especially when it had to do with boys. I remember. I was there!! I hate when we fight, which luckily isn't very often. I really don't want you being mad at me and giving me the cold shoulder. It kills me. So, please—try to hear what I'm saying

Laurie

No doubt about it: although Beth had seen it coming, the letter from Laurie still stung. Laurie asked Beth not to "get mad and give me the cold shoulder." And, to be honest, the bigger, better part of Beth did understand. She had also to admit, at least to herself, that she hated when Laurie didn't listen to her. And yes, she did get upset and "quiet."

Do I give her the silent treatment like the boys used to give me when I tattled on them? Boy, they acted like I was invisible, not even in the room.... Mom did it to me, too, in her own way. I hated that so much! It was a horrible punishment! She'd give me one-word answers to my questions. I knew she was upset or angry, but I felt powerless to change the situation.

With Laurie, I get frustrated and just don't think straight—it's just that she's still so young and vulnerable. I know she thinks Alex has helped her feel more confident—and maybe he has—but she's still immature, still naive.

Alex is older, and seems very smart—but I've seen him around school, and he's so "charming." I can't tell if he's real or fake. But what scares me is that he could really hurt Laurie—and she's my little sister. I couldn't stand that. Yes, she looks older—but she's not! I know she's got to learn about this stuff, but if he breaks her heart—what then?! That could be a real setback. She still misses Mom so much, and Dad...well, Dad doesn't help.. Maybe he thinks she'll figure things out for herself. Like I had to. And even if that is true, Dad was never a teenaged girl—there's so much he doesn't have a clue about!

Alex is driving now—he goes over to see Laurie, takes her out casually—to McDonald's and stuff. Now, he wants to take her to the winter formal. That's a big deal—for a junior to take a lowly sophomore.

Besides! What was wrong with the original plan? Laurie and her girlfriends go together. The dance is open to sophomores, and it's okay to go stag. Since none of the girls has a steady boyfriend, they can go as a little group, get dressed up, even dance with each other if they want. They'd gather at a restaurant, have dinner, then have Robert and me drive them to the dance. Laurie was even going to let us stay and chaperone. I could see the night unfolding, all under my watchful eye. But no! Alex rushes in like a matador, waving his little red flag at Laurie, and that's all she can see. She's decided to think for herself. And what can I do? She's right about how I was when I was her age. Darn it!

Beth knew she hadn't reacted well when Laurie told her about her change of plans: "I decided to go with Alex to the dance. He's going to drive us." Beth and Robert's services would not be needed! Beth had been silently fuming ever since.

And now, Laurie had called Beth on her behavior. She had stood up to Beth, giving her notice that she had her own mind. Laurie would like her big sister's approval, but with it or without it, she'd made her decision.

Beth wondered how much of this was bravado, how much was Alex giving Laurie the words to get Beth out of this picture, and how much was just plain stubbornness on Laurie's part. What did it matter? Beth had to accept it and move on. First though, she decided to talk to her father.

The day after Laurie left the letter in her car, Beth approached Jack.

"Hey, Dad, has Laurie told you she got asked to the big dance at school by a junior boy?"

"Yes, yes, she did. She told me he's the younger brother of a boy you dated in high school. I've met him. He seems like a nice boy, very respectful and all."

"Yeah. I wondered if you're okay with her going with him. He's older and has a car. Do you think she's ready for that?"

"Oh, Bethie, you sound like your mother talking about you. Yes, I trust her. She seems very happy about this. I haven't seen her like this since…what was that other boy's name? The boy from the public school…he had a funny name…."

"Chili?"

"Yeah, that's it. Chili. He sure brought her out of her shell. But boy, you and I both know life has knocked her around, poor kid. I think it's just great that a nice young man from her own school has taken an interest. I know you've been working on her dress, honey, which is real nice of you, with Bobby and Robert and all. It's nice to see Laurie smiling like she means it, for a change."

"She says he has kind eyes."

"Huh?"

"Nothing. So, you're not worried about her, then? I want to chaperone the dance. I don't know if she'll let me, but then I could at least keep an eye on her."

"Well, I'm sure that would be swell. But Beth, if she says no…then no it is! She's got to grow up some time."

So that was that! Jack was unconcerned. Nonchalant. Beth hadn't expected him to say much more than what he'd said. In fact, he'd surprised her by being as aware as he was about Laurie's world.

As for Beth, she had to face the fact of Laurie's emerging strength, though, while she could bring herself to acknowledge it, she wasn't sure she liked it. Was she losing control of the universe she thought she'd set in motion after her mother's death? For over three years now, Beth had worked damned hard to make sense out of confusion, constantly struggling to keep the many balls in the air, struggling hard not to let one—or more—drop. It had seemed to work. But now, she saw that maybe that universe with Margaret, Laurie and her at the center, and Jack occupying a place on the periphery, maybe it was going away.

Yes, she'd taken the huge risk of upsetting things by marrying Robert; still, Beth had thought, by maintaining strict guidelines and by carefully balancing the various parts of her life, she could somehow keep things in order. As long as each player did their part, that is.

She was married Robert, but lived close to her father and sisters. She visited frequently—though not every day--and continued with many of the chores at Jack's. She kept up to date on her sisters' activities and weighed in when she thought she should. So far, so good she had thought, at least for Jack and Margaret. But, in this last year, Laurie had become a question mark.

Soon—perhaps very soon—Beth would be forced to reexamine the decisions she'd made and where they had taken her. These past few years, she hadn't allowed herself to look into the past and more importantly, she recoiled from looking too far into the future. Now she had a child to think about, but when she caught herself musing about Bobby—trying to envision him as a little boy, talking to her, asking her questions—Beth couldn't help but shudder, and hug her infant son to her chest.

Proud as she was of Laurie, Beth had never looked further ahead than a few weeks or months. Unconsciously, Beth had absorbed the idea that the future could not be trusted. "Why plan too far in advance?" she often asked herself. One never knew what lurked in the future anyway. And, so far, that self-advice had worked. The new structure that sat on the old foundation kept her life in balance. Or so she thought.

I guess I'm the only one worried about this. Why am I wading into Laurie's private life, anyway? That's easy: she's my little sister; I love her and I don't want anything to hurt her. But can I actually prevent life from…being life? Dammit! Am I just afraid of Laurie growing up? No! That's ridiculous! Why would I be?

Damn it to hell! Am I just repeating words from the past, words I resented? Words that didn't protect me from pain. Did Mom think that if she kept tight control, protected me from rushing into sex—and its consequences—I would have a happy life? That makes total sense—but…I'm sorry, Mom. That's not the way things went. That didn't turn out to be the problem. Something no one saw coming, something that no one, even—especially—you could control or prevent came and took you away anyway…the worst possible catastrophe.

I have no right to take this away from Laurie—whatever "this" is. I can't pretend I know better than you did about keeping bad things from happening. Anything can happen to anyone, anytime. I need to accept that Laurie's growing up! Focus on my actual baby! God! I've been nagging her about Alex just the way Mom nagged me about the boys I liked in high school.

But that last comment in Laurie's letter about how what all of us have gone through—the accident—has made her grow up fast, made her understand the realities of life.

Unfortunately, I'm not so sure that's what Mom's death did for us, exactly. Yeah, we understand that someone we really love and need can virtually disappear before we can scream, "No! Don't go!" but losing that person did nothing to prepare us for other heartrending realities of life.

Still, I see Laurie's point. I need to trust her. That's what she wants and needs from me. I'm going to have to try if I want her to trust me.

INTERIM

1 WHERE DID THE LOVE GO?

Baby, baby, where did our love go?
And all your promises of a love forevermore!
I've got this burning, burning, yearning feelin' inside me
Ooh, deep inside me, and it hurts so bad…

~ Holland - Dozier – Holland

April, 1971

I'm in shock! Numb. Robert is attracted to someone else! I can't believe it. Is our marriage over? This feels like a bad dream…I can't eat, or sleep—even think.

He says he feels really bad about it, but it was killing him not to be honest with me. "Honest"—what does that even mean here? And that's it?! And she's a kid—a senior! One of his students! He says it's just "an attraction" and that he still loves me and our boys.

Oh, those are the right words, but, somehow, I don't feel love! If it isn't such a big deal, why did he feel like he had to tell me? He says he's confused. I can't even begin to describe my feelings—except I know I feel betrayed and humiliated…like there's something wrong with me. He says it's not me.

How did our marriage—how did we—get to this? I'm trying so hard to be a good mom, but I don't think I ever have a good night's sleep. One of the boys is up every night for something. And I'm working part-time at the school.

I know I get grouchy pretty easily. Robert says I nag him a lot. Maybe I do. So, what does that mean? Is this my fault? He says it's not. So, Mister "I'm-so-confused," how do you think I feel? I mean, seriously! How does he think I feel? I told him once if he ever cheated on me, it would be the end for us. I have to be able to trust him.

The only thing I can say for him is he was "honest" with me. But I still feel like crap! He's just "attracted" to her. Oh, yeah—he TOLD her. He had to be "honest" with her, too, I guess. What did she say? She must've been shocked. I mean, he's her teacher! I know her; she's a nice girl—but how am I supposed to act when I run into her at school?

I just want us to be like we were before her. But how can we ever be like we were before?

I used to worry a little about him and the girls he taught. He's a flirt. And so darned good looking. But he always denies the flirting. It's obvious some of the girls he teaches have crushes on him. I don't like it, but, up till now, I figured "they're kids—so what?" I was more worried—if I was worried at all—about the other young, single teachers around school...the ones with very cute clothes who are never covered in baby spit-up or smelling like the dirty diaper they just changed.

Look at Pam and Jim. That started out as an innocent thing—just a good friendship between teachers—and now she's divorcing her husband for Jim. And then we found out that Jake is having an AFFAIR with a student—the younger sister of one of my good friends from high school who worked on the reservation with me! And what about Maddy—JAKE'S WIFE and one of my best friends from H.S.? We just got to be good friends again since she and Jake moved back from Monterey. She's six months pregnant and has two-year-old Timmy to think about! Doesn't Jake care about that? I don't know how Maddy can say she still loves Jake and wants him back. What does she tell Timmy about why Jake doesn't come home at night? (I don't know where he's staying.) Maddy told me Jake says he loves this student. The student's family is up in arms—even went to Maddy's house looking for Jake. What a mess!

So now what happens for R and me? R says this is just a crush, and "nothing at all" like the other scenarios being played out in St. Joe's Peyton Place. "Nothing at all, but Shelley's one of his students! And she's so much younger than him. According to Robert, nothing physical has happened between them, and he says it's not going to. But when I ask, "Now what?" all he has to say is he's "trying to sort things out."

What about me? What about the sorting out I have to do?! How do I look at our marriage now? How does Robert?! He says this "thing" is over, even though it never really got started. He keeps saying "We're not going to be like Pam and Jim, or Jake and Maddy." He says he loves me, loves our boys; he says he just got confused.

So, am I supposed to help him get through this?

Well, who's going to help me?

I just don't know what to think.

May, 1971

So, it's been a couple of weeks since Robert told me about his not so secret "attraction"—and I've turned into a green-eyed Godzilla. And not the "clinging vine" type. I'm more "Who was that on the phone?" and "Why are you 15 minutes late?" and "What do you think of that girl? Do you think she's cuter than me?" I picture myself as a pea-green octopus, waving her many arms with the "suckers" all over them, just waiting for Robert to make a mistake, so I can attack him with a couple of those tentacles. There! Smack! Take that! Smack! Smack!

I'm turning into the type of girl I despise. The type of wife I can't stand. That's why I said 'we' would be over if he ever cheated: I did NOT want to ever be the wife with zero confidence: shoulders hunched over, mousy hair hanging limp, pimples oozing all over my face. So, right now, I'm using sarcasm to cover up my pain and insecurity. I know I've been on the attack. I feel so immature; I wish I could just listen to him…believe him, and understand what he says he was going through. But I can't. Because I don't. And, well…just maybe, being that way is what got us into this mess in the first place. Maybe I should have stood up for myself instead of "understanding" so much. Who knows? I guess we're both still growing up. (Fairly obvious, Beth!)

I don't know if Shelley told her parents, but R said, a few days after they "talked," she told him she only liked him as her teacher. How pathetic! He said he's so relieved, and that he told her he never should have said anything…that it was a mistake, and he loves his family. Told her to forget about it, if she can.

In a way, I feel sorry for her; I mean, what did she do wrong? As for Robert, he's pretty grumpy most of the time. Says it's because he's focused on coaching. He's not sure he's up for the job of head coach—Jake got fired, so, now R's got the job! Says he's trying really hard to be a good teacher and a good coach. So, lots of pressure. Poor Robert! He tells me he's not really talking to Shelley much now, except when he has to, as her teacher. How awkward!

Does Robert really no longer have feelings for her? It'll be summer in a month. Track will be over; we'll go camping with Bobby and baby Greg, and hopefully some friends. Maybe things will get back to normal. We have two little boys who love their daddy. I have to at least pretend to be happy, for them. But it's just so hard!

The other day, I was painting the living room, listening to talk radio, and the show was about something called "open marriage." Different couples were talking about how "free" they felt in their marriages since they agreed to be "open." This agreement had "invigorated" their love life. I wondered what they were talking about. Then, I realized—the husbands and their wives had made this agreement to have other "relationships." I mean, they were, in fact, talking about sex with people they weren't married to!

This woman had written a book, claiming that having this "open" relationship had improved the couples' marriages by keeping things exciting. If one of them met someone else they were attracted to, they could "pursue" their feelings. One couple that was interviewed said now they don't feel "stuck." Now they operate on the theory that they don't have to fantasize about other people, because they're free to act on their feelings. Somehow, they've stayed stronger as a couple. And this was better for their kids! Or, at least, so they said. I was shocked and felt sick to my stomach.

R and I got married so young and had Bobby right away...and then Greggy arrived a year-and-a-half later. Sometimes, it seems we'll never get a full night's sleep. I just love them so much—and Robert, too, even though I'm hurt and confused right now. I can't imagine having an "open marriage." Just the thought of it makes me double over and clench my stomach!

I guess that, sometimes, I'm attracted to other guys. I suppose I fantasize, too. I mean, yes, I think certain guys are cute. But I love my family. Getting together with someone else—having an "open marriage"—just seems wrong. I find it hard to believe these people are for real, even though they sound so logical and sophisticated. But, then again, how would I know? I've been in my own little world for the past four years.

We had one year in our first apartment. We loved it because it was ours, but I know it wasn't great. Then, after we had Bobby, we moved to a bigger apartment with a grassy courtyard. We loved it, too. It was simple, but we painted some of the rooms bright yellow. Bobby's crib and dresser were hand-me-downs, but we painted them a deep sky blue with white-white trim and put up an inch-thick wall of paneling—which we decoupaged—between his room and the living room. It made everything look so cool and artsy. And we had a big, sunny kitchen. I don't know—we just made it "our" home.

Then last year—right after we had Greggy—we bought our first, very own house, and, over the summer, we started to fix it up. We painted our "TV room" chartreuse; I tied-dyed a sheet, and we covered a single bed mattress with it, then put the whole thing on an old door on cement blocks. Maddy gave us a couple of her old throw pillows, and—voila! Now, it's our couch! We even have beads hanging in the entrance to the room. It's far out, really groovy! And these things were fun—because we were doing them together, and it was all to make our house ours! We don't have much money, but Robert finished college and is teaching, and I take classes every chance I can to finish my degree. I work as a TA at St. Joe's for a little extra money, and I love it.

The point is, we both work really hard. I thought we were happy. It would be nice to have more money, but we do fine. And we have good friends, mostly other teachers. We camp with our boys and friends, and have fun parties. So why would this happen to us? How could Robert be attracted to someone else? What's wrong with me? With us?

2 BE HARD, BE COOL

I've built walls, a fortress deep and mighty
That none may penetrate
I have no need of friendship; friendship causes pain
It's laughter and it's loving I disdain.
I am a rock, I am an island.

~Paul Simon

June, 1972

This morning I was listening to "The Sounds of Silence"—which I love—on the radio. When it was over, the DJ comes on and says that Paul Simon wrote it after JFK was assassinated. Wow! I'd never heard that. But this is one of those songs for me…I mean whenever I hear the lines, "Hello Darkness, my old friend, I've come to talk with you again," I always get transported back to how I felt after the accident. I think about how dark I get when I let myself start to miss her—Mom. What do I mean LET? Usually, the "missing" just envelops me; I don't really LET it; it's just there. And I'm sure if JFK's kids knew that this was written about their dad's death, it would seem really weird to them, yet somehow fitting, too.

And then, a little while ago, another of S&G's songs came on the radio. They were singing "I am a rock, I am an island." I don't get it! I mean, I wonder how? How does someone decide to be hard and cool like a rock or an island? I'm almost 26 years old, and I don't get it. I try, but I fail every time.

It's been a year since I heard the words "I'm attracted to Shelley" from Robert. It's taken time, but our life is mostly back on track. I think Robert kind of hates himself for the whole thing. I've looked at it a million different ways, and when I can be objective about it, I think—okay, I WONDER, really—if he saw himself on a precipice with nowhere to go. Behind him were all the responsibilities: a wife, two kids, new house with a mortgage, students depending on him at school. Maybe he wanted to be that carefree teenager again, so he stepped off the precipice. Only, where he landed hurt people he loves. Taking the step complicated his life more. He still won't talk about it. Says he "can't explain" it. And he has never really said he was sorry for almost ruining "us." Still, somehow, I can feel his love, his commitment to me, to our little family. When I think about Shelley, I think how weird it must be for her.

In those days, I felt pretty good about myself. At one point, Robert confided in me that he was feeling a lack of confidence. I remember saying, all cocky, "Oh, why don't you just go make out with some girl. Then you'll feel better!" Flippant ole me! What was I thinking?

Of course, I didn't mean it. I just thought he was describing what we were both going through: being young parents, both of us working with kids only a little younger than we were. I mean, most of our friends are either just now getting married or are still kid-less. Things were pretty different for us then…and now. Shelley's graduated, but I wonder what she thinks about what happened to her—if she thinks about it at all. I think about it way too much!

I wonder if I'll ever NOT think about it.

Before the Shelley thing happened, Robert and I, as a couple, were a team, working together, moving forward together. Now, I'm not so confident. Robert is movie star good looking. Not only do I think this, but I hear it enough from other females. But since I've known him, I've always been sure he thought I was good looking, too.

After his "attraction" to Shelley, I've looked at Robert differently, to be sure, but I also see myself differently. Robert shook my world up but good! I worry a lot, now. I worry that I care more than he cares…about us, about me, our marriage. I'm pathetic—I convince myself that it's true, then I yell at myself, "Just be cool."

Why should I care so much if Robert's busy thinking about something other than me, than us? I tell myself I've still got 'it.' Why not focus on some other guy? Fantasize. But then I think that, even if I could "focus" on someone else, indulge a fantasy, forget about how Robert feels for a change—what about our darling, innocent boys? And I get disgusted and tell myself, "Stop doing this to yourself! This is not you! It won't change anything. It's not good for anyone."

Still…what if?

I remember right after Robert told me, I told Robert to stay with Tom for a few days…but I was such a mess, so, Laurie came over to stay with me. She helped me so much! I had a hard time paying attention to the boys, but she played with them, kept them busy. We decided to take the boys to the beach just to get out of the house—that maybe that would help my mood.

When we got there, we took off our shoes and started playing in the sand—Laurie and me and Bobby and Greggy. A while later, this guy came over and started playing with us for a little while. Afterwards, we got to talking. When I said we had to get going, he asked ME for my phone number! I remember first being shocked, but then I thought, "What the hell. Screw Robert!" So, I gave it to the guy. I still can't believe I did that. I mean I'm so "Good little Beth."

When "the guy" actually did call a few days later, I felt so weird. I just awkwardly told him not to call again. I knew, inside, even talking to him would be turning a corner of some kind. It scared me...I mean—what had I been thinking?

Sometimes, I get to thinking about Margaret and Laurie, and how, sometimes, I wish I wasn't so attached to them. I wonder if life would be easier for me...for my family with Robert—if I could be cool and hard about them. But there's no way. Instead, I get all worked up. How can Dad just go out at night and leave them at home alone? What kind of family life does he think they have?

I can't imagine being Laurie's age and being alone all the time with just Margaret to keep me company or look after me. (Technically, Frankie still lives there, but he's never home) It must feel so empty! No one's making Laurie's lunch for school the next day or worrying about how she's doing in school. No one's holding her hair back when she's puking in the toilet with the flu. No one gets her a cool washcloth. I mean WHO GETS LAURIE A HOT WATER BOTTLE WHEN SHE'S GOT CRAMPS? OR RUBS HER FEET WHEN SHE'S TIRED AND CONFUSED ABOUT SOME BOY, OR JUST WATCHING TV, JUST FILLING UP THE TIME WITH INANE SHOWS? WHO'S LISTENING TO HER PLAYING HER GUITAR, MAKING UP SAD SONGS?

I mean...Dad must have no clue what Mom did for us. And I don't even know about Margaret.

So many times, Dad talks to me about his square-dancing friends and outings they're planning, places where his dance group is going to dance. I fume and go on and on to Robert who listens and says, "You're doing all you can do. Give yourself a break." But still I think I should be able to change things. I just want to shake Dad! Tell him to "Shut up about fun old dancing! Take your daughters out for some fun!"

I should at least let Dad know I'm not interested in how he's spending his time away from home. Why don't I act cold and distant to him, LIKE "A ROCK OR AN ISLAND"? Would he even ask me what's the matter? Could I even have a real conversation with him, adult to adult?

It wouldn't do any good, even if I could do it, which I can't; I'm a chicken where Dad's concerned. Besides—who am I to judge him, really? He's my father. I'm not in his shoes. I haven't lived his life, borne his pain.

Still…what if he could change? I mean, WHY CAN'T HE? Does he think family life died with Mom?

Oh, why don't I just stop worrying about them all the time and BE A ROCK OR AN ISLAND?!

Sometimes, I wish I wasn't a 25-year-old wife and mother. What if I had waited at least until Laurie got through high school? Could I have filled in for Mom in some way for Laurie? Made her life more secure? At least I could have made her lunch and gotten her a hot water bottle, and rubbed her feet, but would I really have done that? Would she have let me? Of course, she would always miss Mom like I always do. I know I could never BE Mom, but would it have helped my sisters if I had stayed with them a few more years to try to fill in some gaps?!

And what if I had waited to get married…and then met someone when I was older, someone who would really love me? Love me…not just because he was in a car accident with my family and bonded with me and me with him, but love me for me.

And what if I had finished college…been on my own for a while, figured a few things out, gotten through missing Mom so much? Who would I be?

But then I think that's just crazy. First of all, I really did love Robert and he loved me, and second, I was so lost and devastated! Robert was my shining light.

When would I ever have felt good about leaving Dad and the girls to move out on my own? The answer is never! I thought about all of that when I got engaged, and no matter how many times I fantasize about how it could have been or might have been, I'll never know. I'll just NEVER KNOW! For sure, I could never be a rock or an island. Anyway, S&G sound so sarcastic and bitter in the song, I think it's all ironic; that what they really mean is they can't do it either—be a rock or an island.

<u>The Crazy Worried Girl</u>

She's one of those—the crazy girls, whose life is full of twists and twirls;
She cannot see the future, does the endless worry suit her?
Could she change what's on the inside—take the fears, the tears, and then hide?
Act cool, like things don't matter; that there's nothing there to shatter?
Act like things don't hurt or faze her? The shots, they barely graze her—
You know her heart is tender; still, she is her own defender
Who can take the hurt and mend her? She needs someone to befriend her
Outstretched arms that will embrace her—comfort, hold, and then

amaze her
Just soothe and then embrace her. Just soothe and then amaze her.
...just me, B. L.

The Dressing Room by me, B. L.

In the dressing room, I can hear them in the next stall. They must be out shopping together, the young woman and her mother. They're discussing how a dress looks on the daughter. The mom is so encouraging, complimentary. The girl must be giggling at her image in the mirror, asking for reassurance from her mother, who probably smiles a little as she earnestly nods her head, telling her daughter she looks beautiful, "Go ahead, it's perfect on you; get the dress. You've earned it." I open my door as they open theirs. They smile at me, and I gaze at them, one the younger version of the other. They chat about their next stop as we all leave the dressing room, the daughter carrying her pretty new dress. I walk out with nothing. Mom, where are you? I miss you...still.

3 BABY WOMAN ARRIVES

You are the sunshine of my life.
That's why I'll always be around.
You are the apple of my eye,
Forever you'll stay in my heart

~ Stevie Wonder

May 20, 1974—a few weeks after Ellie's birth

I'm in love…with my new baby girl! I'm so, so glad I convinced Robert to have another baby. I know he worried about more sleepless nights. Oh, my God! With the boys coming one right after the other, it was at least three years before we finally got a full night's sleep. Actually, it still seems that one of them wakes us most nights of the week. Robert argued that the boys were finally old enough to be pretty easy kids, so why start over with another baby? And I could see his point. But, somehow, something inside of me still said yes, I did want one more baby. And now, every time I look at her, this gorgeous creature, I'm just in awe!

Mom, you must be part of this blessing. I just feel you here with me, as I do so often—but especially now that Ellie's here. It's as if, through my little Eleanor—named for my hero, Mrs. E. Roosevelt—you found a way to grace me with the light of the angels. You are my particular angel; why do I forget to listen for you? I get caught up in the chaos, I guess. But, right now, I'm forced to slow down to the rhythm of my baby's needs, and I'm noticing signs of you. You are in the quiet…and in the light around Ellie. I'm feeding my girl, nothing else to do right now, and I feel you in this calm that, once in a while, permeates my life. Not too long ago, I was doing dishes, and I could hear the boys playing that they were camping, taking their little boats and GI Joes to the mud-lake in our backyard. I wanted to freeze the moment. And lately, Robert's been taking them to track practice for a few hours after school. Wow. I get to sit alone with my Ellie and look in her eyes, cooing with her in a blissful back-and-forth flow of love. In times like these, you're here. How can I ever forget to look for you?

I ask Ellie why she took so long to arrive. Every day at school, the kids would say, "Ms. D. I can't believe you're still here. Don't you feel like you're going to burst?!" Finally, Dr. Klein said "That's it. This kid is coming into this world!"

For the first time, Robert got to be in the room with me. I must have been turning blue, because he kept telling me to breathe. Poor thing, "natural" childbirth ended up being the most difficult for him! What an amazing experience for Ellie and me, and Daddy got to be a witness! Even throughout labor, which was start-and-stop all day, he was by my side. We watched the Watergate hearings between contractions. Kinda bizarre, but very distracting. I wonder if politics will interest our little girl!

I remember how, after we had Bobby, I wondered how I could ever love another baby as much as I love Bobby. I felt an infusion of love so deep, so mystical, that I still can't put it into words. I know I was a little worried when I got pregnant again. How could I love this one as much as I love Bobby? I needed someone to reassure me, but I felt funny asking my friends. Robert just kept telling me to stop worrying.

Having Greggy was different, yes, but my heart just filled up again at the beautiful little being that had come into my life, conceived by Robert and me and our love! I couldn't have loved him more. Another little miracle nestled in my arms so naturally, stretching and cooing. Just like Bobby did, and just as Ellie does now. And she'll be unique, the same way Bobby is and Greggy is.

Each of the boys is his own person. Where Bobby chatters away excitedly, Greggy seems to think about things. I remember when he was a baby…he'd be crawling along and then just stop, sit, and look around him—and I'd wonder, "What are you thinking about, my beautiful baby boy?" I knew, even then, what an interesting little guy he would be. And he is. He doesn't ask non-stop questions like Bobby does, but his questions are usually pretty deep.

When they're not fighting, I love watching them play. It's clear Bobby loves Greggy, and Greggy follows Bobby all around. Still, each has his own, distinct personality. And now! Now we have a baby girl joining this family! Who will she be? Will she be a talker, a thinker, a do-er—or something else entirely? What interesting things will she do? Will she love her big brothers? (Of course, she will!) And how my boys will love their little sister!

How did I get so lucky? I know it's something more than luck…so…maybe this is what grace feels like.

Amidst all the things I don't know, there are the things I'm absolutely certain of…and the first on that list is this: I want Ellie to know she's as good as any boy, even her brothers. I want her to grow up strong and confident, believing in herself. She's my Baby Woman. I hope I can be what she needs me to be as her mom. I feel so very responsible in a wonder-full and full-of-awe way.

May 27, 1974

Apparently, according to Laurie, the world is really changing for us females. I guess I'm not keeping up, or my values are all messed up, whatever. Tonight, on the phone, I was telling her how Robert made the little room off our bedroom into a baby room, and how I'm decorating for Ellie, and she said, "Beth, you crack me up. You are really stuck in suburbia, aren't you?"

She caught me off guard, and I was kinda tongue-tied. I said something like "Maybe…I guess. What do you mean?" She said something about my wanting to "keep up with the Joneses."

Well, that bugged me, so I said, "You mean because we painted the house?! Or because of my plans for the baby's room?"

Mistake number one: I had let her get under my skin.

Then she let me have it with "Oh, you know, Beth. Maybe I'm wrong, but you just seem so concerned with how everything looks. And dressing the baby in cute baby girl outfits. Now you're having Robert make that little room into a baby girl room. It seems like something out of the 50's. Sorry, I'm sure it'll be cute. Just remember, just 'cause she's a girl doesn't mean she's a doll."

I took a breath and fumed silently, trying to control myself.

She knew it and said, "Uh oh! I guess I shouldn't have said that. Don't be mad. I'm probably just jealous because I don't have all of the stuff you have."

I couldn't tell if she was serious, but I hoped she was, so I said, "You'll have a house one day, Laurie, if that's what you really want. And you'll probably want to work on it like Robert and I do ours. You guys have a neat place, but you're still in school, so it's different for you. But you did kinda stun me by saying Ellie's not a doll. I mean, you know I would never treat her like that."

I think she felt bad because she said, "I know. I didn't mean that seriously, Beth."

But I couldn't stop myself from saying, "I'm going to work hard to make sure she's equal to her brothers. Her room is just fun for me, right now. I can't explain it. Lately, though, Laurie, it sounds like maybe you don't approve of me or how hard we—Robert and I—work to make things nice for our family. And by the way, we certainly don't have a lot of stuff!"

I know I was huffing and puffing by then, and she started to lecture: "Well, all I really meant is I wonder if you're aware of what's going on in the real world, Beth. I mean, there are lots of people without much at all. They don't get to live a nice, middle-class life. Women, in particular, if they don't want to get married, have kids and follow what everyone else does—those women struggle in a big way!"

This made me mad, so I said, "Well, do those women WANT a 'nice, middle-class life' or no? Women don't have to get married. Just work hard. Save."

So, then she got sarcastic. "Oh, man, Beth! You make me laugh. You think it's that easy? Look at me—almost done with college, and the only jobs I can get are working at a burger joint, making minimum wage, or in an office, being a secretary to some man. How far can that get me? And Colin—he's done with school, but all he can get is a part-time job working for a doctor. Luckily, it gives him time to do his applications for grad school and study. But you know how we have to scrape by."

"Laurie, I know it's been hard for you. But what if you get that minimum wage job and use your experience to get a better job? Ya know—work your way up. Maybe you'd feel good about that. Or how about trying to find a job working on campus? Maybe in a professor's office."

Why did I have to say all that? But she really pushed my buttons!

"Beth, you're living in a dream world if you think I can or would do that. Women have to hold out, organize, and demand good jobs with fair pay for what they do. Did you know we only get paid two thirds of what a man does in a job with equal work? You think that's right? You have it easy. Robert—as a man—makes more than you would doing his job. But you still get to reap those benefits to fix up your house and get stuff for your kids!"

I've heard this speech before. We argue, but we get nowhere. So, I said, "Laurie, I gotta go. Robert's giving me the sign…you know, the long-distance thing."

It's so easy to forget she lives "long distance" from us. It's hard for us to keep our phone calls short, no matter how often we talk! I guess that's just the sister bond!

"Oh, okay. So, are you guys coming up next weekend? There's a free play up here near us. It's being held in a barn. It should be fun. And Beth, Jason really misses the boys. And I need to see Ellie. I bet she's grown so much! And I'm having some big problems with the co-op, not to mention Colin. I don't know how much longer I can stick it out with him. Colin needs to see his big brother. Maybe being with Robert will help Colin see he could treat me better. Oh, well, since Robert won't let us talk anymore tonight, I really need you guys to come.

"I'll try, I'm just not sure yet."

"Why not? Is there a problem?"

"Robert has something at the school, I think. I'll let you know."

"I hope it's not because of this conversation. You always say we need to be honest."

"I do want us to be honest. It's not because of that. I'll try to make it work for the weekend."

I do say that about honesty, but do I really mean it? I don't always know. It's complicated. I want us to share our personal stuff—at least, I think I do—we're sisters! But I do get tired of Laurie's judgments or criticisms or whatever they are.

I know I don't have the benefit of her women's studies classes, and I like talking with her about them, hearing the different perspectives she's getting. But I hate it when Laurie talks down to me like this. Robert and I work hard. I only took off a few weeks from my job when I had Ellie, just so I could finish out the second semester. I could've stayed out longer with summer coming—without pay, of course—but I knew we needed the money.

Robert and I watch our pennies and work on our house together. I don't think Laurie understands all the effort he and I put in because she's so focused on herself and her life. She's a lot younger, though, and in a different place than we are. Also, Colin's different from Robert; he's more like their dad—academically motivated. I do think Colin's a great dad, though, and Laurie's a great mom. They just—they come at things differently than Robert and I do—and "different" doesn't make any of us wrong.

How am I going to convince Robert to go? He hates the long drive. Then there's the new kitty. The boys aren't going to want to leave her behind. We can't anyway, because we have no one to feed her. How do we take her in the car? Oh, man. After this conversation, I can't see why I should want to go!

But, then, why does Laurie want me to come? Sometimes, she doesn't even seem to like me! I hope it's just a phase. Why do I still worry about her? I know she doesn't have much, which makes me feel guilty. I'm glad she wants to see Ellie, and I miss Jase, too. We all love him so much, just like Laurie loves the boys. I mean, we really are one big family. The sisters married the brothers…pretty unique! We all argue sometimes, but we love each other. That's what's important. Oh, God! She's so influenced by the Women's Co-op. I wonder if they fill her with ideas that cause problems with Colin.

May 29, 1974

I talked Robert into going to see Laurie and Colin this weekend! He isn't totally crazy about the idea, mostly because his hay fever is bugging him, and he wanted to have track practice on Monday since there's no school. I guess I guilted him into it, but—oh, well. I called Laurie, and she sounded really happy that we're coming. I think it'll be a fun weekend if Robert isn't too grumpy. Maybe Colin will talk to him about sports. They both love their Yankees, the whole "We're from New York" thing, they say. I guess I'll find out what's going on with Laurie and the Co-op.

I've got to admit: those girls—I mean women—make me feel uncomfortable (though I don't plan to tell Laurie that). They all—including Laurie—have hairy legs and underarms, and they don't wear bras or deodorant. Laurie said it's more comfortable for women. I decided to be open-minded, so I tried the hairy legs, no bra thing, but, basically, I just felt weird. I mean, Robert was okay with it (though he did say my legs were scratchy), but none of my friends do any of that, and I just felt really self-conscious walking around that way. I hope I don't have to explain that to Laurie.

Robert has let his hair get kinda long, and he has a mustache and long sideburns, so it's not like we're stuck in the past. We keep up with trends. Some trends. And he's pretty open-minded—but that doesn't mean he gets the whole women's lib thing, much less embraces it. Like other guys our age, he often asks me what's wrong with doing things the way our parents did them? "If it ain't broke, why fix it?" But, then, I've always insisted that we share the work around the house—the kids, for sure, but also everything that seems lopsided in so many marriages—and he's been okay with that.

I mean—why should I be changing diapers and getting food for the kids while he sits around watching a game on TV? As long as what I'm saying is logical—as long as things make sense to him—he's fine. But—like Laurie—I get tired of fighting for these things, and I want the "status quo" to be different for my baby girl. Luckily, her daddy loves to play with his kids and doesn't mind changing dirty diapers and feeding babies.

The other day, I read an interview with Betty Friedan in Dad's Time magazine, about how she started NOW and wrote 'The Feminine Mystique' in the 60's. I've borrowed the book from Laurie, but I haven't had time to read it. In the interview, Friedan says that women in general think they are meant to be wives and mothers, cooking and cleaning for their families—just being homemakers. Yet, she says, her research shows most of these "homemakers" are actually unhappy, because just doing that is unfulfilling.

So why do we do it? She says women are brainwashed by male publishers and advertisers who control what articles go into women's magazines! They make us think we SHOULD want to devote our lives 24/7 to our families. And it's true! I have thought "What's wrong with me?" because I don't want to be "just" a stay-at-home mom, and I'm not all that concerned with cooking the perfect meal, or the latest trends in makeup or decorating, no matter what Laurie thinks. Not that I can afford that stuff anyway.

But then, I also do feel guilty. It's confusing to me. I mean, MY husband

and kids are EXTREMELY important to me—they're my world—but I also get bored just cleaning the house and going to the park. I love teaching teenagers, and getting them to really think about what they read for their English classes. I feel like I connect with them, and it also makes me feel that I'm accomplishing something.

I also enjoy just being with and working with the people at school—some of my old teachers even. I'm learning kind of on the job. It's neat to see all these adults—besides the aides and teachers that are around my age—as real people with issues and lives sort of like mine.

I guess that, when I stayed home after each of the boys came, I was happy at first, but eventually, I got bored. Maybe I'm too young for a slower pace to the day. Or maybe I'm not creative enough to come up with tons of imaginative things to do. Or maybe I just like using my brain and interacting with adults, at least for part of the day.

I guess somehow, I want to do both—be with my kids, and still do something that makes me feel I'm contributing—to our household, yes, but also to something bigger than me and my family. Now, with Ellie, I'm happy to stay home for the next semester—not just for her, but for all three of them. Bobby just finished kindergarten and Greggy wants to go to pre-school in the fall. Time flies by, and they're off. Still, I'm pretty sure that, one of these days, I'll want to spread my wings again.

I'm still young—I'm only 26! —I think I SHOULD be able to apply for jobs that people see as "men's jobs"—though I can't think of any such job I'd want right now. But, definitely, Laurie should be able to be a fireman or policeman—or fire-WOMAN or police-WOMAN, I should say—if she wants to (which she doesn't), but Robert says men are stronger and women can't keep up with them, so it wouldn't be fair to have them take jobs that should go to men. (Actually, he admits that Laurie's pretty strong!)

Some of the women interviewed for the article don't like the idea of other women doing "men's" jobs because they worry that their husbands might have affairs. That made me stop and think because some guys MIGHT be attracted to their female partners. I know I'm pretty insecure, so maybe that's why that issue bothers me.

Anyway, for now—for now! —I'm content. And I'm going to always love my baby-woman to bits and try to teach her to be proud of herself—her self—and not to ever let any guy—even her brothers—hold her back from being who she is or wants to be. And, next weekend, we're going to San Francisco to see my liberated sister and her smarty-pants husband—my husband's brother—watch a play in a barn and have a blast!

4 CALAMITY AND GRACE COLLIDE

Raindrops keep falling on my head
and just like the guy whose feet are too big for his bed
Nothing seems to fit...
So, I did me some talking to the sun
And I said I didn't like the way he got things done
Crying's not for me…

~ Burt Bacharach and Hal David

August 17, 1975

So, our 10-year high school reunion, which we'd anticipated for weeks, finally arrived. We'd made plans with Joe and Diane to go a pre-party with "hors d'oeuvres and cocktails." It sounded so sophisticated! Knowing how excited we were about this night out, Linda had invited all three of our kids to spend the night with her kids! The boys and Ellie love Linda, as well as playing with Paul and Cindy, so this turn of events made our anticipation even greater. And no whining from the kids about leaving them with a sitter! The boys were going to have a blast spending the night with their playmates, and, with Ellie, we were going to play the overnight part by ear. If she missed us at bedtime, we would leave early and pick her up.

With a balmy summer evening and kids excited about their slumber party, we were ready for a night of freedom and fun. And everything went just as planned for a while. Then, just as we were getting ready to head over to the actual reunion, we got a phone call from Linda. Robert went to answer the phone, while I kept my fingers crossed. When he came back, I could see trouble on his face.

"Is everything okay?" I asked, praying nothing would interrupt our evening.

"Bobby took a hard fall off his bike. Linda doesn't think it's serious, but he's crying and wants us. I'll go calm him down and meet you at the restaurant. Don't have too much fun without me," Robert joked.

I can't lie; I was so glad he offered. I mean, I did feel guilty, but I didn't let that stop me. So, off I went with Joe and Diane. Soon, I was mixing it up with old friends, chatting with them about our lives now, remarking on how good we all looked; I even danced with an old boyfriend. Finally, I realized Robert hadn't arrived yet, and I hadn't even called him. So, now, I was anxious and guilty, looking around for a pay phone. He answered on the second or third ring.

"Oh, good! I've been waiting for you to call. How is it?"

"It's nice. But how's Bobby? How come you never came?"

"Well, he was really upset when I got there. I tried to calm him down, but I could see he didn't want me to leave him there, so I brought him home. He's in bed now. I gave him some baby aspirin. He's gonna be okay. Don't rush home. One of us should enjoy the reunion."

"What about Greg and Ellie?"

"They—and I mean Ellie, too—wanted to stay." At least that part was good.

But still, I felt ashamed because I WAS having fun! I was enjoying drinking and laughing with old friends. I actually felt like a teenager again.

As soon as I told Joe what had happened, he said, "We'll take you home. We're ready to go anyway. I've seen enough of our old classmates!" But Molly, who was sitting with us, said "If you want to stay a little longer, Lizbeth, we'll take you; your house is right on our way." So, like a really crappy wife and mother, I told Joe, "Just go ahead. Molly's right. I'm way out of your way." Molly smiled, Joe shrugged, and that was that.

WHY DIDN'T I JUST GO WITH JOE AND DIANE? But I rode with Molly, and didn't get home for close to another hour. When I finally got in, I could hear Bobby moaning. Oh, man! Robert said he'd been doing that for about 30 minutes, and he was getting worried. We knew we had to get Bobby to the ER right away.

It's a bit of a blur now, but we raced to the hospital and waited for what seemed like hours. Then an elderly doctor—he had white hair on the sides of his otherwise bald head—came in to take a look. Though he was cheery and chipper, he was also business-like. He said something like, "I'm Dr. Peters. Okay, let's see what we've got here. Hmm. Does that hurt, little guy? Oh, my, I guess it DOES hurt. Well, what were you doing to get such an "owie"? I hope you weren't skateboarding!" He looked at us. "Because I see so many kids with serious injuries, all because they were skateboarding. Worst invention ever!" We assured the doctor Bobby wasn't skateboarding—although he really wants a skateboard—and the doctor "Hmm-ed" some more and then said, "Well, we'd better get these pants off you, young man, so we can have a better look, and then we'll get you to x-ray." The doctor or nurse—I forget who—grabbed a pair of scissors.

"Wait! Those are his favorite pants!" I yelled—at least I think I yelled it. Anyway, they just started cutting the pants off, while Bobby cried. All I could do was hold his hand and fight my own tears. Robert felt bad that he had left them on him, but what could he do? He hadn't wanted to risk hurting Bobby by taking them off. Seems crazy now, I mean what's the big deal? But the point is, they were his FAVORITE PANTS!

Anyway, we both hugged and kissed Bobby before the nurse wheeled him off to x-ray. I think he was trying to be brave, because he just looked straight ahead. We went back to the waiting room, where we sat like zombies for what seemed like an eternity. Finally, someone in scrubs called us to come back into the cubicle where our little Bobby lay, white-faced.

Soon, Dr. Peters briskly strode in and got right to the point. "Time for some "straight talk," he said, looking at Robert. He asked if we had insurance. Robert said no. Then he told us that Bobby has a "spiral fracture of the femur."

Those words are permanently engraved on my brain.

Because the break was so bad and high on his thigh, Bobby would need his leg in traction for "quite some time." Translation: he would need to stay in the hospital for "quite some time"! I found myself hating this tall, lean, oldish doctor with his "no sugar-coating this news" ways.

"Wait! Slow down!" I wanted to shout. "I'm not grasping this situation! Explain this again, please." When I looked at Robert, I saw panic. I know money—or, actually, our lack of it—drove that look. While the doctor talked on, Robert gave me the "What the hell is happening?" look. I mean—he hated to be leaving St. Joe's, having to say goodbye to his athletes and our old school for a public school, but having medical insurance for the first time had excited him, made him feel responsible. He was turning a page in the grown-up book. The unfortunate catch, however: the timing. Insurance at his new school didn't kick in until October…two months away!

My brain, though, was glued on the nightmarish idea of leaving my little boy here. I just kept hearing the doctor's voice: "He'll probably need to have his leg in traction for…" and then the last three words echoed over and over "QUITE SOME TIME QUITE SOME TIME QUITE SOME TIME…."

I don't think either Robert or I heard half of what Dr. Peters said after his opening salvo. Basically, I looked up to see him walk out as a woman in white gave Bobby a shot of something that made him cry and then fall asleep. Robert and I, too stunned to talk, looked at each other across Bobby's bed, then beat it out of there. We had to do something we had some control over: pick up Greggy and Ellie, and regroup.

As soon as he got in the car, Greggy started in with his questions.

"Where's Bobby?"

"Remember? He broke his leg. We told you he's in the hospital."

"But Mommy, why does he have to be there? Mommy, WHERE is the hospital?"

"Your brother fell off his bike and hurt his leg really badly. The doctor at the hospital is fixing it."

"Are you gonna get him later? I wanna go with you."

"Yes, of course we're going back to see him. You can come, but you won't be able to go in to see him."

"What do you mean, Mommy? I wanna see him. Why can't I?"

Then came the tears.

The boys had NEVER been separated. But being five meant Greggy would not get through the door to Bobby's room. I had checked this out. He just kept asking, "Why not?" Then he'd say, "Please. I'll be good."

At some point, I went back to the hospital. I couldn't stand the idea of Bobby waking up without me there. Meanwhile, Robert called our parents, then took Ellie and Greggy to get Bobby some snacks that Bobby likes, looking for something—ANYTHING—to cheer him up.

We both knew our active and ever-busy boy would be shocked by what this was going to mean for him. At seven, how could he grasp it? "Quite some time" would feel like forever! But then, a great thing happened! A couple of Robert's track kids came by the house. When they heard about Bobby, they were upset. They love Robert, and treat the boys like their little brothers. They told Robert they were going to go see him right then! Greggy heard them, and said he wanted to go with them, but Robert reminded him that he couldn't go in Bobby's room. One of the guys—Mark, I think—shook his head. "That's just not cool, coach! Man, we have to fix this. Leave it to us!"

So—there I was, sitting at Bobby's side, doing what I could do to comfort him, when I see four of the track kids walk into the room with Robert. Mark moved awkwardly, and—despite the August heat, had a big black overcoat wrapped around him. There they were: four big, athletic boys, all giggling. Robert hurried over to Bobby, and whispered excitedly, "Guess who's come to visit you!?"

Once they all got into the room and closed the door, out came Greggy from inside Ken's overcoat. Luckily, Ken's so tall, he just had Greggy grip him around the waist while he held on tightly to him from the outside. The other boys acted as a shield around the two of them as they'd moved through the hospital corridors. Teamwork! We all started laughing—even Bobby! For a little while, he perked up, happy to have his little buddy there, as well as the big boys he admires so much. I wondered where Ellie was, and the boys laughed. "She's playing with Rodney in the waiting room." Robert said. "He drew the shortest straw!"

Luckily, they didn't stay long, because, soon after the boys took Greggy down to the waiting room, Dr. Peters came in to update us on Bobby's condition. He told us an orthopedist looked at the X-rays and agreed Bobby needs his leg in traction for at least a month, maybe two. Dr. Peters looked at Robert and said quietly, "I know, without insurance, you can't afford that."

I held my breath and waited for what would come next. Whatever it was, I knew it wouldn't come with any sugar coating.

"Do you have access to a big station wagon or van?"

Curious, I said, "We do. My aunt has a van. Why?" He asked if it could accommodate Bobby lying down with his leg raised up a foot or so.

Robert and I looked at each other, then Robert said, "I think we can take out the back seats or at least make them lay flat.".

"Okay," the doctor said to both of us. "Make sure. If so, I want you to make arrangements to get that van for tomorrow. You'll have to leave Bobby here one more night, but then, bring the van here in the morning. We'll arrange things with my nurse. We'll get Bobby in there with his leg raised. You'll take him home, and I'll meet you there. Robert, you and I will rig up something to hold Bobby's leg suspended at the proper angle. I'll make house calls to monitor his progress."

We were stunned. I'd been praying non-stop to Mom for something, anything to help us with this situation. This doctor that I had hated for his bad news and abrupt manner turned out to be Bobby's angel…and Robert's and mine, too. I knew I couldn't leave my little boy in the hospital for a month!

Aunt Maudie readily agreed to loan us her van. She even drove it over and picked us up. Robert and Dr. Peters loaded Bobby in the back where Aunt Maudie had folded down the seats. They put his leg up on three pillows. I rode in the back trying to keep Bobby calm. Dr. P. followed us home, and, together, he and Robert set up Bobby's bed with a pulley system with a big hook Robert screwed into the ceiling.

In his bed, leg up in the air, Bobby looked so forlorn. He didn't know how lucky he was. (Thanks, Mom!)

August 31, 1975

Now, we're all home. It's been almost two weeks of Bobby in traction…but it feels like two months! The track guys have been by three or four times; they always check on Bobby, but they're also here for Robert.

They can't believe he's going to start teaching at another school. They joke that they're misfits: a couple are Mexican American, a bunch are Afro American, one moved here from India just before his freshman year—he could hardly speak English. And yet, with Robert, they've become a little family. And because they're kids, they don't really understand that we need health insurance and a better income. Robert can't believe he's leaving them, either…so I guess they all just need time to adjust to the idea.

Since Robert's going to be coaching cross-country at Fischer, he's also been getting together with some of those boys, and on those days, he's gone all afternoon. He comes home pretty downbeat. The good thing is that, when he's home on other days, he's open to my getting out of the house. Last week, I went to Lake Isidore with Joe and Diane. I actually enjoyed myself for a few hours. It was such a relief!

Here's the deal for me, though: we really didn't have a choice about Robert's job, crummy as that might be for him. He's kind of sulking, a little moody, but I want to say, "Buck up, honey! This is all so shitty, but think of Bobby. He's just a kid! We're grown-ups (hopefully). We've got to make the best of this!"

I mean, we have three kids now. I've been staying home with them since Ellie was born, taking on babysitting for extra money. Robert agreed totally with this. I loved working at St Joe's, but childcare for our three kids would be a fortune—way more than I could make as a teacher's aide. We just had to face the facts. It's just extra difficult these days, because I'm not even babysitting. I just can't, what with Bobby so miserable. I mean, the poor little guy is hardly smiling these days. It's so sad, and my nerves are frayed, to say the least. When school starts, Robert will be getting a regular salary again—a much better salary—and we can re-evaluate.

Anyway, Mark, the heart of the team, gave Bobby his special fishing hat, and I know Bobby was happy about it—I mean Mark wore it all the time—and Bobby idolizes him. For the last few years, Robert has taken the boys to practice with him so often that all the boys—the little boys and the big boys—really have bonded. We've taken a lot of these big kids on our family camping trips so they can run at the campgrounds—and they do that—but it's pretty clear they enjoy being with their coach—some of them even call him "DAD"—and our family.

The last time we went to Lake Nacimiento, Mark brought his Dad's fishing stuff, and he took Bobby and Greggy with him to catch some fish. I don't think Mark had ever really been fishing, and that's why he got so excited when he actually caught a few. I said I would definitely NOT clean them, but I would cook them, so Mark threw them back in the lake, which I think relieved us all! Though both Bobby and Greggy love all the boys, Mark is definitely their favorite.

Right now, though, I'm so worried about Bobby. He's so miserable, just lying in his bed. I try to engage him, ask him if he wants to play games or have me read to him, but he says no and just watches TV. Linda has brought Paul over a few times, and Paul brought Bobby a game that they could play. The first time, Bobby played with him, but the next time, he basically ignored Paul. And Paul is his best friend in the world!!

I have to bring the bedpan in when Bobby has to pee or poop. He absolutely hates it, and I do, too. He's so grouchy, and he yells at me sometimes. Sometimes, I yell back at him, or throw one of his stuffed animals at the wall. My stomach hurts so much all the time. I feel like such a failure of a mom.

I've begun imagining Bobby wearing his misery like what the nuns called a "hair shirt." They described saints who wore these things as a form of self-punishment. Their descriptions haunted me at night. In my imagination, I saw something that looked like a long coat, lined with thorns…a coat that hurt and burned something awful.

I could see myself with the coat on—going crazy, wanting to tear it off. It's still vivid in my mind. That's what I see for Bobby; it's so weird! It makes me want to grab him out of his bed and wrap my arms around him. Since I can't, though, I keep moving, keep busy. Get Ellie up, take Greggy to play with a friend, put Ellie down for a nap, wash laundry, dry laundry, fold laundry, pick up Greggy, make lunch, feed Ellie, check on Bobby from time to time—or ask Robert to do it.

I'm too fixated on myself, feeling sorry for me for having to go through this with Bobby. I should remember that he's really yelling at the unfairness of his situation—and I agree with him. He's just a little boy. Why don't I just tell him, "I love you, I love you. I'm here. It's not fair, and I know it. I want to take the pain and boredom away." But no, I point out that we put a little TV in his room, which we would never do under normal circumstances, and he can watch it all day long, which, normally, we would never let him do. But, he's bored and miserable, and we all wish it just hadn't happened. He was riding his bike! HE WASN'T DOING ANYTHING WRONG!

I keep telling myself we'll get through this. Thank God, Bobby's home and okay and his leg will heal. It could be so much worse. God, please—I want to be a better mother to my precious son.

November 3, 1975

Bobby's out of traction! We have to take him in for another x-ray, but we can see the light at the end of this long, long tunnel. Finally!

Dr. P. was so great, coming by regularly to make sure the pulley-thing was staying in place, and that Bobby's leg seemed to be healing. But he must have seen how skinny Bobby was getting. I mentioned it to him—told him Bobby was hardly eating and that it was scary and frustrating. He just said not to worry— "He's young and resilient. Just watch him bounce back!"

But Dr. P is not a counselor. I guess he could be a father or grandpa—I don't know, but his words…well, haven't given me much comfort. I know Bobby is just a little boy whose new world hasn't made any sense to him. How can he comprehend it all? He's angry, and, though I hate to think this, he—a little boy of seven—seems depressed. I mean, I have all the child-rearing books, and this is what I've come up with. I worry like crazy, but then the whole situation has crazed me! And, through it all, where was the person who could help me? Gone, gone, gone—though I talk to her through my tears all the time, it seems.

Though this is the first I've written about it and I haven't said anything to anyone, one pretty big thing happened that I know made everything worse for Bobby. I went along with it, so I know I'll feel guilty about it for the rest of my life. Robert got rid of our cat! Bobby loved that cat.

About a week after the accident, we finally had Bobby home and set up in his room. Robert and I were over the top exhausted from everything. We were trying to balance Ellie's and Greggy's needs with Bobby's, and trying not to think of our own. But he and I were sitting on the couch after all the kids were finally asleep, and Robert noticed Kee-Kee walk by, full belly swinging with her growing teats, and he flipped. In total frustration, he said to me, "Beth, look at her! We can't possibly deal with another litter right now. What are we going to do?" I had no idea and didn't want to even think about it at this point, so I said something like, "What do you mean? What can we do? Let's not worry about this now."

"How can you say not to worry about this? Do you want to have six kittens running around here, besides her? And what if she has another dead kitten like she did last time? That will go over well with the kids, especially Bobby, right?" He was sarcastic and ready to blow.

"Of course not. But remember I talked to you about having her spayed, but you said it cost too much." I wasn't helping! "Let's just let her be, then give away her kittens like we did last time." I didn't want him to take her to the pound. But what he had in mind was worse, when I look back.

"I think I should just take her down to the vacant lot a couple of blocks away and let her go. It's a kid neighborhood. Some cat lover will come along and take her and her kittens in."

"What about Bobby? He loves that cat!" As did Greggy, Ellie and I!

"He's not going to notice with all that's going on," was Robert's reply.

We fought about it for a while. He reminded me of our money problems, as if I didn't how broke we were. He was tearing his hair out. The ER visit, Bobby's few days in the hospital, the doctor's house calls. All of these dollar signs loomed over us, with a giant black cloud filled with question marks ready to burst.

Robert got up with a determined look on his face. I couldn't help him, so I just petted Kee-Kee one more time, then went to our room in tears. I felt so awful, I couldn't even write about it. I just prayed that somehow Robert would be right and Bobby wouldn't notice.

WRONG! If ever anything could have given Bobby comfort, it would have been that cat and a kitten or two. Why, oh, why! did I let Robert go through with it? I guess—no, I know—I was weak. Gave in. A big, fat coward. We didn't know what to do, a PG cat just one more thing to worry about. Robert needed me to figure something out. Between us, I'm more of an animal person. I should've asked Dad for the money to…I don't know what. Something besides this! I could've called Laurie. Why didn't I? She would NOT have let us do this!

While I brooded about how the disappearance of Kee-Kee would affect Bobby, Robert felt bad, too. Only he was focused on what he thought would be Bobby's bigger disappointment: missing what was to be our last camping trip of the summer. Robert had promised him he would teach him to water-ski on that trip. And we were supposed to take some of the track boys again, including Mark. But what could we do?

Robert's prediction came true. Bobby's tears flowed at his disappointment over not getting to camp with the boys and learn to water-ski with his dad. But, also, Bobby did miss our kitty; he asked over and over where she was. Of course, I lied about it—I had to—just kept saying I didn't know, that she was probably off having an adventure. "She'll show up one of these days," I kept saying. And he just kept getting sadder and angrier. God! Why didn't I protest for Bobby's sake? It's the same old thing. Sometimes, it seems like I'm always looking back, questioning myself.

On a brighter note, Bobby was excited to see the kids on Halloween. Robert took Greggy around the neighborhood, while Bobby, Ellie, and I sat by the front door with the candy. Robert was going to pull Bobby and Ellie in the wagon, but it got complicated trying to figure out the trick and treating, especially with Ellie. So, sweet Greggy promised to get Bobby some good candy, and Bobby was good with that. Finally, a good time for Bobby!

November 7, 1975

Dr. P. gave Bobby crutches and said he could start putting a little weight on his leg…and though it would take some time, gradually his leg would get stronger. So, I thought, "Great. Now he can get around. Out of that bed, finally! And pretty soon he'll be walking again." I mean, he hasn't been on his feet for two months!

But, no, he hates the crutches; he won't even try…just gets mad and throws them down. I'm trying not to panic, but he needs to go back to school. I called there as soon as he got the crutches. I thought he'd be going back in a few days. A "home school" teacher had come by in September to leave assignments, saying she'd come back regularly to check his progress.

At first, he tried—Bobby always liked stories that we read to him, or with him, and he likes arithmetic. He's smart at everything, really, and he did well in kindergarten and first grade. But his first-grade class was just beginning to read in June—and then there was summer vacation. He's already been out of school for two months of second grade—he can't afford to get too much farther behind. And, worse, the "home school" teacher did NOT come by to work with him. I tried, but, let's face it: I gave up when he acted cranky and bored. It was just one more thing to upset him; I'm his mom—I just couldn't be his teacher too, especially in his condition!

So, the question now is, how are we going to get him back to school when he won't even try the crutches? It never occurred to me that using crutches is difficult, but then, I've never had to use them! I was an active kid. I climbed trees, rode my bike to school, roller-skated in those horrible things with the skate key that were always coming apart. I had plenty of skinned knees, sure—but never a broken bone.

Bobby's missed so much school, and he needs to learn to read. What if he's lost what he knew at the end of last year? C'mon, WE NEED SOME HELP, BADLY!

Then on top of all this, Robert started his new job at the public school, and he hates it! His students are so far behind and very disrespectful. He says they're wild and rowdy. They move their desks around all over the room, and don't pay attention. He imitates the way they get his attention: "Hey, Dolan!" And, he says, that's if he's lucky! I don't know what they say otherwise—I'm too afraid to ask.

So, Robert's beside himself, and I can't do anything but listen. Truth be told, I don't have much patience for even that. I want him to come home in the evening and cheer me up. I know we're so lucky in so many ways, but somehow, I just can't feel the gratitude. I don't even feel like praying or talking to Mom right now.

November 12, 1975

I'm feeling kinda okay about things…a few things, anyway. Bobby's getting around by kind of crawling, but instead of using his hands and knees, he propels himself with his hands and arms while he drags his legs behind him on the floor. The big problem is that he's still not in school, and I'm getting more worried by the day.

Meanwhile, Robert comes home from school every day upset. He tries to help me with the kids, but it's obvious that he dreads school the next day. He goes to bed and immediately starts worrying about the next day, and tosses and turns for hours.

The other night, he told me he had been thinking about Father Rex. We knew that when Father left our school, he had gone to a parish named St. Matthias. We've never been there because we usually see Father Rex at our house, or at St. Joe's. Anyway, Robert looked it up, and it's somewhere near where he works now. He decided to make some calls during his break at school. Well, he found St. Matthias in the phone book, and called Father

Rex! I was totally surprised—all I could think to say was, "Really, Robert?" "Yeah," he replied, "and I'm so glad I did." I asked him what they talked about, and how it all went. He was so excited.

He told me that Father wants to see us—that he'd said to bring the family to mass on Sunday, and that we'd have lunch after. Robert told Father Rex about his new school, and Bobby, and how tough things have been for both of us.

When Robert said, "He was really concerned—you know how he is," all I could do was laugh. "Um, yeah" I said. "He's the guy who kept me from being a nun!"

"Well, he said we have to come see him right away! I told him we'd come to his mass on Sunday. Father just laughed and said, 'Don't worry if you don't understand much of it. I do my best to say the mass in Spanish, but my Spanish isn't too hot!'"

That was the most upbeat I've seen Robert in quite a while. He seemed so encouraged by Father Rex's invitation. "So… what do you think?" he asked me. "We should go this Sunday, right?"

"ARE YOU KIDDING?" I squealed. "You know how much I love that guy. He pretty much saved my life once upon a time. Not to mention that he married us, and he's the closest thing to Jesus on earth. But Robert—how will we get Bobby in and out of church when he won't use the crutches?"

"Don't worry. I'll give him a piggy back ride."

That's the husband I know and love!

When Sunday rolled around, Robert had us all excited about seeing Father Rex. He was hoping that, somehow, Father would work some magic—or miracle—to help us.

We got there a little late for mass, which was just as well, since we couldn't understand any of it. After mass, lots of people crowded around Father Rex, just the way they had at our parish. Father just laughed and chatted, shaking hands and patting backs. Then he saw us. He waved at us, tousled the hair on a couple more kids, then moved toward us with a huge smile. He grabbed Robert's hands, then gave me a big hug. Then, he knelt down so he was eye-to-eye with Ellie and Greggy, who giggled as he joked with one and tickled the other. Then, he stood up to where Bobby clung to Robert's back. I can't remember his exact words, but it was like, "Wait! This big boy couldn't be little Bobby, could it? You know, I knew you when you were a little snip of a thing, and here you are a big, strong boy. How could this be? Do you know who Popeye is? You must be eating your spinach just like him! Good for you! Well, what do you think, Bobby? You must be hungry, coming all the way over here and sitting through that long old service. I bet I can find something you'll like in my kitchen. Come on with me!"

I didn't know about Robert, but for me, Father Rex was the balm I needed. In that moment, I was aware of the mystery of my life. Just look forward. Trust.

In the rectory dining room, Greggy climbed into a chair, and Robert put Bobby in another chair, while I sat down with Ellie on my lap. Father Rex told us to wait for a minute, and then disappeared. Pretty soon, though, he was back, announcing that his kitchen helper was fixing something special.

"But, my golly," he says, "wouldn't you know, it seems I need your help, Bobby and Greggy. I have a 'watch snake,' and I can't find him anywhere! Would you guys mind looking for him? He's my friend, and he keeps an eye on things for me. Only thing is, you need to get on the floor to find him. Do you mind?"

Well, Greggy jumped right down off his chair, while R helped Bobby down, and Ellie practically slid out of my arms. And away they went! Pretty soon, there they all were, down on the floor—Bobby pulling himself around, Greggy and Ellie crawling, and Father, too! He told them to be sure to look in all the corners and not to be afraid, that this was a special snake that would never hurt them. I couldn't believe the lightness enfolding me after months of darkness. Robert and I just kept smiling and laughing to see all the kids—especially Bobby—on the floor, thoroughly enjoying themselves. Father had gotten a couple of balls for the kids to roll around, one big enough for Ellie to sprawl her body across and push in an arms-akimbo way.

After a little while, a smiling, dark-haired woman came in with a platter of steaming hot dogs. She set down the platter, looked at Father Rex on the floor and laughed. A few minutes later, she returned with bags of potato chips, fruit, and sodas for everyone. We stayed a couple of hours, and though it seems like such a simple thing, it was the best afternoon we'd spent in forever.

On the way home, Ellie fell asleep in my arms, and the boys occupied themselves happily with the "a,b,c" and "find that car" games they love, while R and I marveled at the change in Bobby. Robert confided that he had made a pact with God at mass: he would start going to church on a regular basis if God would help him with his students. I have my fingers crossed for Robert, and I'm praying hard for my family.

This has been a tough time, and I'm trying to have faith that we'll be okay. But, at just this moment, I'm adrift…wondering about something that used to consume me when I was young: that I'm just a tiny speck in a vast universe.

If only I could think about this from time to time, I might do better with understanding that every action I take and every thought I think aren't necessarily so important. I don't always need to be afraid. What comes next, comes next.

Hmm….

5 FIGHT FOR THE KIDS

Somewhere over the rainbow, way up high
There's a land that I heard of once in a lullaby...
Where troubles melt like lemon drops
Away above the chimney tops...that's where you'll find me....

~Harold Arlen and Yip Harburg

March 5, 1976

A lot has happened since I last wrote. I think I got into some kind of funk after Bobby recovered—which seems kinda weird, since he did get better. It was a hard time in his little life, and he had this puny leg that's finally starting to fill out again. So, I should—we all should—feel good. But that's not the case.

I know I'm fairly young—27—with three healthy kids and a nice, good-looking husband. We've had some rocky times, but we love each other. A perfect marriage? A perfect family? Are there such things—because I'm finding being an adult challenging!

When I look at my world, I try to see blue skies, puffy-white marshmallow clouds and the bright yellow sun shining down on me. When one of my kids walks or runs into my view, I feel a shot of warmth inside, which makes me wonder how I could ever complain. Even when it rains and the boys start to gripe, I try to turn things around by making them hot chocolate or looking out the window with them to see how big the puddles are. I turn on music and sing and dance. I suggest they build a fort with blankets and pillows and play under the dining table. I make them let Ellie in, or I go in with her. I try to be and feel like an older version of Shirley Temple's Rebecca of Sunnybrook Farm.

But, right now, my emotions, are dark and dusty. I'm not excited about anything. I wish I could just sit on the couch by myself and stare out the window—and NOT check out puddles or clouds. This makes me pretty disgusted with myself. As a full-fledged adult, I should be able to stand up, tall and strong. I want to offer solace to my children when they need it, to help my husband any way I can. Right now, though, I'm not so sure I'm feeling and acting like the adult I'm supposed to be.

I'm not blind. I do see the blessings that are mixed in with the crises of the past months.

Once Bobby got out of traction, his recovery gave me whiplash. He went back to school, limping on his crutches, which I'd sent with him. And he used them for the first few days, but, then, I picked the kids up from school one afternoon, and there he was, limping toward the car, but the crutches were nowhere in sight.

It didn't take long before the limp was barely noticeable. His leg is still obviously skinnier than the other; Dr. Peters says the muscles atrophied, but they'll develop over time. He also said the magic words "If Bobby doesn't need the crutches, throw them away!" And so, I concocted a little ritual with Bobby; the two of us formally sent them to the garage sale pile. Yay!

He's catching up in school with no obvious problems, although, sadly, my open, affectionate Bobby is absent right now. When I try to hug and kiss him, he gets sort of stiff. Sometimes, he gets angry if I don't let him alone. I'm afraid this isn't normal for an 8-year-old boy. I could use a little of Mom channeling her nurturing self through me to my child right now. I try to pray, but it's hard. I've lost that part of my voice.

And Robert's job never got better. He just couldn't stand the way the kids treated him. He hated to give up, but he couldn't see a way to improve the situation. He missed his "old" kids too much. Overall, even with the kids he was coaching, his confidence had dropped lower than I've ever seen. He talked to the principal, who asked Robert to give it another month—and if his feelings didn't change, he would release Robert from his contract.

So that's what happened. Part of me understands, but another part of me is disillusioned. I mean—isn't this what men do? Whatever it takes to take care of their families?! I know my Dad and his "Dad" had their rough times, but did they quit? I guess I don't really know. Robert's job paid pretty well—much better than St. Joe's ever did. And he had health insurance! With three kids—especially after Bobby's broken leg—he certainly knows how fast bad things can happen! But here we are. Instead, he's throwing our security away to do cement work!

I don't want Robert to know I feel this way.

I DON'T WANT TO FEEL THIS WAY!

I wouldn't mind if it were easier for us for a change.

The worst part—for me? There's no one I can talk to honestly about how I feel. Robert's the one I'd normally talk to. My friends…well, they know the basic facts, but not how I feel about them. I guess I care too much about what they might think. I've talked a little about it to Laurie, but she doesn't see the problem. "Why do you care that he's doing cement work?" At least he's working. She really doesn't understand the insurance worries.

I'd like to tell Dad how worried I am about money and insurance, but I don't want him to think badly of my husband. Already, Dad doesn't understand why Robert quit the teaching job, so I just try to be upbeat. I mean, Dad lived through the depression, and he can go on and on with stories of things he did to make money, beginning when he was 13.

And so, I take my feelings, put them in a cupboard, and shut the door. It's not like I don't have plenty of practice doing that. Robert has to do what he has to do. That's what I tell myself…over and over.

So, for now, he's in the business of tearing out old driveways and putting in new ones, and building block walls. Lately, he's been putting in a tennis court for a well-off couple with a huge back yard. The kids and I have gone to see it, and we've all been appropriately impressed! Though Robert's relieved to be out of the nightmare school situation, this current job is scary. It takes good bidding to make money without scaring customers away, so it's both competitive and physically hard.

Once Robert quit his teaching job, we knew we were going to need the money, so I put my name in again at the kids' elementary school for babysitting. I was lucky—I got a fairly large group of kids, and most of them are at the same school as the boys, so I just pick them up with my kids, and they all play until their parents come for them. I also have two little girls, sisters of an older boy; they're a little older than Ellie, but not yet in school. It's pretty cute how they play with her and "mother" her.

I love the kids, except when I'm disciplining someone for something. I've gotten pretty creative, I must say: when the older kids fight, I warn them once. After that, they have to run up to the corner and back until they're ready to be nice. RAIN or shine! And it works!

Anyway, my nerves are on edge. I KNOW it could be worse, but….

April 5, 1976

Dear God,

I just looked at my last entry. I didn't know how good I had it then! Now, the worst has happened. My baby, my Ellie, is so very sick, and I don't know what's going to happen. I am so, so scared that I can hardly think. She's strapped down on a "bed" in the baby ICU, and she's stark naked—except for the IV. "They" say this is because of the extremely high fever she's running. She's in an "induced unconsciousness" (coma?) and her fair skin is so pale and damp that it looks translucent, Her breathing is very slow and light…she looks like a modern day, baby version of Sleeping Beauty!

God, please, you CANNOT let anything happen to Ellie. I don't know how I'll go on if she doesn't make it. But wait! Oh, yeah—you CAN let that happen. Mom, where are you? I need you more than ever. Spinal meningitis is what is hurting my baby girl. It has her in its grip, clenched so tightly, and, right now, no one knows if it's going to let go, or, if it does, how much damage it will do.

Over the last week or so, all the kids had the flu. Not just Bobby and Greggy, but all the kids I babysit, too. It made sense. Everyone's in school, and the classrooms are just big Petri dishes, with all the kids' germs just mixing in. But all my kids were recovering—until it hit Ellie. She was the last to get it, the last to start vomiting and running a fever. She's younger, more vulnerable, so she got way sicker, and she was burning up. At first, she just wanted Mommy, then, nothing but sleep. We kept thinking, "Babies run fevers. Ellie's got the flu." But she was so listless. None of the kids have ever been like this.

Saturday, Bobby made his first communion. Looking back, I'm glad we hadn't planned to make a huge deal about it, but Dad was coming, and Jimmy and Joanie. Because she hadn't had any energy that morning and was still feverish, I gave Ellie baby aspirin, and asked Sadie to watch her.

When we got home from the service, Robert and I decided he would take the boys to their first Little League game—he's the coach—and I'd stay home with Ellie. After everyone left, I took her temp: 104!

Since I wasn't sure what to do, I called the Emergency Room, but they said NOT to bring her in. "The waiting room is full of sick people. Just give her a tepid bath to bring her temp down and see your family doctor on Monday." That's what someone from ER told me—and it made sense. Now I want to sue the hospital! I shouldn't have listened.

Sunday night, Ellie's temp was back up, so Robert went over to Max's apartment to talk to him about Ellie. Since Max is a med student, we hoped he could reassure us. He looked her over, even held up one of her arms, then let it go, and we all saw it just flop! He touched her belly and tried to get her to talk, but all she would do is look at him. He said it could be SPINAL MENINGITIS but he doubted it. He said it was more likely a bad case of the flu. He said we should try to keep her fever down and get her to the doctor as soon as possible in the morning.

That was already my plan.

When I saw Dr. Klein, he reminded me that everyone had the flu. Ellie's case was probably just worse than most. As he looked her over, checking this and that, I questioned him about her lethargy, and told him what Max had said. He paused thoughtfully, held out Ellie's arm, only to have it fall limply the way it had when Max did the same thing. "Let's rule out anything more serious than the flu. Your friend's right. It COULD be spinal meningitis. No need to panic, though," he said. Yeah, sure! "Take Ellie straight to Children's Hospital. I'll call over there and order the tests."

First, I called home from Dr. K's front desk. Luckily, I caught Robert in the kitchen. He'd just been getting a snack. He said to pick him up and we'd go right over to Children's. I was dying inside. I had never even heard of this illness until Max mentioned it, and now I could see that our doctor saw suspicious symptoms in Ellie that meant she might have it.

Robert was standing out in front of our house when I approached in the car. I pulled to the curb, threw it into park and, hurriedly, got out, handed him my keys, and retrieved Ellie, who was curled up with her blankie in the back seat. On fire with panic, I got into the passenger seat as fast as I could, clutching Ellie to my chest. Robert jumped into the driver's seat, worry creasing his face.

Thirty minutes later, I ran through the ER door as R jetted ahead to the desk, saying who he was and pointing at me and Ellie. At the same time, I heard "Mrs. Dolan?" and "Is this Ellie?" I nodded yes to both questions, and a nurse whisked my sweet baby away from me! The test, I discovered later, was a "spinal tap," what Mom had described to me years ago as a procedure that caused, in her words, "excruciating" pain.

While we waited, I couldn't keep still, so I paced. Robert killed time by calling his parents. At some point, I called Janie. Since she's a nurse, maybe she could reassure me. She's also kind of a big sister. She said as soon as Jimmy got home from work, they'd come over. Then I called Dad. What could he say?

Finally, I sat down and put my head in my hands. Robert kept telling me "Ellie's going to be okay; she has to be. She's our baby girl." But then he said, "No matter what, we'll get through this together." What did he mean by that? When he grabbed my hands, locking eyes with me, I understood.

Finally, a doctor came out, saying they had found milky white fluid in Ellie's spinal cord. Though it was being tested, its color showed that she had the disease. He then sent us to a different waiting room, saying that someone would be in right away to explain everything to us. Robert put his arm around me, and we walked to the other waiting room like zombies.

Five minutes seemed like five hours. I had no patience. I wanted to shout, "Where is my baby?" Just then, a youngish man with a kind face walked in. He quickly shook our hands. "I'm so sorry for making you wait and keeping you from your baby. I hope you can believe me—she's in good hands. Let me explain a few things and then get you both to her. By the way, my name is Dr. John Wong."

Though I can hardly describe my state of mind, I have to say, I sensed this man cared. I trusted him.

"The next 24 hours are crucial for Ellie's life. She has a disease of the brain. Has she been around kids with the flu?" Dr. Wong asked.

We nodded yes. He asked us how old they were. I told him, adding that they were all fine now. "I'm not surprised they're well now. That's the case with most kids and the flu, but, unfortunately for Ellie, the bacteria of this flu germ traveled to her brain, infecting the tissue surrounding it. That's what spinal meningitis is—a terrible infection."

"So, what's going to happen with our baby girl? How serious is this?" I felt myself talking loudly, almost shouting.

"Well, I'm going to tell you the truth, and it's scary. I want you both to ask me any questions you have. Are you ready?"

"Yes, but, I don't know what my questions are. How about you, Robert?"

"I just don't know. So…just…just go ahead, Doctor," Robert responded.

"Okay. The worst that can happen is that spinal meningitis could end your baby's life."

"ELLIE COULD DIE?" My voice echoed in the waiting room. I could hardly grasp that my worst fear—the death of one of my children—now confronted me.

"Yes, or it could mean brain damage, mild to severe."

"You mean she might be behind other kids in development?" I asked stupidly.

"Or…she could…be a vegetable?" Robert croaked out.

"Well, to put it bluntly, yes. Or, it might mean hearing loss or learning issues. But remember, she could also come out of all this completely well."

"What are her odds?" Me again.

Dr. Wong took a deep breath. "I don't like to deal in odds. What if I say she has a 5% chance of recovering completely, but a 95% of something much worse…and then, it turns out that Ellie's in the 5%? You've been picturing your baby as a vegetable for no reason. So…I just don't do odds. I hope you understand."

"We get it, Doctor. So—now what?" Robert asked.

"Okay. So, here we are. As I said, the next 24 hours are crucial. What my team and I would like to do is something experimental. We want to flood Ellie's body with antibiotics—three different ones—for the next 24 hours. We think this has a good chance of arresting the ferocity of this infection. That way, hopefully, her body will be able to fight for itself. Would you like to think about it?"

Robert looked at me intently. "What do you think, honey? I think we should have this doctor and his team go for it. We don't have time to waste thinking about it—do we, Doctor?"

"No, not really. If we don't do this, we will follow the conventional protocol, which means much lower doses of antibiotics, and rest."

"Cross our fingers and say our prayers, you mean?" I asked, wringing my hands.

"Basically."

"Oh, God. Oh, God." I hesitated. "I agree with Robert."

"All right. Your little girl's in the children's ICU. Go see her, but you need to know she's unconscious and restrained. She has tubes feeding her medicine, and shortly we'll get going with the antibiotics. We need to restrain her, so that she won't pull out the tubes when she regains consciousness."

That was…yesterday? No—the day before. Today is technically the end of Ellie's second day in the hospital, and Dr. Wong says tomorrow we will probably see if this is working. I spent last night on a cot in Ellie's room. The nurses made it clear I was in the way, but I don't care. How could I leave her there alone? This is agony, fearing she'll wake up and want her mommy. I know I need to sleep, but how in the hell can I?

It's foggy now, but Robert and I were together at the hospital, until he went home to get the boys from the Brewers and fix them dinner, then get them to bed. He got them off to school today, then came by the hospital mid-morning to see Ellie and bring me food. He said I should come home with him before the boys got home from school this afternoon…both boys missed me and were upset about their baby sister. So…dinner with the boys, and then we'll get a babysitter and come back to Ellie tonight.

I don't think I'm going to stay here tonight. I have to get some sleep, and I can't stand the way the nurses act. I'll come back in the morning, as soon as the boys leave for school. I hate to be away from her. She's all I can really think about right now.

Please, God, and all you angels, too—help us. Mom, I know you're there and have to see that our baby—yours, too—needs some special grace. Can you help? Help all of us—but mostly Ellie—be strong. She needs to defeat this thing.

April 10, 1976

Today, I found myself dealing with emotional quicksand, sinking deeper and deeper into the sludge of my fears and my love. I needed to cry or lash out at someone—but who? I'm not coping well unless I'm with Ellie at the hospital.

Wait. That's not totally true. Once I realize it's time for the boys to get out of school, I start thinking about them. But no matter what, I feel guilty. I have to remember, though—just because I'd feel guiltier if I didn't—how great Ken has been to take care of the kids, both ours and the ones I babysit. I guess he's been taking only the computer jobs that need him in the nighttime. Okay, I just realized another good thing: Ken Brewer! An angel for us right now, for sure!

It's been a week now since my baby girl got a confirmed diagnosis of a disease from Hell. And there's still no way Robert or I can help her.

We're each reacting differently to this situation. It's so hard for Robert to watch her lying there, hour after hour. He needs to stay busy. Plus, he still needs to make money! For me, it's worse to be away from her.

Between hospital visits, Robert's working on a small job he had lined up before. We have no income right now, except whatever he can scrape up! But he always gets the boys from Ken by dinnertime—and I try to come home then, too, unless Ellie is awake. Little chance of that, though, since she's still sleeping most of the time. When I'm away from her, she must wake up to some extent because her IV is in a different place every day. The nurses say she keeps pulling it out when they're not with her—maybe in her stupor. Who knows? She's in her own room now, so anything's possible.

Since that first night, the nurses have made their preference clear: I am not welcome at certain times! Unfortunately for me, they don't come out and specify WHAT times, because the parents are SUPPOSED to be able to come and go. So, I leave at dinnertime and come back after, until it's the boys' bedtime. I feel so guilty, leaving Ellie alone. Is her issue with the IV a message to me: "Get your butt over here, Mommy. This is scary for me!?" In that case, she has no idea how hard I try to be there every minute. And then I think "Of course not. She's a baby."

The really distressing thing for me right now is that no one close to us is here for us! How can this be? I asked Dad to babysit the boys so R and I could go to the hospital together—not to mention how nice it would be if their grandpa wanted to see them, get them ice cream, tell them a story…anything to distract them from the worry at home. And what does he say? "Sorry, Beth, but Sadie doesn't want to miss our square dance class!"

Seriously? Just writing these words makes me want to vomit.

Other relatives? Laurie's up north. Doesn't she know I need her? Frankie? Nothing. Jim and Janie came the first day, then nothing. My two brothers and my sister are our closest family, besides Dad. I just feel so let down. It wouldn't really change anything with Ellie, but the support that mysteriously gives us hope and faith—well, I don't see it. From family or from friends.

The BIGGER picture is this: the sign I had hoped to see by now—Ellie awake and gaining strength—is a no-show! Dr. Wong either pretends or sincerely believes he sees improvement. I pray he's telling the truth and is right in his assessment. I miss my sweet, precious baby girl. Please bring her back to me...I love her so much….

April 13, 1976

It's as if I'm watching myself. I see me moving and talking, but my body doesn't seem to be mine. I say goodbye to the boys in the morning; I say goodbye to Robert. Then I get into the car, drive the 30 to 40 minutes to the hospital, park, walk briskly through the door and down the hall to Ellie's room. I sit next to her bed, stroking her arms, her cheeks, kissing her little head, caressing her hair. I gingerly pick up my little sack of hot potatoes. I sing to her, rock her. I notice the new place the medical people have put the IV. Today marks 6 or 7. She wakes up and looks at me, but nothing dramatic happens. No "Mommy! Mommy!" No attempt to reach up to me. I must be disappointed, but it doesn't show from this perspective.

Eventually, the doctor comes in with a nurse. I see me asking questions, even smiling. But, from here, it seems that I'm operating on automatic. I go to the phone in Ellie's room, get an outside line, and call home. Robert answers, and I talk to him.

"Yep!" I say, "Dr. Wong says Ellie's beginning to come out of it. He must be right, because she definitely sees me. Those big eyes are looking at me! I wish you were here with me. I know…you've got to do this job. I know…I'll see you later this afternoon." I don't know how I pass the day, but I do. I make another call. I talk to the nurses who are in and out; clearly, they would prefer I weren't there. From above though, I'm nonchalant with them. Nice. No one would ever know I'm anything but nonchalant inside.

April 16, 1976

Finally, Ellie's turned a corner! I can see it! It's tangible! I swear—it seems like Dr. Wong's as excited as I am! He's grinning from ear to ear, actually talking about sending my baby home in a few days!!

I took her to the playroom today. I carted the IV down the hall with one hand—now the IV is in Ellie's head! —and pushed her in a wheelchair with the other. She walked around a little, and even went down the red plastic slide a few times. After 30 minutes or so, she signaled in her own way that the toys had lost their allure. I didn't care. All I feel is relief. It's as if I've been blowing up a gigantic balloon, just blowing and blowing out, but not taking any breaths in. I couldn't before, but now I can! And that balloon? It's just flying all over the room willy-nilly as the air comes streaming out.

And Ellie? Well, she's still not herself, but I can see her in there wanting to make an appearance. And she will, soon. She will smile and yawn, and say, "Hi, Mommy," in her sweet little angel voice.

Last night, we tried to be a family after 13 days, have a special moment that would bring us together and also acknowledge the precipice we've been on for the past two weeks. We asked for—and got—some family time with Ellie.

Unfortunately, from the moment the boys stepped into Ellie's room, it was clear they weren't comfortable. I mean, each of them walked right up to her, trying to engage her, but Ellie made no move to do much more than lie back on her pillows and watch them be squirrely; they giggled and pushed each other, acting goofy—like two self-conscious little monkeys. I started to get angry, but Robert stepped in, said not to force them. Then he took the boys to the waiting room where they could play.

Oh, well, or, Oh, hell! Either, I guess—or both! What will be, will be. It's all up to the stars above, I suppose.

April 17, 1976

I spent most of today at the hospital, as usual. But I was home, bustling around—happy for a change—getting dinner ready when the doctor called.

"Hello."

"Hi, Beth. It's Dr. Wong."

"Hi, Doctor. Is everything…okay with Ellie?" He could probably hear my heart revving up with fear.

"Ellie's fine, improving every minute. Don't worry. But I DO have some bad news."

(Shit, shit, shit! What could be so bad NOW?!) "What is it?"

"Well, remember when I told you Ellie wouldn't have to have any more extractions from her spinal chord?" He had shot the bad news; it took a split second for it to hit its target.

"So, what's changing—and why?" How could I sound so calm when every pore was oozing panic?

"My supervisors tell me I had no business making such a promise. Any patient in her circumstances has to be re-tested to show definitively that she is cured. I'm so sorry; I hope you understand. I'm a lowly resident. I guess I jumped the….sorry, what's the word for that…uh…phrase?"

I took a deep breath, "Gun. You wanted to say that you jumped the gun—or rushed to judgment. Actually, that's another cliché. Sorry. I teach this stuff to high school kids. Don't worry, I get what you're saying, and I appreciate it. I don't blame you. I'm sure you can tell that I have a lot of fear surrounding the pain of a spinal tap. It's not your fault. Of course, we want to be positive that Ellie is well…but—Doctor, is a spinal tap incredibly painful—excruciating?" I asked him.

He paused for a minute…and it went on for hours.

"Well, it hurts, but not more than a needle anywhere else. She's still being released tomorrow, provided the results are good. We'll do the test early in the morning. I'll call you as soon as I have the results. Again, I apologize. Good evening."

I sat down, head in my hands, fighting the fear. I thought back to when I had the boys. The doctor then had given me a "saddle block in the spine," and that was about what Dr. Wong described. Wow! Maybe I've been worried for nothing or at least for not quite so much. Anyway, the best news beat the bad. Ellie, our little baby—over two but still, always, my baby—was coming home.

I went back by myself for a couple of hours that night, and Robert stayed home with the boys. He had phone calls for prospective jobs, and the boys needed him, not another baby sitter.

And now…ELLIE'S HOME!

Dr. Wong called me around 9 this morning with the good news: no more milky fluid in our baby's spinal cord. She could come home, he said. So, that's it, then. Ellie's healthy. No apparent brain damage. We won't really know about that for sure until she starts school, three years from now. But, for now, I plan to think positively while keeping my eyes and ears open.

I sort of feel like I'm a million years old, and, for some reason, I also feel kind of pissed off—but I mostly just feel…grateful, relieved…I mean, we have our family intact!

Also, I can fully appreciate this now: for these last weeks, we had two earthly angels keeping us from falling totally apart. The first: Dr. John Wong, who likely saved our Ellie's life and kept me focused on the signs that showed that Ellie was improving. The second was Ken Brewer, whose generous spirit kept life moving along so Robert and I could do what we had to do. I mean, this man stepped up in such an amazing way! From the first phone call Robert made to Ken about Ellie, the disease, and the hospital, Ken just said, "Don't worry about the kids—I've got it covered." He made it clear he meant ALL the kids. He took everyone to school, and watched them all after school for two weeks, refusing to take a penny after Ellie came home!

And now, I'm back to babysitting. Thanks to my little helpers, Karen and Sherry, Ellie is potty training all over again. I'm doing the M&M approach: every time Ellie goes pee in her potty chair, they each get a few M&Ms. It's going great, so far. But really, if it happens next week or next month, or whenever, who cares?

Dear God,

Thank you for my baby. I'm sorry for my doubts, but I've never faced anything like this before. I know it wasn't really fair to ask you to spare my child when there are so many sick kids who need your blessings besides my Ellie. But I did anyway, and she's here, really here. Thank you for the healing of my girl in any way you were responsible. You are the universe and beyond, so all things are possible.

And dear Mom, thank you for watching over her and me. I really did feel you with me so many times, just being present in your calming and comforting way. I know you know that I couldn't stand to lose my mom and my child in one lifetime…though I know there are those unfortunate people who do. I miss you. I love you. Please continue to always be near me.

Your Bethie

6 CALL IT QUITS

I close my eyes only for a moment, and the moment's gone
All my dreams pass before my eyes, a curiosity
Dust in the wind, all they are is dust in the wind…
Now don't hang on, nothing lasts forever but the earth and sky…
Dust in the wind, all we are is dust in the wind….

~ Kerry Livgren

October, 1981

"Hello?"

"Hello, Beth. I…"

"Hi, Laurie! I was just about to call you. I've been thinking—"

"Beth—Beth, wait. I've got something I have to say to you, and it's not going to be easy. Are you listening?"

"God, Laurie, you're scaring me. Is everything okay? Should I sit down?"

"If you mean…if you're worried one of us is sick or something like that, then the answer is we're okay. It's nothing like that. But in terms of me, personally, no—everything's not okay. I need to talk to you about something and I'm hoping you'll understand."

"I'm all ears." Hearing the gravity in Laurie's voice, Beth was suddenly nervous.

"You know I've been seeing Elsa, my new therapist…and you know that I've been looking at some issues that have affected me for a long time."

"Yeah, I know you're unhappy and Elsa…." Beth didn't know what to say next.

"Well, here's the deal: I've come to see that one of my biggest issues is you, Beth."

"Huh? What? Did you say I'm an 'issue' for you?"

"Yes. That's what I said."

The silence gathered weight with each passing second.

"What does that mean?" Beth asked uneasily. "God, Laurie! What's going on?"

Laurie had scolded Beth more than once for perceived wrongs. This felt different.

"Well, just wait a second, Beth, and let me tell you what I mean."

Beth heard Laurie swallow, then take a deep breath before she continued.

"First of all, you have to know I love you. I'll always love you," Laurie said firmly. "It's just…I've come to realize that I can't have you in my life and still figure myself out."

"Wait. What the heck does that mean—you can't have me in your life? Is this a joke? I don't think I'm hearing you right."

"Yes, Beth. You are hearing me right. I'm sorry. But this is how it has to be for me."

"But—Laurie, why? How can you mean that? How can you…we're sisters! We're more than sisters! I mean…!"

Beth stood up and began pacing as far as the phone cord would let her.

"Yes, we're sisters, Beth—but it is what I'm saying. And it is what I really mean. It's time for me to be separate from you." Laurie said this quietly, but deliberately.

"Can you please tell me why? Specifically? What have I done? What is this?"

"You haven't done anything…specifically. It's just that, lately, I always hear your voice in my head. It makes it hard time for me to figure out what's going on with me. I just need…I need to stand on my own."

"How long have you felt this way? Why haven't you said anything? I mean—we talk all the time. I'm always here for you. You call me with your problems. We talk about the kids. Besides, we're family. You can't mean you never want to see me…can you? What did Elsa…. I mean, I just don't understand this at all!"

"No, Beth. I really do mean I can't see you, I can't be with you…ever."

"Give me a break! Don't you think this is extreme? I get that you're working on things, and you need time to figure things out for yourself. Is that it?"

Beth felt her gut clenching; she was breathing hard, and tears had begun to sting, but she continued. "I didn't even know we were in a fight, or that anything was wrong between us. What about us—as sisters? As best friends? Who's going to be there for you like I am? Who are you going to talk to the way we talk?"

Beth felt the room begin to spin and she sat down again.

"You see, Beth? Right there." Laurie's voice was frighteningly calm.

"What you just said is one of the things wrong between us. I don't want a relationship where we're always talking my problems— because you always encourage me to talk about my problems—and you talk to me about your problems.

"What?! —I don't understand what you're saying, Laurie. I just meant that we're close. We share everything. We've been so close ever since Mom died. How can you possibly say you don't want me in your life?"

Laurie's voice was still low, but a discernable tension had begun creeping in. "It's hard to explain, but here it is: You have a strong personality, Beth. You have your opinions, and think you know what's best for everyone. So many times, when I try to talk to you, you think you know what's best for me. But I'm not a little kid anymore. I didn't like it then, and I don't like it now. And it's not just that…."

"Wait just a minute. Laurie! That is not fair and it's not true!" Beth's temper flared.

"…you get defensive; you cannot stand to be wrong, Beth!"

"Oh, c'mon, Laurie! You have to know why I act like I know what's best—if that's what I really do! You've made some pretty bad choices, and haven't had anyone else to step in and try to steer you in the right direction. I've always tried to do that, ever since—"

"Oh, so you know what's right for me. Is that it? You've thought I've always made 'bad choices'?"

"I did not say 'always'! And it's not just me! Anyone with a brain could see that, when you were a kid, you didn't get much direction. I tried the best I could to help you. But I didn't always…."

"No, you didn't always 'steer' me right because I didn't always take your advice. I tried to think for myself, but you confused me. I've been weak and tried to follow you, but I'm not you! I'm done with that weak behavior!"

A deep breath, and Beth spoke as calmly as she could. "Laurie, I think I know what you're saying. I never expected you to follow me. I'm sorry if you thought I did. And I was talking about when you were just a kid, a young teenager. But I never expected you to try to be me or even agree with everything I said."

"Yes! Yes, you did! And you still do! But I'm not interested. Okay? I'm not interested in following in your footsteps. I see that now, with Elsa's help."

"Elsa? Oh, yeah, your new therapist. And do you really think Elsa knows what's best for you?"

"Not necessarily. But that's just it. I'm working on me! I'm deciding that separating myself from people who've confused me and dictated to me or let me down is the best thing for me. And I can't worry about how this makes them feel. I know you've tried to help me, Beth, but I need to stand on my own and figure things out. I feel so much lighter just saying this. I really need you to try to understand."

"Oh. So, I'm supposed to understand your position while you don't have to make an effort to understand mine? Is that how it is? And I'm one of the things you need to toss out? And I should understand that doing that makes you feel "so much lighter"? Beth's sarcasm masked the humiliation she felt.

"So, does this include all of our family?"

"No. Not everyone. Definitely not Margaret. For now, it's just you. And Beth—this is just between us. This is not something for you to go spreading around to our family members. This time, you don't need to go running to Dad like you always do. I mean it!" Laurie was emphatic.

"Oh, Now I get it: you can push me out of your life, but you're gonna tell me I can't talk to my father about this? 'Running to Dad,' huh? This is so crazy! I'm the one who has always talked to Dad about you so he'll be there for you, to try to understand you! God, Laurie, you're making me out to be someone who's really terrible, just a really bad sister. As if I…." Again, Beth fought for control.

"Try to listen to me, Beth. We are too close. It's an unhealthy closeness. I'm too wrapped up with you and our past." Laurie suddenly sounded tired.

"Are you saying there's something unhealthy about the entire family's relationship or just your relationship with me, in particular? Because when Mom died, I tried to look out for you. I was just a kid, and I'm sure I made mistakes, but I did the best I knew how. Was it unhealthy that we bonded in that awful crisis? I think we were lucky we had each other after she died like that."

"I agree with most of that, Beth—but that was then. Now that I'm older, I need to face what's not working in my life. My relationship with you has created something that's damaging to me personally. You and I have really become…it's like we're not two distinct people. We rely too much on each other. We talk about problems too much. I need to change my focus, quit brooding, take action!"

"You're saying you can't change with me so close to you." Beth tried to sound calm, even if she didn't feel that way. "Is that it?"

"Yeah, that's about it.

"What about family dinners at the holidays? Are you NOT going? Or am I supposed to stay away? What about our kids? I know my kids won't understand. They're so close to Jase that he's like their brother. And Ellie—she adores Jase and the baby. Your kids feel like my kids, too. And you and Colin…Colin is Robert's brother as well as my brother-in-law. Does he agree with this?"

"Colin's not a part of this. He has to do what's good for him. And I know what you're saying about the kids…but, with Jase, I don't think…it's not like the boys always include him when he's with them. You know he gets hurt, feels left out sometimes, especially when the other cousins are around."

"What are you talking about, Laurie? They're all just kids. They love him. We all do. It's just kid stuff. They all go through these things. It doesn't mean they don't all love each other. I love your kids as if they were mine. And my kids look to you as another mother."

"The best way I can answer that, Beth, is this: I don't have everything figured out yet. But it will all unfold as it's supposed to."

"'It will all unfold as it's supposed to?!' You're telling me I'm never going to see you again. You're basically saying you're out of my life. So that means you're out of Robert's life, and our kids' lives. God! How can this be happening? Why can't we work on things? Let's agree not to talk so much, definitely about problems. I will really work on not giving advice. I'll go with you to counseling. Wouldn't that be better than doing something so extreme as this?"

"Beth, you're not hearing me! When we talk, you interrupt me, talk over me. You don't really listen. I need to have a relationship—"

"Oh, God, Laurie! I do nothing but listen when we talk! You're the one who has a hard time listening!"

"See, Beth? Like that. Take a breath. Think of what just happened. You got defensive and didn't let me finish. If you can't calm down, I'm going to hang up."

"Okay. I'm trying. I think I just need time to mull this over. This is…I'm about to tear my hair out…I am so…so…frustrated! I just wish I understood this. You can't possibly know how this is making me feel. I can hardly breathe."

Beth stopped crying and sat down at the kitchen table.

"Me, too, believe me. But it's for the best. I think you'll understand if you try to see this from my point of view. Do you remember one time, at the Dolans, we were talking, and I told you I wanted us to start having more fun as families with our kids? You know, play Frisbee, teach them Ollie, Ollie Oxen? You said something like "Uh-huh" and then went right on talking about some issue with Robert or one of the kids. You didn't even hear me."

"I do remember that conversation, and I did think it sounded good, like when we were kids, playing in the neighborhood. I don't remember ignoring you or acting like I didn't hear you. If you remember, it was really awkward at the Dolans that time."

"I remember they ignored me, and they acted like you were an inside member in some family club. You mean 'awkward' like that? The typical 'Sweet little Bethie' who does everything right, and then 'Laurie, the temptress, the one who ruined their son's life?' You mean that awkwardness?"

"Oh, I think you know that's not how it feels to me when I'm there for a holiday!"

"But it's not close to anything like that for me." Laurie's voice was hurt and wistful.

"I know, and I try to bridge the gap for you. But you also know it's because you and Colin did things so differently."

"You mean we had a child without falling into the 'we have to get married' trap? We waited until we thought it was the right time for us, rather than for everyone else. Boy, the Dolans just couldn't stand that! Again, people trying to force us to do what they did! Since I wouldn't do that, they hate me."

"That isn't true. Yes, they can be a little judgmental—"

"A little judgmental? That's an understatement and you know it!"

"Okay! Maybe. I don't know. Does all this have anything to do with that?"

"'All this' involves a lot of things. I suppose the Dolan thing is in there somewhere. I know I'm sick of being your 'little sister' and you 'bridging gaps' for me. I don't need that from you anymore. I'm sick of it. It's not good for me."

"God, Laurie. I can't imagine feeling like you do. I would've loved to have a regular big sister. I love Margaret, but sometimes I fantasize what it would be like to have a normal big sister. I would love to have someone who's known me forever, sees me for me, is proud of me and, yes, at times, gives me advice."

"Fine, Beth. Fine for you! Also, pardon me, but I don't see you as seeing me as I really am and for what I really need. I think you see me—maybe you always have—as someone you need me to be—your little sister—who looks up to you and listens to you and wants to be just like you. That was okay when I was 12, and for a few years after that."

"Laurie, I can't believe you're saying these things to me—that you can think I'm so...calculating and manipulative. Do you think I don't love you?" Beth was crying and trying to breathe without gulping air. "I remember so many good times. Helping each other when we were so sad missing Mom, writing poetry at night, with you strumming your guitar and singing folk songs. Remember the one that goes 'Had a sister Sally…'? There were lots of good times…baby-sitting for our neighbors, playing volleyball in the street, talking the whole time, cracking each other up—just laughing so hard, we didn't even make a sound…."

Beth wasn't really talking to Laurie now. She was off in a kind of reverie.

"Now, see, I didn't mean to upset you."

Beth replied as simply as she could "What did you think was going to happen when you told me you never want to see me again?"

The pause was interminable. Finally, Laurie managed to speak.

"You're asking me to explain my decision, and I said it would be hard. I don't mean we haven't shared good times, and I don't mean you haven't tried with me. I know you have. And, even though I hated it, I know you talked to Dad about me, trying to help. But Dad is Dad, and it just doesn't work for me. I need to forge some kind of relationship with him myself, without you in on it. I don't honestly have much hope that things will change with him, but it's up to me to decide to try or not. Beth? Beth?"

"Hmm?"

"Do you understand any of what I'm saying?"

"I don't know. I'm…I don't know. I need to think about it all. I think this is a big mistake. And it's very painful."

"Well, remember I said I do love you."

"Yeah, I know you said that. This doesn't feel like that. Anyway, I love you, too. I always have."

"Okay. Well, I've got to go now."

"Yeah, me, too."

"Bye, Beth."

Beth hung up the phone. She sat silently for a few minutes, hearing the television in the background. Now and then, she heard laughter from Robert or one of the kids. Must be "The Cosby Show."

Beth got up and climbed the stairs to hers and Robert's room. She threw herself on the bed, starting to cry, holding her face in her hands, squeezing her eyes as tightly as she could, so as not to make any sound.

I can't believe what just happened. I can't believe that Laurie doesn't want to see me again, EVER! I can't breathe! My body hurts. Oh, my God! After all we've been through together, after all the heartache, this is where we're at? How could she do that, call me on the phone and tell me she's decided she's done with me as if I was some boy she was breaking up with! Getting her conscience clear so she's free to date someone else.

I remember her saying not too long ago that they wanted to move here, near us. In the last few phone calls, she's talked about her relationship problems with Colin. Nothing unusual, though. And I probably defended him, which I do mainly to give her another side to consider. But I have no idea if that's part of why she did this. That can't be it. She knows I don't think he's perfect.

She says she loves me, but can't see me, needs me out of her life! How is this possible? She says I don't listen. That I think I know what's best for her. That I'm too dominant in her life, so she can't stand on her own. That I'm why she's unhappy…me and my strong personality! I'll always remember her words, but what did I say? How did I respond? I feel like screaming hysterically. Oh, God…how am I going to go on? She's my sister…who thinks I just want her to follow in my footsteps.

I don't know; do I want that? Have I acted like that without realizing it?

If she only knew…how much I admire and even envy her. I mean, everyone knows how incredibly smart and artistic she is. I guess it's true I wish she hadn't gotten pregnant before she got married, but a big part of me admired her for being independent and deciding that she didn't need marriage; she needed to feel that she and Colin were in a committed and stable relationship. The biggest—and best—thing is that she loves her boys so much. She and Colin have problems, but I don't care. So, do Robert and I. And that's what I usually say. She's it for me in my family. Since Mom died, I've confided more to her than anyone in my life…even Robert. She thinks I'm so close to Dad, but, really, he drives me crazy half the time, mainly because he's so self-centered. But still, she thinks he loves me more, as if that's even possible. I can't imagine loving one of my kids more than another. Yeah, sometimes, one kid is easier to talk to or be with, but never to love. My love for my kids is boundless—for each one of them!

Oh, my God. How can this be happening? It's just like the accident! I'm losing a big piece of my heart again. What do I do, where do I turn? How can she do this? With our history? I mean, how does she just turn her back on her sister—and without giving me a chance to fix whatever it is? I don't really understand. All I understand is that she's walking away from me!

I can feel my heart racing. In a few minutes, I need to put Ellie to bed…go through our sleepy-time ritual. But how am I going to do that? I guess I'll just plaster a mask on my face…for the millionth time act like I'm fine. Robert will be able to tell I'm not okay, and he'll ask me.

And I'll tell him. He'll probably say she didn't mean it…that she'll call me tomorrow or maybe even later tonight and say she didn't mean it. She'll feel bad and explain. Or she'll write me a letter, clearing everything up. "Just give her time," he'll say. "You know how she is. She gets confused, exaggerates. If not tonight or tomorrow, in a few days, she'll call. Just give her some time. Don't call her."

Oh, I won't be calling her. She did not seem the slightest bit confused. Her words were as clear as the water in my glass. And I know from her coldness, not to mention her hurtful words, that she wasn't worried about how I would feel. She had made up her mind. God…doesn't she know what I went through when Mom died?! The answer to that question is yes, she knows, but she doesn't care.

This feels like that…like then. It feels like I'm losing Mom all over again. I'm right back to those days of disbelief that I won't see or talk to her again. And those dreams—of catching a glimpse of Mom in a crowd and her meeting my eyes for a second, then turning away from me, going away from me. And I cry out to her and try to run after her, but the crowd won't let me, and pretty soon, she's gone, just…gone.

I don't know what to do. Right now, I can only imagine this interminable life looming in front of me, the punishing misery, the heartbreak, the wretched anxiety that doesn't melt away with a good night's sleep. Good night's sleep? I have a feeling that kind of sleep won't be visiting me for a very long time.

PART 2

1 OPEN A NEW DOOR

Oh, why you look so sad? Tears are in your eyes
Come on, and come to me now, don't be ashamed to cry
Let me see you through 'cause I've seen the dark side, too
When the night falls on you, you don't know what to do...
I'll stand by you, I'll stand by you, won't let nobody hurt you
I'll stand by you...

~ Thomas Kelly, Christine Hynde, Billy Steinberg

"Grandma, this is Great-Grandpa, isn't it? He looks so happy and...I don't know...excited. What is this? Why is he holding all the balloons?"

I looked over at my twelve-year-old granddaughter, Kate, who sat with me in the midst of piles of family photos, and then at the picture she held. Suddenly, there he was, standing in my brother's driveway, holding a bouquet of balloons with "Happy Birthday!" on them, grinning ear to ear.

I remembered his excitement as if it were yesterday. It was his 85th birthday, his big day. Despite the number, he seemed to be in the prime of his life. The family was gathering to celebrate him, and, if I remember right, he was getting ready for a big trip with Sadie and their square dance group. There he was, out in front of Jim's house, waiting for the stragglers, so he could tell us all together about their plans. The colors sparkled brilliantly in the afternoon sun. Full of glee—a child caught up in the excitement of his celebration—that was Dad at his best, eagerly looking forward. And where was I? Somewhere in the background with my sibs, sharing this moment of joy with our father. Seeing him so alive in that moment, I realized how much and how often I had taken his vitality for granted.

My life with Dad had seemed to go as it had always gone...until one day, which marked a season of significant changes. It caught me unawares and, at first, I was stunned. Though he rarely referred to himself as a "senior citizen" or "elderly"—and then only in jest—Dad's advancing age had begun to subtly manifest in signs and symptoms I could no longer ignore. He'd always walked with a brisk gait, often whistling or humming as he went, impatient for the next thing to spark his excitement. For a little girl, he'd been difficult to keep up with. Often, I'd found myself skipping breathlessly alongside him. Maybe that was why—in my young adulthood, at least—it had always seemed like he had a plan for our family, for adventure, for fun.

Even as we all got older, Dad was still our ringleader. "Hey, Beth, how 'bout you bring the kids over for a swim? I'll get Jim and Frank to bring their families and we'll barbecue burgers and hot dogs. Ask Robert how margaritas sound." I remember when he'd suggested the idea of progressive dinners, since we all lived in close proximity to one other. However…no one had foreseen that we'd drink with every course and, as a result, we'd be pretty tipsy by the time we got to the last house and dessert. When we'd realized the risks we were taking, especially since we were carting the kids around with us, we'd called a halt to those dinner parties.

And there was the time he'd made a "business proposal" to the family.

"What do you think about going in on a ski boat? I saw a cute little used one on a nearby lot. It had a "for sale" sign with a phone number on it, so I called the guy. He says it comes with water-skis and life jackets. I'll buy it, and you guys pay for the gas when we take it out." Dad had called the boat "Rosie" for his favorite flowers, the ones he and Sadie grew in their garden; he was so proud when they bloomed in brilliant reds and yellows.

After a few trips out as a family, my brothers lost interest or found their lives too busy for boating, and since Laurie was still a teenager, Rosie essentially became Robert's and mine. I asked Dad a few times if he wanted us to buy him out, but he said no, that he'd have us take him boating one day soon.

I don't think I fully appreciated it at the time, but Dad's benevolence had, in fact, resulted in boating becoming our favorite family activity. As teachers, Robert and I couldn't afford hotel-oriented travels, but we had Easter breaks and summer vacations off, and we had Rosie. Soon, we acquired a truck and camper and the requisite accoutrements for camping trips, and we were set for years to come.

Now I see that we were engrossed in our own growing family, even as we tried to meet the expectations of each of our families. Looking back, I see that we were constantly in motion, without much thought to all we were doing or why. Robert's parents lived close to us in the early years, as did Dad, and everyone wanted to see their grandchildren, expecting us to drop everything to come over for dinners or pool parties. We wanted to do it all and constantly pushed ourselves to accommodate every invitation.

Over time, my father-in-law was transferred, and Robert and I moved further from Dad for better jobs. Dad and Sadie got older and needier. If I thought about it at all, I guess I just assumed Dad's generosity with the boat—as well as with other things—was his way of paying me back for the attention I continued to direct his way, even though, too often, I did so reluctantly.

I'd often tried to stifle the irritation I felt at his frequent phone calls and requests that I come over "for a visit and lunch out," or "dinner as a foursome." I realize now that I hadn't seen the love behind the need. Sometimes, it had seemed that whatever he said was designed to drive me crazy.

I wish I'd had the wisdom—the heart—to see my father's calls to me for what they were…and for what they weren't. They weren't just phone calls to pass the time—they were his way of entreating me to see him, to hear him, see and hear what was beyond his words.

He came in search of connection, and the return of his love, but I let my life consume me. The demands of my children and my job had to come first, I insisted to myself. I didn't have enough time to be good at everything—and that, unfortunately, included Dad. I wish I'd been more perceptive, that I'd slowed down and paid more attention. My father loved me. I was his child. He had told me that he loved all of his children, worried about all of us. But I know now that a parent can love their children equally and still experience them differently. I'm not sure why—maybe because he liked my spunk, or because I had been his darling post war baby—but whatever it was, he liked me, liked to talk to me. How lonely it is now, to pine for his conversation, to wonder what he'd say about…so many things.

"Gosh darn it! Why can't he ask me about MY job once in a while? He always goes on and on about the store or Jim's job—or Frankie's!—like they're so important. But he never asks me what I'm teaching or how it's going. And Laurie, too. He always feels so sorry for her. That's fine. But does he talk about his experiences in the army every time he talks to one of them? I have all these papers to grade. Now, I'm too tired." Robert would grimace and shrug his shoulders.

And his inattention to Margaret annoyed me no end. Dad says Harold's a bastard for pointing out the spots he missed when he painted the living room, but does he ever tell Harold he's a bastard for treating Margaret so badly? Why doesn't he tell him to quit calling her a 'ree-tard?' Maybe he doesn't even know Harold calls her that. Well, he should! And telling her to stay in their room when she bugs him for some reason? I know I've told Dad about that. When I drove over there the other day and took him and Margaret to lunch, Dad talked non-stop—to ME—with hardly a word to Margaret. He's a grown man, for God's sake. Can't he see he's got another daughter who wants to talk to us about HER life for a change? It can't be easy being married to Harold.

At other times, I'd sympathize with him, touched by his admission that he often tossed and turned at night as he worried about one of us. And I'd admire how he taught Margaret to use the bus system, and to deposit her disability checks, and pay her bills, quietly insuring that she could be independent.

Looking at him from this vantage point, my heart would open up to our family patriarch. He'd hosted holiday dinners as well as informal family parties, and played Santa for our kids when they were little. He'd even paid all our ways to a few amusement parks. At those times, when I heard my brothers or sister poke fun at his loud, boisterous talk or politically incorrect opinions, even though I oftentimes agreed with them, I'd still feel a little sick and confused.

As his birthdays passed, we "kids" had begun to ask Dad when he thought he'd retire. At that, Dad would usually shoot back, "Why would I do that? Holy smokes! What would I do with myself? I've been in the automotive business for over 40 years!" Finally, as his 75th birthday approached, Dad gathered us together to make an announcement.

"I'm turning 75 years old and you all think enough of your old man to throw this party for me. And I appreciate it, though I don't think turning 75 is anything to cheer about. But I am doing something we can celebrate. I'm making a change. I'm not getting any younger, and there are lots of places in this world that I'd like to see. Our square dance group plans some pretty great trips to some of those places. Sadie agrees with me, don't you honey?" To this, Sadie replied, "Well, I guess so, but it's up to you, Jack," in her oh-so-southern drawl. Dad went on, "So, I'm sellin' the business—since none of you wants it. And it's doing pretty well, I might add. Anyway, Kenny's been taking business classes and thinks he's ready to take over. He's got a young family and is plenty motivated to take good care of the store. I have faith in him, so we're making a deal that's good for both of us!"

"Congratulations, Dad! You've been working hard long enough," Jim remarked.

"Thanks, Jim. I guess that's true. While we haven't always had the success I would've liked, it's been good enough to give you all Catholic educations, and help with college. I'm proud I could do at least that. Like I said, business is great now. It's nice that I'll have a pretty good living off this sale. So, anyway, that's that!"

And so, over the next ten years, Dad and Sadie traveled. He brought home pictures of him—all big smiles!—riding a camel in Egypt...of Sadie tentatively holding a Koala bear in Australia...of their group, colorfully dressed and dancing on streets all over Europe—all the places that he had dreamed about since he was a little boy reading adventure stories.

The last big trip he and Sadie planned—and the one Dad looked forward to the most—was a cruise to Russia with visits to Moscow and St. Petersburg, cities whose histories fascinated him. He dreamed of seeing the sites of WWII battles, the graves of the Romanovs, and the famous onion-skinned domes and stout towers. He spent hours reading about what he and Sadie would see on the tour arranged by their square dance troupe.

But the trip was not to be. For a few weeks, Sadie had complained, "My arth-er-i-tus sure is actin' up. Don't know why. But my fingers and toes're just gettin' to achin' over nothin'. I don't hardly think I can drive myself to the doctor." So, Dad had taken her to the doctor, and soon we all knew the bad news: Sadie's "touch" of arthritis had developed into a full-blown case of severe osteoarthritis. She was 86 or 7.

For a while, medication had helped with the pain, and stubborn, strong Sadie had moved through her discomfort. A few months before the Russia trip, though, Dad noticed that she was taking to her bed more frequently. He would call to her, "There's a show on you'll get a kick out of, honey. Come on in here." Or "You just have to see how the roses (or the tomatoes or corn) are growing. I'll help you with the steps. It'll do you good." More and more often, she would decline. "I'm fine just where I am, Jack. You go on ahead out there."

When the doctor had prescribed hot whirlpool baths, Sadie perked up at the prospect of being more mobile—but, each time, she returned home, discouraged that they weren't helping. When her doctor had suggested walking and exercises to ease the pain, she said, "That makes no sense! It just don't! Doesn't he know how I feel? No, because he's never had what I have!" Even when Dad suggested she go out to dinner with Robert and me to their favorite restaurant, she refused, saying, "I'm not gonna let people see me in a wheelchair like some ol' invalid!"

Dad had pleaded with the doctor for additional pain medication, but was told Sadie was already taking all he could prescribe. Dad remained convinced that the doctor could have done more if he'd wanted to do so.

Once, Dad and I took Sadie shopping, having her use the three-legged cane that she'd gotten when she was first diagnosed. Dad had instructed me to park close to the store, right by the women's department. Sadie managed to hobble through the door, but, once inside, almost immediately collapsed into a chair by the dressing room. Dad stayed with her while I brought over loose-fitting pants and soft, warm tops. Sadie showed little interest, but ultimately decided on a top—just to pacify us, it seemed to me.

Much to Sadie's relief, this excursion put an end to any mentions of further shopping trips. Eventually, my father conceded that, if Sadie couldn't handle a short shopping trip, any kind of travel would be out of the question. Disappointed, Dad had prayed that Sadie would improve, and they would still see the spires of St. Basel's. Unfortunately, the answer to that prayer was an unequivocal, "No."

Sometime later, Dad had mentioned to Jim that he'd been having dizzy spells and stiff legs, and just "didn't feel right." Dad thought it would pass, but my brother had insisted that Dad see the doctor, even offering to take him.

Dr. Hemengway said it looked like Dad was in the early stage of Parkinson's, not unusual for a man in his mid-80's. Time would tell for sure. Also, Dad's blood pressure remained high, even with his medication, and he could stand to lose a few pounds. When I tried to talk to Dad about any of this, he evaded my questions. Though no major symptoms had manifested yet, I could see that he was moving more slowly. Perhaps more telling, he'd begun to let home maintenance slide or hired others to do things he'd always done himself.

Sadie expressed her cranky concern one day when I happened to be sitting with them after one of our lunches. Their den faced the backyard, so we were all looking out at their full, healthy tree. "I like that tree, but it sure does need trimming. I think I'll get someone to come and give it a light pruning," Dad declared, mostly to himself.

"I don't think you need to hire some ole guy to trim that tree, Jack. You can do that yourself, just like you always do. And I can help you."

"Honey, I just don't think I'm up to it right now." We both knew Sadie couldn't help with much of anything.

"Well, it don't really need it right now, anyway. It can wait."

"I disagree. I can get Alberto to do it. He could use the work, I bet."

"Who? You mean the husband of that gal, our housekeeper? He's crippled, isn't he? How's he gonna do it, anyhow? He can't hardly walk."

"That gal" was Carmen, a woman Jim and I had talked Dad into hiring and with whom Dad had quickly fallen in love. Carmen's sweet solicitude of Dad, her amusement at his witticisms, her quiet approach to her job, and her willingness to make it possible for him to grocery shop, had won him over. At first, Carmen had cleaned the house and driven Dad to the grocery store once a week. When he'd found it too tiring to walk around the store, Carmen had helped Dad into one of the carts with molded plastic seats and pushed him. He loved food, and this was a chore he had always enjoyed. Alberto, Carmen's husband, had hung Christmas lights for Dad that year, and done a few minor repairs for him.

"Alberto's not crippled, Sadie. He walks and drives and works around his house. He's probably twenty years younger than me. I'm sure he could do it just fine." Alberto, who'd been in an accident that had damaged his spinal cord and left him with a lopsided gait, now did odd jobs and helped his wife with their children and household tasks.

That was not the last time Sadie would express her views on Dad's declining health. Not long after that incident, Dad had prostate surgery; he called it his "Roto-Router" fix. It went well and, after a few days in the hospital, he came home to rest and recover—which meant spending most of the day reading in his red recliner. I was visiting with him and, when he dozed off, had gone into the kitchen. I'd noticed the dishes in the sink as well as the particularly sticky floor when I'd come in. Usually, Carmen kept things tidy, but she had tended to Sadie until Dad came home from the hospital. I guessed she hadn't had a chance to tackle the kitchen. Determined to make myself useful, I looked for a mop, but, all I could find was the generic household soap and some rags. Once I'd drawn a pan of hot water, I got down on my knees and began to scrub the way my mother had taught me long before. There was never any mop for her.

I was halfway through the job, when I heard "Beth, what are you doing on that floor? That's no job for you! Jack can do it." Darn! Sadie had crept up on me! I quietly replied "I'm almost done. I think Dad needs his rest—you know, so he can recuperate." But Sadie would have none of it and grumbled her way into the living room to wake Dad up and tell him what I was doing, as if I was a child up to malicious mischief.

Dad recovered, but slowly, and definitely not completely. For too long, he'd been acting as Sadie's sole caretaker…doing lonely, life-sucking work. On the phone, he would plead with me to help him find something or someone to relieve her pain. I would hang up the phone, overwhelmed and speechless and entirely out of my element. I knew he had no words to convey the crushing reality of his life.

Now I wonder what he'd seen when he looked to the future. The wide world, with all its possibilities, had always thrilled my father; sadly, it had been reduced to a narrow focus: Sadie. I asked friends and colleagues; I asked my own doctor: what relief could someone with debilitating arthritis find? No one knew. Those that did had the same report: news was promising—for the future.

On my occasional day off, I took Dad—and often Margaret, too—out to lunch. Sadie would always decline the invitation, but encourage Dad to go. He could never hide his relief to get a break from the confinement Sadie's condition imposed on them both. He put a brave spin on his life, and continued to read his novels and newspapers, and watch the news on TV. An intelligent man, he had always found local and world news engaging.

About this time, though, another interest took front and center for him: writing poetry. I'll never forget the call I got at work one day; it began innocently enough: "Say, Beth, I know you're at work, but do you have a few minutes for your poor, broken-down father?"

"Hi, Dad. Sure, I can spare a few minutes. What's up?"

"To get to the point: I entered a poetry contest sponsored by our newspaper. Problem is, my handwriting isn't so good anymore. Do you think you could take a few minutes to type it up for me?"

"Sure!" I said. "How long is it?"

"It's a sonnet. Being an English teacher, I bet you know how many lines are in a sonnet." I laughed. "Of course, I do: fourteen."

"Okay, then. What I'll do is stick it in the mail to you, and you can mail it back to me all clean and typed. That work for you?" I said it did, and asked him what had gotten him interested in this.

"Well, you know I've always liked to write. You may even remember back when I used to write silly dramas for the Knights of Columbus socials. Your mom and some of our friends would take parts. It was a lot of fun. Your mom always encouraged me to write more, but how could I, what with a business, and a house, and you kids? Anyway, you know I started sending poems to the grandkids—I'd tuck 'em in with their college allowances. Once in a while, I've gotten a poem back, mostly from your Greg. He's pretty clever! Anyway, I've been writing more, and I thought I'd try my hand at a contest."

Would this guy ever cease to surprise me? I told Dad I loved the idea. And so, a couple days later, I got his poem about Groundhog Day. I chuckled as I read, recalling how, when we were kids, he'd told us a story about Jackie Begorry saving this day for all the groundhogs!

I immediately typed it up and sent it back. He didn't win, but he got a nice, very encouraging letter back. For a while, I got packets of poems from Dad every week or so. When I had a moment at work—maybe a period when I wasn't teaching and had no students pounding on the door—I would take out the packet and start on the next poem. He kept me entertained. His topics included the month we were in, a holiday coming up, animals like hedgehogs and armadillos and, once in a while, a sweet topic like love or parenthood. His poetry was interesting and humorous, even witty. He got to the point and stuck to it.

Soon, Dad graduated to short stories. Now, I could hardly keep up with him.

I had a fairly demanding job, which I loved and at which I worked hard. Teaching demanded time—time for reading and preparing, and time for grading the never-ending stack of papers. Then there was counseling—which required that I give my full attention to students who needed guidance on any number of issues. Add to those responsibilities the inevitable meetings I had to attend. But these stories…well, they demanded time, too. Time to edit and correct, time to type, time to talk to Dad about. At home, life was just as hectic. Still, he counted on me. For the millionth time, I told myself I couldn't let him down.

His short stories and poetry morphed into books, which he wanted decorated and bound, so that he could give them as gifts. He managed to do this for our family for two Christmases. I edited and typed; he cut pictures or illustrations out of magazines. He had the books bound at the nearby Kinko's, and Ellie calligraphed the titles.

When one of my sibs acted nonchalant or unappreciative of these efforts—Dad's efforts—I went ballistic to Robert, my insides coiled in tight knots. I felt sad for Dad, and prayed he hadn't noticed the cool reception his hard work had received; I felt resentful, and hoped I had read someone wrong. And I felt guilty. Maybe I had rushed through the work; maybe I should have spent more time editing. Why couldn't they see how he needed appreciation for using his vivid imagination—for his creativity? Didn't they know he needed recognition that we still valued him?

I wanted to be his cheerleader. I really did. Looking back, I think that, where Dad was concerned, guilt drove me as much as anything else could have. What I know for certain is that, sometimes, I couldn't find it in me to do one more thing for him. My emotions were so mixed up. One day, I would laugh with Dad at his creative limericks and funny stories of life growing up in Minneapolis—of swimming in the muddy Mississippi, and of traipsing through the ritzy part of town on his way to swim in one of many lakes. Another day, I would get off the phone, my heart breaking with him over Sadie's latest medical complication.

My daughterly life never left me in peace. These emotional maelstroms sometimes carried over to my work with my students. As they told me about their confusing worlds and of problems with parents or teachers, I would over-react, projecting my life onto theirs: "Honey, that is unacceptable. You need to tell your parents that you're just a kid. They cannot expect you to shoulder that responsibility. You've already got a lot on your plate with school." Or "Listen, here's what you do: go to your parents, ask them to please call the teacher and make it clear that you need more help with the concepts. Mr. So-and-So can't expect you to learn Algebra on your own! If you need more explanation, he can stay after school and tutor you." I needed to fix something!

I see it now. I didn't let myself see it then.

One day, my brother Jim called to ask what I thought about Dad's "environment." I knew just what he meant. I'm sure I sighed, relieved to know I wasn't alone in concern about this. "Well, I worry about them. Every time I leave their house, I wonder what catastrophe is imminent."

"So, you agree—it's getting to be too much for them?"

"Absolutely. The house is gross. The carpets, Sadie's room. The kitchen. And it seems to me he's having a harder time getting around. He's in no condition to be Sadie's caretaker."

"I agree. Laurie called and said she also noticed all of this during her last visit."

"Yeah? Dad said she visited right before his surgery. Anyway, I'm probably not the only one to hear this from him, but he's so worried about

Sadie. He feels inadequate…I'm sure. He told me he asked Carmen if she would work more hours and help him with Sadie. She said no…says she has two teenagers at home, and she can't see herself working more hours. I felt so bad for him. Dad really loves Carmen, as much as he was against hiring her. And Alberto's been a help to him, too."

"Well, Laurie thinks he and Sadie are in a dangerous situation. They didn't have their meds organized, so she bought pill holders with labels for the days of the week and AM and PM. She says their diet's awful—all they eat are microwave meals. And their house is a mess. She thinks it may be time to move them to a nursing facility. What do you think?"

I wanted to scream "Why doesn't Laurie come down more often and help out if she's so worried?" Because I did spend the most time there, I felt personally attacked—a fallback feeling from the number of times she'd criticized my handling of Margaret. Now, this, too, seemed to be aimed at me. Of course, my choosing to feel slighted didn't help anything.

But I didn't see that then.

"I think it's easy for Laurie to judge since she's not the one dealing with them on a regular basis." I took a breath, then continued. "I definitely do not think Dad needs to go to a nursing home. I agree that they seem to eat a lot of microwave dinners, but Dad always buys fresh vegetables and fruit, and Carmen makes their lunch, so I'm not sure their diet is all that bad. But yeah, they definitely need more help than they're getting right now. I'm just not sure what to do about it."

"A nursing home is an extreme idea, but what other options do we have?" Jim asked.

"I've been thinking about a service, some kind of home health group. I could make some calls, but I don't think Dad will go for it. You remember how hard we fought him just to get Carmen in to help with the housework."

"Yeah, I do. But you go ahead and make the calls, and I'll talk to him. I can be stern when I need to be. And the nursing home option is worse. He'll see that."

I made some calls, gathered some information. It all sounded pretty good: someone who had training in helping elderly people would work eight or more hours a day preparing meals, taking care of bedridden patients, and doing light housework. I reported back to Jimmy who had talked to Dad, so I was prepared when Dad called, fuming and confused.

"What's brought this up now, Beth? I've always taken care of Sadie. I know her. We've been getting along okay. We have Carmen."

"I know, Dad. You're so good to Sadie. She's a lucky woman."

"She would do the same for me, too."

In my ungracious heart, I doubted it. "But Dad, the point is, she can't, and it's getting to be too much for you. You even asked Carmen to help out more. I know you realize what we're all saying is true."

"Jim said something about a nursing home. Do you want to put me—or us—there?"

"Absolutely not! None of us wants that. We want to avoid anything like that. I made some calls and found a couple of agencies. How about if I have someone come over—with me there? Together, we can talk to them and see how it goes."

Dad agreed to that. A few days later, "Marion" came out from "We Care."

Marion began by explaining We Care's mission is "consummate dedication to helping seniors in need." I asked some questions and explained what I could of the situation while Dad listened. Marion assured us their workers were licensed, caring men and women.

After she left, Dad agreed to give it a try.

I had explained to Marion that Sadie had trouble getting in and out of bed and needed help going to the bathroom in particular. For the two weeks that Dad used this group, he had serious complaints. The TLC we had been promised was anything but. Though I registered his complaints and was sent three different workers, nothing much changed: each one watched TV, left dishes in the sink, and fixed uninspired food. Dad tried to be a good sport, but when he realized they were ignoring Sadie, he seethed at me over the phone.

"Beth, I know you think I'm one of the original dinosaurs who knows nothing about how to take care of myself or Sadie, but I fired that god-damned—uh…darned—woman today. I don't want any more of those "We Care" people. The hell they do!"

"What happened Dad? Please—what…"

"That sorry excuse for a human being left poor Sadie on the toilet by herself until she was crying her eyes out. I finally heard her and got there as soon as I could. I tried to yell over the TV for help, but she didn't hear me—how could she with the TV blaring? I had to leave Sadie and get myself to the den, where that infernal woman was sitting on my couch in the lap of luxury, eating her snack or lunch or whatever. I told her to move her goddamned ass and help Sadie. She got Sadie cleaned up and put back to bed, but Sadie, poor thing…she just moaned and cried. I sat on her bed, crying myself. I hate to say it, but it's the truth. The real truth though, Beth, is that your father is an old man, and not much good for anything. I got a sick wife, and I can't take care of her. What'm I going to do?" From anger, he had fallen to dejection.

I listened to this story with pure dread. Though reluctant at times, I usually knew what Dad needed and struggled to hide any negative feelings I had, whatever he asked. Or, maybe my love for this flawed, but strong and amazing man overcame the negatives. I sincerely hope so. "Dad, I'll call the agency and tell them—just in case they didn't get the message—that we don't want their idea of help anymore. Are you two okay for now?" I asked him, praying he'd say yes, but what else would he say? He still had his pride.

"Yeah, I got Sadie some soup and cottage cheese for supper. I managed to get her to watch a little TV with me. She's in bed now. Criminy! Well, I guess that's that. Anyway, Beth, don't you worry about this. I know I put too much on you. It's not your fault or your problem. We'll get by."

I fought tears as I searched for words—to ease his pain as well as mine at my inadequacy! I should have been able to help. I mean, that's who I am. Or that's who I should be. Hadn't I learned by then that I couldn't always do anything consequential for people in pain, even those I loved?

"Dad, please don't say that. Of course, I'm going to help you and Sadie. We'll figure things out. Tomorrow's Saturday. I'll come over in the morning. Together, we'll make sure Sadie's comfortable. Is it okay if I call Jimmy and tell him what's happened?"

"Sure. I guess so. He might as well know his father's a broken down old man, too. Maybe he's right. Throw us in a home and be done with us."

"Please, stop saying that, Dad. You had a setback, that's all. I'll talk to Jim, then call you back. It's going to be okay. Right?"

"Okay. Right. Sure. I'm not going anywhere—that I know of anyway."

Jimmy said he and Janie would check on Dad and Sadie that evening. When I got there in the morning, I would call him and let him know what the new day had wrought.

So that's what we did. I'm sure Dad brightened up to see Janie, with her nursing skills and good humor. I think we all have found it reassuring if Janie has a comment or suggestion on any of our medical questions. Anyway, Dad's mood had improved by the time I arrived the next day, and Sadie felt well enough to be sitting in her robe in the living room. Jimmy came by, and we all chatted for a while over a couple of rounds of coffee.

Sadie told the story of the previous day's harrowing events in her own inimitable way. "Well, the girl helped me to the toilet, ya see. But she left me there, she did. Just left me sittin' there. So, I's waiting for her to come back, and then I start hollering for Jack. 'Course, he's stone deaf, so he cain't hear a word I say." She chuckled at her joke about Dad's hearing, then continued. "Finally, he comes in. By that time, I guess I'm crying. I's just frustrated to no end at that girl. She has no business sayin' she's helpin' people. Anyway, I'm okay. Survived a lot worse than that, I can tell ya." She giggled a little more.

Finally, Dad spoke up. "That's sure right, honey. Don't we know it. You're tough stuff. You might bend, but you don't break! That's my girl!" Dad's love and loyalty for Sadie soared above the degrading circumstances.

Anyway, Sadie went to lie down, sending us off to have lunch, saying she "weren't hungry." She just wanted a rest. By the time I left for home, those two seemed calm and cheery, at least on the surface, but I knew I hadn't fixed anything. When I walked in my front door, Robert read the disappointment all over me. "I just don't know what we're going to do. It's only going to get worse." That's when he came up with the Pennysaver plan. Skeptical, I didn't tell Jimmy or Dad what we had in mind.

Robert and I got up the next day, had a quick breakfast, then drove straight over to Dad's. Right away, Robert asked Dad for the local free paper, the Pennysaver, which both men looked to when wanting a deal on something car- or house-related. Dad and I talked while Robert pored over the ads, Dad oblivious to what Robert was looking for. After a little while, Robert says, "Guys, listen to this. 'Experienced health care worker looking for job in private home.'" Saying it couldn't hurt to call, he asked Dad for his okay and then dialed.

A young woman answered, and Robert dove in. "Hi. I'm looking for the person who advertised home care."

"That's me."

"Okay. I'm not sure how to start. Maybe you can tell me about what you do."

"Well, it depends on what you need. I take care of people who have a hard time taking care of themselves."

"Do you have training to do that? I mean, what's your experience?"

"I'm a certified nurse's aide. I worked for an agency for over a year."

"What happened? Uh…sorry, but why aren't you still working for them?"

"I quit for a couple of reasons. The pay was pretty bad, and I have three little kids. After paying the babysitter, I only made a little bit. It wasn't worth it."

"Can I call you back in a little while? This is for my wife's stepmother. I need to talk to my father-in-law. Could you come over today for an interview if he wants that?"

She said yes, and as soon as he hung up, Robert filled Dad and me in. Now, it was Dad's turn to say, "I guess it couldn't hurt to meet her and hear what she has to say."

A little later, she arrived. Her name was Kaitlyn, and she was a short woman with a pleasant face and bleached blonde hair pulled back in a neat ponytail. Kaitlyn answered our questions directly and simply. She told us what she made at the agency, before taxes, and Dad, ever the businessman, asked, "Would you take that to start? We can see how it goes for all of us, and you won't have any taxes taken out, so you'll actually be making more." He implied that, if she worked out, her pay could be improved. That suited Kaitlyn. Could she start immediately (my question)? When she said yes, Dad said, "Okay, then. Let's go meet the boss. If we can't convince her, I'm afraid we won't have a deal."

I held my breath as Dad led Kaitlyn into Sadie's bedroom and introduced the hopeful young woman to the hopeless old woman. When they came out, Dad indicated they had a deal. He told Kaitlyn he would see her the next day and said goodbye.

I walked her out to her car, fighting the storm of words and feelings that wanted to spew out, beginning with "Do you know what you're getting into? Sadie's a hellion! But my dad is mostly an angel! He's having problems, too, though he doesn't want to admit it. Please—please!—treat him well." Instead, I asked about her kids, telling her I understood the pull to be with them and the need to bring in some money. At her car, she stopped and turned to me, seeming to really see me as she said with a smile, "I think this is going to be a good job. Jack—uh, your dad—seems to be a character. Don't worry about your stepmom. (I blanched at that term. I only thought of Sadie as my Dad's wife.) I'll take care of her. I've worked with older ladies before. (Amen to that! I shouted inside my head.)

Back inside, I asked Dad what had sealed the deal for him with Kaitlyn. "She's a mom who needs work, she knows the work we need and, what's more, she seems to know what that means. Most important, Sadie likes her."

In the days that followed, I made various deals with God. I needed this to work. I hate to admit it, but I was really my top priority; if it didn't work, I figured I'd be on the hook again. At first, I worried that Kaitlyn didn't have a supervisor I could call if she failed to attend to Sadie.

I gave it a few days, then called to see how things were going. "Oh, swell," Dad answered when I asked the question.

And then, a few days later I heard "Beth, those two are thick as thieves. I read the entire paper this morning, with no interruptions. When I looked in Sadie's room, there was Kaitlyn on the bed, brushing Sadie's hair, the two of them talking away."

Life for Dad and Sadie improved significantly as Kaitlyn focused her attentions on her increasingly needy charges. Still, the house continued to deteriorate around them. One day, Jim suggested Dad consider getting new carpeting, bluntly saying the old carpet was filthy and even smelled in places. When he talked to me about it, Dad seemed open, saying, "Yeah, we got it twenty years ago, when we first moved here. Beth, do you think it actually smells?" I tried being diplomatic, but Dad got my drift.

He was on board. What's more, he seemed excited, and so we made plans to go to a carpet store near him. That is, until, as he often said, "Sadie put the kibosh on it." This time, he covered for her with, "Sadie and I talked it over. We don't want to spend the money for new carpeting. What we have is fine. Besides, I paid a pretty penny for it twenty years ago." Later, he let me know he was concerned about the "smell." What could he do? I recommended my carpet cleaner, Tony, and he agreed to that.

Not long after, Dad somehow convinced Sadie to attend her only granddaughter's wedding in Arkansas. I seized the moment and called Tony. With Sadie out of the way for a few days, Jim and I had our opportunity. Besides the carpet, we had Tony clean the furniture. With that work started, we looked around and dug in—walls, sinks—whatever we thought needed a good scrub. When Dad got home, he called me. After his report on the wedding, he launched into a conversation he'd had with Jim.

"He swears he did nothing to the house when we were gone, but, as much as I hate to say it, I don't think he's telling the truth."

"Why do you say that?" I asked him.

"Well, for one thing, the carpet in my bathroom's gone. That's one big reason. What do you know about that?"

"Okay, Dad. First, the furniture…"

"I'm not talking about that. I know Tony cleaned the furniture. I see it on the invoice he left. That's fine. It looks good, and it probably needed it. I'm talking about my BATHROOM."

"Well, I'm not sure why Jimmy didn't mention this, but I think he was checking on things and saw that your toilet had overflowed. I'm pretty sure that's what he told me."

"Oh, for God's sake! Why would that happen? It was working fine when we left."

"I don't know. Maybe he used the toilet and clogged it up."

Dad wasn't buying any of it, but I guess he didn't want to start a big fight, at least not with me, so he let it drop. Meanwhile, when he hung up, I hurried to warn Jimmy that I had made up a cover story. He was just as stubborn as Dad. Let Dad think what he wanted, he said. That rug, well, it had to go! The entire place had been smelly and dirty. How could any of us feel comfortable spending time there? I agreed with him. I just hated to upset Dad.

Somehow, the drama passed. Dad's anger cooled. He resumed his old, enthusiastic ways, continuing to hold out hope for Sadie who refused to budge from her bed—except to get her hair done every few weeks.

All these years later, I can still see Dad in his old red chair, reading, comfortable and at ease, with Kaitlyn nearby, caring for his precious Sadie with concern and affection.

As time went on, I saw more changes in Dad. His balance seemed off, and his brisk step had slowed to a shuffle. He was beginning to look his 88 years. When I look back, I can see the Parkinson's symptoms, but I guess then I didn't want to acknowledge them. He'd seemed plenty healthy to me, just slower, a little off his game. But he still acted pretty much like Dad! He took medications and went for regular check-ups for his prostate and high blood pressure. Everything was under control…until one day, it wasn't.

Greg called to tell me he'd made a date with his grandpa to interview him for a story that he was writing about Dad's life. The upcoming President's Day meant he had a day off from work, as did Robert and I.

"I'm really excited about doing this. I've collected lots of his stories over the years. And do you remember that I interviewed him once before—six months to a year ago?"

"I do, now that you mention it." I said.

"Now, I can fill in some holes. I thought I'd take him to breakfast first. He seemed okay on the phone. What do you think?"

"I think it's a great idea, honey. It's touching."

"But do you think he can handle it?"

"I think so. I take him out pretty often. Just help him getting into and out of the car, and stay close to him when he's walking. He's slow, and his balance is a little iffy. But there should be no problem."

"Would you and Dad like to come? You could leave after breakfast, I mean unless you want to stay and listen to us talk. Not sure if you'd want to hear stories you've probably heard a million times."

I laughed at the truth of Greg's last comment. "Well, I love the idea. Let me ask Dad. I know he has practice sometime that day."

"Taskmaster Dad!"

"I know, right? I've got papers to grade anyway."

When I think about it, I remember the next time I talked to Dad, his excitement at this unexpected visit came through the phone. That was the last time I would experience my father's lifelong exuberance.

President's Day arrived and we all descended on Dad, Robert and I arriving in one car and Greg in another. When he didn't answer the door, I opened it calling "Dad, we're here!" Then I saw him, white faced, lying on the couch, still in his pajamas and robe. Something was very wrong.

"I don't know what happened, Beth. I got up feeling fine, checked on Sadie, then came out here to read the paper. Still, no problem. But when I got up to get dressed, something just hit me."

"What, Dad? Can you describe it?"

"It was just the darnedest thing…I took a few steps, but then I got so dizzy and weak that I fell onto the couch."

"How do you feel now? Any better?"

"I wish I could say yes, but I feel like I've been run over by a two-ton truck."

"I'm going to call the doctor."

When I came back to where Dad still lay on the couch, I had bad news. "They say they're full today. I tried to explain how strange and different you feel, Dad, but they said for you to make an appointment for later in the week."

"Mom, I don't think this can wait." Greg's face registered our shared concern.

"I agree, Beth. Why don't you call Janie? See what she says. She's a nurse; she'll at least have an opinion," Robert suggested.

"Beth, I don't want to be an alarmist," Janie said when I told her what had happened, "but those symptoms sound serious, especially considering your dad's age. I'd call the office back and tell them you're going to take him to the hospital if they can't squeeze him in. That should light a fire under them. If it doesn't, the ER's still where he belongs, given his age."

The next call to the doctor produced the desired effect. "Bring him right over. The doctor wants to see him."

In the meantime, Kaitlyn had arrived and Robert gave her an update. I told her we'd call to keep her and Sadie posted. An hour later, after the doctor checked Dad's vitals, we were rushing Dad to the hospital, with the doctor's word that he would meet us there later. After a test and a blood panel, Dad was found to have an arterial blockage. At least, that's what I think they said. It turned out to be only a preliminary test, but the results were serious enough that he'd been admitted to the hospital for further tests and monitoring.

And that was that…the beginning of a new chapter in my father's life—and mine.

2 TALK STRAIGHT, FOR THE LOVE OF GOD

In the arms of the angel
Fly away from here
From this dark cold hotel room
And the endlessness that you fear
You are pulled from the wreckage of your silent reverie
You're in the arms of the angel
May you find some comfort here

~ Sarah McLachlan

I saw Dad wake with a start. "Okay. This isn't a dream," he mumbled. But he wasn't one to give in to fear easily, and he seemed to force his eyes to focus on his surroundings. At first, he didn't see me watching him from across the room. Looking around, as if taking stock, he noted the wires protruding from various parts of his body. I saw pain register on his face, quickly replaced by irritation at the difficulty of shifting his body in the bed. He must've been trying to get comfortable. Why was I paralyzed, stuck against the side wall?

"Damn it, I'm thirsty," he said to no one in particular.

On a tray beside his bed sat a plastic pitcher sweating drops of ice-cold water. Instinctively, he reached for it, and immediately he lay back, gasping. He told me later he'd felt a piercing, hot pain shock his upper body.

The doctor, who stood looking through the folder in his hand, had sprung into action. "Mr. Lawrence—Jack—can you hear me?"

"Dad!" Finally, I had quickly moved to his bedside.

Dad had closed his eyes and taken in a big breath. He let out the breath as the sharp pain slowly receded.

"Huh? What's the…."

"Dad, are you okay? Can you hear me?" I looked at his ears for his hearing aids.

Now he focused on me and the doctor who stood at my side.

"Yes, yes," he mumbled, once again trying to adjust himself in the bed's cumbersome sheets. "Why do hospitals always have to have so many damn sheets? How can a guy keep from getting tangled up in them?" He licked his lips.

"Dad, what can I do for you? What do you need?"

"Water, just a sip…just a sip." He nodded to the pitcher that was so close to him, but unreachable, all the same.

The doctor was taking his pulse now, listening to his heart, checking the monitors, when I heard Dad comment again "…just so many damn machines." I poured the water, then hesitated, looking at the doctor for permission.

"It's okay," the doctor said to me, then he looked at Dad. "But just a sip Mr. Lawrence."

Jack took the sip as I held the cup for him. He had tried again to reach for it himself, this time tentatively, but had backed off immediately.

"Mr. Lawrence, do you remember me? Dr. Abe?

"Dr. Abe? What kind of name is that?"

"Remember? I told you my name is Dr. Omar Abebe, but you can call me Dr. Abe for short. Most patients do."

"All right. Okay. Yeah, I remember. Funny name…definite accent. What are you?"

"Hmm. What am I? Let's see…a man…an African man. Oh, and I'm an African doctor. I bet you couldn't guess that. Well, maybe you could," he had said, chuckling as he looked at his very dark arms.

"Hmph, my GP is an African, too. His name is Hemengway. Do you know him?"

"Hemengway? Can't say that I do. Though, I'm sure you know, there are many Africans in Africa!"

Dad laughed at Dr. Abebe's humor. "I guess you're right there."

"Listen, Mr. Lawrence – may I call you Jack?

"Sure, everyone else does. Why not you, too?" Weak as he was, Dad could not repress his sense of humor in light of this doctor's refreshingly friendly tone.

"Well, Jack, I think you must know we have a very big problem here."

"Well, yeah, I AM in the hospital. What's more, I feel like hell. Is it my heart?"

"I'm afraid so. We've been trying to stabilize you, giving you some fluids and medicine through that IV, and monitoring your situation. That's why you're in the ICU. You're getting special treatment, you know."

Uh-oh, I thought. I could see that Dad felt patronized, which he did not like.

"C'mon Doc, I'm not a kid. Give it to me straight. I've been in the army,

World War II, for Chrissake. I can take it."

"Okay, Jack. Here it is: it looks like your body's in pretty good shape overall, but, unfortunately, your heart is not. As a result, your body is retaining fluid. Now, we're trying to flush it out—that's why we have you hooked up to a catheter."

"Oh, that damn thing," Dad said, as he fingered the tube but resisted the urge to pull on the line as he had a few minutes earlier.

"We need to run some tests to determine how serious the damage is to your heart, so we can figure out how to treat you—"

"Listen, I don't hear so good. Could you talk a little louder?"

"Sure. I'm sorry Jack. Is that better?"

"Yeah."

"OK. Should I start over?"

"No. I got the gist of it. Body's good overall. But my heart's bad. Collecting water, 'fluid.' What's it gonna take to fix it? Can you operate on it?" He looked at me, and I took his hand and squeezed it. He let go after a few seconds to rub his eyes.

"Well, this is what we're going to find out once we run a few more tests."

"I'm pretty old, I guess. But I don't want to die. People here need me, like this one right here." Dad nodded at me.

"Oh, I'm sure she does. In fact, I'm sure there are many who'd like to keep you around a while longer. Why wouldn't they? A smart, handsome guy like you!"

Dad tried to laugh. I could see he liked this man. Dr. Abe was okay in his book. Not like so many doctors. Sadie's doctor, for instance, was always rushing in, talking rapidly in doctor speak, and NEVER loud enough for him to hear. And if my brother or I were there, the doctor would just aim his words at us, as if Dad and Sadie weren't in the room. Even the doctors that Dad had liked over the years had rarely shown him the patience and respect of Dr. Abebe...Dr. Abe.

3 OLD AGE SNEAKS IN

Memory

All alone in the moonlight…
Life was beautiful then
I remember the time I knew what happiness was
Let the memory live again…
I must wait for the sunrise, and I mustn't give in…

~Andrew Lloyd Webber and Trevor Nunn

Sitting in the hospital waiting room, thinking about the day's events, I realized Dad had been old for a long time. He'd turned 89 on this last birthday—if anything, it should have been difficult to remember when he wasn't old. Strangely, that's not the way I thought of him. In fact, memories of a different man, vibrant and energetic, washed over me.

I'm a little girl in pigtails. It's Saturday morning and, full of childish exuberance, I am the only one up—or so I think as I head for the TV room and cartoons. Suddenly, there he is, in the doorway, dressed in his Saturday morning clothes—army khakis—ready for chores around the house.

"Hey, lil' sis. I see you're up. What do ya think? How 'bout you and me head off to Dooley's? I need some nails and screws for the trellis I'm building for your mom. I think Dooley's might even have some ribbons for those pigtails of yours."

And just like that, we're off on an adventure. It's Bethie and Daddy, not my big brothers or baby sister. Yep! Just the two of us in the big blue truck that he drove back and forth to work, with its gears grinding as he gets going. He places me on the high seat right next to him, and begins to hum, then finally breaks into a favorite song, "Never Smile At A Crocodile." He always goes way down deep with his voice, shaking his finger at me and warning, "Don't be taken in, by his friendly grin—he's imagining how good you'd feel within his skin!" as I glow and giggle.

Once we're at the store, Dad's big, rough hand holding mine, we head to the aisle with the screws and nails. He gathers up a handful, then leads me to the corner of the store where different colors and patterns of ribbons dangle, and he lets me pick out a spool of satiny red plaid. We take the spool with us to be measured, and purchase the bright, shiny strand along with the nails and screws. At home, he oohs and aahs after Mom ties the ribbon into pretty bows in my hair.

Another time, we walk up the big, wide steps at the library—again, just the two of us. Daddy leads me by the hand into a big room, with books on shelves that I just know reach to the ceiling. After showing me the book jackets that will help me discover the stories I want to read, he deposits me in the juvenile section as he heads off to the grown-up books. I barely notice he's gone, as I am very busy pulling books with colorful covers off the shelf. After a while, having picked out a book, I wander a bit until I find him poring over a book with its own colorful cover—one with a boat with many sails in a very rough-looking sea. He looks up to see me, and sets my choice on the top of his stack of books then turns to me and asks "Is that all you want? Just one book? You know, you can always check out more than one," and he shows me that he has four. "One book would never do for me. I have to have enough to last me at least two weeks!" I don't reply, but, grinning ear to ear, I immediately turn back in the direction I have just come from to make one or two more selections.

Outside the library, he commands me to wait at the top of the concrete steps while he hurries down them, then holds out his arms, inviting me to "Jump to Daddy!" And I do, with perfect trust in this man who touches an errand and magically turns it into an adventure.

Immediately, another memory surfaces. We're at the same library, only I'm a few years older. This time, I've brought my friend Grace along. At his command, again I eagerly jump into his outstretched arms. "Hurrah! You made it!" he exclaims as he always does when I land in his arms. Grace looks on, laughing.

Suddenly, I'm…what? Ten? Daddy and I walk out of church on Sunday, heading to the hall where Mom's serving donuts; he grabs my hand as he always does, getting ready to cross the narrow street separating the church from its hall. Suddenly, I'm aware "I'm too big for this! What if someone sees me?" And I drop his hand.

"Oh, I guess you're too old to hold my hand now, huh, lil' sis?" Immediately, I'm sorry. But it's too late. I have taken that inevitable step, and I can't reclaim what I'd had a day or even an hour before.

I have never forgotten his disappointment—or my own.

How was it that I still had these intimate memories? How was it that they blessed me at the time I had needed them so terribly? I realize now, what with my big family and all, that I'd really had very little time alone with either parent growing up. I even remember asking myself then if I had made up these events. But no…I knew I hadn't. These crystalline memories were locked in my heart, as certainly as the knowledge that, under other circumstances, my life would have (should have?) unfolded differently.

I realize now that, for a brief time, my position in my family was clear: I was the princess of the household—my father's princess, the perfect baby of four: two big brothers, one "exceptional" older sister, and then me, the post-war-starting-over-better-days-have-arrived child. I remember being my parents' little star: sitting on Daddy's lap to watch "Sheriff John" when he came home from work for lunch; being Mommy's sole audience as she sang "You are my sunshine" and took pictures of cute little me on the wide red porch as I ate a juicy red apple in my underwear. Am I wearing shoes? Are those hers, too big on my little feet? What was it about that moment that had compelled my mother to do something so extraordinary as take my picture doing something so mundane?

My thoughts returned to Dad, lying in the hospital bed, his worn green gown askew. He slept fitfully, his breathing labored, and again I was struck by the old man before me.

I noticed the time: three-thirty. How could I have been lost in thought for so long? Looking back over the day, though, I had the sense that time—my awareness of it—had escaped me. There was the moment when Robert and Greg had gone for coffee and some kind of egg sandwiches while I waited with Dad in the Emergency Room. Once they had returned with my breakfast—that has to have been two or three hours before—husband and son had said their goodbyes to Dad and me and gone off to do what they needed to do with the day. But not me.

This is what I needed to do: sit and wait. For what, though? To get more information about Dad's condition? Sure. For my siblings to arrive so I could recount…explain…help with something…anything? Was that it, really? If so, why? Who made me queen keeper of Dad? I know the answer to that, now. I didn't even think about it then.

At some point, I moved to the waiting room and sat, alone with my thoughts, feeling strangely calm. I cared about Dad; I knew this wasn't about that. I had two sisters and two brothers, and yet I was the only one at Dad's sick bed. But why did I rush to judgment? Did I even know what my siblings were doing? I had the day off, after all—and I wasn't coming from out of town, really. I only lived 30-plus minutes away, not hours away, like my sister. And I had talked to Jimmy, so I knew he was trying to break away from the office. I'm sure Jimmy'll be here any time now, I'd told myself.

For all these years, I had continued to hero worship my oldest brother. My relationship with him was the healthiest of any I had in the family—by far. We'd babysat for each other when our kids were young, and spent time as couples going to dinner or out for a movie. In more recent years, we'd get on the phone from time to time to talk about situations with Margaret and Harold. At awkward times, he'd managed to navigate family dynamics as he presented some issue pertaining to Margaret or Dad that bothered Laurie, but that Laurie wouldn't discuss with me directly. And, as Dad aged and needed us, I think we both found comfort sharing our experiences of his journey. Mostly, when we came together, our mutual affection and respect was sincere.

Now, peering down the hall, I started as I recognized Jim's compact, still-youthful form hurrying toward me. Relieved, I rose to meet him.

"How is he?" Jim asked as he gave me a quick hug.

"In and out. Cheerful one moment, gloomy the next. He worries about Sadie—then he claims he's fine. He dozed for a while, then woke up crying for Mom. I don't know what meds they have him on, but they must be strong. I'm just glad you're here. We met his doctor, Dr. Abebe. He told Dad to call him Dr. Abe. He's Dad's cup of tea—treated him with respect, joked with him. They're still running tests, so he didn't have anything specific to offer, but he said that, clearly, this heart thing is serious."

"Wow, Beth." Jimmy shook his head. "Sorry I'm so late. Big case going to trial soon. The work on the briefs is going way too slowly. I'm between a rock and a hard place. These young attorneys don't seem to understand what hard work is. Not too happy that I brought them in on a holiday. But you don't need to hear about that. Let's go see him." With that, Jimmy braced himself, took a breath and motioned for me to lead him to Dad's room.

4 SPIN IN UNCERTAINTY

The chains are locked, and tied across the door…
Blue, blue windows behind the stars
Yellow moon on the rise
Big birds flying across the sky
Throwing shadows on our eyes…
Helpless, helpless, helpless…

~Neil Young

Jack had been fully awake for at least 15 minutes. While the pain continued to ebb and flow, it wasn't the physical pain that gnawed at him. It was the incredible humiliation of dependence on these ladies in white, for even the most private of functions. And the most mundane. Just now, he longed for a sip of water.

What do I do? Ring the buzzer? Where is the damn thing, anyway? He groped with his right hand and felt only tubes. Tugging on one, a sharp jolt let him know that it was attached to his penis. Damn it. Should I shout for someone? I don't think I can. Oh, God. I'm too damn weak. Why isn't someone here to help me? Where's Beth?

He was sure his daughter was nearby; even though he didn't see her, he knew that she would never leave him.

I'm her burden, he suddenly thought. Oh, God. Just what I vowed not to be to any of my children. And now here I am, a weak old man. He felt the tears coursing down his cheeks. Anna is the one I really want. Darling, soft, sweet Anna. Maybe I'll be joining her soon, if the last few years of tending to Sadie have atoned for my many sins against her. Strange way to look at it, but what choice do I have? There it is.

Wait … I love Sadie now. She needs me, poor thing. Losing her vision, pain wracking her body with damned arthritis. Why can't the doctor do anything for her? I've asked and asked!

She's given up. Hardly leaves her bed. Thank God for Kaitlyn. I'm so glad I hired her to help Sadie. And Carmen…she really cheers my days, getting me out of the house. I'd be hog-tied without her since the damn DMV took away my license. Confounded driving test. Hell, I was just nervous. Damn kid made me do all those impossible park jobs! I've been driving since I was 13. Never had more than a fender bender, except for that horrible, God-awful accident, which I DID NOT CAUSE! Poor Anna.

Poor Sadie. Oh, it makes me see red, the way she's always talking about her dead husband. I guess I understand. But I don't talk about Anna like that. Sadie acts like he's the only husband she's had. Doesn't she know that it riles me up to hear her go on and on about him? She must know how much I love her, worry about her. When I first really noticed her…wow! So cute and petite…and her sweet southern ways. Anna had been gone for so long…over seven years when I met Sadie.

Anna and I had some life together, though. I adored her from the minute I laid eyes on her. Only here from Michigan "on a visit." Imagine that. Gonna go back "home" and enter a convent. No! Not if I had any say! Just did what I could to make her mine and get married. And her with that heart-shaped face…what a beauty. Those early days were so sweet. How could I get drafted? Me with two babies? A nightmare, saying goodbye when we'd barely started our life together. To see her after she had Jimmy, then Margaret so soon after—her beautiful face with that black hair spilling over the white pillows—what a picture. I'll never forget it. My darling Anna.

Unlike Anna, Sadie's sweet exterior masked a steely core that could be harsh. Her first husband left her a widow with two children, Don and his younger sister, Judy. Years later, in a cruel development, her darling Don had been killed in a hit and run car accident, leaving her with the motel that she had owned and managed with Tom's help. With Don gone, and teenager Judy occupied with schoolwork and glee club, Sadie nursed her bitter grief with long hours of upkeep on her ten motel rooms. Judy was often left to fend for herself, and when she acted out in rebellion, Sadie said she had let Judy know on no uncertain terms which child she wished had lived.

Aghast at first, Jack's admiration eventually overshadowed any disapproval. Sadie had survived her heart-breaking losses just as he had. In time, she sold her motel and bought a cute little house in a well-kept neighborhood. What's more, she maintained a bountiful vegetable garden and did most of the maintenance on her property.

Southern conservative to his eastern liberal, at first Sadie seemed only to see him as a dancing partner at the square dances they both attended.

Tentatively, Jack began to court her. Once Sadie's fierce survival instinct became clear, Jack was hooked. Though she never hid her lack of any deep affection for him, they married and lived together companionably, learning to avoid politics when they could and agreeing to disagree when they couldn't.

At least with Sadie, Jack's life was simple. They had no money issues between them, and no children at home to fuss over. They planted gardens together, maintained their home together and, best of all, square-danced and traveled together. After the long years of loneliness that had followed Anna's tragic passing, Sadie provided Jack with a happy life. Perhaps, more than anything else, they were good company for one another.

Jack remembered how he and Anna had vowed to always care for Margaret. But then Sadie made it clear: no marriage until Margaret was out of the house. Still, once adult Margaret had started wandering the city streets, sending them all into fits of worry, Jack had resisted the pressure from his children to find a group home for Margaret. He had rationalized her behavior: "Remember, she doesn't have what you all have—a family of her own. She's lonely; she's just trying to keep busy when she gets home from work, looking for a little excitement. She's agreed to be home by nine. Don't worry." Yet, he found himself longing for pert little Sadie, and knew he had to find a way.

Then, serendipity got involved, and Margaret announced that she wanted to get married to Harold. Jack knew his children judged him harshly for allowing that to happen—especially Beth and Laurie. He often agreed with the family's consensus: "That man is a bastard!"...but Jack had to look out for himself. And Margaret had cried and begged him. Jack suspected Harold had ulterior motives. How could he sincerely want to marry a woman with developmental issues, even high-functioning Margaret? But maybe she provided her husband something none of them saw.

It wasn't six months after the wedding that "that bastard" had gone after the money Margaret inherited when her mother died. Jack went to court to make sure Harold couldn't touch any of Margaret's funds, then created a blocked account that only Jack could access. But that wasn't the end of Harold. He'd stayed married to Margaret, and according to Laurie and Beth, made her life miserable. Well, that was all water under the bridge. Harold was dead, and Margaret, who lived on her own, was doing okay, as far as Jack was concerned.

Lost in his brooding, Jack didn't notice Beth and Jimmy enter the room.

"Hi, Dad," Jim said tentatively, noticing Jack's glum expression, but unsure how to read it. "How're you feeling?" He got no response—just a shrug of Jack's shoulders, so he continued. "Janie says hi. Says she'll see you tonight. The girls send their love."

At this, Jack shrugged again, muttering unintelligibly and rubbing his eyes. Something in this gesture moved Beth, and she took her father's hand. He squeezed hard and lifted his head and looked at Beth imploringly.

"Your mother..." he faltered. Beth struggled to speak.

"What about her, Dad?" Jimmy asked, moving closer to take Jack's other hand.

"She was so good, didn't deserve...what she got...did she? She worked so hard for all you kids, and me, too. Needed more from me than I gave her." He still focused his gaze on Beth, whose tears now covered her cheeks.

"Mom was good," Jimmy said quietly. "She was better than all of us, and now she understands that we meant to be better to her."

"She knows we all loved her," Beth murmured. "She's been watching out for us all this time, waiting for us, waiting for you, Dad." Something made her add, "You're her Jackie." With that, Jack chuckled quietly, and then Jimmy and Beth did, too.

"Yeah. I had my pet names for her, too."

"I remember, when I was a kid—I thought both your names were 'honey.' I told Sister Mary Frances—my third-grade teacher—that, and she just howled."

"Hmph." Dad smiled, clearly amused, but it was also clear the conversation was sapping the little energy he had.

"I'm glad you're both here. I'm sure I'm going to be fine. Right Jim?"

Now, it was Jimmy's turn to shrug, albeit through a slight smile. But Dad had closed his eyes, nestling into his pillows.

They're good kids. I did okay by them. Here they are, by my side, and soon the others will be here. I'm very fortunate. They love their old man. What about Frank? Will he come? Long drive and all. Same with Laurie...longer drive. Those kids...never gave us a lick of trouble, at least nothing to worry about.

That Anna, boy, she could still worry. About all of them, I guess. Though Margaret...her greatest weight. Thought Anna's heart would break in two when that damn school said Margaret couldn't graduate...had to leave high school early. So hard on Anna, and so hard on Margaret, poor kid.

What was she supposed to do with herself? I was no help. What could I do, with the business such a scramble? But Anna, she had the will of a bulldog when the mother in her got going. Once she heard about that experimental workshop for disabled kids, well...bingo! She and some other mothers got one going for our kids. 'Bout saved Margaret's life. And Anna's sanity.

I encouraged her, listened to her, talked her through the logistics. Did some Saturday driving when the parents got the kids into that bowling league. Margaret's athletic genes kicked in, too. Once I gave her some pointers, her game took off like gangbusters! Guess I did help, after all.

Oh, why'm I so damn tired? Guess I can sleep a little if I want to—I'm in the damn hospital, after all.

Beth looked at Jimmy, mouthing the words "Where'd he go?" Jimmy frowned, lifting his shoulders. But Jack had sounded optimistic, reassuring them for the time being. This is more like him, Beth thought, looking at her father's peaceful face.

Just then, a doctor walked in and took what seemed like a cursory look at Jack's chart. Jack appeared to be sleeping as the doctor signaled for Jimmy and Beth to follow him outside. "I'm Dr. Kaplan, your father's cardiologist. I'll be monitoring his condition as regards his heart, which certainly looks to be the culprit. As soon as all the tests are in, I'll be back with the results. Have you met Dr. Abebe? He'll be your father's primary doctor while he's in the hospital.

Jim looked at Beth who nodded her head 'yes' to the last question.

"Did he have a heart attack?" she wanted to know.

"I can't say that for certain. Dr. Abebe will be in later to give you more information. Clearly, however, Jack's condition is critical. So, for now, give your father time to rest. By all means, visit with him—just keep it short, and try not to excite him."

Back in the waiting room, Jimmy went off for some coffee and a phone call, while Beth sank into a couch and stared at the ceiling. How often had she felt this isolation, this chilling loneliness? She knew it well, though, and had discovered ways to accommodate: lots of distractions! She loved having a family—couldn't imagine life without them!—and, for the most part, that, along with a challenging and fulfilling profession, had kept her going. Since the kids had grown up, though, even with her job, she had more time to herself, more time to "brood," a word for what Jack had often said Anna did.

Dad's in "critical condition." Okay. He's 89 years old. Something had to give, sometime. What did I expect? How do I feel about all this? At the moment, I don't know. I'm tense...wound tight inside. He's sick and it's sad. But my head is filled with thoughts that don't connect. I keep thinking about seeing Laurie, and how awkward that's going to be. And Frankie...God, I love that guy, but I never know how he'll be when I see him. Last time I saw him was at Jim's. Why did he say I tried to turn Dad against him? Why would he think that? Because I moved when he lit up a cigarette?

Why aren't I more upset right now? Dad could die. He's so weak...he looks awful, and he's talking kinda crazy...about Mom, and his regrets. Well...okay...maybe not so crazy. Mom didn't have it easy...but why was that his fault? We had a big family. And there was Margaret. Mom worried a lot. I guess I'm a lot like her.

That doctor…he didn't name what's going on with Dad. But then, he didn't have to. Am I brooding? I hate that word, but it probably applies. I mean—look at me now…thinking weird thoughts. Does anyone else do this?

I remember that time Debbie said I was too needy, that she felt like I was a burden to her. She was mad when she said it, and our friendship seems to be okay now. But we're not as close as we were. I'm definitely more guarded now. I remember how wonderful it felt when we first got close, both having that cancer scare. How good it felt to have someone who seemed to understand how I felt about things, to share our disappointments…her breakup with Matt…and Laurie for me. We confided in each other…we shared our families; we felt like sisters—or was that just me romanticizing the friendship?

I know I've let friends down. No one can really fill the void in someone else. What was it that I read a while ago? Oh, yeah, Scott Peck…and how we each go down our own path, and along the way, we're making decisions—whether we acknowledge them or not. I guess I do that. I try to be a good person. I love my family, but I'm such a jumble inside. I've always tried to be optimistic, self-reliant. But the truth is, in many ways, I'm just a kid…and damn insecure. In other ways, I feel so old.

I remember trying to explain to Robert what goes on inside of me sometimes that I work so hard to hide. Things that make me touchy, demanding …. I promised him I would get help. Try to figure it out. And I did. I found a great therapist!

Rayna helped—what a lifeline she was! I remember when she told me I'd bottled up feelings for forever. And that it had always been chaotic—from a lifetime of pressure to give, give, give. She said that I was looking for love—validation—for my "true self." It all sounded so good and so right…if only I knew just who my "true self" is.

Suddenly, out of nowhere, a familiar voice stirred the heavy air. "Hi, Beth."

"Laurie…."

5 TAME THAT BEAST

Miles from nowhere, I guess I'll take my time
Oh, yeah, to reach there
Look up at the mountain I have to climb…
Lord, my body has been a good friend
But I won't need it when I reach the end

~ Cat Stevens

"Well, I'm here. How's Dad?"

"Okay, so far. I mean—Dad will be happy you're here. It's good to see you."

"Yeah? Really. Huh. Well, it's been a long day."

"How are you? How are the boys?"

"I'm just fine. They're just fine. You remember Anthony, my husband."

Of course I remember him. He's the guy who wrote me that horrible letter once upon a time, the guy who accused me of stabbing you and everyone else in our family in the back—the guy who taunted me, proclaiming that your love for one other was something I would never know, mostly because I wasn't capable of it and didn't deserve it. All that—from a guy who barely knew me.

And what horrendous offense had I committed that time? Of course—how could I forget? I'd written you a letter inviting you and "your family" for Thanksgiving. Well, I hadn't met your stepsons, didn't know their names, and had only met Anthony once, briefly—but my failure to address each member of your family by name was my mortal sin. How could I, instead, refer to them as "your family." How could I have been so cold, so unfeeling?!

So then, of course, you had to send a letter back, full of accusations. Your letter had stung because all I'd meant to do was reach out, and get our family together for a holiday dinner.

It's likely that, in time, I would have come to understand that you'd thought I didn't value the family you had made for yourself, including a husband and stepsons you loved. This meant that you were hurting, too—and I figured I had my fair share of blame for that. But to get such a shockingly angry letter from a man I hardly knew…well…that had certainly left an imprint. Oh, yes, I remembered Anthony.

"Hello, Anthony." He nodded and looked away.

"I asked where Dad's room is. No one seems to be sure."

"Oh, he was moved earlier, some mix-up with another patient. Laurie, you look good. How are you?"

"I told you, I'm fine. I talked to Jimmy. I think you should know he and Janie are meeting me and Anthony here later for dinner. We're going to discuss what to do with Dad when he's ready to leave the hospital. I've already got a call in to hospice. They're going to call me back to discuss the situation. Thought you should know."

I can feel my face flush, grow hot. "Oh. Wow! I've been talking to the doctors, and so far, they haven't indicated his condition is that dire. Of course, I know it's serious, but no one's said anything about hospice. That's pretty extreme. We can all talk to Dr. Abebe later. He's supposed to be coming later to update us."

Laurie smirked. "Like I always say, you know best…where Dad is concerned."

"All I meant is that we can all talk to his doctor together."

"Uh-huh. Fine. So anyway, I've got a question for you, Beth. What happened to Dad, and why didn't you call me? He's my father, too."

Oh shit, here it comes: the accusatory questions, the inevitable blame.

"What, no one told you the details? Jim said he spoke to…well uh, Robert and I went over on President's Day to take Dad to breakfast. Actually, Greg met us there. He wanted to interview Dad for a project he's working on. We were all going out to breakfast. But when we got to Dad's, he was lying on the couch in his bathrobe. He said he felt fine when he first got up. Then, suddenly, he felt so weak he could hardly stand. He didn't seem to have any other symptoms." I stopped. Was I rambling?

"And then what?" she asked.

"I called his doctor's office, but they said they couldn't see him until the following Monday. So, I called Janie to see what she thought, ya know as a nurse….

She said to call the office back, say we were going straight to the hospital if they couldn't fit Dad in. So, I did that. And Janie was right. They did tell us to come on over. As soon as we got to the office—Dad was barely able to walk—they took us into a room; the doctor came in, did a quick exam, and sent us to the hospital ER. The ER doctors did some tests, and said Dad's carotid artery might be blocked. So, they admitted him."

"And, I repeat, why in God's name didn't you call me?!" Laurie demanded, and she looked squarely at me. "I was so upset and worried. If I had known earlier…"

Hadn't she heard the shocking sequence of events I just described?

Damn, I can't find the right words. They're eluding me. Why can't she just understand me. How am I wrong in this situation?

"Look, you haven't talked to me in forever. When I called Jimmy, he said he'd let you know. *And then I felt myself getting mad* I was a little busy with Dad. It took all day. I've been here since morning." *Poor me, poor me!*

"Not too tired to call Margaret, and probably Frankie."

"I told you—Jimmy said he'd call you. I made a quick call to Margaret while Dad had his tests, and I think Janie talked to Frankie. It hasn't been easy, you know?!" *And there I go again.*

"Oh, that's right. I forgot. It's all about you. Give me a break. You don't know what I—I mean, we—went through to get here. And my boys are also busting their butts to get here. We don't even know where we're staying. But we're not worrying about that. Like I said, it's always about you!" Now, Laurie put her head down. She seemed near tears.

"What do you mean, Laurie? I'm sure you're worried and tired, too. I do understand. I didn't mean…. We both love our father." *I felt the ground beneath me shifting, and I fought for control.*

"Yeah, but you always know what's best for him, and, of course, he depends on you, his Bethie." Laurie's arms, folded across her chest, suddenly dropped. Laurie's voice had softened into hurt.

"Oh, God, Laurie. You know Dad loves you. He's been asking for you."

Why am I blubbering like this?. "It's scary for all of us to think of Dad in this condition, but I really haven't heard anyone talk about hospice yet. I mean, they're still doing tests on him, trying to assess the problems. So far, all they know is that it's his heart. When we all know more, you, Jimmy, hopefully Frankie and I can all sit down and talk about Dad's condition and options together."

"Yeah, well, we'll see. I'll talk it over with Jim at dinner. My boys should be here pretty soon. They'll want to weigh in on his future, also. Jason's planning to talk to Dad about his will. He wants to represent him, make sure everything's in order, make sure Margaret's taken care of…well, properly. She's really worried about him, you know."

"Of course, she is. I know that." I tried to soften my voice.

"Well, right now, I'm going to see him, and then I'll find someone who will give me some straight answers." Laurie had mustered her strength again.

"Can you tell Jim I'm here, and he should come to Dad's room?"

Suddenly, I felt light-headed, teary—and VULNERABLE. I looked around for Jim, Robert—someone. At that moment, I just couldn't figure out what bugged Laurie so much, but I was sure it had to do with me. I knew I needed to get away from her. So, I summoned the energy and announced that I was going to the bathroom and told her Dad's new room number.

With my head down and tears streaming down my face, I nearly collided with Jimmy as he strode toward me.

"What's wrong, Beth?" My brother held my shoulders and looked at me with concern.

"Laurie just showed up with Anthony, talking about hospice. She said you are all going to discuss this over dinner with her boys." I took a step back, away from my brother's arms. "Apparently…anyway, I got the impression that I'm not included." *I felt like a child saying that out loud. Just so whiny and puerile.*

"Beth, she called my cell phone just a little while ago, saying they were almost here. She suggested dinner and mentioned talking about hospice, but I told her to wait, to see Dad. We would talk about everything later. She's just worried, that's all."

"Yeah, sure. Well, I'd just like it known that I think any discussion about Dad's future should include all of us—even Frankie, if he ever gets here. And, by the way, Jason's planning to use his newly acquired attorney skills to 'make sure Dad's will is in order' and that Margaret is taken care of "properly"—Laurie's word."

"Jason's here with her?" He ignored the sarcastic drama in my words.

"No, but he's on his way, with Christopher. Doesn't Laurie know about our meetings with the attorney? Doesn't she know Dad already has a living trust? I mean, I love Jason, but what's he going to do that Dad hasn't already done for himself? And of course, Margaret IS provided for properly! I've done what I could to make sure of that."

"Beth, remember that a battle with Laurie will serve no one, particularly Dad. And remember, Jason and Christopher are coming because they love their grandpa and are probably worried about their mom as well.

"Just stay focused on why we're all here. I'm sure this has been a long and tough day for you, whether or not Laurie's thinking about that. The main thing is, Dad. He needs us all united in our concern for him.

"By the way, do you remember the counselor you took Margaret to while back? Laurie had reported to Jim that Margaret was depressed, and he should get me to take her to counseling.

"You mean, the therapist who concluded that Margaret had a pretty positive attitude to life?"

"Right," Jim said. "If I remember right, the therapist also noted that Margaret could be pretty manipulative where you, Dad, and Laurie are concerned. She and Laurie talk. It's just possible that she accidentally planted some false ideas in Laurie's head about you and Dad."

Jimmy's honest, straightforward approach had the desired effect: I felt calm, sane again. In his loving, diplomatic way, my big brother had set me straight. In return, I hope I'd shown him that I knew he was right—never an easy task for me. I mainly remember being tired and annoyed. I wanted him to see Laurie in action. That seems childish now.

I thought—insisted—to myself that what I wanted more than anything was to get my sister back in my life. I thought if I could just figure out the right move or words, I could make it happen. But, from my present vantage point, I see the folly in that thinking. Maybe, what I really wanted was to be right while also getting my sister back in my life. I always was—maybe still am—a control freak. So, of course, that would never have worked. If Laurie were ever to be back in my life, it would have to be because she wanted to be back, and that would require that I be a different me.

And I would say that's taken most of a lifetime for me to figure out.

When Jim asked me about Margaret, I replied that she was expecting me to call her with an update on Dad. "Do you think you can swing by and pick her up and bring her with you and Janie tonight?

"If she tells me where she'll be and when. I don't want to go looking for her."

"Okay, I'll call her and make sure she's planning to come. I sure hope she is. Anyway, I'll call you after I talk to her. Anyway, right now, I'm going to the bathroom. I told Laurie where Dad's room is. She wants you to meet her there." I turned toward the bathroom, and Jimmy headed in the opposite direction.

When I returned to the lobby, I found it empty. Deciding that meant that Laurie, Anthony, and Jimmy were in with Dad, I plopped down in a chair. Soon, I found myself fretting about Laurie.

Why'd she come here with both barrels loaded and ready to shoot? And why is it that it seems like no one else sees her when she acts this way? Maybe she's frustrated, too. Maybe, somehow, the fact that I didn't call really had hurt her. I need to remember that, no matter what, I alone hold the key to the peace and calm I desire…I just need to figure out where that key is and where to put it!

And then, suddenly, Jimmy was back. I hadn't seen or heard him coming.

"Okay. I just talked to Janie. She and I are going to eat at home. Are Laurie and Anthony with Dad?"

"I guess. I haven't seen them. I thought you'd see them in Dad's room."

"I decided to check in at home first. Now, I think I'll step in for a minute, and say goodbye to Dad for now. I'll be back later with Janie."

I'd been afraid he'd say that. I didn't want to be left alone with Laurie at the hospital. Jimmy broke into my thoughts: "Don't you want to go home, Beth, get a little rest, see Robert?" At that, I realized how much I needed to get out of that place. The very scent that screamed "sanitizer" had invaded my body. It cried out for fresh air. I said that I did.

"And Beth—remember: Laurie's here for Dad, same as you. You don't have to do battle. It's not good for you, her or anyone."

Did Jim ever stop being my big brother? To me, he had always been so grown up and responsible. And his solid moral core never ceased to amaze me.

"I know. You're right." Still, I had to add, "Could you just please tell her that?"

"I already have."

6 COME TOGETHER, ALREADY

We are family, get up everybody and sing
We are family, get up everybody and sing
Everyone can see we're together
As we walk on b, and we fly just like birds of a feather
I won't tell no lie…we are family…

~Bernard Edwards and Nile Rodgers

"Margaret? Hi, it's me, Beth."

"Hi-yee. How you?"

"I'm fine, just tired from being here at the hospital."

"How our dad? Is he…is he…umm…he din't die, did he?"

"No. No change. What're you doing?"

"Oh, nothin' much. I do some laundry. I always do it on Tuesdays, ya know. I do three loads so far."

"Good for you," I commented with a chuckle. "How's Mr. Grumpy Pants?"

"Guy, why you call Harold that?"

"Well, he is, isn't he?"

At this, Margaret giggled. "Yeah…guy…sometime, he drive me crazy."

"What else is new?"

"Oh…umm…not much…just doing different things…."

She clearly missed my continuing sarcasm about Harold.

"Yeah. Good. Hey, listen, the reason I called is that Jimmy and Janie are coming to the hospital at seven tonight. They want to pick you up. How about it?"

"Umm. What about my walk?"

Every day, seven days a week, rain or shine, at 4 PM—sometimes earlier—Margaret set out to wander the streets of her neighborhood. At first, it had seemed like a positive move—asserting her independence from Harold, as well as providing a healthy diversion from days spent watching

TV. But, as these excursions grew longer and longer, she returned later and later—and her answers to questions about where she went and what she did while she was out became increasingly vague. Harold started calling Dad, but Dad thought Harold was making the proverbial mountain out of a molehill.

"What do you think, Beth? That guy doesn't want Margaret to have a life!"

"I don't know, Dad. I don't like Harold any more than you do, but she does seem to be getting home later and later at night. When I ask her what she does on these walks, she says she's making friends. In the market, at a coffee shop, at the post office? I'm worried about her, too, Dad."

When I asked a social worker friend, she said people with mental retardation thrive on routine, and that Margaret had probably fallen into a pattern that afforded her some satisfaction, and had become hooked on it. That made sense, but I still wanted to know more. I called the Regional Center and after a few tries, spoke to Margaret's official social worker, Beverly, who asked me some questions, and then said Margaret sounded bored and probably unhappy. She would make an appointment with Margaret to meet up and have a chat. Unfortunately, that hadn't solved my problem. I needed to know what to do NOW.

In those days, I always thought there had to be an answer. My concerns were exacerbated by the fact that Margaret had gone on these walks before she married. When we—her siblings—found out our vulnerable sister had gone to a bar and then had gotten into a car with a strange man, we'd descended on Dad. Dad, in turn, had a serious talk with Margaret…but nothing changed.

Eventually, Harold came into her life. They married, and, when he made her quit her job, she became a housewife. Eventually, she seemed to have arrived at some type of normalcy…but, over time, she must have gotten tired of her soap operas—or Harold. Or maybe Harold took control of the TV. Who knew? Maybe she got tired of his endless criticisms and his impossible expectations.

One time, she called me in tears and told me, with uncharacteristic directness, "I don't think I love Harold anymore." I talked and talked to her. Part of me felt relieved, hoping this meant she would divorce him. I loathed that man. But I simply had no idea how to help. I took her to lunch to talk, but she just cried.

Not long after that, I found her a marriage counselor with fees on a sliding scale. Margaret liked the counselor, and liked talking to her, but I guess her routine had already become too fixed. She couldn't walk away from her marriage, especially after she'd found a way to tolerate it—by getting away from her husband for a while each day. However, that "while" had begun to stretch, such that she was now leaving the house every afternoon, and not returning until 10 or later.

With her on her "walk," Margaret took her "bag." At first it was just her purse; but, soon enough, she'd graduated to carrying a large plastic bag. Eventually, she left the house with a large purse over her shoulder and two or three plastic bags that she pushed around in a shopping cart. These bags held everything she thought she might possibly need to keep herself entertained and productive during her hours away from home: her wallet and house keys, pens, pencils, stationery and stamps; a small bag for business cards she collected; her camera, and an envelope with photos she might want to show some new friend; a calendar, a small notebook and other miscellany. I know this inventory because of the many times I failed to convince her she didn't need to walk around with all that baggage, which, I was afraid, made her more of a target.

As Margaret's walks grew longer, Harold began calling me, whining at me with his nasal voice. Oh, I hated those calls, especially when I so wanted to scream at him for his treatment of my sister! Part of me wanted to call him names and slam the phone down. Another part wanted to hear his frustration, make him wade in worry and concern. But ironically, this time I agreed with him. The more he told me, the more I felt sure that, one day, someone would find Margaret dead in a culvert. But every conversation with Margaret on this subject left me feeling like my brain had spent thirty minutes in a blender.

"Margaret, it's not safe for you to be walking the streets alone at night, especially at ten o'clock and later."

"What you mean, Beth?"

"I mean that you could get hurt. Someone could come after you!"

"Why they do that?"

"Because some people are bad. You know that."

"I know, but I talk to people, you know. They very nice."

"It's true—many people are. But some aren't nice. That's what I'm talking about. What if someone turns out to be a bad person and you're talking to them?"

"I ve-wwy careful, make sure."

No one can compete with Margaret's stubborn streak.

"Listen, I'm just worried about you. Hasn't anyone else said anything to you about this? Laurie maybe?"

"Mm-hmm, I guess. But I okay. Nothin' to do at home, anyway."

"What about Harold? He's worried about you walking home from the mall so late by yourself." It was funny—after passively accepting years of mistreatment from Harold, Margaret had grown tougher and less compliant. So, of course, now Harold was more concerned about her.

"I watch where I go. I look behind me."

"What if someone drove up and tried to get you in a van?"

"What you mean? Dad told me don't go in van. You know, I don't do that."

"Yeah, but—I mean, what if some big, strong man attacked you? He could drag you into his van. He could hurt you or worse!"

"I can run. And I look. I watch. And I strong. Don't worry! I okay. I careful, I am."

"Would you just please think about it?" This is about the point that I would be stand up and begin pacing, wanting to tear my hair out or reach through the phone and shake her.

"Mm-hmm. You mad at me?"

"No, Margaret…I'm just worried. Anyway, will you be ready for Jimmy at seven?"

"Guy-ee. What about my walk?"

"You can skip it for one night, can't you—for Dad?"

"I going to take the bus to Stonewood today."

"What for? What's in Stonewood?"

"Umm. Just for some things I lookin' at."

"Margaret, our dad is seriously ill. He might die."

"Oh. I know. What wrong with him?"

"Come on. I told you before we don't know that yet. That's why he's here. The doctors are trying to figure that out. They're pretty sure it's his heart."

"Oh. You mad at me, right?"

"No, I'm not mad. But this is important. And Laurie's here."

"Oh. Who she with?"

"Anthony. You know, he's Laurie's Mr. Grumpy Pants.

Margaret laughed and promised me not to tell Laurie I said that.

"Her boys are coming tonight. Might be here any minute."

"Where you? You see Laurie?"

"You know I'm at the hospital—and yes, I've seen Laurie. She wants to see you. And so does Dad!"

"How 'bout I think about it? Let you know?"

"Oh. No. No way. I know what that means. Jimmy needs to know now. You really need to do this, Margaret."

"What time Jimmy come?"

"He'll be there at seven sharp. Where will you be? Home?"

Oh…I don't know. I guess so," she said with a sigh of resignation. "Can he drop me at the market after? I have to buy some things, ya know, for tomorrow."

"Fine. Remember, in front of your apartment at seven. See you when you get here."

"Okay. Byeeee!"

Big surprise that, after these phone calls with my precious sister, I would be exhausted and sweating up a storm. I knew I had badgered her, and I always felt incredibly conflicted and guilty. I knew I had been fighting with a child of sorts, and it hadn't been a fair fight. Though I had made my point and gotten what I wanted, I knew it had only been because I had worn her down with an incessant guilt trip. I never thought to try to entice her with something shiny—in other words, with some kind of reward. I sat there in the lobby, stewing, until I heard,

"Bethie? Bethie? Looks like she's sleepin'. I don't think we should wake her up. Should we?"

"I don't know. She's your sister. How should I know?"

I heard this exchange as if from a great distance. I'd just made a quick call to Margaret…and now, here I was, sound asleep with my bag packed up beside me.

"Frank, Marcia. You're here. Guess I was catnapping. The last thing I remember, I sat down for a minute, then had an exhausting conversation with Margaret." I rose to hug Frank and awkwardly pat Marcia's back in a kind of air hug. "I went in to say goodbye to Dad, and the nurses came in to change his catheter, and they—or, rather, he—kicked me out. Can't say I was sorry…seeing my 89-year old father's private parts is one thing I can easily skip as long as I'm not desperately needed." Apparently, I had decided to amuse myself. Marcia looked at me, then started to laugh. Frank looked uneasy, but seemed to make a God's honest attempt to stay in our orbit.

"So, the old man's still kickin'?"

"Yep. He's always been feisty—you know that. He's in room 222, a few doors down on the left. Laurie and Anthony were here. I guess they left. I remember them saying that they'd be back with Jason and Christopher in a few hours. Jimmy's come and gone. He'll be back with Janie. Dad's been looking for you."

I squirmed as I waited for Frank's reaction. Why had I said that? And why had I sounded so accusatory? Immediately, I'd wished I could take back the sting of those last words. Had Frank heard the anger inherent in the statement? Of course, he had. The real question: would he react—or let it go?

"Yeah. I wanted to get here earlier. Got tied up with some things," he mumbled as he started down the hall. Then, looking back: "You coming, Marcia? Beth?"

"I'll be in in a minute," I said, indicating the bathroom.

Truth was, I was nervous about this "reunion." I knew Frank and Dad hadn't talked in a while. Would the room be silent? Would both father and son look to me to fill the void, ease the tension? What was it even about? I only knew Dad usually said Marcia filled him in when he called to find out about the kids—Frank's kids. Well, maybe Marcia could do whatever "filling in" needed doing now.

I still hadn't budged from the hospital couch when I saw Marcia coming back. Hurriedly, I got up and moved toward the drinking fountain. I looked up when I heard Marcia: "God, your dad looks really awful. I didn't expect this. I mean, I knew it was bad, but he's way worse. He can hardly talk, can't hold his head up—he asked Frank to get him a drink of water, even though the glass was sitting on his tray right in front of him."

"How do you think Frankie'll do in there by himself with Dad?" I silently wished Marcia back in the room.

"Damned if I know. Better do okay. That's his father, after all!"

"You're right there," I said, mostly to myself, wondering again about the distance between my brother and father. Whatever had happened?

"I guess I'll go in now," I said.

"Hold on. I'm coming," Marcia called. "It was just such a shock, I had to get outta there for a minute. I mean, I can't believe he's still breathing."

"I know," I replied. What could I do but grit my teeth? I wanted to punch my sister-in-law for her bluntness, but I could feel the emotion behind her words. We were all on edge.

Now, as Marcia and I walked into Dad's room, I took in the scene. There was Frank, in a chair across from Dad. Both sat silently. Frank stared at our father's ashen face glumly, his tightly crossed arms holding his torso rigidly upright. Dad at first appeared to be dozing, but then I saw his eyes open and close as he adjusted his position ever so slightly. Tubes protruded from his nose; his breathing was shallow and raspy. He looked up as my sister-in-law approached the bed. I stood at Dad's feet. When Frank saw me, he stood up and moved towards me, his head shaking, his face lined and sallow.

"Bethie, he's bad. I can't believe it. I don't know what I expected, but not this. I wish…maybe I shouldn't have come." His voice faltered, and he turned away from me.

"I know…I know, Frankie," and I cried quietly, the pressure of the day washing over me. I understood how Frank felt, yet wondered how he could think about staying away when, to my mind, our father needed him so. How could he be so shocked when I had warned him? I cried now for my brother, my forlorn and mysterious brother, whom I loved so much.

"You love him, Frank—don't you?"

"Of course, Beth! Goddam it! Why'd you ask that?"

"I'm sorry—stupid question. The two of you…what the hell do I know? Nothing."

Frank stared at our incapacitated father for a long while, then turned, suddenly, and said "Sorry, Beth—I gotta get out of here." And with that, he was gone.

"He needs a smoke," Marcia said drily.

I wondered then if Frank's attitude toward our dad masked something significant, something that had happened between them, something that neither of them knew how to resolve. It was just as likely that Frank couldn't express his sorrow about Dad's condition. And now that I know about Frank's own fragile health, maybe it had nothing to do with Dad at all. Maybe life in general had become overwhelming: work, family, his own medical problems. How could I really know unless he told me?

Clearly, he wasn't about to do that right now. Why did I find it so important to know, anyway?

7 BREATHE IN THE AIR

Slow down, you move too fast
You got to make the morning last
Just kicking down the cobble stones
Looking for fun and feelin' groovy

~Paul Simon

I had stepped out into the afternoon sunshine; it was bright—almost blinding—and the air was so fresh after the dim, sanitized claustrophobia of the hospital. How I had longed to open a window! "Now, where did I park my car?" I wondered, muttering to myself.

A sense of direction had eluded me my entire life. I don't know if you're born with that ability, but I always quipped "Not in my genes" to my kids and friends when they rode with me. I thank the geniuses out there who made GPS available to us—but it didn't cover things like parking. At this moment, however, my relief at being out of the hospital was so exhilarating that my chronic parking lot confusion wasn't even a minor annoyance.

"I'll find it. I'll just take my time. Get to breathe. No hurry." A few rows away, I glimpsed what looked like Robert's bright red Bronco. "That can't be his. He's not here," I said to myself. Then I spotted the youthful, athletic man emerging from the car.

"Hey, honey! I didn't know you were coming over," I called to him.

"Hey, honey yourself! I didn't plan on it, but look. Here I am." I'm sure he smiled in that cute way he has. Always such a flirt, even with me.

"I'm just leaving—maybe…if I can find my car."

"Your car's right over there, down and across the next row. At least you were going in the right direction," he teased.

I grabbed him for a quick kiss. I was so glad to see him.

"Gettin' a little tough in there?"

"Oh, I don't know. Jimmy was here. Now, he's gone—Mr. Busy Lawyer. And then Frank and Marcia made an appearance. He's out here somewhere, smoking, I suppose."

"What about Laurie?"

A roll of my eyes and a change in my tone. "Yeah, she was here with Anthony."

"Did it get ugly?"

"Not that bad, I guess. I just don't get why we can't be friends—or, at least, friendly."

"Poor honey." He pulled me to him in a comforting hug.

"How come you're here anyway? I thought you were coming with me tonight."

"I was. I am. But on the way home from work, I decided to stop by. I don't know why, exactly. I guess I was worried about you. And—uh…I care about your dad. Hope he's not hooked up to a bunch of machines. It's just, well, I don't know exactly…."

"I know. That's sweet. I'm okay. He's okay, sort of. He'll be glad to see you. But I decided I needed a break from the drama. I'm dog tired."

"Go on home. I'll go on in and say hi to your Dad… and whoever else I run into. I'll see you in a little while."

"Be sure to tell him I'll see him later tonight. We both will."

Finally, tucked into my car and on the road, I found myself alone…really alone. I realized, for the first time in so many hours, that I wasn't waiting for anyone; no one was questioning me. And it was quiet. For a few minutes I just breathed and sighed, aware of my heart rate slowing down. Finally, I breathed deeply, comfortably. I drove slowly, for me, and, for the first time since I walked into Dad's house all those hours ago, I let go of the stress. Another mile, and I put on my blinker, drove onto the freeway and into the steady flow of traffic. I accelerated to a comfortable speed.

As I relaxed, the day unfolded in front of me, giving me a curious perspective. I saw myself from a distance: I had a day off. There I was, planning what I would get done; how I would spend my day. Dad and breakfast for a start; planning my classes and grading for a few hours—maybe even getting in a run at the beach later in the day with Robert. Instead, I'd found myself steeped in a life-threatening crisis. Rather than having the day in my control, I'd found myself out of control, merely reacting to a cascading stream of events.

Wow! Dad! How unnerving to find him like that! Then to jump into motion…get him to the doctor, then the hospital, and Robert, Greg and I holding him up while he tried in vain to walk. Then, in the ER, where they flew into action. Tests—one after another. Finally, he slept, time stopped, and I waited.

And what about that mess back there with Laurie? Why did I quiz her like I did? But then, why did she scold me the way she did? I guess I reacted as I always do with her: like a little girl who thinks she's being mistreated. Maybe she's right—maybe I do think everything's about me.

And my silliness with Jimmy. What got into me? He's such a support to me. Of course, he loves Laurie and hates that his sisters don't—what? Get along? You could call it that, I suppose, though I don't really see it that way.

I think I would give anything to have Laurie back in my life, but would I, really? It seems she doesn't really like who I am, and it takes two to have a relationship. If she doesn't want that, I can't force it.

That scene between Frankie and Dad…so sad. But why did I ask Frank if he loves Dad? How do I know what their relationship is? And Margaret…again, I basically try to control things...stubborn, uncontrollable things.

Oh, the lot of us!—including me!—could we be more out of kilter? How in the world did we get like this? Didn't we all huddle around "The Ed Sullivan Show" on Sunday nights? Didn't Dad and the boys cheer and holler as they watched the Lakers together? I remember dinner time…home always seemed so cozy to me: the smells of food on the stove or in the oven—roast beef or meat loaf—Dad in his chair, reading the paper, some of us doing homework or helping Mom in the kitchen. In a little while, the seven of us would gather around the table, make the sign of the cross, say grace, then dig in as our voices competed to be heard. Outside was darkness and cold, but inside was warmth and light.

Or maybe this is just how I choose to remember it all. I know we weren't a perfect family, but who is? After we lost Mom, Dad kept us together as we married and started our families. Never as close, though, as when we could draw our strength and love from her, from them. Still, things were good for a pretty long time. I thought they were. For certain, we were not the mess that we are now.

After a while, I let my thoughts wander to a little brown-haired girl who ran around the neighborhood in cut-off jeans, imitating her big brothers by climbing trees and fences as she searched for the next adventure. There she was!—running with tow-headed Frankie to see his latest fort, proud that he wanted to show it to her. And the bushes, loaded with butterflies—there she ran after her brother to watch the remarkable creatures as he named them for her and showed her how to catch them without hurting their delicate wings. How they both admired the Monarchs. And those Swallowtails!

A short way down the block, she talked to the neighbor boy with his exotic French accent. Her excitement rose as he showed her his latest Superman and Archie comic books—and she was thrilled that he would trust her with them as she ran home to her backyard patio to stretch out on her dad's chaise lounge and dive into the world of make believe.

That same little girl sang as she played hopscotch with her best friend,

Grace or her next door neighbor Linda. Some afternoons, dressed in clothes they found in the special box in her mother's closet, they tap-danced on the front porch,

And she couldn't wait for her daddy to come home from work at night so she could guess how much money he'd made at work that day—it was their special game.

And maybe the best time of all—coming into the kitchen after dinner, where her mom, was always ready with a back rub or a hug while her dad sat at the table. So often, in the evenings, her mom and dad lingered there for hours over steaming coffee and endless talk. She loved that memory; she knew, as she grew up, she wanted to make that memory real for herself.

And then, there I was, pulling into my driveway, gathering my things and making my way into my house.

In the sunlit kitchen, I thumbed through the mail and checked phone messages, both on the home machine and the voice mail at work. Ellie was on both. Grad school was fine—aside from a few issues. Her advisor had approved her master's thesis. But even the good news was tinged with worry…how was Grandpa...how was I doing? She wanted to be there with us, was looking for a window of time to make the drive home this week. Call, call, call! ASAP!

My heart warmed at my daughter's strong, loving voice. I knew that this woman-child of mine understood, at least on some level, my pain, my confusion.

I could clearly see that my immediate family was coming through for their much-loved grandfather…but it was even more apparent that, knowing my history with their aunt, they were determined to protect and support me as best they could.

Of my three children, Ellie had the words for what she felt and even, perhaps, for what she perceived I felt. I had tried to nurture emotional depth in my children. I wanted them to be aware of others' feelings—and to know that life sometimes betrayed us. I wanted them all to be prepared for the disappointments and sorrows as well as the joys in life, but I never wanted to burden them with the darkness that too often threatened to overtake me. I'm not sure how well I succeeded.

When Ellie was 11 or 12 and found herself confused and disappointed at being shut out by a few girlfriends, I gave her a diary. I explained to her that, in the childhood diary I'd kept, I'd first explored my private feelings about my world—including the challenges of friendships and the disappointments that sometimes accompanied them. Beginning with innocent musings on the thrill of some adventure or the joy of finding a soul-binding friend, I had chronicled what was important to me at the time.

Once, after reading a biography of Amelia Earhart, I wrote with wonder about all the far-off horizons I might encounter one day. Perhaps more important, I poured out my hurts and disappointments in words. Just writing my feelings down had helped somehow, and I wanted that for her.

Often, I'd used writing to express emotions I didn't understand: my early feelings for a grade school crush, and the hurt and confusion that had pummeled me when Grace replaced me with another best friend. A few years later—in absolute amazement!—I had poured out my overflowing adolescent heart at finding love for the first time. Time after time after time, I found my voice in writing: saying goodbye to Jimmy when he went off to the army; longing in vain for my mother at 17; falling in overwhelming and confusing love for Robert in the wake of that loss; doubting myself as a wife and mother—these were among the things I had explored on paper over the years.

And on I wrote. The indescribable loss I felt when Laurie severed ties with me haunted the pages of many journals over the years: anger, bitterness, befuddlement—at times, they hit me like a wave and flung me about like a ragdoll. Maybe I looked for Mom in Laurie; maybe, somehow, as long as I had Laurie, I still had Mom.

What does it matter now? Here I was. What could I do but what everyone always does: put one foot in front of the other. Torn between the bed's comforting invitation for a quick nap and my inclination to reassure my daughter, I reached for the phone and dialed.

"Hi, honey."

"Mom? Good. Finally. How's Grandpa?"

"Up and down. In and out. He's stable for now. Uncle Jimmy and Uncle Frank were at the hospital."

"How was that?"

"Good. I think Grandpa really appreciated that they came. Uncle Jimmy and I even joked around with him some."

"Really? How come you're home? Are you sure you're telling me everything?"

"I'm sure. I just needed a break, a shower—maybe a nap. Dad's there now."

"Did Aunt Laurie get there yet?"

"Yep. And your cousins are on their way."

"That's great. I'd love to see them. How long will they be there?"

"I don't know."

"How'd it go with Aunt Laurie?"

"Okay. She's worried about Grandpa."

"Yeah, of course, but how about between you two? Was it weird?"

"Yeah, I can't lie. You know, it's never easy with her. I just needed a break."

"But what happened? What did she say? Was it really hard for you?"

"It really wasn't that bad. I'll tell you about it later."

"OK. I know this has got to be hard. I'm just so frustrated that I have to be here. Where are my priorities? Maybe I should just screw school right now. Or—I don't know. I think I can come home tomorrow or at least the next day. Mary Lou's meeting with me tonight. Thinks I can turn in what I have, and if it's good enough, and I'm solid and clear in my focus—and I'm sure all this will be fine—then I can work through the next part on my own later. And I think she'll understand. He's my grandfather!"

"I'm sure everything will be fine with the thesis, and that Mary Lou will understand. It'll be good to have you here. Ellie…?"

"Huh? What's up?"

"Nothing. I think I just need to take a shower and stretch out for a little while before Dad gets home. I'm just so tired."

"Sure. But call me later—okay?"

"I promise. Bye, Ellie. Love you, honey."

The water was hot, and I shuddered involuntarily; then came the soothing sensation of deep knots beginning to relent. Then came the images: Dad lying helpless; the doctor standing over him with a mysterious chart. What did it say anyway? I stuck my face into the rushing water, willing it to rinse the images away. Instead, a swarm of faces and emotions threatened to engulf me. I cried aloud "Stop!" and let the steam envelope me, and finally, my body began letting go of the day's tension.

Before long, I was stretched out on my bed, Newsweek in hand. Thumbing through, I found the distraction I needed: the latest obsession with weight. "Good," I thought. "Nothing too personal, but definitely a topic I care about." With that, I fell fast asleep.

Dad was dead. Everyone gathered around his body except me. Laurie softly cried into her husband's shoulder. Frank and Marcia, Jim and Janie, Margaret—even Robert and my kids—stood around, hushed and somber. Then I was in a corridor, looking into room after room, without seeing a familiar face. People crowded the halls. Frantic, I tried to move, but couldn't. Suddenly, someone pointed, and I tried to move in that direction, but my legs—why wouldn't they move? Wait! Was that my mother? Yes! She was smiling, gently beckoning to me as she moved away. Wait! Where are you going? Don't you know I've been searching for you? Wait! Wait! I struggled to pursue her through the crowd. In disbelief, I reached for her, calling—only to see her slip away. Then she was gone.

I awoke, tears on my cheeks. How many times had I had this dream or some variation of it? For a moment, I lay there in pain until the phone punctuated my foggy misery.

"Hello?"

"Mom, it's Bob. What's up?"

"Not much at the moment." I sat up, pushing at the hair in my face with my free hand.

"Yeah? How's Grandpa?"

"Not great. It's his heart. That's all I know. I just came back from the hospital about an hour ago to shower and rest. I'm going back with Dad after we eat something. How 'bout you? How're you doing?"

"Oh, fine. You know Greg and I are going, too, right?"

"Oh, honey, I do know that; that's so nice. Do you want to come with us? Immediate family can visit any time…there are no real visiting hours because of his condition. I mean. There's talk that the hospice people will be there tonight. Or maybe they will have been there by the time I go back."

"He's that bad? How's Grandpa going to deal with that? How're you dealing with it?"

"Well, I haven't talked to anybody official yet. Laurie was there, and she seemed to be intent on making it happen. If someone does talk to Grandpa without me there, I would hope they'd be sensitive about it. Your dad's just walking in the door. We'll probably be ready in an hour or so. Should we swing by your place? What about Greg?"

"Greg'll be here. But Mom—Laurie."

"Uh-huh?"

"How was that? I mean, how're you doing?"

Startled by the uncharacteristic concern from my oldest, who had seemed to have removed himself from me lately, absorbed by his own life with his wife and toddler, I stuttered, "It was weird…frustrating. It's hard to grasp all that's happening. I just had a dream that Grandpa died and I wasn't there. It felt awful."

"Yeah. That's crummy—but, when you think about it, it's not really that weird. Not good, but not weird. Right? Don't have any bad dreams about ME before then, Okay?"

I chuckled in spite of myself. "Good idea. And Bob? Thanks for asking about Laurie. I'm sure she'll be glad to see you. But mainly, having you and Greg there will be a big comfort to me."

"Okay. See you soon," he said, shrugging off the compliment.

I stretched and shook my head, trying to decide if I should get up and get dressed. Instead, I lay back and closed my eyes again. When I heard a rattling, I sat up and looked.

Robert stood at his dresser, looking through the mail. I waited for him to glance my way. Finally, impatient, I asked, "Hey, you. How was my dad?"

"I only saw him for a minute."

His attention was still on a bill-like envelope.

"Yeah, but how was he?"

"OK. I guess."

"Was he awake?"

"Yeah."

Still not looking at me.

"What's wrong?" I was irritated at this non-conversation, yet unwilling to let it go.

"Nothing. Just checking out the mail."

"Yeah, but I mean, was Dad awake? Did you guys talk? Did you see Laurie?"

"Uh, he was awake if you can call it that, and, no, I didn't see Laurie."

Robert still hadn't looked up.

"Goddamn it, Robert! Is the mail really that absorbing?"

"Huh?" His face screwed into an angry frown. "Can't I just have a minute to read the mail without a cross examination?!"

I got up and stomped into the bathroom, slamming the door. Robert was right behind me, opening the door. "Beth, come back here—what'd I do? Did I do something wrong?"

"You really have to ask me that? Am I expecting too much to think you would want to tell me about your visit with my very sick father?"

"God! I'm sorry. Okay?" Then he looked at me, and, more quietly, said, "I'm just tired. It's been a long day, ya know?" He followed me as I walked past him back into the bedroom and threw myself down on the bed again. Then I looked up at him, worried.

"What's really wrong, Robert? Did something happen while you were there?"

Robert's face, a mask moments before, crumpled. "No, No. Nothing happened. I'm sorry. I just can't stand seeing him like this. He's just not…Jack. I can't explain it. Honey, he looked so old and frail. I can't get over it."

"Did he know you were there?" My voice softened…the frustration was gone.

"Yeah, but I couldn't stay long. I don't know what I expected, but it wasn't this. He started to cry, and I didn't know what to do."

"What did you do?" I asked quietly.

"I held his hand," Robert sobbed, his head down, standing in front of me.

I opened my arms to him "Oh, honey. That was the best thing you could have done."

"I don't know if I can go back tonight. I will if you need me to, though. Just say the word. I don't want to let you down."

There it was: my decision. How many times had Robert said he just couldn't go to some event, a kid's teacher conference, back-to-school night, open house…whatever. Oh, I could usually guilt trip him into going—remind him how important it was for the kids to know both their parents cared. But how often had I heard that he was so tired, needed a night off?

Couldn't I just go and fill him in later? And ditto for most of my school events—even the time when the principal had asked me to make a presentation to a group of parents at a school meeting. Come to think of it, had he ever wanted to go to something that didn't directly involve him?

But I was vulnerable now. I needed Robert; needed to be protected, cared for. It seemed that was what Robert needed now, too. Familiar story. I turned away from him…I didn't know what else to do.

"Beth? Say something."

"What do you want me to say? Bob called, said he and Greg are going tonight to the hospital. I said we'd pick them up at Bob's, and go together. Do you want me to go with them? That way, you can avoid the whole scene."

"No." He shook his head. "Definitely not. I'm really letting you down, aren't I? I'm being a big baby. I'm glad the boys are coming. Let me take a quick shower, pull myself together. I'll be okay. It's just been a long day. First with your dad, and earlier I had to deal with some angry parents at practice."

I didn't ask about parents or practice…just sat, drained.

"Just tell me you're okay," Robert said insistently.

"I have to be. I don't have the luxury to skip all this. Turn on the TV and pretend everything is okay. I would give anything if this whole thing hadn't happened."

"I know. And you don't have to be okay. Yell at me. I deserve it. I'm just thinking of myself. Like I said, I'm being a big baby. I'm going with you. It's settled."

"Just take your shower while I warm up some leftovers."

With that, Robert kissed my cheek as I stood to go out of the room; then he shrugged and moved toward the bathroom.

8 ONE DOC WEIGHS IN

Amazing grace, how sweet the sound
That saved a wretch like me
I once was lost but now am found
Was blind but now can see

~John Newton

Robert and I followed Bob and Greg into the hospital lobby, and as we stopped to check in at the visitors' desk, I spotted this evening's cast of my family drama. As I argued with myself about how to act and what to say, Bob interrupted my thoughts: "Hey, there's Jason and Chris. I haven't seen or talked to either of them in a long while. Have you, Greg?"

"No. I think the last I saw them was at my wedding, so…that's over a year ago."

"That's right. Hey, you know what they say…weddings and funerals, right?"

"Bob, don't say that! Grandpa's going to be okay." It was a full-on Mom scold.

"Sorry, Mom. Bad joke."

"Well, let's go over and say hello, why don't we?' And Robert took my hand, leading me over to where Laurie sat, apparently listening intently to her husband. Margaret stood close by, her arms folded across her chest.

Jason was the first to see us approach. With a smile spreading across his face, he held out his arms to Robert and to me, then turned to Bob and Greg for high fives and hugs. Then it was Christopher's turn. Both young men couldn't have been more open and gracious. Margaret, always a fan of displays of affection, giggled and remarked "Guy, when I see you last?" to Bob and Greg.

Finally, Robert faced Laurie, who sat, observing this interaction between her sons and my family. As she looked up, he remarked in an easy-going tone, "Well, hello, stranger. Good to see you, as well as your boys—or I guess I should say, men, right? I always forget how tall Jason is," he chuckled as he looked over and up at his 6'5" nephew. Laurie couldn't suppress a giggle, and as she rose, Robert leaned over for an awkward hug. I wondered if anyone else had noticed that neither Robert nor Anthony acknowledged one another. Anthony sat in his chair while the others in the group stood and chatted amiably, forgetting, if just for a moment, the reason for their reunion.

I looked around for Jim and Janie, and Robert turned to me as I asked Laurie, "Is Jim here, yet? What am I saying. They brought Margaret, right?"

"Nope. Just talked to Janie on the phone. They're on their way."

"How'd you get here, Margaret? Thought you were coming with Jimmy."

"The boys picked her up. They missed their aunt," Laurie said, smiling at Margaret.

I felt a stab of resentment, which I tried to squash. "Okay. Good. Is anyone else in with Dad now? We'd like to go in, but I don't want to overwhelm him with too big a group."

"We just got back from dinner, so I don't think so. We were getting ready to go in ourselves." Laurie's tone had softened; gone was the sarcasm and anger.

Jason met his mother's eyes calmly. "Mom, it's okay with me if Bob and Greg go in. I can wait after that big meal. I bet Chris can, too. I'm sure they won't be long."

I looked at Chris who shrugged, seeming to agree with Jason, and smiled.

"Okay, then, we'll go on in. The boys are anxious to see him. Thanks, guys."

Walking into the room, I could see Dad had his eyes closed. Still, I moved up close to him, put a hand on his arm, and whispered, "Dad. Hi, I'm here. I've brought some visitors."

"Beth, honey." And there he was, my dad, his eyes shining as he patted my hand and tried to sit up. "Say, Bethie, could you pull that lever—prop me up so I can see a little. Don't know why they make things so hard. Then he looked around and smiled. "Well, look who's here. This is a nice surprise." He fumbled at his ears, which started them humming.

I thanked God, he had his hearing aids in. I hoped they were working for this little reunion.

"Hi, Grandpa!" Greg was the first to move close to Dad and take his other hand. "You gave me quite a scare this morning." Greg spoke loudly and right into Dad's face. "I started thinking maybe you didn't really want me to ask you too many questions for fear I'd discover some wild adventures that you'd rather we didn't know about."

Dad chuckled. "No, nothing like that. I wish that was it. Damned heart."

"Hi, Grandpa." Bob, too, had come over close to Jack, to the space I'd occupied opposite Greg. "Sammy wanted to come and see his Papa, but I told him you'd be home soon, and then you'd tell him another Jackie Begorry story." Bob leaned in for a hug.

"Bobby." Dad took Bob's hand. "It's great to see you. Your boy is quite the little man, isn't he? Nothing but questions and exploring for that one. They say that's a mark of intelligence, ya' know. He's just like you when you were his age."

"Yeah? Was I really as active as Sammy?"

"Am I right, Beth? Hey, Robert—is that you over there?"

"Hi, Jack. Just waiting my turn. Don't want to tire you out. You've got a fan club out there in the lobby. What are you, the most popular guy in town?"

Just then, a young doctor strode briskly through the door and introduced himself as Dr. Kaplan. He was the heart specialist who'd visited Dad earlier. I stepped forward to shake his hand and make introductions. Dad didn't seem to remember him.

Everyone stepped aside to allow the doctor access to Dad, who'd closed his eyes as the doctor approached. He glanced over Dad's chart and then placed his stethoscope to Dad's heart, asking, "How're you doing this evening, Mr. Lawrence? You've perked up since I saw you this afternoon. I gather you're happy to see your family."

Dad opened his eyes, "Yeah, I'm swell. Couldn't be better."

"Good, that's what we want to hear," and he smiled at me. "We have the results of some of your tests. I thought I'd come by before I leave tonight. I thought you'd like to know what caused you to become so weak this morning."

Uh, oh, I thought. I knew Laurie wanted to be here for this, and she deserved to be. Assuming she'd think I had maneuvered to exclude her, I considered saying, "Stop! Don't say another word until I get my sister!" But before I could do any such thing, Dad looked at the doctor holding his future in his hands: "I'm ready. What's more, I'm eager to know what's going on with me. Go ahead, let me have it, doctor."

"First, would you like me to talk to you privately? I can come back, or your guests can wait in the hall."

"Hell…er…heck no! This is my family! I'm sorry, doc. Go ahead. Let's have it.

"Okay. Well, Mr. Lawrence, your heart is having a hard time pumping blood, so the blood is backing up in other areas of your body, causing congestion. At the same time, this is causing problems for your major organs, such as your lungs and kidneys, and that's putting pressure on the whole system. You may be having a hard time catching your breath. That's because the blood carries oxygen, but your poor blood flow isn't allowing an easy flow of oxygen throughout your body. All of this has made you feel overly tired and weak. That's the bottom line here. Your heart problems are causing congestion throughout your body. Am I making sense, Mr. Lawrence?"

"Did I have a heart attack?"

"Not exactly. You have what's called Congestive Heart Failure."

"My heart's failing?"

"It is, but that means it's failing to do its job the way it should—the way I just described. It's not pumping the way it used to when you were younger."

"Okay. That sounds pretty bad. So, what can you do about it?"

"Well, I have to say I'm not sure yet. But I think because your body is so weak, it limits the effectiveness of the conventional treatments that we would normally try. What I mean to say is that you look healthy; your body is muscular, and I think if you didn't have these problems with your heart, if it were some other part of your body, we could consider a number of options. Given that it's your heart, I just don't know." Dad glanced at me, then looked away. I stood there hardly breathing. "Dr. Abebe will be talking to you more about this. I know it's all a bit overwhelming. He'll be here in the morning." He patted Dad's leg through the sheets, saying, "Get a good night's sleep." Then he started to leave.

"Say, Dr. Kaplan, could surgery fix this thing with my heart?"

"Honestly, Mr. Lawrence, I hate to make predictions. As I said, your heart is trying very hard just to keep you going."

"What do you think, though?" Dad wanted a straight answer.

"I don't recommend it, Mr. Lawrence. Your age. Your high blood pressure. But talk to Dr. Abebe. He will be here tomorrow. He may suggest another approach."

"Okay. Thanks." Dad lay back, closing his eyes.

Dr. Kaplan nodded at me, then walked out of the room just as briskly as he had entered it.

"Grandpa, uh…I think I'll head out to the waiting room. You have some other visitors. I'll check in on you in a day or two." Bob looked at his brother.

"Me, too, Grandpa. I need to get back to Gina and the baby. Maybe I'll bring them by tomorrow if you're up to it."

"Sure, sure. I would love that. You boys are a great comfort to me. You might not know it, but you are. Thanks for coming, but I am really tired." Again, Dad closed his eyes.

That left Robert and me with Dad. I sat down close to him, trying to keep my voice even. Why did I always think I had to act strong? "I know you're tired Dad. And that was a lot to digest."

"What? What did you say about the doctor?" I had startled him with my words.

"I said that what the doctor just said was a lot to digest," I continued the strong stance, head up and voice loud and steady.

"Yeah, Jack," Robert said as he came up beside me. "There will be plenty of time to talk to the doctor.

"I think I should go get Laurie and see if Jimmy's here yet."

"Yeah, say, tell them to take their time. I need to rest my eyes for a minute. That doctor did wear me out."

Robert looked at me, indicating he would stay there with Dad.

I was nervous that I would have to give Laurie this news alone, so I walked to the bathroom first. When I emerged, I felt better, calmer. What had really changed? We had one doctor saying the test results showed Dad's heart was working too hard. His weakness limited what the doctors could do for him. But he hadn't had a heart attack. I didn't know if that mitigated the seriousness or not. As I approached the glass in the door leading to the lobby, I saw only Jimmy and Janie with Bob and Greg. Bob and Greg had both pulled out their wallets, displaying pictures of their little ones. While Janie oohed and aahed, Jimmy turned toward me.

"What's up, Beth? Did something happen?"

"Did the boys tell you what the doctor who just came in—the heart specialist, Dr. Kaplan—had to say?"

"No. What?"

"Well, he gave Dad the results of the tests. Said Dad has Congestive Heart Failure. He didn't have a heart attack. When Dad pressed him about his options, he pretty much avoided answering. He didn't sound hopeful."

"Why? What do you mean?"

"Dad asked about surgery. He said—" my voice began to crack—"he wouldn't recommend it for Dad, though it sounded like what's usually done. He…uh…didn't want to speculate on what Dad should do, and said Dr. Abebe would be here in the morning to talk to Dad. It didn't sound good."

"How's Dad doing?"

"He said he needed to close his eyes for a minute. I swear, the doctor came in one minute after we walked in. I didn't have time to come out and get Laurie and you. Robert's with Dad now. He seems really weak, but lucid. I don't know, he's just more with it than he was this afternoon. Have you seen Laurie? She needs to know this."

"Don't worry, Beth. You couldn't help the circumstances. Anyway, Laurie and Anthony went for a walk, said they wanted to stretch their legs. I'll get Janie and Margaret. We'll check in on Dad."

"Okay, will you call me later so we can talk after you see him? The boys need to get home to Gina and Lisa and their little ones. And tell Robert we're ready to go, okay?"

"Sure, we can't stay long, but I know Laurie and her boys will be back soon, so I'll make sure she knows what's going on. Maybe we can all talk tomorrow after Dr. Abebe weighs in. It's Saturday so I should have more time."

"Yeah, right. I mean Dr. Kaplan didn't really say anything new, except the words 'Congestive Heart Failure.' I don't know what to think."

Jimmy put an arm around my shoulder, "Well, we're in this together. We'll take it one step at a time."

9 THE HOSPITAL WAIT

Mama, take this badge off of me, I can't use it anymore
It's getting' dark, too dark to see
I feel I'm knockin' on heaven's door…
Knock, knock, knockin' on heaven's door

~ Bob Dylan

That night I lay in bed, bewildered. I had been quiet on the way home from the hospital. Though the doctor tonight had sounded alarms, the doctor in charge of Dad's case would evaluate things in the morning. Wait, Bob and Greg said, and see what he had to say. Their grandpa was 89, but he was tough, steely, and his strength would surprise us all.

Of course, that was all true. Dad had survived so much. Surely, there were other options for Congestive Heart Failure besides surgery. I thanked them for their words of encouragement, but mostly for coming to the hospital. I recognized that it was difficult for Greg to leave his wife and infant at home, and no easier for Bob with his little man, probably running his mom ragged with Daddy away.

"Mom, I meant it when I told Grandpa I would bring the baby over to see him tomorrow. Nothing's more important than having her see her great-grandpa," Greg said as he hugged me goodbye.

"Honey, that's so sweet. Tell her I want her to see her Grandma Beth, too!

"That's a given, Grandma."

Bob chimed in, "I'll be here too, Mom. Gina wanted to come tonight, but she had a paper to do for school. And I told her I should check out Grandpa's condition before we bring our little tiger over." Bob's brown eyes shone with sincere affection.

"You guys are the best sons—and grandsons! I feel so lucky. What do you say, Robert? Aren't they the best?"

"Of course, honey. Thanks, you guys. Grandpa said how much having you at the hospital meant to him. That goes for your mom and me, too."

Chatting with the boys, we all sounded so positive, but I couldn't shake the sense that the heart specialist was trying to convey to us that this was it for Dad. I wondered if I should have stayed and spoken to Dad with Jimmy. No—the boys had to get home. Besides…the day had exhausted me, and that I couldn't stomach any more discussion about Dad's condition.

I told myself I'd face the music tomorrow...which, being Saturday, let me hope Robert would come with me. I really didn't want to face Laurie without him, concerned that I would react out of lingering resentment. I guess I thought Robert would step in if I started to erupt at something she said. Soon enough, though, my thoughts turned to Dad. God, please be with him; he must be scared. But the boys were right: he is tough…stronger than I could ever be.

We pulled into our driveway, got out of the car, and said our goodbyes.

"Well, thanks again for coming tonight, guys. Say hello to Gina and Lisa. Tell them thanks for letting you come," Robert said, hugging his sons.

"I love you guys," I said. "Maybe we'll see you at the hospital tomorrow. How 'bout I let you know what Dr. Abe says before you head over?"

"Okay, Mom. We all love you…and you, too, Dad," they said almost in unison.

As we drove off, Robert patted my leg and asked, "So, honey, how are you? You've been unusually quiet. You must be beat! I sure am."

"I am. I guess I'm just thinking. Dad is old. I can't expect him to go on forever. But it's hard to see him like this. He's hardly ever sick. I remember one time when I was little, he had the flu. He was in bed, and Mom wasn't home. He called for me. He gave me a note and a couple of dollars and told me to go to the little store at the end of our block. 'Hand the man this note. Tell him this is for your father. He'll give you a cup of Coke syrup. Bring it back for me.' I don't know where Mom was, but it scared me. He looked so pale and awful."

"What do you mean, 'Coke syrup'?"

"You know, Coke that hasn't been diluted or carbonated. I tasted it, and it tasted like Coca Cola, only really, really strong and thick. I have no idea how it was supposed to help him. Anyway, he looked like that today."

Later, strangely, even in my exhaustion, I couldn't get comfortable in bed. I had called Ellie as I said I would, but kept Dad's condition vague. Then Jimmy called to say he planned to be back at the hospital in the morning to talk to Dr. Abebe; Laurie would be there as well. I said I'd see them there.

By the time I came up to our room, Robert was in his pajamas and brushing his teeth. He fell asleep as soon as his head hit the pillow. Not me. I lay tossing and turning, any semblance of rest eluding me. Finally, giving up the fight, I opened my eyes, put my hands behind my head, and let my mind wander.

How surreal this is, seeing Dad this way—the father I've admired and doted on…and been angry with, and judged…the father I sometimes wished would listen more, care more, treat me more gently…the father who would go through fire for me any day of the week.

This was also the man who once hung his head and wept that it had been Mom who had died instead of him. Through his tears, he'd said he'd gone over and over it, but still didn't know what else he could've done. Things just happened. Awful things. Yet, people endure. He knew that from experience.

And it's much worse for lots of people. Why am I so dramatic? Yes, I've had heartaches, known loss. And I know there's nothing to do for it. You're born—hopefully to parents who love you. But you can just as easily be born to drug addicts or mentally ill parents. You could be orphaned at an early age, or rejected, left outside some hospital door, or on the streets, or in a trashcan. I'm lucky not to have lost both parents in that terrible accident.

I could've had a father a whole lot less of a man than Dad is.

I thought about Dad's childhood. On the rare occasions he'd spoken about his parents and their problems, he used the old cliché that "they couldn't live together, and they couldn't live apart." His dad gambled, and couldn't live without that, either.

As a kid, Dad was sick with rheumatic fever and lost a year of school to a dreary bed. He'd been "puny," and been called "four eyes" because of the glasses he had to wear if he wanted to see. In baseball, he was "always relegated to the outfield," he'd say, looking down, sighing. But he spoke of these things matter-of-factly and didn't dwell; in fact, he said he was "a good little outfielder."

Instead, he focused on how much he loved to read—even made it through "The Odyssey" while still a young child. Even now, he would excitedly relate the story—quote actual lines if given half a chance.

After high school, his mother had encouraged him to start at UCLA, but a job Dad wouldn't refuse cut his college career short, even when she begged him to stay in school.

A thrombotic stroke took his mother suddenly at thirty-nine, while Dad was working for a newspaper in Sacramento.

Dad would recount any of this only if I asked him about his young adulthood or my grandmother, which was rare. Then, he would shake his head, take off his glasses and rub his eyes. If I tried to learn more about my grandmother's death, he would get a pained look on his face and, mutter, "How would I know? I wasn't there. I shoulda been there."

As I recognized the pride and love I felt for my father, my tears started to flow.

He's a remarkable man, heroic in so many ways. His grandkids sure look up to him. Dad's not the dad I sometimes wish he'd been, but he provided a good life for me, for all of us. He did the best he could, and he is, after all, human…flawed…just like I am.

The boys talk about him being "remarkable." Good word for him. Remarkable. Wonder if they would ever say that about me. What difference does it make? The end result is the same.

No—it does make a difference. It has to. Dad worked hard all his life. He loved Mom, put her on a pedestal, bought her candy on Valentine's Day, and kept a standing date with her to grocery shop every Saturday that I can remember. He lived a devoted and faithful life for twenty-five years. Always tried to make Mom happy. When she died, he seemed to forget to smile for a solid year, at least.

He loved us kids, made a good home for us, full of his mirth and big voice. He showed us how to be concerned about the world, to believe in justice and fairness. But he also showed us—when Frankie got passed over for that basketball award, and when Robert and I got conned out of our '57 Chevy, and then. when all of us had our mother taken too damn soon—he showed us that life is unfair sometimes. "But what can you do? Shrug your shoulders, get on with life."

I never asked him—just how do I do that? But actually, he showed me how. He got out of his red chair, went back to work, slowly started to smile again. Then he married someone who seemed to be like Mom but wasn't, really. He decided to love her anyway, and started growing gardens with her and dancing and traveling with her. Then she got sick, and he stayed home and doted on her…even when she grew bitter and mean.

Isn't that some kind of comfort for Dad—that he has been a good and brave and loving man—now that the final curtain may be falling on his life? But is he ready for this? Am I? I don't think I am. How can there be a world without him in it?

Finally, I had worn myself out. I wiped at my eyes, then snuggled into my pillow, whispering, "Good night, Dad. God bless you and keep you close. And all you angels, please surround him through this night and always. I love you Dad, I really do."

10 GIVE THOSE MARCHING ORDERS

All day, all night,
Angels watching over me, my lord…
Now I lay me down to sleep, angels watching over me, my lord
Pray the lord my soul to keep, angels watching over me
Sleep comes over me, oh, my lord
Pray my soul to keep, angels watching over me

~ Traditional lullaby

The next morning, I awoke alone—I couldn't believe Robert had slipped out of bed without waking me. Still drowsy, I nestled into my pillow and closed my eyes for another minute, but, before long, my mind had started playing its tricks, and I started to imagine all that could go wrong that day, starting with uncomfortable exchanges between Laurie and me. Soon, I began giving myself some logical advice.

Jimmy's right: be the bigger person. There's no need to act or speak out of anger. Put Laurie out of my mind. Focus on the person who needs the attention and care. Poor Dad—what must he be thinking and feeling? This is HIS life we're talking about. I know he's not going to shrink from the truth, whatever it is. We have a general diagnosis—now he needs to know what to do about it. The doctor last night made the situation seem so bad; he was clear that he didn't think Dad could live through surgery. Was he implying Dad should do nothing except plan on dying?

No. I can't get ahead of myself. Dr. Abebe will give us some straight answers. Dad's faced so many challenges …this is just one more. A new phase for him—and me! I pray to God I can handle whatever it turns out to be. One step at a time; but first: get moving.

Robert was downstairs at our dining room table, eating a bowl of cereal and reading the sports page. When he heard me come down, he looked up and said, "Hey, honey—look at you, already dressed and ready to go."

"I want to get to the hospital early. I don't want to miss Dr. Abebe when he comes by to weigh in on Dad's prognosis." I poured myself some cereal and sat down to eat with Robert. I found the metro section and read while I ate.

A few minutes later, Robert stood up. "I'll go get dressed and be right down."

"Are you going with me?" I asked tentatively, knowing that, often, on the weekends Robert had a game or something planned.

"I was planning on it. You want me to, right?"

"I definitely do. I'll feel so much better having you there. I want to stay positive—but how can I not be worried? I just want to get over there with Dad."

"Okay, then I'm gonna get dressed. I made coffee…don't know how good it is. Are you going to call the boys?"

"In a minute. You know—I don't know if they should go, what with him getting the diagnosis last night and then waiting for Dr. Abebe to weigh in on how we should proceed."

"Why don't you tell them you'll call them after you know more. See how this morning goes. Maybe they could come by this afternoon. That is, if they're planning to go. We don't even know if either of them actually plans to go."

"Good idea." Before I could pick up the phone, it rang. Bob had talked to Greg already, and each had decided that he needed to stick around home, at least for the morning. They would wait for me to call one of them with an update on their grandpa.

When Robert and I walked into the lobby and got in line to sign in, I discovered Dad had been moved out of the ICU. As we walked towards Dad's new room, I heard Jimmy's voice. He looked up at me with a smile. "Dad's having a pretty good morning, aren't you, Dad? Tell Beth," Jimmy said loudly, pointing at me.

"Sure. Sure. I've had my orange juice and coffee. Janie and Jim are here, the nurses couldn't be nicer, and now you and Robert appear. I guess your old man has got himself a fan club. How about that?"

We all chatted for a while about inane stuff until a nurse arrived and addressed Dad with a wink, declaring, "Mr. Lawrence, I know you're popular, but I need to have a little alone time with you. Do you think you can ask these nice people to go have a cup of coffee? I need to get you all cleaned up for them. I promise they can come back."

Dad returned her flirtatious banter, "Well, I should say it's okay with me. To be alone with such a gracious lady? You kids don't mind, do you?"

Jimmy and I laughed. "We know when we're not wanted," I said, and out we went. In the cafeteria, we got coffee and sat down. I asked Jimmy if he'd heard anything more from Dr. Abebe. Maybe it was just the hospital, but I couldn't shake a gloomy feeling.

"No, he hasn't come by yet today. Since it's Saturday, do you think there's a chance he won't be here today?"

"I don't know. The other…the uh…the heart guy, Dr. Kaplan, said Dr. Abe would be here to talk to Dad. He seemed certain."

Janie chimed in. "I'm sure he'll be here. CHF is serious, and not many doctors I know would let their patients stew for a whole weekend after receiving that diagnosis."

"Well, I don't want to be too far away from Dad and miss Dr. Abe."

"It won't take long to change his bed and give him a quick wash down. We should take our coffee and go back to his room. We can at least wait outside," Janie added.

On the way back to the room, Jimmy told me he had talked to Laurie right after he got to the hospital. She was on her way. At this news, I felt my stomach clench up. Sure enough, we got off the elevator, and, down the hall I could see Laurie and Anthony, apparently waiting outside Dad's room as we planned to do.

"The nurse said we can go in in a few minutes. I think they're cleaning Dad up," Laurie said mainly to Jimmy.

"Yeah, we were shooed out of there ourselves," he said, giving Laurie a welcoming hug. "Where are your boys?"

"They're having breakfast, giving us time with Dad. I can't believe he has CHF. We went to the library this morning to research it. I had a feeling this might be his last hurrah," Laurie said firmly. "He's old, and this is really serious…." I was reminded of Aunt Maudie's perpetually warning tone, and suddenly missed her, lost to breast cancer twenty years before.

"Well, I hope not," Jim said levelly.

"I'm not ready to think like that," I said, "I want to hear what Dr. Abe has to say."

"We'll see, won't we?" Laurie's eyes met mine. No one else seemed perturbed by the comment.

When I look back, I see how immaturely I had viewed it all. But I also see why I had: teenage dramas went down more easily than wondering what my father's actual alternatives were.

Just then, Dr. Abebe walked up, greeted us all and told us to follow him into Dad's room. The nurse grabbed the rumpled sheets and other detritus and left. Now, the six of us gathered around Dad's bed.

"Good morning, Jack." Dr. Abebe's boomed warmly. "You are, indeed, well loved. Look at this group gathered here to see you. And I understand this is only a small portion of your family—am I right?" His skin shone as he rocked on his heels.

"You are, Doc. I'm a lucky man!"

"Jack, I know Dr. Kaplan, our heart specialist, saw you last night, and he told you that your condition is called Congestive Heart Failure. It sounds serious because it is serious."

"So I've heard. What are we going to do about it? I hear I'm too weak for surgery. Is that right?"

"I'm afraid that is right."

"Have I reached the end of the line then, Doc? Am I supposed to gather up my marbles and call it a day?" There wasn't a hint of self-pity in Dad's tone.

"That is one option. In this case, I recommend something called hospice. Forget all these drugs, these pills. Spend some quality time with your family. You are—as you say—a lucky man, Mr. Lawrence. You have such a big and loving family. Reminds me of my family in Nigeria." He looked straight into Dad's face. "Do you know what hospice is?"

"No, I don't."

"Well, medical professionals come to visit you in your home. They monitor you and keep you comfortable. They make sure you have as little pain as possible."

"I don't get it. That's it? Do I just go about my business? I can't get better without doing something, right? I understand my blood's not flowing so good. Depriving important parts of my body of oxygen. That's why I'm so weak and tired."

"Congratulations, you are now an expert on this disease," Doctor Abebe chuckled, clearly appreciating Dad's fighting spirit. "But, to be serious, yes, you are right, Jack. You cannot get better without doing something. Unfortunately, those approaches do not bode well for you because of your age and weakened condition." Dr. Abebe looked around at all of us.

"Mr. Lawrence, with hospice, you 'go about your business' as you say, as best you can. But there's little chance that you will get better. It's more likely that you'll get weaker and weaker. The hospice workers will be there to make you comfortable and keep your pain to a minimum. You can stay at home with your loved ones."

"Wow! I appreciate your honesty and directness, but it's a helluva lot for a guy to swallow. What about surgery for my heart? They fixed my prostate with surgery."

"Did they now? How long ago, was this?

"Last year."

"Really. Hmm. Well, you do look like a strong man, Jack, but I'm guessing that your heart was in better condition when you had that surgery, and your heart could help your body heal. These days, though, your heart is not functioning as well. Have you been tired lately?

"To tell you the truth, Dr. Abe, I've been tired all the time, even before this episode. Is this why? Anyway, what are my chances of making it through an operation on my heart?"

"This heart condition makes you feel pretty tired in general. But I'm afraid your odds of surviving surgery in your condition are about ten percent. That's my best guess, Jack."

"Well, hell, Doctor, if I do this hospice, I'm giving up. I have a sick wife at home. Who takes care of her?" With his question about Sadie, he'd raised his voice, full of passion.

Now, the doctor looked up at us. Jimmy spoke: "Dad, we'll figure that out together. Don't worry about that now." I could see Laurie bury her head in Anthony's chest, while I gulped, trying to breathe.

I don't remember much after that. The doctor left. The rest of us stood or sat. Laurie left to call her sons. I think she was crying. I know Dad fell asleep a little later, and we dispersed to the lobby.

Stunned and stung by the exchange between my father and Dr. Abebe, I asked Jimmy, "What are we going to do? Hospice? I can't believe it."

"Beth, I say let's get a second opinion. We have no reason to drop the subject here."

"What do you mean?"

"I mean, let's call a heart specialist—besides Dr. Kaplan. We already know what he thinks. What do we have to lose? Dr. Abebe says he puts Dad's odds at surviving surgery at ten percent, right? Well, let's see what another heart specialist has to say."

"Absolutely."

Jimmy's words lifted the pall that had enveloped me. I can't say they filled me with optimism, but I was grateful for a possible reprieve.

"What have I got to lose?" Dad responded when Jimmy presented him with the idea of seeing another heart specialist. "Let's do it. You with me, Beth?" he asked me. I smiled and nodded. I wanted to be hopeful, but I was scared.

Privately, I asked myself a hundred questions. What if this doctor gives us the same bad news as Dr. Abebe? Who will or can take care of Dad—besides hospice? And what does hospice actually do? How much time do they actually spend with their patients? When Dr. Abebe said the hospice people would be there, what did that mean, exactly? What about Sadie?

When Dad had first gotten the dire news about his heart, I'd wondered how Sadie would take the news. I didn't know what Dad had told her about his condition, nor, at the time, did I have the strength to ask him.

After a few days, family members went their ways. Laurie and her family went home. My children, including Ellie, who had come home the day after Dad went into the hospital, visited a few more times. It was difficult for them, knowing the hospital doctor's grim suggestion for hospice. Meanwhile, Jim had looked into heart specialists, and found one with a solid reputation. I assumed everyone supported Dad in his decision to get another opinion about his gloomy prognosis. On the morning that Dad was to check out, the hospital social worker asked to speak to me—a routine conversation, or so I was told, so I wasn't expecting what she had to say.

"Beth, I know you and your brother are getting a second opinion," she began. "I think this is good. You should know what your options are. I hope you know I wish the best for your father and your family, but I want to caution you: your father's condition could worsen quickly or he might go along, even improve some. But please—don't discount his age and the strain this has been on him. I understand he has an invalid wife, also elderly. Right?"

"Yes, she has severe arthritis, hypertension, and reflux. She's in constant pain, and can hardly see because of macular degeneration. Weekdays, my dad has a caregiver come in for her."

"Twenty-four-hour care?"

"No. Kaitlyn's there Monday through Friday, morning till evening. Dad and Sadie have Carmen, another woman who works part-time who does the cleaning and grocery shopping. They manage simply on the weekends," I said feebly. How could I sufficiently describe this relationship? "Dad's very devoted to Sadie—and they get by pretty well. My brother or I usually visit on the weekends when we can."

"Well, you know your father's overall condition has worsened. Congestive Heart Failure is progressive, so your father has very likely had it for some time. This episode landing him in the hospital like it did should tell your family that his condition is dire. If your father tries to continue his present routine, it could speed up the process. It's up to your family, of course, but I would urge you all to consider hospice. At the very least, look into it, because, if not now, the day will come.

"I understand."

But I understood nothing. I could hardly think. Though I knew the social worker's words were meant to help, they produced guilt feelings in me tantamount to a big, red flashing sign: "Bad daughter!" Should I be taking better care of Dad, getting more help for Sadie? Yet, it wasn't up to me—or was it?"

Jim had managed to get an appointment pretty quickly with a second heart specialist, and so, one morning, he, Dad, and I went to see Dr. Doyle for what we all hoped would be a more positive prognosis. After handshakes all around, Jim calmly explained that we were there hoping to find an alternative for our father other than hospice.

The doctor got to work, first looking over Dad's file. Then he listened to Dad's heartbeat, checked his blood pressure and had him breathe in and out several times while he listened to Dad's lungs with his stethoscope.

After reviewing specific pages of Dad's file, Dr. Doyle looked up and directed his comments to Jimmy and me: "I have to agree that your dad's not a good candidate for surgery. But I do have another suggestion which

I—"

Dad chose that moment to interrupt. "Hey, Doc. Could you speak up? My hearing's not too good, and I think I need to hear what you're about to say. Especially since it concerns me." Dad's words seemed to make the doctor uncomfortable, but, after a moment's reflection, I applauded Dad. The doctor's patient was sitting in front of him. Shouldn't these life-or-death comments be directed at him?

Dr. Doyle continued, but now he addressed our father, raising his voice and slowing down his words.

"Of course, Mr. Lawrence. Here's what I can do—but it won't be an easy approach for you. I propose an intense round of medication. You know that having CHF means your heart isn't working the way it should, and your body is accumulating too much fluid. What I can do for you is prescribe medications that will lessen that accumulation, giving your heart a better chance to do what it needs to—pump your blood.

"With these medications, what's my prognosis? How much time would it give me?"

"Right to the point, eh? Well, someone younger and in better overall condition could have another five years, maybe more. For you—at your age and in your present condition—I'd say you could have another two years." Dad looked at Jimmy and me and gave us a funny kind of smile.

"Hmm." He sighed and said, "Doesn't sound too bad to me. It's better than what the doctors at the hospital said. I'm on board."

On the way home, we didn't talk much about what had just transpired, except that Jim offered to fill the prescriptions Dr. Doyle had just written. I asked about Sadie and Kaitlyn, and Dad talked cheerfully about the changes that Kaitlyn had brought about in Sadie.

"She even talked Sadie into having her nails done along with her hair. I think her appointment's tomorrow. And Carmen and I grocery shop this afternoon—I wouldn't want to miss that. I'm gonna need a nap, though…that appointment wore me out!"

"Dad, are you sure you're up for grocery shopping?" my brother asked.

"Don't worry. Kaitlyn pushes me around in this cart the store has. It's like I'm a kid again, riding big toy car with my mother pushing me—only the car is attached to the shopping basket! Whee!"

I laughed and then reminded Dad that he had a lot of dietary restrictions now. The doctor had given us a printed list of foods he had to avoid. I knew this would be a tall order for my father. He loved food—salty and spicy food, in particular. He would not be happy with a regimen that denied him the full pleasure of one of his favorite activities: eating. For now, though, he wasn't worried about that.

"I'll take the list with me. We'll be fine, don't you worry."

I smiled, but only to mask my uncertainty. The plan seemed too easy. I wondered how this doctor could be so sure that a change in diet and a few more prescriptions would keep dad going for two more years. Dad was so relieved, though. I didn't want to be the one to give voice to doubt.

11 GO BACK TO THAT ROOM

I'm just sitting here watching the wheels go round and round
I really love to watch them roll
No longer riding on the merry-go-round
I just had to let it go…

~ Paul McCartney and John Lennon

At first, Dad was enthusiastic about his new regimen; he'd bartered for more time, and he was determined to make the most of it. Soon enough, however, he shrugged off the new restrictions because, though he'd had a catastrophic event, his daily life hadn't really changed.

Although his shuffle was more pronounced now, and he paused frequently when walking through the house, Dad's condition didn't make an impression on Sadie. Perhaps she just couldn't absorb the seriousness of his condition…or perhaps it was a streak of stubborn mule that ran through Sadie.

Years ago, I'd sized her up as a woman who insisted on being the one with the most needs and problems. Yes, she had a debilitating illness—more than one, in fact—but why make this a competition? Her husband had been given a gloomy prognosis—couldn't she be sweet to him for a change? No. She was as demanding as ever, expecting him to take care of her as he had before he got sick. And, God knows, he tried to where he could.

I've nursed some bitterness about this, which is unfair. It was their life, not mine.

Dad's morning routine had been to make coffee and toast, then take Sadie's meal into her room where he'd help her sit up to eat. When she was finished, he'd go back to the kitchen for his own coffee and toast, then head to his red chair to eat while he watched the morning news. A little later, Kaitlyn would arrive, bringing in the paper, and Dad would happily devour the LA Times for the next hour or so while Kaitlyn tended to Sadie.

After Kaitlyn left in the early evening, he would serve the meal she'd prepared, leaving the dirty dishes in the sink.

But now, the signs that even this routine was too much for him became immediately apparent. Easily winded, he'd stop frequently as he moved from one room to another—and there was no way he could carry anything with him. Now, Dad, as well as Sadie, were both increasingly dependent on Kaitlyn. Dad had a walker and no qualms about using it. If the sun was shining, he might ask Kaitlyn to take him outside. "I've got to build up my strength," he'd say. Otherwise, he stayed inside with Sadie. When I visited, I wanted Dad to myself—but if we were with Sadie, he would try to draw her into the conversation, or talk endlessly about her bravery in the face of her ailments.

Many weekends, Robert and I brought lunch over to them. Robert would wipe down the picnic table and benches, the patio's dust and grime from disuse so clearly visible. Then, with our help, they hobbled out to the backyard where we would eat, chat, and ignore the growing disorder around us.

For almost a month, their household maintained a workable rhythm. Then, one day, the rhythm broke when Sadie took a fall. Kaitlyn rushed to her, trying to help her up, only to see Sadie gasp for breath and clutch her chest. Kaitlyn yelled for Dad to call 911.

Sadie had suffered a heart attack. When I got to the hospital that evening, there sat Dad, in a wheelchair at Sadie's side, holding her hand. I couldn't tell if she was non-responsive or asleep. I tiptoed over to him, and gave him a hug. He looked up at me and spoke quietly, "It's Sadie's birthday tomorrow, Beth. She'll be 90. Can you imagine that?"

Sadie made it through the night…but, in the early morning, she was gone. I got the call, notified my principal, and went back to the hospital to get Dad. As I pushed his wheelchair down the hall and out the door, he sadly said, "Sadie made it to 90. And that's something. I know she wasn't your favorite person, Beth, but you treated her well. I know you did it for your old man, and I appreciate that."

He couldn't see the tears flowing down my face at the truth of his words. Sadie had never been my favorite person. When Dad married her, I had entertained a fantasy that she might play "Grandma" to my kids. I even had them call her that for a month or so. It didn't take long, though, for me to see that Sadie had no interest in being their grandma.

Disappointed, I let it drop. Over the years, I sized up Sadie as someone with little warmth or depth. Clearly, I had failed to conceal my lack of affection for her.

What could I say in reply to Dad's comment? Had he chosen someone else, life might have been very different for our family. "Missed opportunity," I often thought when I remembered Ginger, whom he had dated and loved for a time. We all cared for her, especially Laurie. Ginger had lost her husband a few years before, and she and Dad seemed to be "simpatico." Her warmth and kind attention attracted all of us. She had three sons—one my age and out of the house, and one Laurie's age. I think Laurie saw this as a new family to fill some of her loneliness. To be sure, Ginger had eased some of my still-aching heart.

Still, there were obstacles, and it was Dad's life after all. Though he loved Ginger, he had decided that raising a second family would put distressing pressures on him—at least, that's what he told me after he broke off the engagement. Doing something strictly for his children would never have been his way. Even if he had put aside his doubts and married Ginger, who's to say how it would've turned out?

Life presents us with possibilities; ultimately, we have to choose, and then live with the consequences. Still, I saw Laurie's hurt at this new loss. I also felt it, but I had Robert and, by that time, Bobby, too. What did I know, really, of Laurie's pain or Dad's misgivings—but I held it against him, anyway.

The days after Sadie's death are still clear to me. It was the end of March, and, while I'd focused on Dad, Robert had made plans with his parents and our children to spend a few days of our Easter vacation at a nearby resort. I'd agreed to this, but now I was torn.

Dad's medications and restricted diet had already caused him to lose weight and feel increasingly weak. Add to that his grief over losing Sadie, and facing his own mortality.

Understandably, Robert didn't want to cancel on his parents, and, since the service for Sadie would be held after we returned, he thought I should take advantage of the opportunity to spend some time with our busy children and their paternal grandparents. It was all planned: I could stay in touch with Jim by phone, and besides, what would change over the four days I'd be gone? We had given Kaitlyn some time off, and Laurie was coming down to help Dad. If I remember right, Jim was taking some time off work to help with arrangements for Sadie.

What was I doing? Going off on a vacation!

And what about Frankie? Sadly, he didn't figure into much of this part of Dad's life. At the time, I didn't know why, and I didn't give it much thought. Eventually, I decided to find out why he hadn't visited or called, so, one evening, I phoned him.

"Frankie, it's me. How's it going? Everything okay? We haven't heard from you. You know Sadie died, right?"

"Yeah, sorry, Beth."

"Yeah, it was kinda sudden…wait…what do you mean?"

"I…uh…was gonna call…uh, when's the funeral? Or is there a funeral?

"We're putting a memorial together—that's what Dad wants. Laurie's coming down for a while to help Dad. Is everything okay over there?" I repeated.

"Yeah…no…not really. Don't worry. It's just…I haven't been feeling so great."

"What do you mean? What's wrong?"

"I don't know. I'm going to the doctor," my brother replied. "In fact, I've been going to a few doctors. It's just that…I have pain. No one's figured out why. I can't really talk now, Beth. It hurts just to stand here. When you know, can you call and tell us when the service is?" I said I would and hung up, not knowing what to think. Something was wrong with my brother, but he wasn't providing much information. I didn't know any more than that.

Dad was at loose ends; he wanted to mark the passing of Sadie, the strong, independent woman with whom he'd shared so many contented years…but he didn't know where to start. He took for granted there would be a service, which he wanted, especially since he'd been hospitalized for Mom's church funeral, thirty years before. Unlike our Catholic family, Sadie had been a Baptist, though her illness had put an end to her going to services—and Dad had never once gone with Sadie to her church. He had no idea about any of her church friends, or a pastor.

Jimmy called her church, but the new pastor said he'd never met Sadie; still, he would officiate at the service, and scheduled it for the week after Easter. I offered to write Sadie's eulogy. Sadie's daughter, Ann, planned to fly in from Michigan to take her mother's body back to be buried in the family plot with her first husband. I figured that Ann could give me any details I needed about her mother's life—those that Dad didn't know, that is.

The day before Robert and I left for the resort, I'd gone to Dad's, where I found Laurie trying to put Sadie's room into some sort of order. She stood in the middle of piles of half-full medicine bottles, latex gloves, and dirty clothes. Laurie offered that Jimmy had taken Dad to get his hair cut, and, when I surprised myself by offering to help her sort through the mess, she didn't decline. She talked about wanting to take Dad to visit some retirement residences, saying her mother-in-law had recently moved into a place that offered wonderful activities. She thought some place like it could be great for our father. "You know, Sadie really kept Dad from so many of the things he loved. It would be great for him to live in a place with other people who love music. I can just see him sitting at a big piano in a bright, sunny room plunking out his tunes." A heart-warming picture, to be sure, but I had misgivings. I kept quiet.

For the first time in so long, my sister and I were experiencing a momentary reprieve from conflict. Out of love for our father, we seemed to operate in a neutral zone. I told myself I would have plenty of time to weigh in on Dad's living situation; besides, certainly Dad's grief and poor health had to be considered before any big changes were considered.

I've learned that what seems ill-advised to one person can seem like a practical solution to another.

I stayed in touch from the resort, calling during the afternoons. I remember one upsetting conversation with Dad—he'd sounded downcast and confused, talking about moving and homes and Sadie and 25 years of marriage. In another conversation, Jim told me Dad had had a troubling incident: he'd gone over to a neighbor's house in the middle of the night, upset and confused. "Out of his mind, according to the neighbor" Laurie had reported to Jimmy, who had driven over to help her get Dad home and to bed. Apparently, the new meds were exacerbating Dad's problems, making him agitated and restless.

In the morning, though, Dad had seemed much better, and so Jimmy and Laurie took him to see a couple of residences that Laurie had found in the phone book. Jim said Dad was ambivalent, but he didn't seem upset. In fact, he had seemed open to the idea. I asked Jim not to make any decisions until I got back. He assured me he would wait, and that we would all talk it over with Dad then.

To my dismay, I returned to a done deal. Laurie had needed to leave the day before, and she wanted the plan in place for the "home" they had found—New Horizons, "for seniors who could still live independently." Bottom line: Dad could afford it. It offered limited care; the staff would be there to make sure Dad took his meds and came down for meals. They had a piano that Laurie thought Dad would enjoy and a cheery group of caring workers and volunteers. Dad would adjust and do fine. Anyway, that was the thinking.

I had a presentiment of doom about it all. I couldn't imagine myself in his shoes. How would he handle all these changes? His body still in a stage of recovery after his prostate surgery ….

Jimmy, Janie, Robert and I took Dad to his new home a few days after Sadie's memorial. After Dad signed the rental agreement, Jimmy led the way to his room as the rest of us followed. We settled him in, and then Jimmy and I helped Dad into his pajamas and tucked him in.

I was the last to leave the room. He had his hands behind his head, looking into space. I bent over to kiss him goodbye and told him I would call him in the morning to check on him. For one of the very few times in my life with my father, he had no words for me. He gave me a half smile and a little wave. I left in tears.

When I think about it now, I'm amazed at the speed of his decline. In a matter of months, he'd struggled with early signs of Parkinson's, then, soon after, he'd suffered a major medical incident that had resulted in a diagnosis of terminal heart disease. One doctor had suggested he resign himself to the imminent end of his life. Then, just a few days later, another doctor says, "Wait! Hold on! I can give you a reprieve!...if you go on a diet of ten to twelve medications daily and eat bland, tasteless food." Dad opted for the extension of his life, but without considering what it would do to the quality of that life.

Then, boom!

He lost the second love of his life, the woman he'd chosen to give his life renewed purpose after the loss of his first love in a tragic accident. How did he grasp the abrupt turn in his circumstances? Did he feel as if he'd been thrown into a rushing river and left to thrash around, with no choice but to bear the blows from all sides?

I was in shock, and blamed everyone—myself, in particular. Why had I gone on vacation? Why hadn't I begged off and let Robert and the rest of the family go? I should have been there, involved in caring for my father at his most vulnerable time. I should have been available when Jimmy and Laurie were struggling with crucial decisions.

How could Dad be expected to leave his home of so many years, so many memories? Did anyone wonder if he truly understood what was happening? Yes, they probably had. But he couldn't afford to stay in his home without Sadie's contributions to the household expenses, and he clearly needed to be where he would be monitored. Somewhere safe. They had acted out of love and good intentions. Really—what would I have done differently?

The irony of the situation wasn't lost on me. Dad's physical heart was breaking, losing its ability to sustain him. At the same time, his loving heart was breaking at the loss of the wife he'd doted on so tenderly. His natural armor of energy and pride, which had so long enabled him to fight life's battles, had fallen away, leaving him vulnerable. I saw it all, felt it with him, but didn't know what to do. My brother and sister had not been wrong, but he'd needed me to consider another option, to offer another way…at the very least, to console him. I argued, I cried, but the decision had been made. I had to accept it.

In the following months, I got in the habit of going to visit Dad after school a few times during the week, then once on the weekend. I knew Jim and Janie were frequent visitors, too. Robert and I frequently planned family outings to include Dad. Bob lived pretty close to the retirement home, so we took Dad there a few times to watch sporting events on TV. Once or twice, our family went to a nearby park for a picnic.

At first, Dad seemed to enjoy this…or maybe I want to remember it that way. I saw how hard our children tried to make him feel included and comfortable, and he clearly appreciated their loving attention. As time passed, however, his lack of any real joy stood out as clearly as his fatigue and discomfort.

The "rose-colored glasses" that had us seeing Dad regaining his passion for life without the burden of his sick wife were faulty. Being surrounded by other seniors, some still full of zest for living, did not improve Dad's health or loneliness.

I see now that I'd failed to fully consider the dire state of his heart. Worse, I hadn't given due consideration to the advice of the hospital doctor who, just a few months earlier, had advised us to take Dad home, get hospice care, and let him die peacefully, surrounded by his family. Instead, we had uprooted him and transplanted him in completely unfamiliar surroundings where he was alone in a room. Was he doing anything more than swimming in a pool of grief and isolation?

Dad called me frequently, usually because he couldn't figure out how to work the multiple remotes that he now needed for his television. Robert would get on the phone and patiently walk him through the steps. Then, when we visited, he would go through it again. He even wrote the steps down, but "that damned infernal machine" would rarely cooperate. When Jim visited, he went through the same steps and routine with our father. I know this because we stayed in touch, sharing stories and comparing notes.

Many times, I sat with Dad through his dinner; sometimes eating with him. He had a tablemate, George, a vet like Dad. An interesting man, George must have decided Dad feigned his lack of hearing. Either that, or George had just decided not to put himself out to be agreeable to Dad. This man refused to speak so that Dad could hear his voice, though Dad told him repeatedly that he was hard of hearing. When I visited, however, George carried on lively conversations—with ME.

I tried to bridge the gap between the two men, but without success. Dad asked to be moved to another table. "When we get an opening, Mr. Lawrence, we'll move you," went the promise. I got the same answer when I asked. As for the meals—they seemed fine, in general, except they were bland, and came with an explicit warning to Dad: do NOT add salt. The words might as well have been: do NOT enjoy! Mealtime for Dad—something he once relished—became a chore. One day, as I was getting ready to leave, he called me back with a question: "Beth, is this what my life is now…that room?" And he pointed up the stairs.

I had no answer.

Jimmy and I took Dad to his doctor's appointments. Dr. Doyle maintained that the fluid around Dad's heart had lessened, and that his condition was on track. Unfortunately, because of the combination of "water pills" he now took every day, Dad had become incontinent, an indignity he railed against. He refused to "wear any damned diapers," no matter how often the staff at the residence insisted.

One day, he announced to me, "Beth. They want me to wear diapers. Imagine—me, a sergeant in the US Army. I fought in WWII, for Pete's sake. A man has his pride. I ain't doin' it."

"Dad. I'm sure it's awful to wear those things. I mean, I can't imagine," I started to say, but Dad cut me off.

"That's right. You can't!"

"Wait, Dad—let me finish."

I'd run out of patience. I'd taken a couple of periods off from school, driven thirty minutes over to New Horizons, gotten him in and out of his wheelchair—and the wheelchair in and out of my car trunk—to take him to the doctor. On our drive over, he had re-lived WWII battles and their brave heroes—and just as he'd finished with one story, with a "Can you imagine that?" shaking his head, he'd start up with another one. On our way back to New Horizons, staring out the window, he had begun with the complaints.

In frustration, I continued: "Do you know how many times those ladies who change your bedding and wash your pajamas have talked to me about this? Can you imagine what it must be like for them, having to change your bed every day, often more than once? How would you feel if that was your job? No—imagine if you knew that was MY job?"

Quiet filled the car as my words reverberated in the air. Then, a much calmer Dad murmured, "I never thought about it like that."

When we reached his building, I got his wheelchair from the trunk. I wheeled it up to him, feeling a mixture of dissipating anger and growing regret. Good God! How could I talk to him like that?

"Here, Dad. Let me get the brakes on this thing. Okay. We're good." I reached for him, but he didn't move. Instead, he looked up at me and said, "You're right, Beth. When you're right, well…you're just right. I'll give the damned things a try."

I got him in his chair and wheeled him in. Immediately, up came a darling young girl with shiny dark hair and a ponytail. She wore a pink jumper, white tennis shoes and a nametag.

"Well, if it isn't Mr. Lawrence. I've been looking for you." She reached down and gave Dad a kiss on the cheek. He beamed. "This must be your daughter, right?"

"It is. This is Beth."

"Hi. I'm Shelley. I just love your Dad. He always makes me laugh. I'll see you in a little while, Mr. Lawrence. I'm staying through dinner." She gave another little wave and off she went, ponytail bobbing and bouncing.

"Okay. That's a date, Shelley. I'll see you later," he called after her.

12 COME ON HOME

When the night has come
And the land is dark
And the moon is the only light we can see
I won't be afraid, oh, I won't be afraid
Just as long as you stand…stand by me

~Ben E. King

This next part of my story isn't unique, but it looms large in my life. Some events stretched and bent time as I navigated my way through them, while others were a blur. What always stood out clearly during this time was my home life. It was a time of soul searching for me—not work that I consciously set out to do; rather, things would dawn on the me somewhat frozen in her spiritual development.

Though I attended religious services frequently as a teacher at a Catholic school, I can't say I had a deep interior life. I was moved by the liturgy, and yet I ignored tenets in Catholicism that I didn't like and nursed grievances where I felt my religion fell short. I made jokes about being a "cafeteria Catholic" as many born-and-bred Catholics do. And I was okay with this for a long while, as I ignored the bigger questions that deep faith compels.

Now, with the changes in my father's life, I found I was unable to stave off the moments of reckoning facing both of us. As Dad stared at death, I found I couldn't avoid doing the same.

It occurred to me that, as a middle-aged adult, I had deep questions about God. Although I had held on to the childhood comfort of a spiritual dimension to life, however superficial, He or She didn't make complete sense to me. And I didn't talk about my doubts. To some extent, I faked my faith. Now, in my father's last days, I was becoming a crucial player in his life in a way I'd never been before—up close and personal.

As I look back, I see that it was then that I began to experience the warmth of God. In my young adulthood, I had faced the cold, unforgiving winter of God's mystery as I vacillated between blind love and angry denial. I held onto my faith simply because I was terrified to let go of it. It was only as Dad set about the process of passing away from this life that I began to see God's beauty shining in my dying father.

It began with a morning phone call from New Horizons. Though he could hardly hear, needed his walker to get anywhere at a painfully slow pace, and couldn't get into his adult diapers by himself, Dad lived "independently." New Horizons Retirement Home required it. Thus, my father lived on the edge. While there was no mistaking that he required help, he could get to and from his meals with his walker and take his daily meds. Most importantly, he had all his faculties and could talk and joke with the volunteers and staff. Though his needs could be challenging, the facility could look the other way while dealing with these inconvenient issues.

Until one day.

On a lazy morning in early summer, Robert and I sat drinking coffee and reading the paper, when the phone rang. "Mrs. Dolan, your father took a fall," the voice reported. "We need someone in your family to come right over." Apparently, just as he had for the previous three months, Dad had risen at 7AM to the knock on his door. The aide had helped him dress, checked to see that he had taken his morning meds, then handed him his hearing aids and walker. She hadn't noticed any difference in his demeanor, and wished him a good day before leaving to help the "guest" in the next room.

Dad had slowly made his way to the elevator and down to the room where he took his meals. On this particular day, though, as he started toward the tables, something had happened. According to the residents gathered there, Dad sort of "crumpled."

Staff members had rushed to help him, quickly determining that he couldn't get himself up. They took him back to his room, and helped him into his bed, where he lay disoriented. There were no apparent injuries, but he was clearly struggling for air. The on-call doctor checked him, putting him on oxygen and giving him a shot of something similar to adrenaline. She strongly recommended moving him to the nursing wing where he could be monitored, "unless, you'd rather take him to his doctor or the ER."

All I knew was that I wanted Dad under someone's care right away. "I'll decide about that when I get there. For now, please take my father to your nursing wing," I said. Before I hung up, the other voice on the phone said clearly, "Mrs. Dolan, your family needs to know that your father's current condition changes his living situation here. We're going to need you to make some decisions your father is too weak to make."

I hung up the phone.

"Dad took a fall and couldn't get up," I told Robert. 'It sounds like he's in bad shape. I'm going to call Jimmy, then head over there." I made a quick call, but Jimmy had already left for work. Janie said she would have him call my cell phone as soon as she reached him.

Before long, Robert, Ellie—who'd moved home temporarily—and I were on our way. I've never forgotten Ellie's role in the decision to come later that day, and I'll always be grateful she insisted on joining us. As the miles passed, Robert and Ellie talked quietly while I stared out the window, wondering how bad this would be. They'd described Dad as weak and disoriented. Why didn't they call 911? Should he be in a hospital rather than their nursing wing? Is he dying? The heart specialist said Dad SHOULD have two more years!

When we arrived at New Horizons, we went straight to the office; Shirley greeted me warmly as I walked through the door.

"Your father's resting, Beth. But I must tell you, he's not coherent enough for a conversation. When he discovered he couldn't get up, he became agitated. The doctor has given him something to help him relax."

"Can we talk to this doctor?"

"She's waiting for you. Is any more of your family on their way?"

"No, I couldn't reach my brother, but he'll call when he gets the message. I don't want to wait."

The three of us followed Shirley to a building adjacent to the one where Dad lived. In the elevator, Shirley introduced herself to Ellie and made small talk. A quick walk through non-descript corridors, and then we were seated opposite a woman whom Shirley introduced as Dr. Schrader. Shirley said she would give us some privacy, but would be close by.

Dr. Schrader had Dad's file open in front of her. I remember the high points of our conversation.

"Mrs. Dolan, your father's been diagnosed with Congestive Heart Failure. You know this, yes?" I appreciated Dr. Schrader's direct approach.

"Yes. Please call me Beth."

"Okay, Beth. You've been taking your Dad to a…Dr. Doyle, a heart specialist. Right?

"Right."

"So, you know your father's taking a regimen of medications designed to keep his heart pumping and to prevent fluid from collecting throughout his body. While they have done an adequate job to that end, I'm afraid the overall state of his medical condition has not improved. His heart is giving out, making him very weak—so much so, that he's finding it difficult to exert much energy. This is my preliminary observation after examining him and interacting with him."

I hated what I was hearing, and reacted accordingly.

"Why wasn't he taken to the hospital? When Shirley called me, she said they called you instead of 911 because they knew his medical condition and why he had fallen. Shouldn't the hospital be running some tests or something?" I was clutching at straws.

"I'm a hospital doctor over at Mercy.

"Oh, I didn't know that." This changed things for me.

"As I was about to say, all I had to do was look at your father's records—which, of course, New Horizons has—and do a cursory examination to determine his condition."

I knew this—and that there was no cure for his condition—but I still struggled with this death sentence. "The condition your father is in is readily observable with only a few tests—which I've done."

"I understand what you're saying, Dr. Schrader, but Dr. Doyle said that with these medications, Dad could go on for another two years. It's only been a few months…." I begged for a different appraisal. Who cared now what Dr. Doyle had said? That was then.

"I'm sure he's had some success with his approach," Dr. Schrader said carefully, "but, unfortunately, it's not working for your father. Of course, you're free to take him back to this doctor."

"What do you recommend?" At that, Robert took my hand to steel me for her answer.

"I'd recommend a nursing home and hospice. They have him in this wing now. They offer 24-hour attention. And hospice will keep him comfortable. Of course, this is a decision for you and your family."

"Can I see my dad now?"

"Of course, though he may still be asleep."

At that, the doctor got up and opened the door. It's a bit blurry, but I hope I thanked her. Shirley reappeared, and we all shuffled into the hall. I know Robert put his arm around me. I, in turn, patted Ellie's back—the domino effect of loving concern.

Shirley spoke: "I'll take you all to Jack's bed. Take a look around as we go. We have a pretty full house, but we can make room for one of our favorite residents."

We walked slowly down the hall, which smelled of disinfectant that failed to masked a faint urine odor. We passed rooms with TVs blaring as people lay in beds with eyes closed, a few in restraints. Two women in wheelchairs were parked against the wall; as we passed, I tried to make eye contact and say hello. Both had stared ahead, unresponsive. Finally, we got to Dad's room. I walked up to his bed. His face looked pale, especially without his glasses.

"Mom, Grandpa doesn't look good at all. I haven't seen him in a few weeks, but I'm really shocked," Ellie whispered to me. I held one of Dad's hands in mine

"I know, honey. Dad, we're here. It's me—Beth. Robert and Ellie are with me."

He didn't open his eyes.

"Beth, why don't we get some coffee? Give your dad some time. Come back a little later. They can call your cell phone when he wakes up. We need to talk," Robert urged.

"Okay. I'll just find someone to tell."

We left the building and headed to a coffee shop down the street. With breakfast ordered, Robert said, "There's no way we can leave your dad there, Beth."

"I agree, Mom. He can't stay there—he just can't!" Ellie's eyes filled with tears.

"Then where? What do we do?" I looked at them, searching for answers.

"Bring him home, to our house," Ellie said unequivocally.

"I agree. We'll figure it out together. It's the right thing to do," from Robert.

"Really? Robert, you're sure? Ellie?" They both nodded, and I knew they were right.

I talked to Jimmy a little later. I told him about the doctor's evaluation and the conclusion she had drawn: Dad was not going to recover from this episode.

"As for New Horizons," I told him, "we have two options. They said Dad needs around-the-clock care. Bottom line: he needs to find somewhere else to live." I told him I had decided, with Robert's agreement, that "somewhere else" would be with me. I assured him that now that I was off work for the summer, I had time to devote to Dad. Robert would be right by my side. Jimmy said something about heading over to see Dad so that he, too, could talk to Dr. Schrader.

We agreed to talk more about Dad's treatment and future after that. I could tell he had reservations about my taking Dad in—maybe he worried it would be more than I could handle. In the meantime, I said I would read the materials Shirley had given me on hospice and make a few phone calls. In the end, Jimmy agreed with me about hospice. I don't remember calling to get agreement from our siblings, so he must have done that. I do remember Dad's reaction when I told him he was coming home to live with me: he smiled, finally opening his eyes. "Oh, Beth. Thank you. You don't know what this means to me."

Over the next couple of days, I questioned myself constantly. How would Dad react when he heard the word "hospice?" How would he face what that meant? Hospice seemed to be about minimizing pain. Would it really do that for Dad? Could I actually believe that my father, with whom I'd been through so much, was dying? Unlike the seventeen-year-old girl of so long ago, I now knew what that meant. Could I deal with what this decision—that I would go with him to the end of his days? Who really knew the answer to that question? What choice did I have?

I knew I could only be me and do what I could. I prayed hard, though. I prayed that God would help me to face whatever came with love. I would need help. I couldn't expect Ellie to postpone her life, but Robert, my rock for so many years, would be there. My father was coming to die with us…with me.

Shirley helped us set up a meeting with hospice in our home. It was important that Dad understand what this meant for him going forward.

We understood just how fragile and weak Dad was; we practically carried him up the steps into our house and into the family room. After seeing the single bed we'd set up was inadequate, Robert immediately ordered a hospital bed. The nurse who followed us home to help us get dad set up explained what I should do with Dad's IV and oxygen. That taken care of, she said quietly, "Your father is very ill. Take your time coming down in the morning. It won't be surprising if he passes away in the night. Sometimes, all someone in his condition needs is to know he's where he wants to be. He may relax and let go."

I didn't sleep much that night, fearful of the nurse's words. Then I worried whether I'd remember all her instructions about the IV. Was Dad's life in my hands? More than that, was I ready for this next phase of my father's life—his death?

As father and daughter, our lives were inextricably linked, but so much more had bound us over the years. I often wondered what my life would have looked like had I traveled the route my early years had projected, all the while having two parents mentoring and nurturing me as I found my way to adulthood. I could only wonder.

Somehow, with the premature loss of my mother, roles had gotten muddled. Far from the life I might have had as a daughter with two supportive parents, my life shifted this way and that, usually without much warning. When Dad remarried eight years after Mom's death, my life assumed a bit more stability, but it never really "normalized." I just went along, doing my best to adjust to the shifts and trying to keep my focus on whatever was required.

Now? I'd forge ahead. I knew, though, that this time, this circumstance, would demand much more from me than any other. I would be returning in a profound way to the questions I had asked forty years ago, after Mom's passing. Now, though, I would attend to these questions without the shock or naïveté.

13 JUST MAKE THE DECISION

Would you know my name
If I saw you in heaven?
Would it be the same, if I saw you in heaven?
I must be strong and carry on
'Cause I know I don't belong here in heaven.

~ Eric Clapton

"I know I've given you a lot of information, Mr. Lawrence. Any questions?"

Dad had been sitting at our dining room table with Jimmy, Janie, Robert, and

me as a woman from Heart to Heart Hospice Care went over their program.

I liked Emily Coleson, instantly. As she walked through my front door, I was struck with her warmth and cheerful demeanor. She'd reached for my hand, smiling and introducing herself, and immediately covered my hand with her other hand. Then, as she peered into the living and dining rooms in front of her, she complimented me with a question: "Do you regard your home as a refuge?" When I laughed and said yes, she responded, "I can tell. Your home, even at first glance, just feels comfortable and serene—everything seems just right. And may I see where your father's sleeping?"

At that, I led her into the bright, sunny family room where Dad's bed sat facing the TV, just under one of the room's big windows.

"Lovely! Lots of sun—good for reading…this seems like just the place for your dad."

"Well, Dad's a reader," I told her, "and if you ask him about it, he'll probably tell you how he got his first library card at five."

She smiled at that. "I like to see where our clients live. I like to see a comfortable space with easy access to people. Too often, patients are isolated in some boring back room."

"Well, Dad just got here, and already my kids have visited him. We're a pretty social group, and he likes being the center of attention."

"Good. I'm happy to hear that. Let's go sit down with the others and then your father can get some rest before his afternoon visitors arrive."

We moved to the dining area, and Mrs. Coleson set a binder on the table. "We're here to give you all—especially, you, Mr. Lawrence—an overview of how we at "Heart to Heart" can help you at this time. You're the patient, so it's most important that you understand and agree to our services." With that, she opened the binder and began her presentation.

Two days had passed since we brought Dad home to live with us. From that first morning, when he, Robert, and I divided up the newspaper and started reading, he appeared calm, relaxed, and grateful. When I sat at his bedside, he smiled into my eyes, nodding. One time, he whispered, "Beth, you don't know what this means to me."

Now, he sat quietly at the table as Mrs. Coleson spoke. Throughout the presentation, he looked down, appearing less engaged by the minute. At first, he had politely smiled at the woman, but, as she described their services—repeatedly emphasizing the words hospice and palliative care—he'd begun to slump in his chair. I couldn't tell if he was physically uncomfortable, emotionally uncomfortable, or both.

The print on the binder pages was large; it didn't take much to see the phrases in bold letters. The first page proclaimed: A CARE PLAN, NOT A CURE PLAN. Bullet points followed, outlining the three major categories that Heart to Heart addressed: symptom control, pain management, and comfort measures. As she leafed through the pages, Mrs. Coleson talked about medical assessment services, home health aides, and much more. To me, it all sounded reassuring and helpful.

When she closed the binder and turned directly to Dad, she seemed to be asking, "Well? Are you on board?" But Dad didn't respond. I remember feeling awkward. He had looked around the table at Robert and me and Jimmy and Janie, as if to say, "What do I care? You all figure it out and let me know." I guess we took his silence as permission, because the four of us had lots of questions.

Jim wanted to know if Dad would still see his primary care doctor, Dr. Hemengway. The answer was not clear-cut.

"Our job is to make sure your father's needs are met with frequent visits from our hospice care team," Mrs. Coleson answered. "He won't really need medical appointments, but, of course, if he wants that, he is welcome to work that out with the doctor." She now spoke directly to Dad: "Mr. Lawrence, we're going to keep you comfortable and pain-free. You'll see." And she had smiled at him tenderly. I'll never forget that, because he had smiled back as if to say "You understand…I can tell."

I asked about how I would regulate his pharmacopeia of medications. "The new approach now, with hospice," Mrs. Coleson told us, "will include a reduction in your dad's medications. He'll take only those meds designed to keep him comfortable."

Janie wanted to know, "What did you say the time limit is for hospice care?"

"Generally, six months—but each case is unique. We have no strict time limit."

"So, if he improves…." Jim paused.

"If he improves, that will be wonderful. It happens more than you would think, and, if and when it does, we adjust our approach. This is a distinct possibility."

So, there we were. We all had at least a general understanding of hospice. The woman had been professional and caring with all of us. She had answered all the questions we could think to ask. We all sat, silent.

Mrs. Coleson somehow intuited our vague unease. She began speaking, assuring us that, though the Heart to Heart staff were professionals, they were also caring people who wanted to help us in this, the toughest job we might do. What we were giving Dad was the most loving and beautiful gift we had: a home.

She emphasized the importance of all of us pitching in. It was going to take all of us to do this. "And I do mean all of you." She looked directly at me. "Be sure to keep your siblings informed and included, Beth. Remember, I'm here for you. Call me with any questions. You're a lucky man, Mr. Lawrence," she said, taking Dad's hand. She continued gently: "Mr. Lawrence, if you're comfortable with the idea of hospice, and if you want the care that we're offering, we would like you to sign and date this contract."

At that, Dad took the pen she held out to him and signed.

After the woman left and we got Dad into bed for a rest, the four of us sat on the living room couch, drinking coffee and talking. "I'm not sure why, but I'm exhausted. How about you, Beth?" Jim asked. I replied that my poor brain hurt.

"Jim, that was a workout, am I right?"

It didn't occur to me then, but I realized later, that, as siblings, Jimmy and I were sharing one of the most elemental aspect of life there is: our father's decline and death. Though I had occasionally witnessed Dad's vulnerability, this was unlike anything else, and while my father had always impressed me with a particular brand of toughness, this situation, called upon all his inner strength…and ours.

As a kid, I had often come upon Dad working on a household project. He might accidentally hit his thumb hard with a hammer; did he swear up a storm and shake it violently? You bet! But a few minutes later, he was hammering away again. Many times, at his store, I observed him bang the phone down after conversing with an ornery customer; he'd take a breath, calmly put the other phone up to his ear, and talk cheerfully with another customer, who'd been on hold. And I never walked through that door when there weren't two or three customers waiting at the counter. Still, when I did walk through the door with a friend in tow, he always smiled and tossed me the keys to the coke machine. At home, he didn't want to hear any whining about helping out around the house, or we'd be sorry. I knew I didn't really want to know what he meant by that.

Once we were out of the house, he displayed a different kind of strength. Having resolved to keep our family close, he did it with regular family gatherings for which he did much of the cooking. And he was a presence not to be ignored. Whether plunking out a tune on the piano during any holiday season, or whistling while he built a closet for Sadie's square dancing petticoats, he let anyone near him know his determination to conquer life's challenges and enjoy himself along the way.

He talked fast and walked fast, and took people as they were. He enjoyed whatever he did, and never complained that he hadn't had more of anything: money, opportunity, prestige. Even as he grew old, he only really complained for Sadie. Why did she have to be in so much pain? Why couldn't her doctor help her vision problems? Why didn't her daughter call more often?

Yes, he had his flaws, which I recounted to Robert and close friends. Over the years, though, my respect for his decency, integrity, and strength far outweighed the negatives.

Once, when I asked him why he and Mom hadn't brought Mom's sister to live with them after she suffered a debilitating accident, he looked me straight in the eyes and said, "Kiddo, believe me, we wanted to…we really did, but, ya know, we did the best we could under the circumstances." He had gone on to explain that the accident had taken place during the war when they had two small children and one on the way, and Dad was preparing to be shipped overseas. Three years later, he came home to three small children, one of whom, at five, still couldn't talk. He and Mom had set their priorities. Faced with many painful decisions, this philosophy must have helped him—and Mom—through them.

Only a few weeks before he came to live with me, Dad had bitterly called himself a "useless old man." On the heart specialist's regimen to lose weight, he'd also lost much of his strength and his ability to walk more than a few steps without tiring. He'd also lost his ability to control his bowels. This angered him no end. He demanded to know when he would feel like himself again. I could only shake my head as I watched his sturdy, barrel-chested frame and ruddy complexion fade away.

I can see now that he had gritted his teeth and clung to his life. Those of us close to him conspired to sustain him, willing him, "Do this Dad. We want you alive!" until, finally, we had all been forced to acknowledge that he was, inevitably, on a final decline.

I taught my high school students that, in a battle between man and nature, nature always wins. I was facing this battle with my father.

Now, what mattered most to Dad was rest, relief, and time with his family. He hadn't given up on life so much as he'd trusted us to do what was best for him. Jim and I had agreed not to suggest seeing the heart specialist again, and, since Dad rarely asked about Dr. Hemengway, we deemed his agreement implicit.

We hadn't spoken much about that initial visit by the hospice people, and I wondered at times if maybe that had been a mistake. Though Robert and I welcomed the almost-daily visits from one of the medical staff, Dad had a hard time with them, especially if he was unusually tired or feeling out of sorts. "Oh, what do you want with me now?" he'd complain.

From my vantage point, they were friendly, professional women, there to do anything it took to make him more comfortable. But it occurs to me now that he had a point: they would take his temperature and blood pressure, turn him in his bed, and encourage him to get up and walk a bit. From his perspective, though, they were the interlopers to his peace and quiet. Our household, nevertheless, soon settled into a routine, with the women coming and going, informing us of upcoming visits, telling us to call with questions, and complimenting Dad. Then there was my saving grace: the social worker.

Sonya was a tall, slim brunette in her late 40's or early 50's. She had big, dark eyes that crinkled when she smiled. She called or came by from time to time to check up on things. She always inquired about Dad first thing. If I said he'd had a tough time with something that day, she'd ask for my reaction, then say just the right thing to let me know she understood how I felt.

I distinctly remember one time when the nurse's aide put a catheter in Dad. She'd explained to Dad what she was doing and why, and I'd asked him if he understood. Though out of sorts that day, he'd indicated he did. I left the room, and a minute later I heard, "Goddammit! Why'd you do that?' followed by the aide's murmured explanation. A little flustered, she emerged, and I went back in to check on Dad. As I approached his bed, he turned his head and closed his eyes, dismissing me.

"Well," Sonya said, "it sounds like a reasonable reaction to a very uncomfortable moment for him. I bet you felt bad about the whole thing—for both of them. Am I right?"

I told her I did feel bad for both of them—and confused. "I wanted to scold Dad—tell him to give the woman a break, that she was just doing her job. But, you know, it was my fault he got the catheter. He was going through so many sheets. Robert and I have been doing at least two loads of laundry a day, changing and making and changing and re-making his bed.

The aide said this would take care of the problem. But I didn't think about how uncomfortable it would be for Dad. Now, it seems selfish of me!"

Sonya assured me it was important Robert and I to save our energy for the more important jobs we faced taking care of my father. "Yes, a catheter is not very comfortable for your dad, but there are worse things, Beth. You don't need to get burned out doing laundry."

Then she put a question to me: "Are other family members pitching in to help you care for your father? You know, this is something you should be sharing with your siblings or extended family. You can't do it all by yourself, even with the help of your wonderful husband." Though we were on the phone, I could just see those kind eyes as she talked to me so earnestly. I thought about her question.

I had no easy answer. Jim and Janie visited Dad frequently, but besides that, what was I supposed to do? Call them and ask them to drive forty minutes to come and help me do laundry? I mean, I didn't know whom else to call even if I felt I could do that. I didn't have a relationship with Laurie. Frank seemed to be struggling to figure out the cause of his own health problems. Who did that leave? Ellie still lived with us, but she had her own busy life, and my other kids came over often, always going straight to their grandpa's bed in the family room. As the months passed, I had many more conversations with Sonja. Each time, I hung up the phone feeling acknowledged and encouraged.

Despite the occasional mishap, I remember this time in my life with warmth. Dad had arrived at my house the first of July with the serious admonition of the nurse accompanying us. He made it through the first night, and the next day, we met with Mrs. Coleson and signed on for hospice. The rest of that day, Dad had seemed weak and subdued. I felt myself moving around on eggshells, holding my breath.

Two days later, however, on the Fourth of July, he woke up refreshed and eager for the day. Our son Greg had invited our family to come over for a barbeque and watch fireworks from his yard. I worried it would be too much for Dad, but when I put it to him, he enthusiastically agreed. "It's just what I need, Beth. I wouldn't miss it. But I sure would like a shower and shave, first."

How could we pull this off? We knew he wasn't strong enough to take his own shower. He needed the walker to get from one room to the next, and he moved slowly. Robert, ever creative, thought about it and said one of our plastic patio chairs might work. Pretty soon, he had put one in the guest room's walk-in shower. He put on his bathing suit, got Dad undressed, into the chair and turned on the warm water.

Once he had Dad out of the shower and wrapped in a towel, he called me, and I came in. We got Dad dressed in comfortable clothes and to the kitchen table. Robert got his shaving things and shaved Dad's face. I'll never forget Dad's elation at this. "Robert, I feel like a new man. Thank you. Thank you,!"

Soon, Ellie, Robert, Dad, and I headed over to Greg's. For a few hours, Dad seemed like Dad: talkative and relaxed. The next day, he cheerfully recounted being at Greg's, especially getting to hold his great-granddaughter, while Greg's loving wife, Robin, looked on and smiled.

One day in early August, Bob called to ask if we were still going on our annual camping trip. We had been camping in the Sierras every summer since friends had invited us to join them 25 years before. The group had grown over the years, and now a substantial number of families and friends packed up trucks, campers—and a boat—and headed to a campground nestled in the forest. There, we played in the streams and lake for four or five days, water-skiing, hiking, swimming, and generally basking in the magic of nature. No one in our family—extending to at least one of Robert's brothers—liked to miss it.

Robert wanted us to go. I was nervous about it and called Sonya. What did she think? "It sounds like the perfect break for you and Robert. First, make up your mind that it's okay to go. Then get on the phone and make it happen. You really need this, Beth." I decided to call Jim. Nervously, I explained that I wanted four days away, and wondered if he would consider staying with Dad for that time. "Or," I suggested, "you could call Laurie and tell her I will be gone, and she could have time with Dad. Another option." He said he would talk to Janie and get back to me. Before long, I had my answer: yes, we should go. They would work it out—with or without Laurie. My brother had just given me a wonderful gift!

I have to say…I felt weird the entire vacation, though I loved being with my family and playing with my little grandson in the grandeur that surrounded us. But we were somewhat isolated, a big part of what we all loved about the place. We had no phone service at our campground and only a small store about ten minutes away. While I rejoiced in the freedom from routine and the invigoration of the crisp mountain air, I had to fight feelings of unease.

Hard as I tried, I couldn't break free of imagined catastrophes. And the thought that I had abandoned my father and dumped a responsibility I had chosen for myself on my brother nagged at me. It was as if I stood outside myself, looking at this person laughing, lounging in the sun, splashing in the water with two-year-old Sammy, and asked, "Who are you, anyway? Why aren't you with your dying father?"

Still, the respite did me good, and I returned with new energy.

I continued to worry about anything and everything that summer. Early on, Dad asked me why he didn't have to take "all those pills" anymore. "Remember, Dad, with hospice, you don't have to take all those pills anymore. The ladies check up on you and make sure you have what you need."

He acted like he'd forgotten—and maybe he had—but I wondered if he really understood what hospice was. Another time, he mentioned the doctor he had been seeing for years. "Say, Beth, when am I going to see Dr. Hemengway again? Maybe he can do something with my toenails! They're so thick, it'd take my wire-cutters to trim them."

Confused, I just said, "Well, we'll have to see about that." Though I was pretty sure what they'd say, I went so far as to call the office; the doctor's nurse said she thought Dad was under hospice care. When I replied "That's right," she said that the doctor wouldn't see him unless his status changed. I waited to see if Dad would say any more about Dr. Hemengway. He didn't, so I didn't.

Soon, the new school year was upon us, and I had to make a decision. Dad's health had stabilized. Sonja had confirmed this. "Your father's comfortable, out of pain, clearly happy to be where he is. He might go on for a long while." His prognosis was, for the moment, unclear. While he was still weak, his death did not seem imminent.

With only a few weeks of summer left, at Robert's urging, I called Kaitlyn. "She'll never want to drive all the way over here to take care of Dad," I'd said. "Maybe I'll just have to quit my job."

"You don't know that. Just call her and see. She probably stayed home with her kids all summer and is looking for a job right now." Before I took the drastic measure of quitting a job I loved and had been doing for over twenty years, I picked up the.

"Robert, you were right," I said when I'd hung up the phone. "It's just what you said. She needs a job, and as long as she can be there when her kids come home from school, she'll do it. In fact, she sounded happy to hear from me and concerned about Dad. I made sure she knew the complete situation with him. What a relief!

Oh, but there is one thing. She has to talk to her mom about her little girl, Becky, only three. She's not in school yet, so Kaitlyn will need her mom to watch Becky while she's working here. She's going to call me back." Not long after, Kaitlyn called back to say her mom was on board. One step at a time, we agreed.

I knew it was one step at a time for Dad and me as well--and wondered what challenges the new school year would bring.

14 SAY GOODBYE, FOR NOW

My pa can light my room at night with just his being near
And make a fearful dream all right by grinning ear to ear…
His arms are house and home to me, his face a pretty poem to me
My pa's the finest friend I ever knew, I only wish that you could know him too…

~ Michael Leonard and H. Martin

The mystery of it all is how easily and quickly those next days and weeks passed. Our days were filled with a familiar routine that included rising, dressing, breakfast, Kaitlyn's arrival—I even kissed Dad goodbye as he had done with me when I was a child.

At school, the outer office would be filled with teenagers vying for time with one of us counselors. While they breathlessly explained their latest concern, I unlocked my door, got my coat off and put my purse away. I'd motion these faces into chairs and try to answer their questions. "Mrs. D, will the colleges penalize me if I take the SAT again—my scores stink!" "Would you read my essay—how can I make it better?" "I don't think Ms. Koch likes me. I have a D in Algebra." "Can I change English teachers, pleeease? I just don't get the way Mr. Brown explains anything."

Then there were my hangers-on, who looked at me as a surrogate mom.

On any day, Amber would drop in at random times, plop into one of my chairs, sigh and launch into the latest indignity: "I can't believe the homework Mr. Reyes expects us to do. Doesn't he know we have other AP classes? You should talk to him, tell him what you're making us do for English. Why are you making us do all those literary terms, besides reading the longest book ever? Doesn't Dickens know it doesn't take three paragraphs to tell us Pip loves Estella? God!"

Emma would usually call out from her office across the hall, "Hey, Amber. You know Mrs. Dolan isn't your mom, right? She's way too nice to you." Amber would just respond in kind, "Yes, she is my mom. She forgets that sometimes. Like when she calls on other people when I have my hand up."

Eventually, I'd send Amber on her way, telling her I'd see her in class. With a quiet moment, I might sit back, and, if she wasn't busy with kids herself, Emma might sing out, "Rox-anne!" in a squawky, screechy imitation of Sting, making me laugh uncontrollably.

And so, the day went. No boredom, and little, if any, downtime. I was grateful that the distractions of my job actively engaged my mind in things other than medicine, care-givers and the approach of death.

I vacillated between wanting desperately to stop time and wondering when it was all going to end. Sometimes, I forced myself to forget the fragility of Dad's situation and the permanent emptiness I would experience when he left me for good. Particularly when Robert and I were engaged in mundane, daily activities with Dad, I could almost forgot why he was there: eating dinner…chatting about our days…calling out the answers as we watched Jeopardy…sitting at his bedside while he recounted the day's reading.

One day, this last revealed something about Dad that I'd never known.

I'd always been amazed at how fast he read, and how well he remembered details. One day, he looked up at me, put his book down, and said, "Oh, Beth, I just read the most amazing thing," and he went on to describe a scene about the storming of the beaches of Normandy. I could see from his bookmark that he'd read about two thirds of the book, and I knew he had just started it a few days before. When I expressed surprise, he replied, "Oh, honey, I've read this book before. Sometimes I just like to I start at the end, and work my way back to the beginning." I smiled. "Dad—that's cheating! I can't believe I never knew you did that." He just chuckled.

Some days, I marveled that we managed so well, particularly as Robert and I were constant captives to Dad's needs.

One Saturday, we were watching Sammy for a few hours. Sammy's potty training hadn't been going well, so this day he had diapers on. I happened to carry Sammy into the family room, where Robert was talking with Dad. Robert stopped, looked at me, and remarked, "Phew, I smell something. Don't you?"

"Yeah," I replied. "Sammy had a big accident. I need the diaper bag so I can change him." I found it next to the couch, got out the changing pad, lay my grandson down on it, and changed the soiled diaper. That done, Sammy got down, went over to Dad, and announced, "Papa! I'm building a fort outside with Grandma!" and ran off.

"Wow," Robert remarked as I left the room, "that was a big one." A little later, Robert found me outside with Sammy. "Beth, I think your dad needs changing. Don't worry—I know you don't want to do it—but where are his Depends?"

"Robert—are you sure? I can get them for you, but how can I ask you to do this?" Robert had heard me say many times this was a "No-Go" zone for me.

"Well, what other options do we have?"

I had dreaded this day. I just didn't think I could see my father's "private parts," let alone clean them. Robert picked up Sammy, and, as we walked into the house, Dad called to me. We were already walking into the family room with the Depends, when he said, "Uh…I hate to say this…but I think I've had an accident, just like Sammy. Are the ladies coming today?" It was Saturday, a day they didn't come unless something critical had happened. As this didn't qualify, we were on our own. Casually, Robert broke in.

"Jack, don't worry. I've got this."

"Oh, no, Robert. You shouldn't have to…."

"Don't worry. Beth just changed Sammy. There's nothing to it!" I helped Robert get Dad in a position where we could get the diaper under him and turned to walk out. Then I stopped, turned around resolutely, and said, "I'm going to help you, honey."

"Beth, I never wanted you to see me like this," Dad lamented.

"I know, Dad, but it's no big deal. Like Robert said, I just changed Sammy. It's not so different, except you're bigger. Besides, I'm sure you did this for me more than a few times."

At that, Sammy piped in, "Papa has diapers, too!"

Then there were challenging days of a different kind. I remember one day, I'd been needing a break from the everyday responsibilities of Dad's needs, and I'd gone to school with a case of "Poor me." As usual, the kids had quickly distracted me, and I had begun to settle into my school routine, when the phone rang.

"Hello, this is Mrs. Dolan."

"Uh, Beth. This is Kaitlyn. I'm sorry to call you at work, but the hospice ladies are here. Jack won't do what they're telling him, and he's swearing at the ladies." Kaitlyn was trying not to laugh.

"He can have quite the potty-mouth, can't he? Okay. Let me talk to him." Kaitlyn took the phone to Dad, and I asked him what was wrong."

'It's these damned women. I'm tired and I'm… blocked up, Beth. I don't want them to…pardon me, but I don't want them to…stick something up my ass. Then, they expect me to walk around until the damned thing works! I'm not going to do it, and that's that!"

I'd heard the defiance and finality of the last part of that statement from him too many times to count, most often with my mother when she tried to convince him to hold off on the salt or the globs of butter, or when she tried to convince him to drink the carrot juice she had made for him with her fancy juicer.

"Dad?"

"Beth, it's me, Kaitlyn, again. He just put the phone down."

"Okay. Tell the ladies I'll be right there." I told the other counselors I'd be back to teach my class and out I went.

It only took a few minutes to get home, and I walked directly into the family room to everyone waiting quietly. I went straight to Dad's bedside.

"Dad, what 's up? This isn't like you. You know these ladies are here to help you. I know you're constipated and uncomfortable. Don't you want them to relieve that for you?"

He looked at me, a little sheepishly. "I didn't want you to come home from work, for Chrissake, Beth. I guess…yeah…I suppose I'm being childish. I just don't feel so good, ya know? I don't feel like doing any of this. I'm a grown man…and this makes me feel like a damned kid. He lay his head back on his pillow, looking at the ceiling again, groaning a little.

"I don't really know any more than you do—but I do remember that Sadie used to have these same issues. I know it's no fun when your plumbing's clogged, so to speak." He chuckled a little at that phrase. "And I'm sure I'd hate this as much as you do." I tried to hold his hand, but he wouldn't let me. "I want you to feel better, and so do they. The bottom line is, will you let them help you?"

"I guess I have no choice. I'm sorry everybody. Old Jack's gonna be a good boy. So, do what you gotta do!" With that, I told him I was sorry for the whole ordeal. He smirked, without looking at me. What else could I say?

When I got back to school, no one was in the office. It was eerie; unless we had a meeting or an assembly, at least one of the counselors was always here, but there was nothing on the schedule. At first, I tried to go about my business, but I couldn't concentrate, so, I started calling the other offices, looking for my people. Just then, two of them walked in, chattering excitedly. "Where were you guys? How come you didn't leave me a message about what you were doing?"

"Oh, Christy called and asked us if we wanted to see the latest educational program they just got in the front office. It's going to be much more efficient to locate records and things. She said she'd come down later and show us how we can use it here in our office." This from Holly, our head counselor.

"Why? What's up?" Emma asked, now looking at me seriously.

"I don't know. I just came in, and I didn't know where you all were. I would've liked to see the program, too. You could at least have left me a note. I was calling all the offices. I…I just felt like I was missing something important. I would have liked to have been there."

I remember how I felt, but I don't really remember how petulant I must have sounded. I'm sure it was pretty bad.

"I'm sorry, Beth. We didn't know when you would get back. We thought it would only take us a few minutes. Really, we weren't there very long. And it wasn't that big a deal. You didn't miss much." Holly had seemed genuinely concerned about my reaction. I knew I'd needlessly caused her to feel bad right along with me.

"Don't worry about it." Now I felt foolish. My emotions were so out of whack. Emma went into her office, and I got ready for class.

After an hour of Dickens, I was back in my office. My books and papers on the file cabinet, I dropped into my chair. Just then Emma walked in, closed the door and sat down close to my desk.

Uh oh. Now I'm going to hear about my shitty behavior.

"Beth, are you okay?" Emma began. "That was so unlike you. What is it? Did something happen with your dad when you went home?"

I looked at this wonderful gift of a friend and nodded. "Well, you're gonna love this. My dad couldn't poop, so, since he was miserable, everyone else had to be miserable, too. I'm sorry for being such a jerk."

"It's okay. I love it when you're a jerk and vent on me—then I don't feel so bad about being a jerk and venting on you!!" At that, we both started to laugh. Emma has never been one to let an opportunity for a joke pass. "You know I'm kidding, but—God, Beth, did you ever think we'd be sitting here talking about your dad's bowel movements?" This time I laughed so hard I had to hold my stomach. Finally, she said "I know you're going through a tough time. I understand."

"Yeah…but then, I'm so lucky to have him with me." Emma knew what I meant. "Pretty confusing, huh?" she said.

Hearing the kindness in her voice touched me. "Emma, I don't exactly know how to explain it. I'm so sorry that I jumped on you and Holly. It seems stupid now. I don't know why it bothered me to have to go home and help with him."

"So, what did you do?"

"Mostly, I listened to him. Then I explained that all they wanted to do was help. He's usually so cheerful, but sometimes, when he's frustrated, he acts out—like a rebellious teenager…although, I'm no fun, either when I feel frustrated, AS YOU KNOW!"

"So, you calmed him down? He's okay now?"

"I wouldn't say he's okay, but he decided to cooperate, for me. That's really it. He felt bad that I came home from work to deal with him, but I also think he wanted and needed me to come and hold his hand and help him with a crappy situation. Excuse my pun!" We both giggled at that one.

"I swear, Beth. Getting old is not for weaklings, is it? God, I learn so much from the stuff you're facing. You're just that much closer to the things I'm going to go through. It must be especially hard to talk about stuff like this with your father." Emma's ten years younger than me, though

I never think of her that way.

"In some ways, it might be easier with your mother. But the basic truth of it is that Dad said he felt like a baby instead of a grown man. The thing is, Emma, it's true. He needs the same basic help as a little child. I guess the only way he can assert himself is to be stubborn. I feel for him, but at the same time, I'm so exhausted mentally and emotionally."

"It sounds like what would help you right now is a break from it all. I don't know how you do that, though. I wish I knew what to say to help you."

"You help me just by being so darn great, Emma. You couldn't be a better listener. Thank you for being my friend. Really." I meant this with every fiber in me. She knew just what I needed and was there to provide it.

"You know, I still feel the same respect for Dad. In fact, more than ever before. I just get cranky…I don't know exactly why. I don't want him to die…but…."

"You wish he could do more for himself or at least cooperate with the hospice ladies without complaining."

That was only part of it.

"Yeah, for sure. But Emma, if I were in his shoes…. I couldn't stand to lie in that bed in that little room, needing help for the simplest things. Like…he'll say 'Say, Beth—a little of that pink lemonade you've got would sure go good right now. Just about an inch, that's all.' When I bring it to him, he smiles and says, "That's just swell. It really hits the spot." When I really think about it, I can't imagine what it would be like to…you know, have to ask for something so mundane. And he's so darn sweet about it. It makes me feel so guilty."

"Yeah, I don't know how I'd be, either. But remember, you're doing a great thing for him. He could be in a nursing home."

"Oh, that would make me want to shoot myself, for sure. I just couldn't do that to him. You know, he's turning 90 in a little over a week. We're thinking of having a party for him, provided he feels up to it. In fact, I hope he makes it till then."

On the way home that day, I questioned myself. What's wrong with me? I asked for this. And I love Dad. He's relying on me. He's so happy in our home. He says it over and over. I can always call Sonja. Heck, it's like I have my own personal social worker! And Robert helps with Dad and rarely complains. We have great friends who call and try to get Robert and me to play tennis or go to the movies. Of course, no one can really grasp what this situation's like. I mean, how can we go to a movie? We can't leave Dad alone for more than an hour. He tells us he's fine, but he doesn't really know that. Still, our friends listen and care. What more can I expect?

I scolded myself for allowing the self-pity to set in.

When I got home that afternoon, Kaitlyn said things went better after I left. The ladies had relieved Dad's constipation. He'd taken a nap and when he woke up, his demeanor had changed for the better.

When Robert got home, he suggested we take Dad out to his favorite restaurant, give him a treat. At first I was enthusiastic, and Dad acted excited, so I got ready to go. But then I started to worry. What about the logistics of the wheelchair? Would Dad be overwhelmed by the crowds and the noise? Robert assured me it would all be fine.

We got there early, but the dining room was already filling and we were seated in a busy section. As we sat there, I noticed Dad's urine bag on the side of his wheelchair, and tried unsuccessfully to hide it; my embarrassment made me nervous and impatient.

Dad did his best to be cheerful for a while, but the discomfort and fatigue soon got the best of him. Finally, we decided to get our food boxed to go, and call it a night.

Later that evening, I called Sonya, and related the events of the day. I hadn't behaved well, I moaned to her. How could I miss the big picture of what this time meant—the good fortune with which I had been blessed at having my father close to me. She listened, she laughed, and, most important, she understood. But it surprised me when she echoed Emma's words that I needed a break—just a short one. It had been a while since the camping trip.

She wanted me to arrange for Dad to go to Jim's for a few days. I should take a breather at home. She pointed out that Dad's condition had stabilized. His life with us could go on for a long while. It had already been over two months. Generally, he felt pretty good. He didn't seem to experience pain, though he felt discomfort from time to time. I let myself think about her idea for a few hours, and then talked to Robert after Dad went to sleep for the night.

"I think it's a great idea, if you're okay with it. I sure wouldn't mind a break."

"I don't want him to think we're tired of having him here. I know how lucky I am."

"Why don't you call Jim and see what he thinks."

I said okay and called my brother. Once again, Jim understood, promised to talk it over with Janie, and call me back. The next day, he called to say they would be happy to take Dad for a few days.

"Jimmy, what am I going to say to him? Do I try to explain how I feel?"

"Look: Dad's birthday is coming up. He knows we're having a party for him. Just tell him Janie and I want him to stay for a visit. No—wait… I'll tell him we want him to visit for a few days."

So, that's what we did. At first, Dad resisted, saying he was comfortable where he was. But, Jim sealed the deal by calling him to say he and Janie were excited about the party. They missed him and wanted him to come for a visit. Anyway, Dad agreed.

The next weekend, Robert, Ellie, and I took Dad to Jimmy's for the party. Most of the family was there, including seven grandchildren and two great-grandchildren. Jim had even invited Steve, the man who had bought Dad's store fifteen years before.

After we sang to Dad and Sammy had helped him blow out his candles, Steve toasted Dad. He'd brought his wife, Amy, and their two little girls with him. Now, he held Amy's hand as he told us all what a great man we had in our father and grandfather, the man who had believed in him and taken a chance on him. He spoke of his respect for Dad, and his gratitude to him for his example of what a true man is. I could tell Dad was visibly moved.

I sat in Jim's big backyard with the sun sparkling on the green foliage as Dad laughed and joked with the grandkids and held the little ones on his lap. It was a perfect moment. I have pictures of that day in frames around my house, but the pictures in my mind have the soundtrack as well. I can hear Dad laughing with us, thanking Steve for his kind words. I can see him opening presents and exclaiming over one more novel that he would never read, one more shirt or pair of slippers that he would never wear. I can feel him looking around at his legacy, the family that he loved, that he made.

After the party, I kissed him goodbye and said I'd be back to get him in a few days. Though I noticed the party's heartening effect on Dad, and though the reprieve from responsibility had lightened my mood somewhat, the darkness that plagued me did not release its grip easily.

Come Friday, I was more than ready to bring Dad home.

For the next month, Dad seemed to have more energy. He began talking about taking us to Hawaii over Thanksgiving break—even going so far as to call his travel agent and inquire about airline tickets and hotels. He insisted that he felt stronger, and, though I couldn't see evidence of it, I rejoiced in his enthusiasm. I even talked with Robert, asking him if he thought it possible that Dad could make a trip like that. Cowardly me thought about being away without the hospice ladies. How would that work?

By the end of October, Dad's energy had begun to wane. His battles with the hospice ladies had never really subsided, but he submitted to them more readily. I worried about him constantly. When I went to bed at night, I could hardly sleep for fear I'd find him dead in the morning. But then, there he was, reading away, when I poked my head in the family room. "Good morning, Dad." I'd say, relieved. "Ready for a little coffee?"

"That sounds good. Maybe in a little while, Bethie."

Once, I walked into his room to find him in the middle of an animated conversation—with the air. When I asked who he was talking to, he just said, "Oh, no one, really...." but he had a vague smile on his face. I felt sure his conversation involved my mom, though it might have been his sister,

Aunt Maudie, or, possibly, Sadie. It might even have been the drugs, although I don't believe that for a minute.

The combination of worry and lack of sleep got to me. I tried to ignore the little voice that kept repeating, "You can't keep doing this. Who are you kidding? You're falling apart".

And I knew it was true. My heart would start pounding when I drove up my street after work. I snapped at Robert over nothing. I prayed I didn't show my state of mind to Dad, who was sleeping more and eating less. He kept insisting he was hungry and could make it to the dinner table—and, with the help of his walker, he would. Then, not long after, he'd ask me or Robert to take him back to bed.

He'd never liked using the oxygen machine that hospice had prescribed, but now, he'd call to me, saying, "Beth, maybe I should use the oxygen—just for a few minutes." Before, I noticed he'd take the tubes out of his nostrils; now he left them in for longer periods of time. Kaitlyn concurred; she was experiencing many of the same things with Dad. Still, the hospice ladies saw nothing alarming in his status quo.

Then, one morning, Kaitlyn called to say she couldn't come that day, offering a vague excuse. She didn't come the next day, either. I had run back and forth from school both days to check on Dad and let the ladies in, and now I was worried about Kaitlyn. I feared there was something she hadn't mentioned. Perhaps the job had gotten to be too much for her? On the third day, she came back. Relieved, I told her how worried I'd been that she might quit.

"Now that you mention it," she'd said, "it is getting pretty hard. I mean…uh, I don't know if I can do this much longer."

"What do you mean? What is it? I thought that, with the ladies coming over, you didn't have to do anything too hard." I knew that wasn't the issue, but I was in denial.

"It's not that. It's just that, well, the drive is hard. It takes me a long time to get here, and it's worse when I go home in the afternoon…and, uh…my mom complains about the kids." She looked away from me. "It's kinda hard seeing Jack like this. I think I might need to quit." My heart lurched. Finally, I said, "Would a break help?" At that, she'd nodded.

Not long after my conversation with Kaitlyn, Sonya stopped by. She'd already checked in with Dad, and hospice, too. Then, she said, "Okay, Beth, I know how your father's doing. He's doing pretty well, considering. Nothing's out of the ordinary. But, now, I want an honest assessment of your health. You don't look like you feel well."

"I'm okay. I'm just tired. I can't help but worry constantly about Dad. I'm also worried about Kaitlyn. She says it's all getting hard…that she might need to quit. I suggested a break. I mean, I know she cares about Dad. I don't think she'd say this unless she really needed it. God, he would feel so bad to lose her. He's really attached to her. I probably should've quit my job or asked for some kind of leave, if our school has such a thing. I don't know what I was thinking. Maybe I should still do that, you know, talk to my principal."

"Okay Beth, let's not get drastic here. Is there anyone who could relieve you for a little while…so you and Kaitlyn could catch your breath?"

I could feel the tears welling up. "No. I can't think of anyone. I don't know what to do. It seems like we just had a break from Jim and Janie."

Sonya comforted me, then said firmly, "That's been a while. This is intense work, Beth. It's a lot of pressure for you, and Robert, too. "How's he doing?"

Her question hit me hard. "He's great with Dad, Sonja." I said, starting to cry. "But he's getting pretty sick of my grouchiness, dark moods, and outbursts."

"I'm sure you're right—because this isn't easy for him either—but it's pretty clear he loves and supports you. More than anyone, he understands what you're going through. I'm wondering if you've been praying…and if that helps at all."

It seemed she'd read my mind. I'd been so busy with doing what needed to be done that I hadn't slowed down to consider the profundities of this moment…what all this meant to me. Every day, my father grew closer to the end of his life. What then? Had he faced that question? What did I think? I knew then that I needed time to let myself think…pray.

"You have to call your sister or one of your brothers, Beth. This is important for all of you. What you're doing is a definite strain on your health, your relationship, and on Kaitlyn. You all need a time out, a respite."

I reminded her about Frank's elusive illness, and Laurie's geographical as well as emotional distance from me. I couldn't even remember if we'd had one conversation since Dad came to our house the previous summer.

"Well, then, you need to turn to Jim again. He understands the gravity of the situation for all of you. He's involved. What's more, he wants to be."

"Do you think it's okay for Dad to make the drive to Jimmy's again?"

Per Sonya's advice, I spoke with the head hospice nurse. Martha cautioned that sitting up in the front seat, could be hard on Dad at this point, but, beyond that, moving him to a different location—especially one with which he was familiar—shouldn't be a problem. She suggested medical transport, which would allow him to lie comfortably.

When I called Jim, I focused on Kaitlyn needing a break, and he'd said "Let me talk to Janie. We need to find out if Heart to Heart has hospice people near us to continue their routine with Dad. We might also need someone to help Janie monitor Dad throughout the day." I told him I wasn't expecting the "break" to take more than a week, but I could see that he was thinking it might be longer. I resisted the idea.

I made arrangements for a medical transport and immediately questioned my decisions. But what choice did I have? Kaitlyn might well bolt if she didn't get a break. Worse—much worse—I didn't know if I had the stamina for the continuing drama…or its conclusion. Still, I hoped that if I took deep breath and did some spiritual preparation, then I could go with Dad to the end of his days. It didn't seem imminent, so, for right now, I needed to slow the chaos that swirled in my head, and start anew.

I chose my words carefully as I told Dad that, because Kaitlyn had some things she needed to take care of—and because I couldn't take a week off of work—he'd be going to Jim's, where Janie would watch out for him. He didn't say much, but I knew he wasn't happy with the news.

The following Saturday morning, I had Dad's bag packed, and we were waiting for the transport. I busied myself with last-minute things, and when the transport arrived, I helped him into his wheelchair. As I held my arms around him, he looked at me, and said, "I'll be fine, Beth. Don't you worry." Did he read the guilt I felt in every fiber of my being? I repeated my mantra that this was only for a few days, and he would be home soon. In the interim, I would visit him in a few days.

I walked alongside him as the men wheeled him to the van, then lifted him onto a gurney. We were both crying as he whispered he loved me, and I said it back to him, over and over. The van pulled away, and I walked back into the house.

Ellie, who sat, eating her breakfast, looked up at me. I leaned against the kitchen sink, crying and debating whether I should follow the van to my brother's house to help Dad get settled in, and to reassure him I was not abandoning him. Ellie said she would go with me if I wanted to do that.

I sat down, looking across the table at her. "I just need to know if I made the wrong choice. And I know you can't answer that. I know Grandpa didn't want to leave us. I don't know how I could send him anyway, except for Kaitlyn—and my own crazy frame of mind. I thought I was a stronger person than this, Ellie. You know?"

She got up and hugged me. "Mom, you are strong. Just think—you took this on. And the fact that Grandpa's been happy to be here means you made a good choice…for him. Right now, though, you just need to do a little recovering…and so does Kaitlyn."

A few hours later, I called Jim, who relayed that Dad seemed tired and lethargic, and, so far, had had little to say. He didn't think Dad was up for a phone call right then. Jim and Janie had hired a nurse to help keep Dad comfortable and assist with his care; she would be over in a few hours to meet Dad. The hospice people would be over on Monday.

"I'll be over on Monday or Tuesday after work. I told Dad that, but remind him. I'm going to call him again tomorrow, and he can call me any time he wants." Jim assured me he'd be fine and not to worry. I'd been telling myself that in vain for hours. Days.

When I called Dad the next day, at first he said little. After enough questions, he finally began to talk, telling me Jim had rented a movie the evening before. It was a World War II movie that he had always wanted to see, "The Thin Red Line."

"Oh, how was that?" I asked him.

"Okay, I guess. But the funny thing is, he didn't watch it with me." He sounded disappointed. He told me a little about it, and before we hung up, I reminded him I would be there to see him on Tuesday or Wednesday, and we could talk more about it then.

Over the next few days, my brother and his wife got Dad into a new routine. They had set up hospice visits, and, on a daily basis, instead of Kaitlyn, he now had Michele the RN tending him. To hear Dad talk, Michele thought she knew everything. And what's more, he grumbled, "She just won't leave me alone! You'd think I was twenty and able to run a marathon, the way she tries to get me to move around on my walker. Didn't anyone tell her I'm tired and sick, Beth? And she's constantly mumbling something or other to me. Doesn't she know she has to speak up—or at least give me my damned hearing aids?"

I hung up, anxious and worried. But when Robert and I went to visit on Saturday, though far from energetic, Dad was all smiles and no complaints. I figured he'd just had an "off" day. I told him I missed him, and he'd be back with us soon.

Meanwhile, I worked in earnest to get in touch with what lay at the heart of my anxiety. I journaled when I got home from school; I took walks by myself, listened to soothing music, and made my way to the chapel at school during lunch time. I slept better, and spent time snuggling with Robert. I even took long baths. After roughly two weeks, I felt a spiritual presence growing in me. I realized, once again, what a minute speck I was in relation to the enormity of God and the universe. I slowed down enough to feel the presence of the love I'd been missing. I felt peaceful.

I called Kaitlyn on Tuesday of the third week and got a lukewarm answer about her returning to our house and her job with Dad. I told her I knew the work she was doing for us was difficult, and I offered her a raise. She'd seemed to brighten at that.

Next, I called Jim and told him we were ready to have Dad home—Kaitlyn was eager to come back, and we were making our preparations. My heart fell at his response.

"That's not a good idea, Beth. He's just not in good enough shape for that. He's so weak, hardly eating, not talking much. We've seen a definite change in him in the last few days." It felt like someone had taken a torch to my brain—all I could think was that I had to get over there and confirm for myself that Jimmy was reading Dad wrong. He must be missing me. I can fix that. I told Jim I would be over the next day.

Where had my newfound peace gone?

The next day, I couldn't wait for school to end. When Emma had asked me how I was doing that day, I could only shake my head.

Why had I done it? I contrasted myself to my brother and his wife, and saw in them two adults patiently dealing with a difficult and painful situation, while I, on the other hand, had melted into a mass of frenzied emotions. Unable to figure a way to make it through a challenging time, I had let my father down as I went off to search for God.

That evening, when I approached his bed, Dad turned his head away from me. I bent over and kissed him. He continued to ignore me when I asked how he felt. I teased him, "C'mon Dad, you can't ignore me. I drove all the way over here just to see you."

Then it occurred to me that he might not have his hearing aids in. I looked on the bedside table, and sure enough, there they lay. "Dad, hey! Look here. I found your hearing aids. That's why you're not talking to me. You can't hear me. Let's put them in!" He took them from me, put them in his ears, and finally looked at me. "Hello, Beth," he said. No cheery greeting, no "Well, look who it is! It's Beth. Isn't that swell!"

Awash in guilt, I sensed that he wanted me to know he'd been angry and hurt that I'd sent him away. He'd been comfortable and secure where he was—how could I do that to him? Didn't I know he was sick? Didn't I know he was grateful? I could imagine him saying, "I'm the only father you've got" as he'd said in jest so many times. Only this time I'd know he wasn't joking.

Determined to bring him around, I shook off my messy feelings, and took his hand. I decided to bring up something I'd always wondered about. "Dad, I was thinking about the night you came home from the war. How'd you get home? You said you came back from overseas to a base in San Pedro, didn't you? How'd you get from there to Compton?" At that, he rubbed his eyes, asked for his glasses and a sip of water. Shifting about in the bed, he finally looked at me and made a kind of noise, "Hmph. Let me see. Well, I'd gotten to the base a few days before. You can imagine how anxious I was to get home to your mother."

"Did they let you call her?" I asked.

"Oh, sure, but I couldn't tell her much because I didn't know how long they were going to keep me."

"Why were they keeping you there?"

"Oh, heck if I remember now. I guess it had to do with making sure we were all healthy. Remember—there were a lot of us coming home from overseas. Anyway, finally, I got the okay. They gave me some money and, a couple of hours later, I was on the train.

It arrived on the outskirts of Compton, a couple of miles from our house on Pearl Street. I realized pretty soon I had a problem—the train took all the money I had, and I had to carry two big duffle bags with all my stuff in them. They were heavy, and it was awkward walking with them, so, I flagged down a taxi. I was in uniform, carrying these heavy bags, but the taxi that stopped, well, that driver, damn bastard, he says, 'no money, no ride.' What kinda guy does that? Couldn't even give a vet who hadn't seen his wife and family for three years a ride! So, I just walked the whole way."

"What time was it, Dad? It must've been late by the time you got home. Was Mom expecting you? Waiting up for you?"

"Oh, I'd called her to let her know I would be home in a few hours, but she didn't drive then, so she couldn't pick me up. Anyway, our car had been up on blocks the whole time I'd been gone. Nobody drove much—to save the gas. She walked everywhere, and when she went to the hospital to have Frank, your Aunt Maudie and Uncle Ralph got her there in the nick of time."

He chuckled, lost in thought for a moment, then continued. "Anyway, I made it to our pretty little home on Pearl Street. A sight for sore eyes, I'll tell you. Even in the dark. It was maybe 10:30 at night. I knocked on the door, and, of course, she came flying into my arms."

He paused again. Jimmy had walked up to the bed, listening with me to the tale of this momentous event in the life of our parents. We waited for Dad to go on. "Your mother took me to see my children—sleeping, of course. But there they all were, in one little room."

"Dad, I remember this." Jimmy said. "I must've been five, but I remember waking up and seeing you standing in the bedroom doorway."

The moment, so precious…suddenly I could see it, too. And it remains with me, indelible, to this day.

I was the first to speak. "Wow, Dad. I can only imagine your reunion with Mom."

"We stayed up half the night just talking, getting reacquainted. We had so much…just so much…to talk about, after all that time. I had a family, for Pete's sake, that I didn't know. And yet, your mom had told me so much in her letters, her sweet, sweet letters. My Anna."

Dad wasn't angry or hurt with me after that. We talked until he was too tired to talk anymore. I had work the next day, so I headed for home after telling him we'd all—Robert, Bob, Greg, Ellie and me—be back on Saturday to watch the big football game with him.

Then, I said, we'd make plans to bring him back to our home. That seemed to satisfy him, though, by that time, he'd settled into a routine at Jim's.

Thursday and Friday passed, and I anticipated a lively time at Jim's on Saturday, watching the game with Dad and the families. I had decided to call for another medical transport to pick him up on Sunday and bring him back to our house, but on Friday evening I got a call I hadn't anticipated.

"Beth, I've got bad news."

"Jim, what is it?"

"When I came out to the family room this morning, Dad was non-responsive. There's been no change all day. I've tried waking him, but Janie says he's not going to wake up. We called hospice. They said just to let him be. He'll let go when he's ready."

"Oh, Jim," was all I could say. It couldn't be over.

"About tomorrow—you know, the game. You might suggest that the kids don't come. You might not want them to see him like this."

"I'll let them decide. I'll tell them what to expect if they still want to come."

I told my children their grandfather seemed to have left us. We didn't expect him to return. Each said if he was still breathing, they wanted to be with him, doing something he would want: watching the team he loved. Rooting for their grandpa.

And so that's what they did. The day passed, we watched the game, we talked to Dad, we kissed his head, held his hand. At some point, the kids left. Robert and I stayed until close to midnight. I didn't want to go. What if he left while I was gone? But finally, I knew I needed a change of clothes, my contacts cleaner, and other sundries. When we came back a few hours later, Dad was still breathing, his chest rising and falling with the help of the oxygen machine.

Margaret came over. Janie made coffee. Jim got the Sunday paper. Robert went out to the patio. Jim and I joined him. We could see Dad's bed from where we sat in the breezy warmth of my brother's patio. For some reason, sitting there with my brother, watching drowsily while our father let go of his life was not unpleasant. Maybe strange, but there it is. I must have closed my eyes for a minute, because I opened them to Jim quietly saying, "Beth, Beth…Janie says Dad's not breathing."

We joined Janie at Dad's bedside and saw the truth of it for ourselves: he'd left us.

Margaret joined us, fidgeting nervously. "Guy…he gone, right?" She looked at me. I nodded my head, and moved to her. She held on to me, so I took her hand. "You think we should pray?" she asked. Sometimes, she is so smart!

Holding hands, we all said the Our Father.

After Jim went to call the mortuary, I walked closer to his bed and stood looking at my father's face. I touched his cheek, his forehead, patted his chest, then smoothed his soft, wavy hair. Where was he? I wondered. Did he hover over us wanting to comfort us? Had he already gone to join Mom…Sadie…Maudie and the rest? How long would it be until the painful realization set in? I knew it didn't matter, I felt the peace returning, the realization of the beauty and love in it all. I would be okay; we would all be okay.

For the next few weeks, the business of death preoccupied Jim and me. We had to let Frank and Laurie know, notify the others who knew and cared about Dad. Go to the cemetery, pick a casket and gravestone, make arrangements at the church for the funeral…and all of the other details. Eventually, though, that busy-ness subsided, and the missing of him set in.

This time, though, the loss was different. Over thirty years had passed since a new, unique relationship with my father had begun to form.

At a tender age, I had been called to stand at Dad's side, and I had answered that call. That decision had seemed to set in motion the decisions that followed, though I know now I'd always had choices.

I could have said no anytime, to so many requests. But then, who would I be? As it was, I had a husband with whom I'd shared life's rocky roads, , ferocious hairpin turns and deep cavernous valleys. We had grown up together, and we were still in love, for good, for keeps. We had an active, boisterous, loving family, three children who were just beginning the roller coaster ride of adult-hood. We knew the incredible, breathtaking love of two small grandchildren. And we had so much ahead of us. We were blessed.

Sometimes, I'd brooded over how to change my father, change us. Silly me. I had envied friends their father-daughter relationships, and the roles they took for granted. I envied their clear definitions of parent and child; for Dad and me, the lines could be amorphous; the complications often muddied things between us. So what?

I had learned to stow away my resentments. During those times when I was startled by the realization that I couldn't figure out who I was in the world, it was easy to shift my focus, to blame Dad's expectations of me for my contradictory instincts: "Be brave and strong, even when feeling weak and alone. Be cheerful and loving, even when feeling sad and unlovable. Be sweet and good, even when feeling anything but."

Be available to Dad; listen to him always, always, always.

And yet, I was the fortunate one. I had learned so much from him. I loved him; he was my father.

"I'm the only father you've got," he'd say, and the truth of that statement sings in my heart to this day. In all his complexity, he had offered himself, unadorned, authentic, unapologetically to the world, to his family, to me. And for this, I am thankful.

Made in the USA
Las Vegas, NV
05 April 2023

70222009R00225